In the Weeds

Mark Ozeroff

Open Books

Published by Open Books

Cover image "Still Life With Psychoactive Botanicals – 2014" © by Jurassic Blueberries

Learn more about the artist at flickr.com/photos/ jurassicblueberries/

ISBN-10: 099-842-7497 /ISBN-13: 978-099-8427492

For Pop, to whom I "stretched the blanket" many a time.

Contents

Prologue

The Cessna rocked in the hot wind blowing over the Atlantic, thirty feet below. I held a course of 280 degrees, steering largely by the sun but referring occasionally to the compass. As I approached the three-mile limit ringing Florida, the bales of high-grade marijuana in back, grown by my friends the Morales family, had me slightly on edge. I rocked the wings up, banking first left and then right to make sure I had no company. Those boys in the DEA were a force to be reckoned with.

I shot over the empty beach at one hundred-fifty miles per hour, quickly heading inland over unoccupied countryside. I knew better than to aim straight for my home field; the days when you could bring a load of contraband into a Florida airport were long gone. DB and I practiced a better method.

We'd arranged a rendezvous a few miles west of the little town of Farth, and I struck up a more northerly course, aiming for that patch of palmetto scrub. Our habit was to never land with a load of weed, but rather to dump it from the plane into the waiting arms of Oso, somewhere out in the sticks. Or at least as close to Oso as I could get, without putting a twenty-five pound bale of *sinsemilla* upside his head.

Of course, it would have been difficult to fly a plane at low altitude and dump marijuana out of it at the same time, which is where DB came in. DB—short for both Dante Berto and Doggy Breath—was Oso's kid brother and my kicker. His job was uncomplicated; kick the weed out on my command. It was a simple and hopefully foolproof system.

It was less than ten minutes flying time in my Cessna 180 from the coast to the drop zone, and I knew that Oso wasn't far away. I told DB to prepare the load.

He unstrapped himself and climbed into the back, which in most Cessnas was occupied by passenger seats; I'd opted for cargo instead of passengers. DB released the tiedowns which prevented the load from shifting en route, removed the modified baggage door, and awaited my command.

Oso heard the approach of the 180, speaking a single word into his radio. "Puke," I clearly heard. I spotted him waving the red bandana, and then nodded to DB.

He began to kick bales out the baggage door, laughing all the while. I could hear his raspy muttering over the engine noise. "Barf," he grated, then, "Spew...vomit." Every time a bale parted company with the Cessna, he uttered another synonym. "Upchuck," he giggled. Much of the English DB used concerned throwing up, thus the inspiration for the nickname Doggy Breath, as well as the reason for his roughened voice.

"Heads up," I spoke into the microphone.

DB was an efficient kicker—twelve bales of marijuana

were out the door and on the ground before we were far beyond the marker.

"Towel twelve," I spoke over the radio, indicating to Oso that it was time to clean up the mess. I kept the plane headed on the same course, just in case anyone was following us unobserved. The DEA boys were beginning to use high altitude surveillance aircraft, difficult for us guys doing buzz jobs to detect.

DB took great care in sweeping out the baggage area with a whiskbroom before replacing the door then rejoined me in front. We were infinitely careful not to bring back the slightest trace of illegal substance to our home field.

"*Gracias*," I said.

"*De nada*," he politely, though malodorously, replied. The Morales boys had all been thoroughly instructed in proper manners by their mother. Had she been here to witness it, Dolores Morales would never have tolerated the display of vomitous invective just employed by her son.

I would have given DB a breath mint, but I knew from long association that he would just have to throw it up. DB regarded anything edible, even a breath mint, as food and thus something to regurgitate once swallowed. So we flew back to the short dirt airstrip outside of Farth, satisfied that we had once again gotten away with an illegal though thoroughly enjoyable flight.

DB was a close friend, as well as my kicker. He was an unusual guy; he was the only Cuban I knew who suffered from bulimia. While many people on the island of Cuba were thin, very few of them sought out that thinness, let alone obsessed about it as DB did. DB's bulimia went a long way toward explaining his fascination with vomit. I'll give DB this much, though; while he may have thrown up with great frequency on the ground, never had he done so in the air. Barf bags were not on our checklist for these Bahamian flights.

For all his quirks, DB was as smart a guy as one was likely to run across. He was self-educated, interested in a wide variety of subjects. He played the meanest game of chess for miles around, and it was a noteworthy day when I could defeat him. He was a fan of the Beat poets, writing his own verse, which he chose not to share. He spoke almost exclusively in Spanish, thus hiding his intelligence from most residents of Farth. I guess he figured that if people didn't want to take the time to understand him, he just didn't give a damn.

Oso was the first member of the Morales family I'd met. His nickname meant Bear, despite the fact that Oso was small and not particularly hairy. He'd acquired the nickname because he usually slept fifteen hours out of every twenty-four. His family was fond of saying that he hibernated on a daily basis. Oso washed dishes in a little restaurant called The Hair of the Dog. He also was the frontman for the Morales family, most of whom resided in the Bahamas. On Chico Cay, they grew the most potent marijuana in the hemisphere.

The family had originally come to the Bahamas from Cuba, after Castro had taken over. Knowing full well that the Communists would disapprove of the family's marijuana trade, they'd moved to Chico Cay seeking artistic freedom. Chico Cay proved very good for the family, the soil rich and well suited to growing marijuana. The quality had never been higher, nor had the people who smoked it.

The Bahamian government also was good to the Morales family, allowing them their privacy so long as the family was prompt in the payment of taxes. *Don't worry, be happy*, seemed to be the official motto both of the government and the Morales clan.

But I'm getting way ahead of myself here.

One

My parents were Russian émigrés displaced during World War II when Hitler attacked Stalin despite their treaty swearing that no such thing would ever occur. They'd fled east, barely escaping Operation Barbarosa, the pits of Babi Yar, the siege of Stalingrad, and the fate of most of the Jews of Eastern Europe.

When they came to the easternmost reaches of Siberia they jumped the puddle, continuing onward when they landed in US territory. I suppose they'd simply gotten in the habit of moving toward the rising sun. Finally there came a time when Sacha and Minka Kisov could go no further without getting wet.

They settled in the town of Farth, Florida, probably because it was not only as far from Russia as they could get, but because it was as unlike Russia as any place they'd ever been. It was hot, and Sacha and Minka had had their fill of the cold. It was tropical and lush, unlike their home village of Pochep. And, since Farth had no indigenous Jewish population, both felt that the organized anti-Semitism they'd fled would be unlikely to disturb their new existence.

So they set up housekeeping and bore a son, Menachem Jakov Kisov—*me*. I was a rambunctious baby, spidery and homely, but my parents loved me very much. Like Spanish moss, I grew rapidly in the fecund surroundings, secure in the all-American small town environment.

My first clear memory is of a crop-duster in a biplane, spraying a field of Florida corn. He was good; I distinctly remember that he flew under some telephone wires at one end of the cornfield on several passes. The sight fascinated me, and I begged my mother to let me watch until the pilot emptied his bin of insecticide and flew away. I watched him grow small in the distance and disappear, knowing all the while that I would fly when I grew to manhood. I was four years old.

When I learned to read, I devoured every book I could find on the subject of aviation. My favorite then and now was a book titled *Old Soggy Number One* by Slats Rodgers. Slats had done pretty much everything you could do with a small airplane: exhibition flying, flight instruction, crop-dusting. But far and away his most interesting exploits involved smuggling liquor from Mexico into Texas during Prohibition. The freedom, the sheer exuberance of his flying experience, was intoxicating to me. I, too, would fly liquor over the border when I was old enough, I told my father one night.

Pop chuckled, and in his heavy accent said, "Menachem, you can't do dat in today's world. First off, smuggling is against the law. No good!" He wagged his finger at me. "Secondly, liquor is legal now. Anyone can go to the store and buy as much as dey wish! You got to pick anudder job you wanna do when you get older… Slats." He poked me in the stomach with his finger.

I was heartbroken. I knew there would never be anything I wanted to do as badly as live a life of harmless banditry from the cockpit of an airplane. But one thing came of our conversation: from now on, I would be called Slats. That was good, since none of the crackers that lived in Farth could come near the correct pronunciation of *Menachem*, despite a lifetime of tobacco chewing and the spitting thus required.

I grew up, never losing interest in flying or in Slats Rodgers. I graduated from William Henry Harrison High School in 1967, a turbulent time whose issues were just beginning to penetrate as far as Farth. I was faced with the question of what to do.

My parents wanted me to attend college. Although I was not totally committed to the idea, I enrolled as a Liberal Arts major at the University of Florida. This satisfied my parents and also gave me a student deferment, allowing me to avoid the draft for the time being. But I wasn't completely happy in college. I lasted two years, growing more and more displeased with the increasingly anti-war sentiment of my fellow students.

It wasn't that I was particularly militaristic, but I'd grown up listening to my folks talk about how bad life under the Communists had been. And according to them, Communism was difficult to differentiate from Fascism when it came right down to it. I thought it must be a little like Magellan's voyage around the world—he sailed so far to the left that he ended up on the right.

With the Vietnam War now in full swing, the date of my birth guaranteed my being drafted. So I asked myself the same question I asked every time I was in doubt: *What would Slats Rodgers do?*

Well, Slats *had* faced a similar situation. When World War I broke out in 1914, the naturally pugnacious Slats had applied to the Aviation Section, US Signal Corps. But the Army had turned him down, and a disappointed Rodgers returned to Texas.

Today's military was not about to make the same mistake with me. I went to the Air Force Recruiting Office in Vero Beach, presented myself to the sergeant there, and announced that I was available at their convenience.

"Sign me up, Sarge," I said with a grin. "I wanna fly airplanes."

So the Air Force taught me to fly. At the time, there was a shortage of Forward Air Controllers, the guys who directed fighter-bomber and artillery attacks from the air. I was assigned from the get-go to do this job, and this specialty fit me from several standpoints. For one thing, I had only two years of college under my belt. It was barely sufficient to qualify during this time of war; I could be an officer, if not a complete gentleman. And secondly, Slats Rodgers flew his entire career in lightplanes—good enough for him, good enough for me.

The plane of choice for FACs was the Cessna O-1 Bird Dog. The O-1 was perhaps the least respected aircraft in the US inventory, being smaller than a primary trainer. It was also armament-challenged; the firepower doubled if a second man climbed in back, wearing a shoulder holster. Those in the know, however, were fond of calling the O-1 the "most formidable weapon known to man," because they were used to call down an almost biblical level of destruction on the enemies of the United States.

I wasn't taught the usual things, like aerobatic maneuvers or cargo carrying. I learned low-level flying, winding the little Cessna through the trees and cutting grass with the propeller. I learned short and rough-field techniques, shooting landings on unimproved fields and beaches. I took to flying like a kid takes to jelly beans—I was good at it, and I couldn't get enough.

I also learned how to mark targets with tiny missiles the Air Force called Willy Petes, military jargon for white phosphorus. They had very little explosive effect; they were only good for making white smoke on a target that jet jocks would then vaporize with larger missiles or bombs.

To me it was a game. I'd played a similar game as a child, spit-bombing piss bubbles in the toilet of my home back in Farth. I was good at hitting piss bubbles, and I was good at hitting targets with Willy Petes. Willy Petes were more fun—*this* game you played with an airplane!

I thoroughly enjoyed playing these new games, right up until the Air Force shipped me to Vietnam. They didn't have piss bubbles—or toilets for that matter—in the Vietnamese boonies.

Two

On first impression Vietnam felt a lot like Florida. Hotter than hell, humid as a greenhouse, and full of bugs. Upon debarking at Tan Son Nhut Airbase, my first sight was row after row of aircraft of all descriptions. There were F-4s, F-105s, Hueys, CH-46s, C-141s, A-37s, AC-47s, T-28s… and off by themselves, on the very edge of the field, a row of O-1s. It was a regular Bird Dog ghetto. These were well-worn examples; the lineup reminded me of Farth's nastiest used car lot on Ribbon Street. I wanted to get my hands on one so badly I could almost taste it.

My second sight was a little more sobering. Rows of plain metal caskets awaited loading into the very same transport we had just vacated. It was plain to see that in Vietnam, one could either hit piss bubbles or become a piss bubble.

I reported to a clerk in an air-conditioned office lost in the jumble of the huge base. He quickly glanced over my orders, in the world-weary way that minor functionaries of all armed forces no doubt employ. He rustled around in a filing cabinet, made a few desultory stamps on several papers, and then handed me back my orders.

"You will be briefed on what you need to know as a FAC and officer of the US Air Force in Vietnam," he told me in the smug way of the noncombatant. "Welcome to the Nam."

The next morning, several of us so-called Fucking New Guys were given a briefing by an officer in the know. Such esoterica as field maintenance of the aircraft, the correct use of the military radio, life with the native peoples, and shitting into a barrel were discussed. As FACs, we were destined to spend our year of duty living in forward bases, without the amenities officers enjoyed on bases like Tan Son Nhut.

We were also thoroughly briefed on ROEs, the Rules of Engagement. These were the impenetrable regulations under which the US was expected to fight. Trying to remain within these rules, which the pilots referred to as Romeos, was going to be considerably more difficult and uncomfortable than crapping into a fifty-five gallon drum.

I was more interested, though, as he moved on to operational information. Calling in air and artillery strikes on Viet Cong or NVA troops, sometimes so close to friendlies that you held their lives literally in the palm of your hand.

You might fly during either day or night as a FAC. Some specialized in working the Ho Chi Minh Trail, a highly dangerous assignment. The officer threw in the fact that several FAC units had suffered casualty rates higher than fifty percent, causing one of our number to swallow his chaw.

And the captain told us we'd have occasion to assist with Search and Rescue missions. SAR was simultaneously the most dangerous and the most rewarding of missions. Everybody's morale was boosted when a pilot was successfully extracted after a shootdown.

"It could be you down in the boonies tomorrow, boys," he told us. A couple of guys looked as if they could use one of the previously mentioned barrels about now.

We were then given our assignments. I was destined for a forward base not far from the city of Hue, assigned to return a plane that had just undergone overhaul.

It was a beautiful day with just a slight haze, the O-1 smoothing along under scattered cumulus clouds. I could see for eight miles, not bad visibility for Vietnam. I followed a small stream meandering through the countryside, thoroughly enjoying the chance to be airborne once again. I had my shades on, as it's practically against regulations for a pilot to take flight without his Ray-Ban Aviators.

Even in the early morning the heat was apparent. As I flew over alternating patches of shaded and sunny jungle, I could feel in the seat of my pants the strong thermals that tried to balloon me upward. In automatic response, I pushed forward on the stick to maintain steady altitude. Quickly I would pass through the thermal into an area of cooler air, where I'd apply back stick lest I lose altitude before encountering the next column of rising air. I felt akin to a hawk soaring still-winged in the rising heat.

The map said I was about fifty miles short of my destination. Radio aid to navigation was just about nonexistent here, which was just as well with me. I liked flying the way Slats Rodgers had flown, fifty years ago.

The Vietnamese countryside looked peaceful as a Rotary Club picnic. I saw no evidence of the war, even at my low altitude of fifteen hundred feet. Here and there small villages dotted the jungle; if my passing overhead bothered them I saw no evidence of it. Though I was flying but a Bird Dog, I puffed myself up as some sort of latter-day Smilin' Jack, piloting a warplane over a land caught in the throes of civil war.

For the sheer hell of it I executed a loop, venting my youthful exuberance in rebel yell. "Yeeeee-*hawwww*!"

The gods must have dribbled urine into their undergarments upon catching sight of my foolishness. Displeased by both my display of abandon and their now-sodden drawers, they allowed a single bullet—probably fired from some ancient relic of a rifle—to enter my cockpit and shatter the altimeter. I stared stupidly at the smashed instrument. I peered over the side of my plane at the jungle below. Neither showed anything of use to my befuddled mind. I continued on my way toward the field, chastened.

I was calm by the time I arrived at my new home. LS 151, more commonly referred to as Baccardi, was a dirt landing strip carved out of the heavy growth with several Bird Dogs disbursed to one side in readiness for the occasional mortar attack. I taxied up to the line, pulled the mixture back to idle-cutoff, and watched the prop coast to a standstill.

A pilot looked on as I unfolded myself from the cockpit, brushing altimeter glass off my lap. "Bust your bong?" he inquired. At my blank expression he grinned, sticking out his hand. "They call me R&R."

"Slats Kisov," I said, shaking his hand.

R&R's strong grip belied his skinniness. Tall and very black, wearing a red bandana, the man looked a lot like Jimi Hendrix. "R&R stands for Rock and Roll, although you'll hear other interpretations." He leaned into the cockpit and, seeing the bullet-hole in the altimeter, repeated the same phrase the clerk had used back at Tan Son Nhut. "Welcome to the Nam."

"This to a newly-intimidated warrior."

"Hell, this ain't jack, Jack. You got it outta the way early. You can coast now, brother. For a while…"

I made an exaggerated motion of shaking out my pants leg, and R&R laughed deep in his throat. "*Shee*-it." Then he quit the shuck and jive routine, indicating a shack with a nod of his head. "Come on over to operations and we'll get you introduced around."

Inside the tent, R&R made the intros. "This FNG is Slats Kisov, boys."

The biggest of them, wearing a three-day growth of beard, said simply, "Meat." It seemed impossible that he was capable of wedging himself into the cockpit of a Bird Dog—Meat was the size of a grizzly.

"I'm the Ops officer, call me Sammy. You bring me a nice, shiny airplane?" Sammy was young but already developing a potbelly.

"Well…" I began.

"Mofo done got it shot up already," R&R interrupted.

Sammy's expression soured. "Goddamn it, that was just overhauled!"

I must have looked hangdog, because R&R slapped me on the back, telling Sammy, "Ain't shot up bad, just the altimeter. We don't go high enough around here to need one."

Meat laughed. "Can hear cockroaches fart at our operational altitude. Long as the dude didn't lose a nut, it's okay."

I began to think that maybe things would be pretty tolerable around here. Provided I didn't lose that nut, of course.

Three

Bright and early next morning, R&R took me on my dollar ride, the euphemistic term for one's first combat flight as a backseater. He gave me a quick tour of the current hotspots around our patch of sky, showing me how a master FAC did things.

About half an hour into the flight, we were contacted by Direct Air Support Center, the ground-based FAC controllers, who informed us that we would soon have a flight of F-4 Phantoms under our control. "Suspected enemy location at Tango Delta 686220. Tomcat flight ETA 10:44 hrs."

"Roger," R&R replied. Referring to his map, he turned us toward the coordinates given by DASC, and we proceeded there at the amble that comprised the Bird Dog's cruising speed. We were at an altitude of four hundred feet.

"Down there, somewhere," R&R said.

I could see nothing other than trees. "Where?"

"You'll see now how we do things out here," he told me. I didn't much like the sound of that. R&R pitched the O-1 over, diving down to sixty feet above the jungle canopy. "We gotta troll for 'em."

What he meant, I learned to my dismay, was that we flew low over the suspected position trying to attract ground fire from the enemy troops. Once we encountered that fire, we marked the target with Willy Pete and radioed for the F-4 jocks to drop ordinance on our smoke. Easy.

Simultaneously, we spotted muzzle flashes; they were down there, all right. R&R rolled the plane into a vertical bank, bringing us around to a perfect position from which to launch a marking rocket. With a small burst of flame one of the Willy Petes ignited then left its launch rail underneath the wing. A slow moving rocket, it was visible in flight all the way to the ground.

"*Got* your ass, Charlie," R&R whispered over the intercom. "Hit my smoke from the west, Tomcat," he told the F-4 jocks over the radio.

We flew off to one side, looking expectantly westward. Specks in the distance rapidly enlarged into F-4 Phantoms carrying an assortment of bombs. One at a time, they dove on the enemy location.

All hell broke loose. Concussive waves were visible for an instant in the humid air, and then the target was obscured by airborne debris. After the initial passes with iron bombs, the F-4s sowed the area with Cluster Bomb Units, which broke apart over the target and distributed thousands of small anti-personnel bomblets over a wide area. Those North Vietnamese soldiers not killed outright by the high explosive were dispatched by CBU fragment. A most impressive display of aerial weaponry had played out before my eyes.

No muzzle flashes threatened us when we made the next pass. R&R scribbled matter-of-fact notes on the side window of the O-1 with his grease pencil, the all-important Bomb Damage Assessment.

"Now what do you think of your new job?" he asked.

"Goddamn, R&R ..." was all I could say.

I did a lot of solo flying during the next several weeks. I learned fast, realizing I wouldn't last long in this environment otherwise. I couldn't help but feel that Slats Rodgers would have fit right in around these parts.

R&R and I grew to be fast friends. He was always pulling something off because, despite being an officer and a gentleman, he claimed to have "larceny in his heart." For one thing, he smoked a lot of marijuana, a not-uncommon habit among US troops in Vietnam—here one needed to find relaxation wherever he could. The Southeast Asians grew some wild weed, and when R&R got high he liked to pull out his guitar and play the blues. I learned to savor the music of guys like Leadbelly and Pinetop Perkins.

"You'll like this one," he'd say, beginning to flatpick. He could play lead, too, not just rhythm. Needless to say, in the Vietnamese boonies a good musician was worth his weight in liquor.

"Play some Pat Boone!" Meat roared one night from across the compound, drunker than a Methodist.

"You got to be kiddin', mofo," R&R yelled back. "I'd rather be butt-bumped by Ho Chi Minh, and I do mean ho!"

"Dope fiend!" Meat bellowed. "Reefer madness," he explained to his companions, drinkers all.

I myself enjoyed vodka on the rocks, although out here rocks were found only in the clouds. Yet I found myself hanging around with stonies instead of fellow drinkers during our few hours off. Inevitably, one night I tried some marijuana.

I found it to my liking. Weed didn't leave one with a debilitating hangover the next day, and morning came early for a FAC. It made R&R's music all the more intense. And Thai stick sure was easier to find out here than vodka.

"Blew up a missile sight today," R&R reported, in between hits on a fat joint. "Thud pilots didn't have nothin' but napalm. When the Thuds left, you could tell that Charlie was demoralized."

BJ, accepting the joint, asked, "How the hell can you tell from the air that Charlie was demoralized?"

"Well, for one thing they were runnin' away," R&R replied. "For another, they were on fire." The pilots all broke up, filing such witty repartee away for future use on unsuspecting prey.

"Gimme that joint, Bogart," I politely suggested. R&R leaned back in his chair, hit the opening chords to John Lee Hooker's "Boom Boom" on his axe, and all was right with the world, at least for a little while.

———————

I flew what was fast becoming my standard workday. I directed a flight of Skyraiders onto a truck park, and then a second flight of A-4s onto a platoon of North Vietnamese regulars engaged in a gunbattle with some Marine grunts. I called in coordinates for an artillery strike on a suspected ammo dump, the secondary explosions making it look like Charlie had commenced Fourth of July festivities. It was tiring but very rewarding work, helping the guys on the ground.

Idly glancing out the window while returning to base, I noticed a large boar rutting for food in a clearing below. I'm not sure what sparked my recollection that the mark of an excellent pilot during World War I had been snatching a hawk from midair in the crossed bracing wires of a biplane's wings. Inspired, I determined to create the Vietnam War equivalent, air-to-pig missile hunting.

I dove down. Most animals would flee in terror at the close approach of an aircraft, but not this magnificent tusker. He resolutely held his ground, squealing defiantly at me. I banked vertically, got him in my sights and fired my last remaining missile. In what was no doubt a lucky shot, the Willy-Pete flipped him ass-over-teacup through the air. He landed quite dead, and more than slightly singed from his white phosphorus shower. I flew the remaining five miles to the field and boasted upon landing of my new game.

"You know where that sucker is?" the crew chief asked.

I looked questioningly at him. "Sure, I could find it."

"You know how good freshly killed pork tastes?" He had an avaricious look in his eye. "We could either eat pig slop tonight, or we could eat pig."

"Damn, Sarge, why didn't I think of that? Let's go get that sumbitch!"

I scared up R&R, the three of us commandeering a jeep and some M-16s. "Where the hell are we goin'? I ain't no ground grunt," R&R complained.

"You won't be disappointed," I assured him. "Not unless you're secretly a Black Muslim."

We retrieved the pig with no complications. Hell, he was even partially cleaned and cooked. We threw an impromptu luau that evening, and the chef of our little one star restaurant outdid himself. The boys were properly appreciative of my skill and made plans to take up the new sport.

But the CO scotched those plans immediately. "You'll hunt from the air again when pigs fly!" Buck said around a mouthful of forbidden game. I tactfully refrained from pointing out that I had seen this very pig fly only hours before. In the face of boos backed up by a spontaneously rude blues riff from R&R, he remained adamant. "It's too damn risky playing around out there. You know what Charlie would do to any FAC he could get his hands on?"

No one could argue the wisdom of that statement. Charlie would do things to us that would make what we did to the pig look like a massage and facial.

―――――――――――

That fact was on the minds of FACs, maybe not continuously, but often. We took all sorts of precautions against the possibility of going down in Indian country. We went out armed, some of us to the teeth. I carried a short-barrel .38—others packed 9mms, carbines, sawed-off shotguns, even grenade launchers. I knew one pilot who claimed that the Vietnamese would never take him alive—he carried his own golden BB, the last round in the clip of his Colt .45.

Others carried good luck pieces, fetishes, or religious icons from one faith or another. Vietnam being largely Buddhist, some pilots employed tiny versions of the Buddha, blessed by local priests and worn around the neck. Meat scorned such policies, and I privately agreed with him.

"Fuckers've gone gook on us," he would sneer.

One way we lessened the chances of Charlie realizing

who we were in the event of a shootdown was to adopt a nickname. Names commonly were chosen to denote fierceness, usually in a humorous and often crude way. It was Meat who came through for me.

"Slats Kisov, eh?" He raised an eyebrow in my general direction one night, while in his cups. "We'll call you Sierra Kilo."

"Not too inventive, Meat. I've heard you come up with better nicknames than initials," R&R observed.

"It don't stand for his initials, dumbass; it stands for Shit Kicker. I heard about how Slats handles himself on his flights. Yeah, Shit Kicker," he rumbled, sounding pleased with himself.

Although the unwritten code forbade my taking notice of the compliment, I was flattered. At least I was until Meat used the short version.

"Yo, Shitman, get me a beer, will ya?"

"Sure, Meat," I answered, trotting off to fulfill his request. I returned quickly, handing the can to him. He took a grateful swig, turned red in the face, and blew the mouthful of liquid over half the clearing.

"What the fuck?" he managed to croak.

"Did I get those cans mixed up?" I asked innocently. "Sorry. The cook was cleaning out the grease trap, and I must have picked up the one he was draining into."

"These things happen on occasion, Slats."

I got Meat a real beer, since he was understanding enough to use my actual name. Also, because it's not smart to piss off the biggest guy in camp.

I got the chance to make it up to Meat soon after, when he

was blowing hell out of some VC humping cargo down an offshoot of the Ho Chi Minh Trail. They were pushing bicycles loaded with several hundred pounds of cargo, using a bamboo tiller tied across the handlebars to steady the load. When they reached their destination and unloaded, the bicycles were ridden back for more—it was a prime example of the way North Vietnam conducted their war.

I learned the details of this story later, from the horse's mouth. Unbeknownst to Meat, a 12.7mm heavy machine gun had been moved into position. As he directed the attack, Meat overflew the emplacement and absorbed a long burst. His engine was hit; trailing smoke, he quickly turned away to put some distance between himself and the outraged VC.

Meat looked over the engine instruments—oil temperature rising and oil pressure rapidly falling. "I'm in deep shit now," he muttered to himself. "Them little bastards are gonna peel me like a banana."

As if to justify his prediction, the engine chose that moment to quit. As he began to settle into the sea of trees, Meat worked the controls, attempting to milk every foot of lateral distance he could from the hornets' nest of North Vietnamese.

He spotted a tiny clearing and banked toward it. It was far too short for a landing, but it beat going into the trees. He pancaked in, ran immediately out of room and caught one wing on a tree trunk. The aircraft whipped around as the wing tore off, hurtled into some brush and came to an abrupt stop.

Meat was momentarily stunned. When he came to his senses, gasoline was pouring from the ruptured tank, seeping along the fuselage and sizzling on the hot exhaust pipe.

With the strength of his size and his equally great alarm, Meat effortlessly tore the cockpit door from its hinges. He scrambled away from the wreckage and into the overgrowth, putting some distance between himself and the O-1 carcass. Uppermost in his mind was an observation taken from the Air Force manual: "It is generally considered inadvisable to go down into an area you just bombed."

A muffled whump was clearly audible behind him; Meat knew the wreck had caught fire. Perhaps it would take the VC a while to realize he wasn't in it, giving him more time to escape.

As the initial adrenaline seeped out of his system, he became aware of pain in his left knee; he looked down to find his flight suit torn and bloody. Apparently, he'd injured it in the crash. He could feel it beginning to stiffen. Concealing himself in a clump of bushes, he removed the emergency radio from his survival vest.

"Mayday, mayday…" He spoke quietly but urgently into the transceiver. "FAC down near Yankee Golf 527884.

To his immense relief, a voice immediately answered him. "FAC, say designation."

"This is Mike Juliet," giving the phonetic ID for his nickname, Meat Johnson. "Out of Baccardi. Get Search and Rescue goin', guys. I'm too fuckin' close to Charlie and I got a banged up knee. And tell 'em to watch out for a 12.7 on the Trail; that's what got me."

"They're on the way. Remain calm."

"Rog," he replied.

I was in the air, and DASC immediately informed me of the shootdown. I stood my O-1 on a wingtip and headed for the coordinates. I knew that nothing could be as helpful, or as welcome, as a FAC on the scene.

DASC had a Jolly Green Giant CH-53, a flying barn of a helicopter, headed for the area, and was diverting some A-1E Skyraiders to suppress ground fire. The A-1, a propeller aircraft we referred to as the Spad due to its antiquity, was the best plane to use for SAR cover. It carried an immense load of bombs, was armed with four 20mm cannon, and could remain on station for hours if necessary. Its slow speed allowed the Spad to achieve tremendous accuracy with its weapons.

I switched to 243 MHz on the radio, the standard military emergency frequency, and spoke into the mic: "Yo, Meat. What the hell you doin' down there, workin' on your tan?"

"That you, Shitman? Get me a beer, will ya?"

"Wish I had one to drop. I'll get one for you in a while. This time, no grease."

"I ain't fallin' for that one again. I'll pop my own top from now on."

"Roger that. Got some Spads due any time, and a Jolly Green. Hang on."

"You ain't gonna tell me to remain calm too, are ya? Do you *believe* that asshole radio operator? Like I ain't got enough friggin' trouble!" I swallowed my laughter, imagining the face of the SAR radioman as he listened to Meat's profane exasperation.

"Better get here fast," he continued. "I can hear yellin' and shootin' in the brush. Gonna put a little more distance between me and the Indians," Meat told me. "I'm east of the crash site. You'll know where that is, 'cause its marked with black O-1 smoke."

I could see the smoke column, not far ahead. I overflew the crash site and made a quick assessment: lots of VC. It looked like a fire ant nest had been kicked apart, except these ants had AK-47s. I made a wide circuit of the area to conceal the direction Meat had taken.

In monitoring the operational frequency, I soon heard a joyous sound in my headset. "Shit Kicker, you got Elbow Bender here. Four Spads, with an order of Snakeeye and nape for Charlie."

I couldn't have custom ordered a better load of ordinance. Napalm was always good, and Snakeeye bombs had drag fins that popped out of the back to slow them down—they were pinpoint accurate.

"Drop some nape just east and west of the smoke, Elbow. Approach from the south." While they were getting Charlie to duck and cover I switched frequencies again, orbiting east of the crash site to look for Meat.

"You're right over me, Shitman."

"I can see a clearing about one klick further east. Your leg okay to take you that far?"

"I'm there already. How long for the Jolly Green?"

"He'll be waitin' on you."

"On my way," Meat replied.

I flew back to the crash site to see that the Spads had made several good passes—the odor of burning napalm was strong in my nostrils. Charlie had his head down, and some of those heads wouldn't be rising again.

Tracer fire reached out for me. "Elbow Flight, they've moved up the 12.7. I can see tracer coming from the treeline on the west." I rolled over, snapping off a Willy Pete. "Hit my smoke with a couple of Snakes."

"Roger, Sierra Kilo."

Again I orbited east, and as the A-1s dropped their bombs I caught a glimpse of Meat moving through the trees. For a guy with a bum leg, he was making remarkably good time toward the pickup site.

"More than halfway there, Meat. Pretty good wind sprint."

"Leg's startin' to hurt," he wheezed with effort. "Think it's fucked up. Nothin' a few beers won't help, though."

"Well, the Jolly Green's just waiting. You take your time, though. No hurry."

"I hear somebody in the trees behind me." Meat sounded worried. "A few of 'em must have sneaked by."

"No sweat." I rolled out of the turn and passed directly over him, firing another Willy Pete.

"Elbow, I need you to strafe, starting on my smoke and going west. Hit a wide swath, but be damn careful. The FAC is down there just east of the smoke."

"Wilco." Elbow Lead lined his flight up and shot all but Jesus out of the jungle.

"That 20mm is awesome," Meat transmitted. "Glad I ain't over there."

"The chopper's almost here. Expedite," I urged.

The CH-53 arrived before Meat made the clearing. I thought it best for them to extract Meat immediately. "FAC is two hundred yards west of the clearing. Get him now, Charlie is too close for comfort," I told the pilot.

"Roger, Sierra Kilo," he responded, the big helicopter lumbering westward.

I fired one more Willy Pete into the jungle just to the

west of Meat, directing the Spads to make several strafing runs from north to south, cautioning them to beware the CH-53. Charlie loved to hit rescue helicopters almost as much as he did FACs, but the 20mm would eliminate accurate ground fire.

"You are over target now," I radioed. The chopper eased into a hover above the jungle canopy, and the cable winched down. "You got it, Meat?"

"Right here in front of me. I owe you big time." The relief in his voice was palpable.

I could see the CH-53 reeling him up, like a fish from an algae-covered pond. Swallowing the lump in my throat, I replied, "Anytime."

In a manner I could not articulate, I felt I'd ... *adopted* Meat.

Four

That night at Baccardi, I got word that Meat had been evacuated to a rear-area hospital. Apparently, his knee was more banged up than he'd realized, and his run through the jungle hadn't helped.

"Think it's a million-dollar wound?" R&R asked. He was referring to that sought-after injury, serious enough to bring an immediate end to one's tour of duty yet not life-altering.

"Meat certainly used up a lot of luck today." I hit on the joint that R&R held out. "I'm just glad that he's alive and out of the jungle."

"No complaints, SK. You did all right. I just hope you're in the air in the unlikely event Charlie ever gets me." No one believed he'd get hit, let alone killed. If a FAC felt vulnerable, he was definitely in the wrong business. "Meat has just one problem—he's too goddamn big. Charlie can't go on missing a target that size." R&R played a rendition of "Little Red Rooster," changing the lyrics to Big Ass Redneck.

We all laughed at R&R's parody, and wished Meat

well in the Million-Dollar Wound lottery.

———————

Just three weeks later, though, Meat walked back into the compound. He came right over to me, wrapped his huge arms around my chest in a bear hug, and picked my one hundred pound frame effortlessly off the ground. In his best imitation of the Skipper from *Gilligan's Island*, he said, "I missed ya, little buddy. Just wasn't the same with you on other side of the island."

"Put me down, you damn *go*-rilla," I laughed. "Or I'll make another deal with the cook for grease. You'll be drinkin' it for the rest of your tour."

"Okay, Shitman, don't get excited. I just wanted to thank you with this bottle of Absolut vodka. But if you don't want my thanks…"

"I'll take that. You don't want to stress out your leg, carrying something that heavy around. Boys, drinks are on me," I said expansively.

R&R surprised me by accepting one. Holding his glass up in a toast, he said, "Here's to Meat; we missed you, dude." He threw down the vodka in a single gulp then reared back and tried his best to smash the paper cup against the corrugated side of the ops shed, as if hurling a crystal glass into a fireplace. We all followed his lead.

Meat surprised me even more by accepting the joint making the rounds. "Leg still hurts," he explained sheepishly. "Maybe this is a medicinal herb."

"All right, Meat!" R&R enthused. "Mofo got smart in the hos-pi-*tal*," he told the rest of us in an aside.

We proceeded to have a fine welcome home party for the wounded warrior returned to the fray.

The following day, we staggered out to the planes and began the preflight ritual common to pilots the world over. The guest of honor looked less hung over than the rest of us— Meat was largely impervious. Being in better shape, he finished his preflight first, taxiing out to the end of the runway. He ran his engine up carefully, testing the controls and finding everything to his liking. I turned to watch as he advanced the throttle.

He proceeded to execute a textbook short-field takeoff, using barely three hundred feet of runway. Skimming the grass, he allowed the airspeed to build and zoomed sharply upward. He climbed to an altitude of one thousand feet and banked toward the field. Feeling the exhilaration of being airborne again, he began a display of aerobatics. He looped then did a split-S, throwing in a couple of barrel rolls for good measure. The O-1 was no stunt plane, but it could maneuver reasonably well.

We all watched as this fine pilot came to his finale. The most difficult maneuver for the little Cessna to perform was a snap roll. Usually, the result was a stall followed by a spin. Not this time, though.

This time we watched in horror as the right wing separated from the fuselage. With Meat sawing frantically at the now-slack control stick, the one-winged plane spun tightly into the ground and burst into flames. Meat never had a chance.

Slowly the disembodied wing fluttered down.

Five

It was determined that Meat's wing spar suffered from the effects of corrosion, and that no preflight would have shown this, however thorough. In rotation, all of the Bird Dogs were subjected to a complete check of the airframe; those not first in line for airframe checks were handled with kid gloves on our operational flights, insofar as possible.

At first, Vietnam had seemed like an incredibly venturesome summer camp. Meat's shootdown had injected a strong dose of reality. In directing his rescue, we'd been joined closer than brothers. But things got grim after my friend burned—no Vietnamese had caused his accident; no golden BB could be blamed. I sensed Meat, an unseen copilot, peering over my shoulder on each mission. I began to drink and smoke a great deal.

"Snap out of it! He was my friend, too," R&R advised me one night, after strumming "I'll Fly Away" as a tribute to Meat. "You've got to keep your mind on what you're doing around here, if you're going to make DEROS." He was referring to the Date of Eligible Return from Overseas, that magical future day every serviceman in Vietnam marched toward, when he returned to The World.

"Stay real, Slats. Stay focused. Meat would tell you that if he were here. Concentrate on your flying, and your job. We're going to have more losses; it's inevitable. I don't want you to be among them." R&R playfully punched my arm. "No one likes my guitar playing as much as you do."

He was not only referring to my drinking and smoking. I'd also begun to take more chances in the air. I flew lower and more wildly than I had before, collecting bullet holes in my aircraft as carelessly as a kid collects pennies in a tin pig. It was almost like I was defying the VC. In the process of taking these risks I was killing a lot of Vietnamese troops, though. My BDAs became more and more impressive.

Even the CO took me aside. "Slats, you're doing a bang-up job here. Just don't bang yourself up in the process."

"Not a gook in the Nam got a chance of hittin' me when I'm doing my thing. Besides, I've got help now," I said, displaying my new good luck piece. I showed him the pinky ring I was wearing, made out of a stainless steel fitting from a Bird Dog. "Got this from Meat's wrecked plane, boss. It's a talisman."

He looked skeptically out from under his eyebrows.

"I know it sounds nuts, but I'm tellin' you that, somehow, I can feel him watching out for me." I must have had a sheepish expression on my face, because Buck said something strange.

"I can still feel him around here myself, from time to time. You're not nuts." Then he added, "Any more than the rest of us."

———————

Two days later, I was directing some A-4 Skyhawks in a

bombardment of an NVA company attacking a Marine patrol. The North Vietnamese Army was more traditional in their military approach than the Viet Cong, though less effective one on one.

But they were better armed, particularly regarding heavier weapons. This company had several ZPU 14.5mm antiaircraft guns, and one 37mm cannon, an especially effective weapon. Anticipating a fight, I subconsciously pushed the sunglasses up on my nose.

The A-4s were Blue Flight, originating from the carrier Enterprise. As the flight neared, I rolled over and dove on the enemy concentration, firing a Willy Pete onto the eastern flank of the NVA position. "Blue Leader, approach from the south and hit my smoke."

"Rog, Sierra Kilo," Lead responded.

Attacks of this nature were generally carried out in line astern formation, one aircraft diving after another. While the initial pass might be a surprise to the enemy, they knew where subsequent planes were going to come from. Thus, the last plane to make a pass had the greatest chance of being hit, the enemy gunners having had the chance to get their range.

And so it went on this day. The ZPUs and the small arms were putting up an effective curtain through which the A-4s had to fly. A veteran must have manned the 37mm, though, for his aim was accurate from the very first. When the number four plane, the slot man, made his initial pass, his aircraft absorbed several cannon hits. He had no chance—the plane dove straight into the ground and exploded; no chute was seen.

I blew up. I knew the proper thing to do would have

been to mark the position of the 37mm with smoke and call in a strike. Instead, I jerked the stick to the left, banking sharply around and headed for the position myself.

As I neared, I yanked the throttle back and pushed sharply over into a steep dive. The pip centered on the cannon, which now began to fire at me. One round from a 37mm would eviscerate a Bird Dog, but I maintained the dive. I had a sense of déjà vu, as though I'd been in this precise position before.

Screaming below a hundred feet, I waited until the last instant before firing the Willy Pete and pulling sharply back on the stick. I looked back over my shoulder in time to see the missile explode on the carriage of the cannon. The gunner jerked around in his seat, covered in burning phosphorus.

Now I realized why it seemed I'd been here before—this was how I had killed the pig! Here was my game, forbidden by the CO, taken to the next level. It may have been more dangerous than pig hunting, but it was infinitely more satisfying. I'd undoubtedly saved future targets from a far-too-skillful antiaircraft gunner.

"Damn, Sierra Kilo, I never saw a FAC take out a gun position by his lonesome," Blue Leader radioed. "You even need us to stick around?"

"Piss bubble shouldn't have gotten me mad," I muttered to myself.

I'm not sure how or why, but the higher-ups heard about my action against the 37mm gunner and I found myself in trouble. I was called up on the carpet, which pissed me off almost as much as the Vietnamese antiaircraft gunner. Before I left for Da Nang Air Base, I got good and stoned in an attempt to assuage my anger. I also pocketed a couple of joints, not knowing how long this ass-chewing session might take.

I touched down an hour before I was due in the colonel's office. I killed some time watching a line of Hueys doing endless landings and takeoffs. Then the pattern was cleared for a medivac chopper. It thumped hurriedly in and discharged some stretchers bearing ground grunts that had been caught in bad crossfire—at least one had bought the farm, if the rictus on his face was any indication. This was the last thing I needed to see. I headed off to renew my buzz.

I stepped behind the nearest row of latrines and fired up. It took an entire joint of good Thai stick to start feeling better, after which I headed off to my appointment with the colonel. Sitting in the outer office, I had to laugh at myself: I felt like a junior high school student called in to see the principal. The intercom buzzed and the corporal waved me through.

I guess I'd gotten used to the lax discipline practiced at forward airbases like Baccardi. I barely straightened up then threw a lazy salute in the general direction of Colonel Marion Ralph. He must have already been mad, because he jumped up and glared at me. "What in the hell is the matter with you, Lieutenant? You're as undisciplined in the office of a superior officer as you are in the air!"

My anger sliced right through my buzz. "I don't even know why I'm here; this is a total waste of time. I did my job, which in this case was to destroy an antiaircraft gun that had just blown some poor Navy pilot to smithereens. Not to mention that my unit needs every FAC they can put in the air—we're still short-handed after losing Meat."

Ralph screamed, "I don't know what a 'Meat' is, and I don't give a hoot in hell! You will come to attention and give me the respect I deserve!"

My gaze pointedly shifted to Ralph's jacket (noticeably lacking wings and combat ribbons) as I hissed, "Meat was the best FAC in the Air Force. He died in the line of duty, which is a lot more than you'll ever be able to say... *sir*."

Furious, he jogged around the desk, stuck his nose three inches from mine, and prepared to ream me royally out. He never started, though. Instead his nostrils flared suspiciously, and Ralph's face broke into a smirk.

"Are you wearing some sort of exotic after-shave, Lieutenant? Tell me I'm *not* smelling marijuana."

He didn't intimidate me, though he undoubtedly should have. "Yeah, that's weed you're smelling. You'd probably smoke it, too, if you'd ever had to fly in combat."

The smile melted right off his face. "I'm going to see that you get a dishonorable discharge for this, Kisov. Or should I call you Shit Kicker?"

It was my turn to grin. "You can call me Shit Kicker if I can call you Colonel REMF."

Ralph's face turned a most interesting shade of purple. For some strange reason, the colonel didn't appreciate being referred to as a "rear echelon motherfucker." And that's how I found myself in the Da Nang Air Base brig. At least I still had that last joint in my pocket.

It took Richard Nixon to bail my ass out.

Six

I'll say one thing about the VC, they were not idiots. When US forces created too many casualties, Charlie just picked up and moved to a new neighborhood. This time, he chose to take up residence in Cambodia.

That's where Nixon stuck his foot in the door. Against the advice of many top advisors, the president decided to invade Cambodia. Of course, we'd been carrying on secret operations there for years. But now we went public, in what would come to be known as the Cambodian Incursion. Naturally, this meant a major bombing campaign, and if FACs had been in scarce supply before, we now became a commodity more precious than platinum.

Orders came through that every able-bodied FAC should prepare to take to the air and stay there until further notice. I'm sure that Colonel Ralph was not pleased at this development, but I sure was—I missed my Bird Dog.

First thing we needed was a new landing strip closer to southeast Cambodia's so-called "fishhook" region, so we could maximize our time over target. It didn't take engineers long to carve one out, and it took even less time for us to vacate Baccardi. We were in place by early May for the start of Operation Rockcrusher.

The VC must have sensed our intentions, because there was very little resistance at first. Charlie moved westward, until the B-52 squadrons reached out and started pounding them. Knowing they couldn't outrun the Buffs, they turned to face us in earnest. Now came the need for tactical strikes by fighter-bombers, which meant it was time for us FACs to do our thing.

Losses on both sides began to mount steadily.

I had a renewed focus for my anger. The VC were cutting down my fellow soldiers—who better than me to funnel bombs and rockets down on them? With this thought in mind I slanted into the sky, launch rails filled with Willy Pete, and took up a course of 295 degrees. As I neared the assigned coordinates, I could see the muzzle flashes of a widespread firefight raging.

DASC radioed, "1st Air Cav Division helos approaching from the northeast—suppress ground fire."

Looking in that direction, I could see a group of dots that quickly resolved into a flight of Hueys. They began their descent, preparing to disgorge infantry into the thick of fighting. I overflew the landing zone, spotted a large number of muzzle flashes, and fired a Willy Pete onto the VC position.

I spoke to a formation of F-105s out of Tan Son Nhut. "Cowboy Flight, you got Sierra Kilo here. Hit my smoke from the east and see if you can suppress some of that ground fire for the slicks."

"Roger that, Shit Kicker." I must have worked with these guys in the past—they knew my name.

As I orbited safely to one side the Thuds streaked in, and huge smears of napalm blossomed below. The Hueys came in and hit hover, disgorging their troops as quickly as possible, then tipped forward into maximum performance takeoffs. The infantrymen immediately began to take withering fire.

I laid down another Willy Pete, transmitting, "Cowboy Flight, hit my smoke from the northeast."

As I stood off again to watch them strafe in single file, I heard the distinctive sound of bullets hitting my aircraft, like gravel rattling on a tin roof. The O-1 entered a shallow dive, and I pulled back on the stick to level off. But the stick was slack in my hand—I realized my elevator cable must have been cut. I was only six hundred feet up—I frantically began to wind the trim control upward, managing to at least slow my descent. As I still had control over ailerons and rudder, I started a turn away from the fighting. If I was going down, I at least wanted to be as far from the Viet Cong as possible. Better the frying pan than the fire.

But the breath whooshed out of me, and I doubled over in pain—something had kicked me hard in the gut. I watched the jungle canopy rise inexorably toward me, realizing that my luck had run out.

My last thought before sinking into the trees was of Meat.

———

My eyes blinked open, and I dimly perceived faces peering down at me. *Shit! The gooks got me,* I thought bleakly. But as my vision cleared, I could see that I was in the hands of the 1st Cav.

"We're gonna put you on the next outgoing chopper, Lieutenant. You'll be okay."

"Where was I hit?"

The private's eyes shifted nervously, before he said, "Mr. Charles fights dirty, sir. You took a round in the groin."

"I don't feel any pain."

"That ain't surprising, seeing as how we shot you up with enough morphine to keep the Rolling Stones grinnin' for a week. You FACs have helped us enough times—we're glad to return the favor."

"I sure as hell thank you guys for getting to me before the VC." He smiled then ducked as a bullet whipped through the elephant grass. I flinched as he ripped off an entire clip from his M-16 then lay back to listen to the answering pop of distant AK-47s.

It wasn't long before I heard the distinctive thump of Huey rotors approaching, sweeter music than even R&R could produce. The first one dropped and skidded in before discharging its men, and I was dragged over and dumped unceremoniously onboard. A couple of rounds tinked through the fuselage as we took off, but the pilot was beating feet too fast for the VC to zero in, and I was quickly out of danger.

———————

So I moved my residence again, this time to a hospital in Saigon. The docs told me that I'd lost a testicle to ground fire, but was otherwise intact. As was happening with increasing frequency, another memory of Meat flitted through my mind. On our first meeting, upon hearing my altimeter had been shot out, he'd said that I'd be all right as long as I didn't lose a nut.

Well, I had my million dollar wound. Of course, I had to deduct about nine hundred and seventy-five thousand dollars from that account because a nut comes with a mighty big price tag.

At least one of my problems resolved itself, though. I guess Nixon figured he needed to sell Operation Rock-crusher to an American people growing ever more unhappy with the war. So he decided to use one of the first casualties to promote his expansion into Cambodia. Now, I hadn't done one thing more than any other FAC, except getting one of my own rocks crushed, and having an O-1 shot out from under me in the process.

But it did make me laugh out loud to imagine the face of Colonel Ralph, when he found out that I'd slipped his grasp with the help of some ribbon and tin. Medals might not be a big deal to me, but this one must have made the colonel mess his pants.

Sumbitch wasn't about to press a dishonorable dis-charge on a guy who'd just been awarded the Distinguished Flying Cross, by order of the Commander in Chief.

Seven

My return to The World was through San Francisco. With a huge weight lifted from my shoulders, I walked down the boarding ramp and into the terminal. I'd never been here before, and my plan was simple: I intended to ring 1971 in properly, with some Absolut.

Ahead of me I spotted several denizens of Haight-Ashbury who reeked of weed, and I instantly revised my short-term goal from getting drunk to getting stoned. Their scruffy jeans and beaded shirts provided a sharp contrast to my dress uniform and ribbons. One of them stepped forward and, clearing his throat, prepared to deliver his welcome speech. I broke into a wide smile.

He let fly a gob of phlegm that hit my nose, oozing down to form a gooey stalactite, before snarling, "What are you grinning at, baby-killer?"

I lost it. I balled my fist and punched him with all the pent-up angst of a year spent in a hellhole. I put every bit of adrenaline-laced fear I'd experienced in Vietnam behind the blow. He went down with an imprint of the ring I'd taken from Meat's wrecked aircraft stamped onto his face, bleeding and blubbering for help.

An airport cop heard the commotion and evaluated the situation in an instant. I started to explain my actions, but he cut me off by whirling me around and slapping a pair of handcuffs onto my wrists. So instead of getting drunk or stoned, my return to the US began in a jail cell populated by bikers, wife-beaters, and some frilly guy who invited me to visit a bathhouse with him after our release.

With regrets to the bathhouse host, I chose instead to arrange bail with an Air Force representative. The sergeant told me that my welcome home was a common one, and not to let it get me down. Knowing good advice when I heard it, I headed to a store for a fifth of cheap vodka, and then asked for directions to the nearest bus station, where I bought a ticket all the way to Farth. I didn't give a damn that I was breaking the law by leaving the state while out on bail—if I wasn't enjoying myself, it was time to leave the party.

I stayed drunk all the way to Florida. If anybody boarding the bus eyed the seat next to mine, I grimaced and placed my survival knife between my teeth. The only passenger to sit down over the next twenty-seven hundred miles was a burly Marine, who apparently saw pulling a blade as a mannerly way to break the conversational ice.

So I shared my liquor with him.

Much the worse for wear, wincing behind my sunglasses, I staggered off the bus. First person I ran into was Gene.

Gene was an institution in Farth. Largely retired now, he'd earned his keep most of his life as a traveling undertaker. There were many black towns in the county too small to have their own funeral parlor, so they'd call Gene any time of the day or night to embalm the recently deceased. Gene liked moving around, which came in handy for his second job as well—he was as talented a harmonica player as he was an undertaker. Somehow, the jobs of blues harpist and embalmer seemed to mesh. When he wasn't practicing either of these skills, Gene served as Farth's unofficial historian.

Gene eased himself off the shady bench next to a telephone booth that served as his office, and tottered over. "Back from the wars? Welcome home, son," he said as he shook my hand.

"Thank you, sir. But it feels like the war's being fought inside my skull."

"I b'lieve I can help you declare an armistice. Nothing like a little sippin' whiskey to help you through rough times." Gene let a bottleneck peek out at me from his jacket pocket. "A little food wouldn't hurt you none, either. You put yourself in ol' Gene's hands, boy."

"I don't know—most of the people who end up in your hands are headin' for the stone orchard."

He laughed as we started slowly up the street, and pulled the cork. "Well, this ain't embalming fluid." He passed the pint over.

I took a nip, grimacing as it burned its way down. "You sure?" I passed it back.

He tipped it briefly, frowned, and said, "Come to think of it, no. You take another little sip, though, and see if it don't help you out." I followed instructions, and the whiskey did begin to ease some of my pain. "See? Now we'll try a little coffee and food." He steered me into a restaurant that had opened during my absence.

Aptly named The Hair of the Dog, it was a tiny place with a counter and five tables. We were outnumbered by the three employees, one a small Hispanic dishwasher who looked as stoned as anyone I'd ever seen. The tired-looking waitress eyed me but addressed my companion. "Hey, Gene, who's your good looking friend?"

"This is Slats, Darla. He'll need some of your home cookin' to restore his equilibrium—scramble him some eggs with bacon and toast. You didn't go kosher on me in Vietnam, did you Slats?" he asked in an aside. I shook my head, and Gene finished ordering, "We'll start with a cup of high-octane joe."

Darla gave the order to the cook then brought our coffee. "Here you go, soldier." She looked on with approval as Gene added a dollop of whiskey to both cups.

"Since I don't have an oxygen tank on me, this'll have to do." I raised my cup to Gene and sipped gratefully.

"I know what it's like to come back from overseas." At my questioning look, Gene continued, "Back in the day, I fought in the war to end all wars."

"I didn't know you were in World War I, Gene."

"I was a Buffalo Soldier with the 92nd Infantry. The Huns gassed us at Soissons, back in 1918—pretty near killed, I was. But these old lungs were tougher than the docs thought, and I'm still drawin' breath these fifty-some years later."

"I understand. A gook shot one of my nuts off with an AK-47."

Gene winced. "Lord a'mighty, son, *that* must have hurt.

But I reckon God knew what he was doin' when he doled out lungs and balls in pairs." He clinked his cup against mine and tossed back a slug. "Here's to spare parts, eh Slats?"

By the time my food arrived, I was feeling good enough to eat. Gene was right—this was just what I needed. Over my objections, he insisted on paying for my meal, and I praised him as a gentleman and a scholar. He smiled, and then passed the remaining rotgut, saying, "Least I can do for a man that served his country." I have to say that I much preferred my reception here to that of San Francisco.

Taking my last piece of toast to munch on the way, I went to see my folks.

That's when I ran into the dog. He stood in the middle of the sidewalk, pugnaciously blocking my way. I tried to sidestep him, but he shifted position like a prizefighter, countering my move.

He was the scruffiest looking critter I'd ever laid eyes on. He resembled a Scotty, except that his tangled coat was white under all that filth. Bow-legged and snaggle-toothed, he was slobbering enough to be a mad dog. It wasn't rabies that made his salivary glands spill over, though—he was staring, hypnotized, at my toast.

I broke off a piece, bent over to give it to him, and damn near lost a finger as he went for it like a shark after chum. He wasn't mean though, just ravenous. I broke off another piece, threw it down, and watched him pounce and snuffle it down his gullet, then wag his tail hopefully for more. All too quickly, I was empty-handed.

"Sorry, boy, that's all I have." He stuck his lower jaw out and digested my words for a moment, then squatted down to defecate right on the sidewalk. To punctuate his protest, he dragged his ass across the cement, leaving a skid mark that would've done a NASCAR driver proud.

"You're not the most mannerly dog I've ever run across, but I get your message. Come on, *Tailskid*, maybe we can find you something more filling."

We strolled over to the Gas'n Grub convenience store, where the closest thing to dog food I could find was beef jerky. I knew the dog didn't care because he leaped up to snatch the bag from my hand, ripped the top off and wolfed down the contents. Then he accompanied me to my childhood home, farting contentedly the entire way.

I'd neglected to forewarn my parents of my arrival, so when my mother answered the door, she took one look at me and swooned. I hugged her, partly in sheer happiness but also to keep her from falling down, and then guided her over to the couch. What revived her more than anything was the dog, who trailed us inside, promptly hiked his leg, and began to urinate. And I'm here to tell you that not even a defibrillator will resuscitate a Jewish mother faster than dirt being introduced into her household.

"Dat thing is *pishing* on my rug!" Ma screeched.

"He seems overly wrapped up in bodily functions," I explained.

"He's a Cossack. Get him outta here!"

After I dragged the dog out, Ma stood on tiptoe to plant a kiss on me. "You are thin as a rail. Doesn't the Air Force feed you? Come, I'll fix you something to eat." She pinched my cheek fondly.

"I just had breakfast with Gene. Tailskid could use a good meal, though."

"What's a tailskid?" she asked

"Usually, it's the landing gear on back of old airplanes. But in this case, it's the dog's name."

"Do I wanna know how he got dat name?"

"Probably not, Ma," I grinned. So, while I related the tale of my truncated military career, she scraped together a plate of leftovers for the hairy little pisher.

———————————

I might not have access to an airplane, but the next best thing was available. I strolled out to the garage to visit my old thumper. She was a 1957 BSA Gold Star, a single-cylinder thoroughbred of a motorcycle. Five hundred cubic centimeters of pure performance, this British beauty might look a little worn but she would embarrass the hottest Harley clean off the road.

I'd been careful to drain the fuel tank and float bowl before I left for Vietnam, to avoid clogging up the carburetor with deteriorating gasoline. I siphoned some gas from Ma's car into the bike's fuel tank, and then sanded the points and spark plug lightly. Tickling the carb until raw fuel dripped onto the crankcase, I set the choke. I kicked the engine around to top dead center, hit the compression release, and switched her on. Rising as high into the air as possible, I belted the kick starter with all my strength. The Beezer rewarded my efforts, lighting off with a roar from the bullet muffler, before settling down to a contented warm-up blat.

I looked down to see Tailskid standing next to the bike.

He all but smiled at me, tail happily wagging—he didn't seem intimidated in the least by the racket. I revved the throttle, and he howled in response.

I took off down the road, heading to see my father. Six days a week—from nine o'clock in the morning until six o'clock at night—Pop could be found at Kisov Hardware, his tiny shop located on the corner of Ribbon Street and George Washington Carver Avenue. Like many small Southern towns, Farth had but a single Jewish family, and as was the custom, we operated a mercantile establishment. In the easy vernacular of the old South, this was known as the "Jew store."

I roared up on the BSA and switched off, leaning her on the kickstand. I barely made it out of the saddle before the door flew open and Pop launched himself at me, grabbing me in a bear hug. He whispered in my ear, "*Mine zun, mine zun...a dank, Porets.*" As so often happened when Pop was moved, he'd spoken first in Yiddish. "Thank you for my son, Lord," he repeated, planting Russian kisses on both my cheeks which were so wet that they sent my face in search of a sleeve.

Wiping tears off his own face, he mussed my hair affectionately. "So, you can't call first, tell your mother you're coming?"

"I didn't know how long it takes a bus to get from San Francisco to Florida, Pop. Besides, you know how much I hate telephones," I grinned.

"This from a guy whose job it is to talk on radios?" He laughed, and then continued, "I hope you feel as good as you look, Menachem. How was your trip? So, what's dis ribbon for?" He dragged me into the shop, talking nonstop the entire time. I was back in the fold of my family.

Eight

I relaxed for a couple of days, but soon I was nagged by two needs—to find a job, and to get back in the air. So I threw a leg over the Beezer and headed for the most logical place where I might accomplish both needs, Farth Air Park.

I don't know who came up with the idea of calling this oily patch of crabgrass a park, but the name had certainly stuck—the place was known to one and all as the Airpark. Home to a seedy bunch of planes and pilots, most of them were crop dusters and banner towers. Presided over by an ancient wooden hangar wearing a shredded windsock, the airfield stank of moldy fabric-covered aircraft, eighty octane avgas, and greasy food. This was my kind of place.

I wandered into a shack whose only decoration was a faded hamburger painted on the door and seated myself at the counter. A waitress, wearing equally faded paint and a nameplate proclaiming her to be Patty, said, "Welcome to the Farth Air Park Bar and Grill. What'll you have?" I ordered a burger and onion rings.

The guy in stained coveralls seated beside me turned and said, "The Farth Air Park Bar and Grill was too long to fit on the door. We usually just call this place the Cow Patty."

Patty put her hands on her hips and snapped her gum in reply then hollered at the kitchen, "Hockey puck with o-strings!"

I shook the hand of my dining companion, introducing myself. "Slats Kisov, recently retired pilot extraordinaire for Uncle Sugar."

"John Wilkes Booth. Also employed by Uncle Sam, back during the Korean Conflict. I can't fly 'em though, I just wrench on 'em."

"Your name is John Wilkes Booth?"

"My folks had what you might call a Confederate sense of humor. I usually go by Wilco."

"Even if I can't fly 'em at the moment, it's at least good to be back at an airport." Patty dropped my food off and, talking around a bite of what indeed tasted like hockey puck, I asked, "Uh … I don't suppose you know of a flying job around these parts?"

"Let's see, the fishing trawlers just lost their part-time aerial spotter. Sumbitch was flyin' plastered, as usual. Went straight into the drink with a smaller splash than Esther Williams, and hasn't washed up yet. They need a new spotter, but you gotta have a plane."

"I don't even have a place to stay yet, let alone a plane. I'm not totally without resources, though." I'd saved almost every dollar I'd made in the Air Force, and with the military disability benefits I'd be drawing I was in decent financial shape.

Wilco scratched his stubbled chin. "Finish your plateful of excrement, and then I've got somethin' for you to see."

Several minutes later, having been led behind the

hanger, I stared at the sorriest excuse for a flying machine I'd ever seen. If this were a dog rather than an airplane, it'd make Tailskid look like a Westminster purebred. The battered 1955 Cessna 180 squatted forlornly in the sand, with only a skeletal motor mount projecting forward of the cockpit. The disembodied engine lay on the ground, a mangled connecting rod peeking shyly out of a hole in the crankcase.

"Jesus, this thing ain't much more than a weathervane!"

"Looks pretty bad, I admit. But feast your eyes on this." He whisked a torn tarpaulin off a misshapen piece of abstract art.

It had once been a crop duster. But the entire rear fuselage had been wrenched off—literally all that held it on were the control cables. The left wing was bent sharply upward, in an ironic salute.

"I don't know which one I like better, Wilco. Maybe you can weld 'em together to make an Erector Set plane!"

"You don't understand, Slats. This duster is an AgWagon." At my blank stare, he added, "A *Cessna* AgWagon."

So Wilco tutored me concerning AgWagons. About ten years back, Cessna had decided to start manufacturing crop dusters. Knowing the profit margin would be small, Cessna minimized design costs by using as much structure as possible from a model already in production. The model they chose was the 180—the airframe was very similar, the engine and accessories all but identical. As I listened, my expression went from condescending to puzzled, then enlightened.

"That's right, Slats. The AgWagon is powered by a

Continental O-470, just like the 180. Only real difference is this AgWagon has a fixed pitch propeller instead of the 180's constant speed prop. Good news is she'll still fly like a champ, just a bit slower."

He told me the 180 had suffered a catastrophic engine failure, the pilot barely stretching the glide far enough to reach the Airpark's runway. The owner had no insurance and no money for expensive repairs, so he'd left it here hoping someone would eventually buy parts from it to help defray his loss.

The AgWagon had recently caught a power line with its tailwheel, while dusting a field. The wire had slowed the plane in midair, almost like the arresting cable of an aircraft carrier, before the rear fuselage tore away. The rest of the plane's energy had been dissipated by the wing collapse, which also prevented a prop strike from causing engine damage. The pilot actually had to shut down the engine before climbing out of the wreckage, unharmed but cussing his head off.

Wilco stared meaningfully at me. "Everything you need to put this 180 back in the air is right here. Won't be the prettiest plane flyin', but she'll be one hundred per-cent mechanically sound. I'm sure I could talk the 180 owner into selling his plane cheap, if you can scrape up the cash. The AgWagon can be had for even less. What do you say, Slats, should I make some discrete inquiries on your behalf?"

What could I say but, "Hell, yes!"

Wilco got back to me pretty quickly, and I headed over to

the Airpark. As he'd predicted, both owners had jumped at the chance to sell their planes. "You can get 'em both for six grand, Slats."

"I have most of that, and I think I can get my hands on the balance. But what's it gonna cost me to join these two in happily wedded bliss?"

"I'm willing to extend you a line of credit, for my services as justice of the peace. My rates are fair, ask anyone in these parts. You can pay me after you start earning your aerial keep." We shook hands on the deal, and I helped Wilco drag the bride and groom into his hangar.

"Now, let's talk about how you want your aircraft set up."

I'd already given this matter serious consideration. "In keeping with the simplicity of a fixed pitch propeller, I want the panel stripped down to basics. This bird's going to earn her keep doing contact flying, so get rid of all the blind flight instruments except the turn and bank indicator. I want equally simple engine instrumentation; toss everything but the tachometer, oil pressure, and oil temperature gauges. I'll keep the radio, though—if I have to, I can fly blind and do instrument landings with just a radio and a needle/ball. Keep the Automatic Direction Finder, too—I like listening to music in the air.

"While you're at it, remove the second set of controls. I don't like copilots—they're glorified backseat drivers. Hell, maybe I can even find cargo to run on occasion. I want this plane to be as basic as my old Bird Dog. My philosophy is, *If it ain't there, it can't break.*"

Wilco grinned. "Simplicate and add lightness, eh? One thing though, Slats. Them Federal Aviation Administration boys won't be happy about the engine switch, since this particular O-470 model isn't certified in the 180. But we can work around that. I'll pencil-whip the papers so everything looks good to go—just don't do anything that'll get your plane inspected."

I pasted my most innocent look onto my face. "I'm the soul of discretion when it comes to flying," I assured my friend.

Again, Wilco wasted no time. Barely a week later, he called me back to the Airpark. Wearing a smug, self-satisfied expression, he invited me into the hangar to meet my "new" aeroplane.

My first impression was that she looked a little like the bride of Frankenstein, with her faded, peeling paint. There wasn't a single frill on this dented airplane, neither prop spinner nor wheel pants. I had a look at the cockpit, which reinforced my impression—there were more blank covers than instruments on this panel. A hole stared back at me from where the propeller control had once protruded. I continued my walk-around, peering at the entire airframe.

I opened the cowling to find an engine that had been cleaned, adjusted, stripped of unnecessary accessories, and safety-wired. I stuck my head inside as far as possible, inhaling the intoxicating scent of well-maintained precision machinery. Then I refastened the cowl, standing back to rest my eyes on a structure that had been pared down to the essential, and let my thoughts wash over me. Hot rodders call a machine like this a "sleeper"—it might look scabrous, but it was in perfect mechanical condition.

"You ain't disappointed, are you, Slats?"

"I think I'm in love." I couldn't see him, but I felt the radiance of Wilco's smile beaming like summer sunshine on my neck. I added, "Only one thing left to do. We got to take her up for a test flight, son."

As we pushed her out onto the ramp, Wilco told me that he could locate no maintenance log for the engine. "But all six cylinders show good compression, so I'd say this is a mid-time engine with maybe eight hundred hours on it. You have a lot of flying time left until overhaul."

Having already performed a thorough preflight in the hangar, we belted ourselves in. I put on my Ray-Bans and began the familiar engine start sequence, switching the fuel selector to right tank, then cracking open the throttle. I set the mixture to full rich, magnetos to both, and gave her a couple shots of prime. I shouted out the open window, "Clear prop!" No one yelled back in alarm, so I turned on the master switch and hit the starter button.

The engine caught immediately, my eye automatically going to the oil pressure gauge, which came right off the peg. I pointed this out to Wilco, who nodded profession-ally. I nudged the throttle to briefly get her rolling, and then hit the brakes to test them before continuing onward.

I turned into the wind just short of the runway. Running the engine up to eighteen hundred RPM, I tested both magnetos, and then the carburetor heat. A final check of oil pressure and temperature showed everything in the green—this engine ran superbly. Checking the controls for freedom of movement, I set the trim and flashed my companion the widest of shit-eating grins.

"You ready to shove everything up into the kitchen?" Wilco nodded in answer.

I eased us onto the hard-packed sand that served as runway, pulled on two notches of flap, and opened up the throttle. We surged forward, the tail came right up, and after a short run I popped the yoke back to bring us off the ground at minimum speed, then skimmed the sand to accelerate in ground effect. As soon as we hit best angle of climb airspeed I pitched abruptly up, and we slanted steeply into the sky. I bled off the flaps and leveled at two thousand feet, allowing the speed to build before easing the throttle back to cruise setting. The airspeed stabilized at one hundred-fifty miles per hour, and I trimmed all pressure out of the controls.

I banked steeply right to look for any aircraft hidden by the left wing, and then abruptly reversed into a high G left turn to peek under the other wing. Clear of traffic, I pulled the throttle back to idle. As the speed bled away, I applied ever-increasing back pressure on the yoke to maintain altitude. The aircraft trembled as the airflow began to burble off the wing. We hit sixty-two miles per hour just as the yoke came fully back, then the wing stalled and the nose pitched sharply over. I pushed the throttle and yoke forward simultaneously to allow air to again flow freely over the wing—we came slightly off the seats in negative G, despite our lap belts. With the nose down the speed came right back up, and I pulled back to arrest our descent. We were flying again.

I glanced over to see that Wilco, more than a little green around the gills, had clamped himself to his seat with both hands. I immediately apologized for my enthusiasm.

"Sorry, I didn't mean to throw you all over the sky like that. I guess FACs aren't used to considering a passenger's well-being."

"I never was real comfortable in the air, Slats. But I

promise not to toss my cookies in your lap."

"Who cares if you're not a natural born flyer? What matters to me is that you're a natural born mechanic. This plane might look like a decrepit crate, but she runs like she just came off the factory floor."

Green or not, he looked mighty satisfied upon hearing my compliment. So I flew him gently back to the Airpark, never banking more than twenty degrees.

As we climbed out, Wilco breathed a sigh of relief at being back on solid ground. I said, "I couldn't be more pleased with this plane. But my ancestry makes me ask, did we run over cost?"

In answer, he dug a considerable wad of money out of his pocket. Handing it over, he said, "She came in *under* cost."

In astonishment, I counted seven hundred and twenty-six dollars. "I don't understand..."

"For a guy whose father sells hardware for a living, I'm surprised at you. You didn't take into account the value of the leftovers, Slats. I know a lot of mechanics, and I made a few calls. The 180 had a decent instrument package—the avionics I removed were worth a buck or two. The busted engine still had lots of good parts, too. Then there were the usable airframe parts from the AgWagon—crop dusters are ham-handed, and mechanics need lots of spares. And don't forget the scrap value in sixteen hundred pounds of aircraft-grade aluminum alloy. That all toted up. You still owe me for the work I did, but not until after you start earning. This'll provide some working capital to get you on your feet. Make me one promise, though, buddy."

"Name it."

"Don't ever take me flyin' again, Slats!"

Nine

On a natural high from my return to the air, I took myself to lunch at the Hair of the Dog. As I rolled up on the BSA, I spotted the dishwasher in the alley, peering redly out from a billowing cloud of smoke. He whipped the joint behind his back, putting on his best insouciant expression as I strolled over to him.

"My first instinct was to grab a fire extinguisher." Then I laughed and stuck out my hand. "I'm Slats Kisov."

He shook my hand warily, mumbling, "Oso Morales."

"Oso, I haven't smelled anything that good since I left Vietnam."

"Didn't I see you in here, wearin' a uniform?" he asked suspiciously.

"I flew with the Air Force for a while. But I'm a free man now, ready to start flying as a civilian."

"You got a plane?"

"I just got one today. Ain't pretty, but she flies real nice."

Oso's eyebrows shot up, and he broke into a cautious grin that displayed two gold teeth. "I always want to try flying. Hey, you want a toke?"

"Sir, it would be impolite to refuse a kind offer like that." I reached out for the proffered joint, inhaling a sizable hit.

I'd never tasted anything quite like it—the smoke was thick as a milkshake, sweet and pungent. It shot straight from my lungs to my brain, producing a buzz unlike any I'd ever experienced. This even beat Thai stick! I was zonked before I finished exhaling. I passed it back to Oso.

"Good, yes?"

Dreamily, I nodded.

"It is called sinsemilla—that mean 'seedless.' You won't find nothin' like this around, *ese*."

"I'm sorry to hear that. I'd love to get my hands on some."

Oso passed the joint back, nonchalantly inquiring, "You, uh…lookin' for a sack?"

"Son, if you gave me a choice right now between a beautiful woman and a bag of this fine weed, I'd take the weed."

"This stuff ain't cheap, amigo." Oso rubbed his fingertips together. "But maybe I help you out with a little taste, on the house. If you wanna pay me back, take me for a plane ride sometime."

"When's your next day off?"

"Tomorrow."

"Get ready, 'cause I'm going to show you another way to get high—in an airplane."

And that's how I found myself in possession of a quarter ounce of the finest weed I'd ever run across, encountering the first of the Morales brothers in the bargain.

I met Oso the following day at the Airpark. I waved him

over to my 180 on the ramp. He eyed her uneasily for a moment. "This thing look like a fifty-year-old hooker named Kristi."

"Sometimes an older woman can show you a few n-ew tricks."

"If you say so, ese."

I kicked the tires, lit the fires, and taxied out with the yoke pulled back into my stomach to keep the tailwheel firmly grounded in the gusting wind. After a quick run-up, I goosed the old girl and honked her into the air.

Oso proved to be a more eager passenger than Wilco. He wasn't intimidated in the least by his first flight—his head was on a swivel from the get-go.

"Man, you can see forever! Can we go out over the ocean?"

"Sure. How about a ride down to Miami?"

"I never been there before; let's go. I brought some joints for the ride." He pulled one out and passed it over, leaning back in his seat with both hands behind his head, like the world's most seasoned passenger.

As we crossed the beach and flew out over the water, the air smoothed like satin. I spotted some sharks feeding in the shallow coastal water, banking over so Oso could look straight down at them.

"*Madre de dios!* This is better than Marineland."

"What do you think of flying, Oso?"

"Coolest thing I ever did! You get paid for this?"

"I'll admit it is a pretty good gig." I lit the joint and passed it over to Oso, then tuned the ADF to WQAM, Miami's best radio station. We kicked back under the high wing that shaded us like a porch roof, bathed by cool sea air wafting in through the open windows. The beach was our compass; rock and roll, fine weed and the endlessly changing scenery below our entertainment.

We flew into southern Florida's crowded airspace, and I contacted Miami approach. They vectored us through Ft. Lauderdale, and straight onto Runway 30. As we taxied in to the general aviation ramp we passed Corrosion Corner, where many an old Douglas and Convair airliner had ended their days, now serving as spare parts bins for those of their brethren still plying the airways. I found an empty tiedown and cut the engine.

"Come on, Oso, let's find a cab."

"Where we going, *compañero*?"

"You ever hear of a head shop?" Oso stared blankly at me. "Never mind; you'll like it. Uh, maybe you better leave your weed in the plane. We won't be gone long."

The cabby cruised down 7th Street in Little Havana, until I spotted the first head shop. "Pull over there, and keep the meter running. We'll be right back."

We entered Kiss the Sky Emporium, where a guy who looked like Cousin It in a dashiki welcomed us. "What's your pleasure, gents?"

"I'm looking for a bong," I replied.

He indicated a shelf loaded with elaborately blown glass sculpture. "We got some really nice Pyrex ones."

But I zeroed in on the shelf below. These bongs were much more in keeping with my basic KISS design philosophy: Keep It Simple, Stupid. I picked up a green plastic bong with a slide-on, one-hit bowl. It was plain, cheap, and tough, like my airplane and my motorcycle.

"This one will do," I said, laying eight dollars on the counter. "Keep the change."

We ran back outside and jumped into the cab. "Take me to the airport, *effendi*. It's time to leave Casablanca—we have our letters of transit."

In no time we were back in the plane, heading north.

"What, joints ain't good enough? Where I'm from, rollin' is an art form," Oso stated. "Most Cubans roll the cigars, though, not the joints," he added.

"Marijuana like this is far too valuable to watch half of it go up in smoke," I sniffed. "I don't wish to waste one iota of this sublime substance."

"You talk funny sometimes."

"Don't get me wrong, I ain't prejudiced," I grinned. "Let's fire up another joint and see how it tastes."

"That I *comprende*," he said, Zippo in hand. He took a hit and passed the joint. "You never asked me where this shit comes from."

"I'm not one to pry. I figure you'll tell me when you're ready."

Oso sized me up. "I think I trust you. My family grows this weed," he stated.

"You *grow* this stuff? Damn, you guys really know what you're doing."

"My father teach me…his father teach him. When Castro take over, my family get outta Cuba. We…" He groped for the right words. "We seek *artistic* freedom."

I laughed, but Oso was deadly serious. "This is our art, ese. And, it is how we put food on our table. But if we stay in Cuba, maybe the Communists make my family political prisoners." He sounded like McNamara, describing why the US had come to Vietnam.

"So you're freedom fighters?" I asked.

"Right! We move to Chico Cay in the Bahamas to make it a little piece of Cuba. My brothers and my sister all work in family business. My mother is boss. In America, we find many people that like our art. The money we make is safe in the bank. But there is a problem, hombre: we lose our carrier."

"Carrier?"

"*Smuggler*. We had a friend with sailboat, who took the *hierba* from Chico Cay to Florida. We don't know what happened—the boat and the weed just disappeared. Now we need a new carrier, amigo."

"So you want me to fly the stuff in."

"A plane would be faster than a sailboat. Probably safer, too. You're a good flyer—you could make a lotta money as carrier." Oso, reading the interest on my face, added the kicker. "And, we make sure you always got fat sack of this stuff." He passed the joint.

I took a deep, thoughtful hit. I'd had my plane for only one day, and I'd already been offered high-paying work. This job seemed to have it all: unadulterated freedom, exuberant flying opportunities, money. It was an aeronautical ice cream sundae, with sinsemilla on top. In the end, I did what I always do when important issues arise: I asked myself, "*What would Slats Rodgers do?*"

Talk about a rhetorical question...

Ten

To tell the truth, I was already growing bored with everyday civilian life. I actually missed the excitement of combat flying and wondered if I had become a little too indoctrinated to military life.

Crazy or not, I needed a place of my own. I also needed to find a hangar for the 180. I couldn't just keep tying it down on the Airpark's ramp, especially if I was going to start smuggling weed. I thought it would be convenient if I could combine house and hangar in one isolated location, so I borrowed a page from Vietnam flying and reconnoitered the area west of town.

This was mainly cow country, with a lot of open grazing fields. I'd been in the air for half an hour when I spotted a small ranch about five miles southwest of Farth. What caught my eye was the barn with a dirt road running alongside it; these might serve well as hangar and runway. The house was occupied—it had laundry drying on a line—but the rest of the ranch was going to seed. There wasn't a cow to be seen.

I circled the place several times, and a woman ran out

of the house and stood in the yard, shading her eyes from the sun as she looked up. I waggled my wings at her, and she waved back.

Throttling back, I performed a full stop landing on the road I later learned had been christened Roadapple Lane by some long-dead wag. Taxiing up to the yard, I swung the nose into the wind and simultaneously cut the engine. As the prop clattered to a halt, I hopped down from the cockpit. The woman approached the fence.

She was thin and plain, well into her forties but not unattractive. Unadorned with makeup or jewelry, her eyes shone with excitement at this unaccustomed incursion. "Are you having engine trouble?" she asked.

"No, ma'am. You could say I'm on a sort of reconnaissance mission."

"I beg your pardon?"

"I've only recently come back to Farth, after serving in Vietnam. I just bought this airplane, and I need every dollar I can spare to set myself up in business. I figured it would be cheaper to find someplace like, well, like this, instead of paying for hangar space at the airport. To tell you the truth, I want a quiet place for myself, too, after the craziness of war." I wasn't above spreading it on pretty thick to get what I was after.

Her eyes widened. "You want to fly your airplane from my ranch?"

"I saw your place from the air. It looks like you aren't doing much in the way of ranching right now. I thought maybe you'd consider renting your barn, as a hangar. I could easily use this stretch of road for a runway—my plane is built for rough field flying."

She stroked her chin, muttering, "That's the most novel proposition I've ever heard."

I let the idea sink in for a moment, and then asked, "Could I have a quick look at the barn?"

"Why not?" She led the way.

"My name is Slats Kisov, ma'am."

"First thing you have to do is stop calling me ma'am. My name is Jelly Rawlins."

"Jelly?"

"My mother wanted to name me Jemima. But Papa thought it would've been condescending to give a black girl that name. Besides, he was a huge jazz fan. Papa especially liked the music of Jelly Roll Morton, so he insisted on Jelly. When I married Henry Rawlins, Papa said I'd come fully into my name—he took to calling me Jelly Roll-ins," she laughed.

As we strolled toward the barn, I said, "I suppose I don't have any room to talk, not with a name like Slats." She laughed again, a sound like wind chimes in a gentle breeze.

"Here's the barn. It hasn't been used since my husband died. The whole place has gone to hell in a handbasket since Henry passed."

"I'm sorry to hear about your loss."

"It's been a long time now. We weren't married for long, but I still miss that man."

Jelly rolled one of the doors open. Dust motes flickered in shafts of sunlight, beaming through the cracks between boards; it seemed expansive as a cathedral. The double doors opened wide enough to accommodate the Cessna's wingspan. There was even a tack room off to one side, with a little pot-bellied stove. All it lacked was a cot from the Army-Navy store, a chair and a table. Add a hot plate and a radio, and it would be more than sufficient for my simple needs.

"Jelly, this place is perfect. Would you consider renting it to me?"

"You want to *live* in here, too?"

I got down on one knee, almost as though I were proposing to her. "I want to move right in. After livin' rough in Vietnam, this place seems like the Ritz."

"You are the craziest man I've ever met. You drop from the sky and want to convert my ranch into an airport, and now you're trying to turn it into some kind of country condominium." She assessed me, hands on hips, and the wind chimes tinkled again. "I may be a fool, and I may be asking for trouble, but I guess I could stand some company out here. A little extra money won't hurt, either." She nodded. "You can stay, Slats."

Oso had told me a crop would soon be ready to harvest. So, snug in my new digs, I studied for my first smuggling run.

I bought a sectional chart, the standard aeronautical map, which covered southern Florida and the Bahamas. Oso pointed out the approximate position of Chico Cay, a name well suited for a place too small to show up even on a detailed map. Located two hundred miles southeast of Farth, not far from Fanny Cay, it was just a hop and a skip away for my 180. I could use the ADF to find Chico Cay, cross-checking between radio stations in Miami and Nassau to determine a fix.

Once again I turned to Slats Rodgers, using his book as a primer on smuggling. I needed to establish the legitimacy of my aircraft, and of its being flown offshore. I could do this in a variety of ways, but time was of the essence in this circumstance. Maybe Oso knew folks in the Bahamas who would buy some kind of cargo for a small profit. Then I could pick up a much more profitable load in Chico Cay, for the return trip.

I needed a safe way to offload the weed in Florida. Slats Rodgers had once dropped smuggled watches out of his Curtiss Canuck, much safer than landing to unload contraband. This was easier to do in an open cockpit aircraft like the Canuck, but with a little ingenuity perhaps my 180 could do it too.

So I paid Wilco a visit, reasoning that since he'd already helped me get around the law by registering a plane with an illegal engine, he might not ask embarrassing questions now. I told him what I wanted and, scratching his head, he considered the possibilities. Strolling over to the plane, he popped the baggage door open to study it.

"Y'know, this wouldn't be hard to modify so that you could take it off from inside the plane. Then you could kick stuff right out, like C-47 cargo planes used to do back in Korea."

This struck me as brilliant, a sort of smuggling secret weapon. The most exposed and vulnerable time—offloading on the ground—would be eliminated. "How soon can you make the mod, Wilco?"

"Hell, won't take more'n a day or two."

While Wilco worked on the baggage door, I went back to see Oso. I outlined my idea, telling him I needed someone to assist me in making airborne drops.

"My little brother can help, ese. He's kinda different, but he's a good boy."

"I can't depend on someone who isn't intelligent."

Oso assured me, "Dante is the smartest in my family. He just ain't... *ordinario*."

The first time I laid eyes on him, Dante was confidently pushing a rook across a chessboard. Solemnly, he intoned, "*Jaque*."

His opponent considered the options for a moment. "Check, hell. Looks like checkmate to me." He left, ruefully shaking his head.

Oso handled the introductions. "Dante Berto Morales, this is my friend Slats Kisov. You talk *Inglés* with Slats, don't mess around," Oso cautioned, fondly cuffing his brother's head.

My first impression of Dante was less than stellar. Sloppily dressed, his hair was cut shorter than a Marine recruit. He was beyond thin—the guy was an organic scarecrow. I wondered if he had the strength necessary to move bales of weed around in a cramped cockpit. He also had the worst halitosis I'd ever encountered. When he opened his mouth to speak, the breath of death swept over me like an olfactory plague.

"It is my pleasure to make your acquaintance, Señor Slats," he rasped.

I matched his formality. "The pleasure is mine, Dante Berto. Would you care to engage me in a game of chess?" This must have been the right tack to take with him, because Dante grinned happily at me, gesturing at the recently vacated chair.

We set up the board, Dante graciously allowing me

the first move. I slid a pawn forward, and then said, "I am wondering if you might help us in a business proposition."

Dante squared his shoulders. "What sort of proposition?" He countered my move with a classic Sicilian Defense.

"It seems I will soon be transporting some of your family's, uh ... *artwork* from the Bahamas. I was wondering if you'd care to accompany me?"

"In what capacity, señor?"

"I require your services as kicker." He looked inquiringly at me.

I hunched forward, describing the kicker's responsibilities and quietly outlining my plans. He asked the occasional pertinent question, meanwhile proceeding to kick my ass up one side of the chessboard and down the other, three times in succession. As we bonded over this ancient game of strategy, I realized that Oso had not been joking about his brother's awesome intellect. This guy was not just whip-thin, he was smart as a whip, too.

Finally satisfied as to a kicker's duties, and also because he'd shown me who was boss on the chessboard, Dante Berto and I sealed our bargain with a handshake ...

Eleven

Which was how I found myself bound for the Bahamian archipelago with a load of eight-track tapes and a bulimic Cuban.

I trusted my aircraft, but only to a point. So I climbed to seventy-five hundred feet and kept an eye peeled for boats to ditch beside, if the engine should suddenly pack it in. I had life jackets on board too, which we could don during our lengthy glide to reach said boat.

Never having been out over the sea in a small plane, DB was clutching his flotation device to his chest like a Teddy bear. "You can relax; this machine is in pretty good shape," I told my uneasy passenger.

"I will relax when I can step onto solid land again. I cannot swim, Slats."

"You can't swim? I'll teach you when we get back to Florida."

"I do not displace enough water to float properly. I am afraid that swimming is beyond my capabilities."

To distract DB from his aquatic disability, I tuned the ADF to WQAM in Miami. We smoothed our way southeast to the melody of Los Lobos' "I Got Loaded."

Nodding toward the cargo area, I asked, "So, who's this guy we're gonna meet in Nassau?"

"He sells items in the marketplace. He will buy these tapes at a modest profit to you, and draw up a receipt that should satisfy the US authorities."

"Excellent! We'll start an official paper trail to divert any suspicion about what we're really doing."

"I am looking forward to seeing my mother again. It has been too long since I've eaten at her table."

"You're looking forward to eating?" I was surprised that DB was capable of this.

"It does her heart good to watch me eat," he explained. "Besides, her food tastes better than any other when coming back up."

"You're the only vomitous gastronome I've ever met." My companion emitted a gravelly giggle, then settled comfortably on his seat.

Taking our brisk tailwind into account, my dead reckoning navigation indicated we'd need just over an hour to near our destination. I tuned in Nassau radio station ZNS-1 to cross-check with Miami, confirming my calculation.

I contacted Oakes Field, reporting that I was inbound for landing. It was pretty easy to sequence into position, since mine was the only aircraft within fifty miles. I landed and taxied to Nassau customs, where a bored official strolled out, glanced briefly at my load, and made a notation on his clipboard. I then taxied to the general aviation ramp, where Joseph Cockburn awaited us.

DB performed the introductions, and right off Joseph asked, "Have you been through customs?" I showed him the form I'd been given. "The Commonwealth places a lot of importance on their paperwork," he explained.

We transferred the eight-track tapes to his pickup, and Joseph peeled three hundred dollars off his bankroll and handed them to me. We shook hands, and I assured him, "We can do this again, if you're inclined."

"It won't take more than a couple of months to sell this. I'll get in touch with you through Oso when the time comes."

"It's been a pleasure dealing with you, Joseph."

With that, DB and I climbed back into the plane and headed northwest for the forty-five mile flight to Chico Cay. Steering outbound from Nassau on a course of 327 degrees, it took only a few minutes to pass over my checkpoint, Whale Cay. I traded altitude for speed, and within ten minutes spotted a tiny island, dead ahead.

"Is that Chico Cay, DB?"

We swept overhead at a thousand feet, and DB said, "Yes! There's our house, and my brothers are working in the field!"

I banked and dove, and one of the brothers waved wildly at us. I waggled the wings, and he pointed toward the western side of the island, where I could see several hundred feet of outlined sand that must be the improvised runway. I circled out, reducing the throttle and adding a couple of notches of flap, and then bounced the wheels on the sand several times. It was soft, but packed firmly enough to do the job. I circled again and lined up on the strip.

I dragged in low and slow, carrying full flaps and some power, almost like a Navy pilot shooting a carrier landing. Crossing the runway threshold, I chopped the throttle and eased fully back on the yoke, the plane thumping solidly in.

I immediately raised the flaps, transferring weight to the wheels so that they dug in and shortened our ground roll. We slowed well before the end of the runway, and I taxied toward the men that I learned were Tomas and Carlos.

As the prop clattered to a halt, DB leaped from the 180 and began to jabber happily with his brothers. A slim older woman ran out of the house and, weeping with joy, threw her arms around DB. I diplomatically poked around in the cockpit, allowing them all a private moment, before climbing out.

The woman wiped her eyes and, regaining her composure, spoke formally in Spanish. DB translated, "Mama bids you welcome to Chico Cay. She says that our house is your house."

I solemnly shook her hand. "I am pleased to finally make your acquaintance, Mrs. Morales. Thank you for your generous hospitality."

She replied, "May this be not only the start of a profitable business venture, but also the beginning of an abiding friendship, Mr. Kisov."

Beaming, I said, "That is my deepest wish, too. And please, call me Slats."

The formalities concluded, Mrs. Morales led us inside. "Please, sit. You must be hungry after your long trip." Turning toward the kitchen, she yelled, "Julieta! Bring some refreshments for your brother and his friend."

Julieta brought a tray of *cafecito* and guava pastries. A pretty girl of fourteen or so, she had soulful brown eyes that beamed at me like spotlights. Julieta batted her long eyelashes, smiling shyly.

Her mother quickly put an end to the flirting, swatting

Julieta on her coltish bottom. "Stop that behavior and serve our guest!"

"Mamaaaa ..." Julieta objected, rolling her eyes.

"You will behave like a young lady, or you'll get more of the same!" Mrs. Morales apparently believed in firm guidance for her offspring.

Knowing wisdom when she heard it, Julieta put the coffee tray on the table and fled.

Mrs. Morales turned her attention back to me. "Mr. Kisov, my sons tell me you've recently returned from serving in Vietnam. Tell me, what makes a military officer want to participate in a venture like ours?"

Feeling a little like I was applying for a part-time job, I replied, "Vietnam was a serious place. I guess I just want a job where people don't shoot at me—at least not regularly. Besides, I've tried your sinsemilla and I find it to be ... *masterful art.*"

I'd apparently taken the right tack with Mrs. Morales, who beamed at me. "Masterful art ... I like that. I believe we can do business, Mr. Kisov."

I gave up trying to get her to use my first name. But I knew the boss had hired me.

―――――――

Tomas and DB took me into the fields, where I got a quick introduction to Morales-style marijuana farming. Translating the narrative, DB said, "Sinsemilla is grown using exclusively female plants. By uprooting any male plants before they reach maturity, the female plants are kept perpetually virginal. In this way, they become very potent."

"You make the plants sound downright horny," I joshed.

"That is exactly what they are. Every harvest, we use cuttings from the plants to start the next crop, rather than growing it from seeds. Thus there is a much smaller chance of getting male plants, which could ruin an entire field if they were not uprooted in time. After we root the cuttings in glass jars, we transplant them. That has just been done in this field."

"No offense, but this field stinks."

"That's our fertilizer. We use night soil, to give every field a good start."

"Night soil?"

"Human excrement."

"Jeez, DB."

"There are no sewers on this cay. Even if there were, it would be a sin to waste the richest fertilizer available. We also gather the dung from the animals we keep, mixing it with leftover food scraps and vegetable matter to make compost. Even hair cuttings and fingernail clippings are mixed in—*nothing* is wasted. After the plants have matured a bit, we switch from pure night soil to compost. In the later stage of maturity, we supplement the compost with a nitrogen-phosphorus-potassium fertilizer."

"You grow throughout the year, DB?"

"Yes, it's possible to do so in this climate. Every component necessary for crop growth is optimized. If the summer is sunnier than usual, we shade the field with canopies during part of the day, to adjust the amount of sunshine to ideal levels. If the season is dry, we irrigate the plants."

"You guys have this process down," I observed.

"It is a blend of art and science, perfected over generations of trial and error."

"How long does it take to grow a crop?"

"It depends on the season. The average is about four months."

"And how big is each harvest?"

"After we take cuttings for the next crop, trim the stems and leaves, cure and dry the sinsemilla, then put some aside for our own use, we get an average yield of about two hundred-fifty pounds. We are slowly adding field space, to increase the harvest. But to ensure each crop the proper level of care and supervision, we will hold the maximum yield to no more than six hundred pounds."

"What do you get for a pound of this wonderful smoke?"

"It varies according to buyer and the amount being sold, but we usually get around four hundred dollars per pound. The price is going up, though."

I did some mental finger-counting, and then whistled. "That's three hundred thousand dollars a year!"

"A little more," DB grinned. "You forgot to take Oso's pay from dishwashing into account."

———————

That night, we celebrated at Mrs. Morales' table. She really kicked out the chocks, cooking a multi-course dinner that had my salivary glands gushing as I sat down.

She started off with *hors d'oeuvres called pastelitos, a sort of Cuban wonton stuff*ed with tangy ground meat. Then she served a salad made with lettuce, tomato, fermented green beans, and avocado. For the main course she'd cooked a delicious shredded-pork dish called *ropa vieja,* served with *Moros y Cristianos*—rice and black beans—and a fried *vianda* made from potato and yuca. Dessert consisted of candied guava in rich syrup. We washed it all down with the purest filtered rainwater.

Now, my own mother was no slouch in the kitchen, but this was the best food I'd ever put to tongue. Mrs. Morales' meal had me humming like an electric motor. She brewed strong Cuban espresso afterward, and then sat at the head of the table like the regal matriarch she was.

Lifting her cup, she said, "I give this food to you in nourishment, in much the same way as we nurture the plants in our fields. My children water the cuttings with the sweat of their labor, just as I have used their placentas and umbilical cords to charm the plants into growth." She cast a sharp glance at DB, who was furtively slipping back into the house. "Even Dante feeds the crop, just as the mother bird feeds her chicks: from the stomach." We all laughed at her razor wit.

Her face turned doleful as she continued, "My husband paid the dearest currency of all. He paid the artist's debt in hearts-blood, giving the fields his life force." She swallowed, before continuing, "Sinsemilla has sustained generations of our hard working family artisans. But we learned to our sorrow that it could also motivate those with baser instincts. They preyed upon us, forever depriving my *familia* of its beloved patriarch. I pray that we never be taken unaware again." She tossed down her espresso, and we all followed suit.

The next day, I watched the baling of the dried and cured weed. We'd decided that twenty-five pound bales were optimal, being neither too heavy for DB, nor so numerous that they spread far and wide during an airdrop. The sinsemilla was never compressed, as this would cause mildew and harm the taste of the product. Instead it was loose-packed in several layers of burlap bag to allow air circulation, and to prevent bursting as the bags hit the ground.

As the baling progressed, I gently inquired about Mrs. Morales' comments the previous night. "Your mother said that your dad paid for his art with hearts-blood. What did she mean?"

DB's face fell. "Papa was murdered in the fields."

"I didn't know, DB; I'm sorry."

"I saw it happen when I was a boy. The pistol firing; gunsmoke drifting on the wind; my father's blood spurting over the green plants. Every night in my dreams, I see it happen again."

"Who did this terrible thing?"

"Bandits… They were after our sinsemilla. We were harvesting the plants in the field when three of them converged on us from different directions. Papa was outraged that they would disturb us; harvest time is almost holy to us. He attacked them with the machete he was using to set free the plants. They didn't even blink; one of them raised his pistol and shot Papa in the chest.

"I was too small to help with the harvest. I was just a little boy, eating guava and watching Papa and my brothers accept sinsemilla from the earth. Since that day I have never been able to eat without thinking of Papa, without feeling a need to bring up the food."

I don't know why my mind filled with the image of Meat's one-winged plane spinning down. I felt again my own helplessness at watching tragedy unfold, at being utterly powerless to stop it. I realized that DB had these same feelings, almost as though he'd experienced his own kind of warfare. There was nothing to say, so I just squeezed his shoulder and shook my head.

My aviation philosophy has always been to chip away at foreseeable risk. For the return flight, I'd brought a couple of five-gallon jerrycans of auto gas to replace some of the fuel we used coming over. While it wasn't aviation fuel, it would mix well enough with our forty or so remaining gallons to give us plenty of reserve. As we used to say in Vietnam, the only time you can have too much fuel is when you're on fire.

I did a preflight, paying close attention to the cargo tiedowns—it wouldn't do to have the load shift in flight. We said our goodbyes, Mrs. Morales hugging DB tightly to her bosom. "You take care of yourself, Dante. Here's food for the trip. Keep some of this in your stomach, my son."

We'd pushed the 180 to the edge of the strip, so we had every inch of available runway. There was a brisk breeze directly on our nose to help us along. I let the engine warm, waggling the controls and pulling on two notches of flaps. When oil temperature was well into the green, I waved everyone back. I shoved the throttle forward, easing the tail up. At minimum speed, I popped us off and accelerated in ground effect, then zoomed sharply upward. Milking the flaps up, I circled around at low altitude and buzzed the family, dipping the wings as they waved us on our way.

I took up a northwest heading, crabbing a few degrees into the wind and starting a slow climb to altitude. Using by-guess and by-gosh navigation, I figured we had about an hour and twenty minutes until landfall. I turned on the ADF and tuned in WQAM just in time to hear "Donkey Jaw" by America. Inhaling the intoxicating scent thrown off by the fresh sinsemilla, at the controls of a fine aircraft, I leaned back in my seat in the knowledge that all was right with the world.

DB apparently wasn't feeling the same. "How are we going to get away with this?"

"This is no time to get squeamish," I laughed.

"I'm not amused, Slats. I don't think I'd do very well in jail."

"Look at the bright side; you'd be the best chess player in the joint."

"Usted es un maldito idiota!"

I didn't know exactly what DB had said, but I doubted that he was complimenting my wit, so I dropped the jokes and told him, "Trust me, DB. I've flown through war zones while everybody and his brother blasted away at me, and gotten away with it."

"You were shot in the *cojones*," DB pointed out.

"Yeah … there was that one time. But I've given this a lot of thought, and I know how to sneak us past any trouble. No one will even know we're back, until long after the weed is safe with Oso. Just relax and enjoy the flight," I advised.

"How am I going to relax with two hundred-fifty pounds of sinsemilla sitting right behind me?"

"Maybe you can eat a snack."

DB eyed me like he was going to cuss me out again in Spanish, but then he laughed. "It's hard to stay mad at you, Slats."

"That's more like it, buddy."

DB pulled a spiral notebook and pencil stub out of his pocket, and began to jot down some of his strange poetry. I figured he was probably trashing me in free verse, but it beat being cussed out in a foreign language, so I concentrated on my flying.

As we neared the coast I started letting down to low altitude, to avoid being picked up on radar. I also started cross-checking my position with a second ADF station to get a precise fix, as I wanted to come ashore over a predetermined deserted section of beach. As we descended below a hundred feet, we were bounced around in turbulence. I was glad DB had a strong stomach.

The coastline materialized ahead in the haze. As we penetrated the Air Defense Identification Zone, I rocked both wings up to make sure I didn't have unseen company. We rocketed over the beach, passing quickly over the narrow strip of land that held highway A1A, and then crossed the Indian River into mainland Florida just south of Wabasso. I kept us headed west for several miles, then angled north toward the drop zone.

"Get everything ready," I told DB. He climbed in back and released the tiedowns then removed the baggage door.

A firm believer in IFR—I Follow Roads—I was looking for the distinctive intersection of Babcock Road with the drainage canal flowing from Stick Marsh. When I spotted it, I banked to follow the canal west until all signs of civilization petered out then turned again to a heading of 285 degrees. I throttled back and added flaps, decelerating to ninety miles per hour so as to minimize the distance between bales when we airdropped.

Three minutes later, I saw a man waving a red bandana step out from a clump of palmetto bushes, and I made a small course correction toward him.

I hollered, "Throw 'em out!"

"You want me to throw up?" I heard DB's raspy laugh as he started to kick bales out of the plane. "I can do that—peristalsis is my specialty!" he said.

It took only seconds to clear the cargo area of marijuana. When the bales were out, I kept us headed in the same direction for several minutes, to throw observers off in the unlikely case that there had been any. DB cleaned up in back, while I raised the flaps and accelerated to cruise speed again. Finally, I eased us up to twelve hundred feet and headed for Jelly's ranch, a big smile splitting my face.

Using a kicker worked even better than I'd thought it would.

Twelve

It was time to relax after a hard week's work. I threw a leg over my BSA and rode into Farth, aiming for the Hair of the Dog. I wanted a decent meal, but I needed something else even more.

Darla was working, as usual. "Hey, soldier, long time, no see. What'll you have?"

"I'll have a western omelet with some wheat toast. And throw in a side of tasty waitress."

She batted her eyes, smiled widely, and said, "That dish is on the house."

"You busy tonight?"

"Why, *no*."

"Maybe we could go to a movie or something."

"We could do… something."

"How 'bout I pick you up after work? If you don't mind riding on a motorcycle…"

"I've never been on a motorcycle before."

"It vibrates a lot, and makes your hair stream back, and then brings tears of joy to your eyes."

"Sounds like fun, honey."

"If you think motorcycles sound like fun, you should try flying. You climb upward, upward, upward, until you're higher than you've ever been. Your heart begins to pound and you breathe faster and faster until you feel like you might swoon. You level off, just floating along, and then— *wham!* You push forward and drop so fast, your eyes snap open. The blood is coursing through your veins, your whole body trembles and, and…"

"And what?" she breathed.

"And then you become one with the universe."

"Ooooh, you're one of them sweet-talkers, ain't you? Just give me half an hour to get cleaned up after work, sugar. I get off at five."

"You may be done with work at five, but it'll take a little longer till you get off."

———————

I roared up to the address she gave me at five-thirty sharp, and Darla was waiting outside. She was in a pair of blue jean cutoffs that showed lots of slim leg, a halter top that jiggled enticingly, and just a touch of makeup. She might have been a few years older than me, but getting out of that waitress uniform and letting her hair down worked wonders.

"You look great, Darla. Where would you like to go?"

"I could use a drink after work. You know any good bars?"

"No, but one of the nicest things about motorcycles is that looking for places is almost as much fun as arriving." I leaned the idling bike on its kickstand and, always the gentleman, strapped my helmet on Darla's head. "This will keep your pretty hair from getting messed up." I unfolded the passenger footpegs and helped her onto the saddle, then climbed over in front of her and revved the engine a couple of times.

"I see what you mean about the vibration," she cooed in my ear. I grinned and snicked the bike into first. Darla slid her arms around my waist as I eased away from the curb, aiming the front wheel toward US 1 and points south.

As soon as we hit the highway, I accelerated hard through all four gears. Darla hung on for dear life, and at ninety-plus it didn't take long until we were on the outskirts of Gifford. We passed a sign that proclaimed:

**Get-off Time at the Missile Lounge
with the Tall Tan Soul Man
1 buck getcha 2 slugs**

It was an omen. I hit the brakes hard, Darla fetching up against my back, and U-turned into the parking lot. I cut the switch and we were enveloped by a sudden silence, punctuated only by the rapid tinking of a hot engine cooling down.

"So, what do you think of motorcycling?"

"Jesus, it felt like we were doing a hundred!"

"We damn near were. Now, let's get some of those fifty-cent drinks, Darla."

Gifford was a mostly black town, and the Missile Lounge reflected that demographic. Over the earsplitting blast of Bill Withers' "Ain't No Sunshine," the bartender asked us what we'd have. Darla yelled, "Something sweet, with rum!" I nodded and held up two fingers, and the bartender showcased his mixology skills with a delicious rum punch.

Darla took a sip, and said, "Damn, that's good." She took a bigger swallow, closed her eyes, and sighed, "That's even better!" She chugged the rest of the glass, grabbed me by the hand, and maneuvered me onto the dance floor.

The tall tan soul man switched to Smokey Robinson, as Darla pulled me close and laid her head on my shoulder. I inhaled one of my favorite smells—the clean scent of a freshly-bathed woman—as we began to swirl softly to "The Tracks of My Tears."

I'm not much of a dancer, but I could fake a slow dance well enough. It felt good to slide around the floor with Darla. But neither of us was concentrating on dancing. Something was beginning to grow between us…

"Are you trying to have your way with me, sir?"

"Now, that ain't *my* fault, Darla. That dude was mindin' his own business till you woke him up."

She looked at me from under her long eyelashes and said, "I'm an old-fashioned girl. It's a compliment when the tube snake nods at you."

I looked down Darla's halter top. "Looks like you've got a couple of pygmy rattlers of your own seeking release from confinement."

"You know what they say: 'Seek and ye shall find.'"

As unobtrusively as possible, I slipped a hand in and lightly caressed her breast, and Darla momentarily sagged in my arms. "Your nipples are sensitive, aren't they?"

"Those aren't nipples—they're clits."

"I think we should move Get-off Time back to Farth," I huskily suggested.

"Let's have another rum punch first."

"Only if you promise to drink it as fast as the first one…"

In response, Darla raised an eyebrow and honked my horn.

A few minutes later we were back on the Beezer and headed for her house. Every time Darla's hand strayed below my belt, the motorcycle throttle autonomically responded, and we broke our own recently set speed record during the return trip.

We squealed into the driveway, scrambled off the bike, and ran onto the porch. But rather than going inside, Darla led me over to the porch swing.

"It's a nice night, Slats. Let's sit on the swing a spell."

"But, but…"

"Shhhhh. We have to be quiet or the neighbors will hear us." She reached back and untied the halter, and then slipped it off over her head. She had tiny breasts that were at least half nipple, aimed enticingly up at me. "I know, they're way too small," she pouted.

"You have beautiful puppies—they must be pointers." I bent down to kiss her, Darla tickling my tongue with her own. I moved lower, taking one of those outsized nipples into my mouth. Darla gasped, collapsing backward onto the swing. Feeling more than a little exposed, I peeled off my clothes and sat beside her.

I had never been more rigid in my life. Darla looked down and said, "That's no tube snake, that's a cobra, sans hood. And he looks ready to spit." A puzzled look crossed her face as she leaned closer. "Where's your other ball?" she asked.

"It was shot down over Vietnam," I explained. I'd been apprehensive that my wound would be a major turn-off for women. Now I was face-to-scrotum with just such a possibility.

"Oh, honey, that's terrible. I didn't know you were wounded. I'm so sorry." I began to wilt, thinking my worst fear had been borne out. I started to explain that I understood if my disfigurement put her off, but Darla spoke first. "The last thing I want to do is cause you any pain. Can I ... can you ... can we still do it?"

In answer, the cobra reared his head anew. Darla just smiled and removed the rest of her clothing. She straddled me, and then eased herself down. "I guess that answers that," she moaned.

As her slow pumping increased in vigor, Darla's breasts began to bounce merrily. Worried about losing an eye to a nipple poke, I reached up and took gentle hold of them; I felt her contraction deep down as she gasped again. I held her nipples in place while, back arched like a cat, Darla moved her body just enough to stretch them out and up, out and up. She froze for a moment, trembling, and then trilled a rich vibrato as she bucked over the edge. I went happily with her.

When we caught our breath, I said, "Well, *that* should give your neighbors something to talk about."

"Those busybodies *need* something to talk about," she grinned. "But maybe we should move inside for round two ... Priapus."

Thirteen

I love to swim, and I considered it a huge plus that Jelly had a pond big enough for me to have a vigorous workout. I'd bought a Speedo for myself because, as a wise man once said, you should never skinny-dip with snapping turtles. I'd already lost more than enough equipment.

I whistled for Tailskid, and we headed to the pond. Tailskid was an enthusiastic observer, but he never went into the water. He let me know in no uncertain terms that Westies were earth dogs. Swimming was too much like bathing, and Tailskid would rather take a beating than a bath.

Tailskid paralleled my course around the pond's periphery, while I vigorously stroked for more than a mile. When I finally swam to shore, there he was, head cocked and tongue lolling. I stretched out on a patch of grass, and he sat beside me, licking pond scum off my forehead every time I bent low.

I lay back to air-dry my hair, which I hadn't cut since leaving the Air Force. It was getting pretty long—soon I'd have to start tying it in back to keep it out of my eyes. Tailskid lay beside me, rolled onto his back and immediately started snoring. I think he liked the ranch even more than me—he could hunt and crap here to his heart's content, just like any other redneck.

Exercised and relaxed, I turned my mind to business. I knew I'd made a good start in legitimizing my airplane by hauling the load to Nassau. But I realized that in evading US customs, I had only half the paperwork that would lead me down the road to legality. So I considered ways to make a clearer trail of evidence. I needed to cover my tracks for the much more profitable illegal trips.

Wilco had told me that local fishing boats sometimes hired aircraft to fly over the coastal waters and spot schools of fish from low altitude. That would provide enough hours and income to help my case.

Just before sunset, I rode the Beezer over to Sebastian Inlet. I watched several trawlers returning to the dock, and received unceremonious turndowns to my ad hoc job applications. The last, a decrepit old tub called the Winnie Mae, belched black smoke from its stack as a deeply tanned graybeard backed the engine. I approached, and the first mate threw me a line.

"Tie us off, will ya buddy?"

"I don't know any maritime knots, but this slipknot keeps my airplane tied down pretty tight, after I'm done flying."

"Hey, Cap'n, we got us a pilot here!" he yelled up to the wheelhouse.

The captain came down and shook my hand. "Used to have a guy that could spot fish for us. But he deep-sixed his plane a few weeks back, and now we've got to find our own fish."

"I heard about that from a friend of mine, sir. I don't suppose you're looking for a replacement?"

He scratched his chin, saying, "Maybe. It's not a full time job, though, and it don't pay much."

"That's okay, Captain. I'm just starting my business, and I need every dollar I can get my hands on. I'm Slats Kisov."

"Name's Buxton. You got any experience?"

"Not with fish spotting, but I was pretty good at spottin' Viet Cong. Fish don't shoot back, do they?"

He chuckled. "Last feller got himself shot down by a bottle of whiskey."

"Well, I make it a policy never to drink and fly."

"Good enough. Can you start tomorrow?"

"Yes, sir!"

"Then I'll give you a crash course in fish spottin'. Ain't much to it—you fly low over the water until you see a school of fish. Usually some seagulls or pelicans are after 'em too, so that'll help to point 'em out for you. Now, my trawler has no radio, so we use sign language. Once you spot 'em, fly over us low, then fly straight back toward the fish and start makin' circles. You gettin' this?"

"It's not all that different from my last job."

"Okay. So then we'll motor over to the fish to see if they're a desirable species. If they ain't, the mate will wave you off to continue the search. If they're good fish, like mackerel or seatrout, the mate'll give you a thumb's up. Then you stooge around in the air for a while and give us time to see if the school's big enough to give us a good day's catch. If it ain't, he'll wave you onward, and you find us another school. But if it is a big school, the mate will cut his hand across his throat, and you're done for the day. You understand?"

"Seems like the better I do my job, the less I'll get paid."

"That's the sad truth, son." It's a good thing I wasn't relying on this job to put food on the table.

The captain concluded, "We get away from the dock a little before the sun comes up. Meet us out over the water two miles east of the inlet at about 6:45 tomorrow morning."

"I'll be there, Captain."

———————

The sun was low over the horizon when I took off. I'd left time to dogleg over Farth—I wanted as many folks as possible to witness me heading out to sea. I caught sight of Darla going into the Hair of the Dog to start her workday, and I dove as low as possible without knocking down television antennas to waggle my wings at her. She blew me a kiss and, fortified for the workday, I winged eastward. I buzzed both sides of the inlet, where a few dedicated surfers were already catching waves. Finally finished with my tour of the area, I headed toward the rendezvous point flying at five hundred feet.

My timing was perfect, as the Winnie Mae was just reaching the two-mile mark. I overflew them and pulled up to a thousand feet, a good altitude for observation, and began to circle. I made sure to keep an eye peeled for other aircraft, a habit learned while flying over the jungles of Vietnam.

I didn't see any schools of fish, or much in the way of birds either, so I widened my search. Several miles northeast of the boat, a huge shadow moving under the surface caught my eye. I circled, and was startled when the shadow surfaced and blew a cloud of mist into the air. It was a whale.

I knew that whales were occasional visitors to Florida waters, but I'd never seen one before. It was a hypnotically beautiful creature, moving in an almost regal manner through its natural element. I couldn't take my eyes off of the whale, until I realized my circling might attract the attention of Captain Buxton if I didn't break away. Of course, he'd never try to hook something so big that the hunter would become the prey. Mental pictures of the Pequod, being drawn down to watery destruction by Moby Dick, played through my mind.

Realizing I was being paid by Captain Buxton to find fish and not mammals, I headed further out to sea. I'd cruised aimlessly for another forty-five minutes when I spotted another shadow beneath the surface. This one resembled a diffuse snake, and as I arrived overhead I realized I was seeing my first school of fish. It looked to be pretty big, too, so I beat feet toward the Winnie Mae. Diving down to wave top height, I flew straight at the trawler, pulling sharply up only at the last moment. As I cleared the smokestack, I wildly rocked my wings and banked toward the school. Looking back, I could see the boat ponderously turning to follow me.

I flew straight out to my find and circled tightly. Then I throttled back, knowing the trawler would take some time to reach the fish. Widening my turn, I flew lazy circles until the boat caught up to the airplane. I watched the mate winch down the nets and begin to scoop up fish. I saw the mate give me a thumb's up—these were good fish! The mate cut his throat with his own hand, and I'd been released for the day from my already boring new job. It felt like I'd been flying all day, but in actuality I'd only been at it for a few hours.

Smuggling was one hell of a lot more fun than tracking down fish. But at least now I'd become a legitimate overwater pilot.

Fourteen

I took myself over to the Hair of the Dog, intending to see Darla and eat an early lunch. But I ran into Oso taking a weed break in the alley and, knowing a good thing when I saw it, paused for refreshment.

Oso broke into a wide grin, holding out the joint. "Come over here, ese, and get some of this fat dad."

"Don't mind if I do," I accepted his offer. "I've been fish spotting this morning, which was boring as hell. But I did see a whale a couple of miles offshore."

"Damn! How big is a whale, anyway?"

"About the same size as the trawler. She was huge, but she was beautiful."

"I'd like to…" Oso and I were rudely interrupted.

"Hands in the air, hippie!" I swiveled around to find a uniformed man pointing a large caliber revolver straight at my head. Oso's reaction was instantaneous: he popped the lit joint into his mouth, gulping it down like a circus fire-eater.

"You're gonna be sorry you did that, you gudd-amn beaner."

"My friend is an immigrant from Cuba; he isn't a 'beaner,'" I observed.

"A Cuban ain't nothin' but a nigger with a worse accent."

"Now, we might be breakin' the law, in a minor sort of way, but there is no cause for a crack like that, Officer... Pistle," I said, reading his nametag. I'd heard that name somewhere, though I couldn't quite place it.

He approached me, hissing, "I'm the Police Chief here, and I reckon I'll say whatever I want to a longhaired stinkin' greaser!" He punctuated these words by cracking me in the forehead with his gun barrel, and everything went fuzzy.

When my vision cleared, I found myself bleeding, hand-cuffed, and stuffed in the back seat of a patrol car with Oso. The chief flipped on the siren and took off at high speed, which I thought was overkill given that the stationhouse was only two blocks away. As we accelerated I saw Darla's face framed in the window, mouthing a silent O.

Staring at me in the mirror, the chief said, "In *my* town, we don't tolerate no hippies or beaners pissin' on 'Merica."

"We weren't disrespecting America, Chief. I love my country, and Oso here fled the communists in Cuba for freedom in this country, just like my parents fled Russia." Then I added, "Besides, about the only place I'd care to piss right now is on your grave."

"You better watch your mouth, boy, or you'll get another taste of my pistol barrel upside your skull when we get to the station!" Oso shook his head at me—I understood I was only making things worse, so I followed his silent advice and shut up.

Upon arrival, Oso and I were dragged inside and cuffed to a bench. The chief rocked back and forth on his heels a few times, apparently well satisfied with the morning's haul. "Startin' here and now, we gonna get hold of this drug problem that's croppin' up in Farth."

He sat down at his desk, paused to cram a wad of Red Man into his cheek, and then pulled some forms from the drawer. "You got any ID, hippie?" Using my free hand, I dug the pilot license out of my wallet and handed it over.

"They give you a license to fly a plane? *Shee*-it! They must hand these things out to just about anybody."

My head throbbed, but I wasn't about to give an inch to this blowhard. "I'll have you know I got that license out of a very expensive box of Cracker Jacks."

The chief directed a nasty spurt of tobacco juice into a Budweiser can. "Y'know, back in the good ol' days when I was a Military Policeman, we knew how to handle smart-asses like you. Right about now, you'd be spittin' teeth on the floor of the brig."

"You were an MP?" I asked.

"Four years. I got the Good Conduct Medal to prove it," he proudly stated.

"It's common knowledge that MPs are the biggest *mo*-rons in the military."

The chief's face clouded over—he stood up and pulled his gun again. "If you didn't learn your lesson the first time, I can teach you one you won't forget."

I changed tack, asking, "Isn't that a New Servi-ce revolver?"

My question threw the chief off balance. "What? Why, uh…yes, this is a Colt .45 with a seven-inch barrel. What's a hippie like you know about guns, anyway?"

"I know that some guys use 'em for penis substitutes.

You must be a real needledick, if you need to strap a horse pistol like that to your hip."

The only thing that stopped the chief from murdering me right then and there was a quickly suppressed giggle. I looked over to see Darla standing in the doorway, hand over her mouth. "He's got you there, Bobby Ray."

The chief looked down at the Colt, then helplessly around for somewhere to put it, finally slipping it back into his holster. "What are you doin' here, Darla?"

"I've come to bail these boys outta jail."

"*Huh*? What do you care what happens to these scumbags?"

"Well, Oso here works for us down at the restaurant, and the dishes are gonna pile up quick if I don't bring him back. And Slats is my new boyfriend."

I beamed at Darla, and then turned my smile on the chief. "Personally, I make it a policy never to argue with a woman. And Darla is *all* woman!"

The chief looked like he wanted nothing more in the world than to pull his Colt once again and empty all six rounds into my thorax. "Why in hell are you goin' out with a dope smokin', draft-dodgin' sleazeball like this?

"Draft dodger? Are you nuts? Slats was wounded and decorated in Vietnam!" The chief all but coughed out a lung, as some chaw went down the wrong pipe. "That's right, Bobby Ray—you just beat up an officer of the United States Air Force, one who received the Distinguished Flying Cross from the president himself."

"Why didn't you tell me that?" the chief finally managed to choke out.

"Because it's none of your goddamn business," I replied.

"But if it makes you feel any better, you did do one thing right," I added, glaring up at him. "You blindsided me. If I'd seen you comin', I would have knocked your dick right in the dirt."

It was Darla's turn to shoot me a warning look, so I again changed the subject. "You seem to know this guy pretty well," I said, tilting my chin up at the chief.

"I ought to…Bobby Ray is my ex-husband." It was my turn to be bowled over—only now did I belatedly place the name Pistle.

"You were married to *him?*" I shook my head, swallowing my astonishment, and turned to the chief. "Jeez, now I understand why Darla was laughin.'"

"Boy, the name Bobby Ray Pistle means somethin' in this neck of the woods!"

"Same thing as the name Ernst Roehm meant to Germans in the 1930s?"

The chief might not have understood my reference, but he damn sure knew it wasn't complimentary. He stared daggers at me, while a dribble of brown juice made its slow pilgrimage down his chin.

Darla interrupted the chief's violent fantasy by noting, "Y'know, I saw what you did, Bobby Ray. I don't think it was legal—or very sporting—to pistol-whip someone who wasn't putting up a fight."

"I'll be the judge of proper police procedure," he replied. Nonetheless, the chief reluctantly unlocked Oso and me. "Get 'em outta here fast, Darla, before I decide to feed this sumbitch to the gators out at Stick Marsh!"

"That's mighty white of you, Chief…*Piss Bubble*, or whatever your name is," I said.

I then beat a prudent retreat, before I'd pushed him too far.

————————

Darla drove back to the Hair of the Dog and dropped Oso off to finish his workday, none the worse for his adventure through the American legal system.

Turning to me, she said, "That's a pretty nasty gash. Want me to take you to a hospital for some stitches?"

Truth be told, I was dizzy, and a bit nauseous. But as a Purple Heart recipient, the unwritten rules made me say, "Nah, I'm good to go."

"That's gonna leave a bad scar, Slats."

I shot a glance at my crotch, noting, "I got scars that bother me more than this one ever will."

"At least let me take you to my place to bandage that cut—and don't sass me."

"Yes, ma'am," I acceded, as she drove off.

I didn't mind Darla bandaging my head. What I minded was the disinfecting process, which consisted of lots of hydrogen peroxide poured into my open wound.

"Stop fussing, Slats. I'd think a wounded warrior would be a little tougher."

"Quit using so much of that damn peroxide!"

Darla's expression grew serious. "You know, you've made a real enemy today. Bobby Ray won't forget about what you said to him."

"Somebody ought to teach the chief that if he wants to engage in a battle of the wits, he should arm himself first."

"He doesn't have a whole lot of humor in him, Slats."

"What was a smart, funny woman like you doing with an idiot like that?"

"Much of the time getting beat on for being smarter and funnier than him."

I'd been beaten and arrested by a redneck with more power than brains, and I was already less than thrilled. But upon hearing that Darla had been abused, I found myself growing furious. Nothing made me angrier than violence directed at women or children.

"Your treatment is done, Slats. How about we move on to the therapy part of the procedure?" She kissed me, and then led me by the hand toward her bedroom.

Fifteen

It had been several months since my confrontation with the chief, and things had settled down. I'd done more fish spotting, and my exuberant flying style had gained notice.

As had become our custom, DB and I were playing chess in the park one Saturday afternoon. Gene and I were splitting a sandwich from the Hair of the Dog. The proximity of food made DB nervous, a ploy I was using to distract him and thus increase my chance of winning.

"Must you eat while we're playing?"

"I'm hungry, DB. And Gene has to keep up his strength—I hear that Donita Williams is sweet on him."

"I'm seventy-three years old, Slats. I don't have the strength to deal with the Williams sisters any more."

"That's why I'm fortifying you with food, Gene. Any man who's still above ground has to chase women sometimes."

"I think I'm in love," DB quietly dropped a bombshell.

Curious about my friend, and hoping to further divide his concentration, I asked, "Who is she?"

"Graciella Bellaventura. She is Guatemalan, and she is as beautiful as her name. I can't get her off my mind."

"Have you gone out with her?" I asked.

"No. In my culture, such matters take time. First I must meet her family, and then ask permission of her father."

"Does she at least know you're interested?"

DB reddened, squirming as he admitted, "I've written her a poem, to let her know."

"I know some poetry. 'There once was a woman from Guadalajara; she was hairier than Che Guevara...'"

"It isn't that kind of poem, Slats. I write free verse."

"Let us hear it, DB. We might not know much about poetry, but we know a little about what women like," I observed.

"I'm not sure any man alive can make *that* claim," Gene demurred. "But I'd like to hear what you wrote, DB, if you feel like sharin' it with an old timer."

And DB surprised me by reciting one of his poems for the first time.

"Resplendent, dark
silence blankets the ground,
footfall you can scarce hear

treads Graciella the trail late.
Moon illumes all
Earth bathed in sundry silver'd shade,
scent or sound intrudes naught...
nocturnal beauty, akin to dream."

DB fell silent, looking shyly up at us. Gene spoke first: "DB, you are a true poet. If that doesn't melt the girl's heart, I don't know what will."

Even I couldn't poke fun at my friend. "Gene's right;

don't change a word. Now I know that DB stands for *da Bard*."

DB soaked in our praise, nodding his thanks. Then he moved his queen beside my king, saying, "Checkmate."

———————————

Oso let me know it was time for another trip to Chico Cay. This suited me fine, as I was hungry for a tasty Cuban meal, some tasty Cuban bud, and for that best treat of all—adventure! We made plans to exchange the bales out in the weeds west of town, several days hence.

I'd had an idea that might help bend the odds in our favor. I had Wilco rig up an aircraft radio for Oso's car, complete with magnetic antenna and single-plug electrical connector, so it could be removed easily when not needed. I'd chosen several little used frequencies that we could rotate, and instructed Oso in the use of simple code to throw off any eavesdroppers. I also advised him to monitor the radio for a while after I'd dropped the bales, in case I spotted any suspicious vehicles he should know about.

DB and I topped off the fuel tanks at the Airpark, before departing. I headed offshore at low altitude, as though going on another fish spotting flight, before turning southeast for Chico Cay. About ten miles out I started my climb to seventy-five hundred feet, automatically passing DB his life jacket.

"Gracias," he responded.

"De nada." Thinking to distract DB from his aquatic worries, I asked, "How are things going with Graciella?"

"I am not sure. Women confuse me; I don't always understand what she is talking about."

I laughed, "Welcome to the club."

"Graciella did not seem to be impressed with my poem."

"What did she say?"

"At first, nothing. When I asked her what she thought of it, she shrugged and used a word I do not know." DB's brow knit as he asked, "What is 'lesbian,' Slats?"

I know DB didn't miss my flinch and the resulting altitude loss of a hundred feet. I could feel my friend's eyes on me, as I carefully phrased my response. "That isn't good, DB. It means that Graciella, uh … well, she doesn't like … *guys*. She prefers women to men."

As comprehension dawned, DB's face fell. There was little I could do to shield him from this revelation, so I did the only thing I could think of—I lit a joint and passed it to him. DB wasn't usually much of a smoker, but he drew deeply and repeatedly this time. I switched on the ADF and turned up the music, giving him acoustic privacy to come to terms with this unfortunate development in his love life.

I concentrated on getting us to a place where DB could be enfolded by family. In due course we arrived, and I shot a short-field landing on the sands of Chico Cay. The brothers met us as I switched off, though this reception was somewhat muted by DB's pensive mood.

As we walked to the house, Carlos questioned me on the sly. "Is something wrong with Dante?"

"He's had some bad luck with a girl."

"My brother has much bad luck with women. He is someone who does better by himself."

"I think you mean a 'loner.'"

"*Sí*, he is loner. I wish I could help my brother. But DB will get over it—he always does."

I changed the subject. "How is the crop this time?"

"We got good crop, amigo."

"Excellent!"

"But we see something lately…"

Carlos was interrupted by the appearance of Mrs. Morales, who ran down the steps to embrace DB. In the way mothers do, she had immediately sensed his mood and, nodding over her shoulder at me, drew him into the house for a private conversation.

"Mama has a way with Dante; she makes him understand." Giving a worldly shrug, Carlos added, "As much as any man can understand the woman."

He led me into the kitchen. Julieta's eyes lit up and she bounded over to give me a tight hug, which lasted too long for comfort. Carlos' eyes narrowed, but I kept my hands at my side and put a comically helpless expression on my face. He softened, rattling some rapid-fire Spanish at his sister that must have translated to something like, *Stop pestering our guest, or I'll put you over my knee!* Julieta reluctantly released me.

"Get Mr. Slats some coffee, Julieta!" She jumped to it, like a properly chastened sister turned good hostess.

Quickly changing topics, I asked, "Carlos, you said you'd noticed something lately?"

"Yes, yes. A couple times, we've seen boats. Somebody might be watching the island."

"Do you know who they might be?"

"No. But we always worry, after the *homicidas* shoot Papa."

"This might be nothing, Carlos. But you never know; it could mean trouble. I believe in being prepared. Does your family own any guns?"

"Mama never liked guns. But maybe now she will change her mind, if you talk to her."

"I hardly know your mother. Why would she listen to me?"

"She likes you, Mr. Slats. And she respects that you was in the army. You talk to her. I think she will listen to you."

The day was warm and the sea inviting, and I decided to take a swim. Changing into a Speedo, I grabbed a towel and headed for the beach. Exercising would not only feel great, it would relax me for my talk with Mrs. Morales.

I dropped my towel and ran full speed for the water, diving through a breaking wave and stroking hard into deeper water. I swam out and paralleled the beach—this way, I could stay out of rip currents but keep conveniently near the cay. I ended up swimming entirely around the island, about a mile and a half.

Coming ashore, I did some stretches to iron out the kinks. As I finished I caught sight of Julieta, spying on me from a clump of palmettos. I didn't want to hurt her feelings, but I thought I needed to end this infatuation before it got me in trouble with her very traditional family. I walked up to the bush, Julieta eyeing me up and down the whole time. I started an explanation, only to be drowned out by a high volume screech.

"Julieta! *Esto debe parar inmediatamente!*" It was Mrs. Morales, crimson face spewing invective while her body language screamed even louder—she was hotter than hellfire. What really caught my attention, though, was the large butcher knife she was waving.

"*Tu comportamiento no es mejor que la de un cochino*

común! Vas a actuar como una verdadera dama, o te daré una lección de comportamiento que no vas a creer!" Mrs. Morales punctuated every word of what obviously was a lesson in unladylike behavior with viscous stabs of the knife, barely missing her daughter.

Julieta was no fool. She backed away as fast as possible from this mother-turned-madwoman, but the palmetto bushes hampered her progress. Luckily, Mrs. Morales was focused entirely upon Julieta, and I was able to step up behind her.

The next time her arm fully extended I looped one arm around her waist, then grabbed her wrist with my other hand, doing my utmost to immobilize her knife hand. But Mrs. Morales had the strength of the righteously pissed off, and I quickly realized I would not be able to hold her for long.

"Run, Julieta, run!" I hollered.

She may not have understood English very well, but she received my message with crystal clarity. She turned on her heel and fired herself through the brush like a Willy Pete, leaving only a girl-sized hole in the undergrowth.

We fell to the ground, and I spoke as soothingly to Mrs. Morales as I could, while straining to hold her down. I wheezed that Julieta's actions were those of an innocent child, and that I would never do anything to compromise her family's honor. Mrs. Morales thrashed about for a moment, but thankfully her stamina did not match her anger, and she finally stopped struggling.

"Are you calm now? Please stop fighting, ma'am, I'd like to let you up."

Though she didn't understand me any more than

Julieta had, my reasonable tone seemed to get through. Mrs. Morales dropped both the knife and her murderous frame of mind. I loosened my grip experimentally and she remained in control of herself, so I let her go. We both lay there panting, just as Carlos belatedly made it to the scene of the almost-crime. He looked at me, shrugging helplessly to indicate that he understood what had happened, as he helped his mother up and led her away.

———————

I approached the dinner table warily that night. I figured that having wrestled the family matriarch to the ground might prove detrimental to a convivial meal. But I didn't need to worry; apparently, Mrs. Morales had forgiven my lapse in gallantry. After an excellent meal of *fabada asturiana*, I brought up an interesting topic for dinner conversation—protection through superior firepower.

DB translated. "Mrs. Morales, I understand that there may be people watching the island."

"We are not sure of this. But we have become worried."

"I hope you'll consider taking steps to protect yourselves. I'd like to bring you some guns."

"We have never before owned firearms, Mr. Kisov; we are not people of the gun. However, I will admit that this thought has already crossed my mind."

"I understand your reluctance to change tradition. But if you'll allow me, I can teach you to shoot properly and safely. Please consider my offer, ma'am. I speak from experience when I say that in times of real danger, a gun can be more comforting than a Teddy bear or a bible."

While Mrs. Morales seemed a bit annoyed at my

irreligious statement, she did nod at the wisdom behind it.

I tied weed bales down in my 180 the next morning, proudly watched by the Morales family. Seeing a load of sinsemilla off always provided them a feeling of fulfillment.

Mrs. Morales took DB and me aside, saying, "I have reluctantly come to the conclusion that you're right, Mr. Kisov. I will accept your offer of firearms and training."

"I'm glad to hear that, ma'am. I'll get some guns together, and bring them to you soon."

"You are taking the only thing of value on the island with you; we should be safe for the moment. Thank you, and Godspeed."

DB and I were in the air quickly thereafter, Farthbound. As I switched on the ADF, I spotted a boat close to shore. I circled it suspiciously, but the two men onboard just seemed to be fishing. DB said this wasn't unusual, so I set course for Florida. Tuning the ADF to WQAM, I fired up a single pipe hit from the latest crop, to the opening chords of Black Sabbath's "Planet Caravan."

"Damn, DB! Your brothers have outdone themselves this time! Want some?"

"No, thank you. I'm more concerned with Mama's request for guns."

"I think it's a good precaution to take."

"So do I. I'm just afraid that Mama will go after Julieta with a pistol instead of a knife next time she gets mad."

I laughed. "Maybe I should stress that using a gun to discipline family members violates every safety rule."

"I hope you are successful."

After an uneventful flight, we slipped into the country, dropped the weed to Oso, and headed for Jelly's ranch. The radio had worked well.

And that's when the trip took a turn for the worse.

Sixteen

Approaching the ranch for landing, I could see a police car parked in the driveway. I considered buzzing it and flying away, but then I saw Jelly standing next to the chief. She appeared to be in handcuffs.

I could take being harassed, and I could even understand the Morales brothers getting some heat, but now the chief was messing with an innocent woman, and I was pissed. I made a wide circle around the ranch, dumping the several joints I still had on board, and then landed on the dirt road. Taxiing up to the barn, I pulled the mixture control back to idle-cutoff and jumped out. Tailskid ran up and barked his usual hundred-decibel greeting, and I stooped to scratch him behind the ear, taking several deep breaths to prepare myself.

"Well, well, if it ain't the hero and his Mex."

"DB is Cuban," I corrected, standing to face the chief.

"Whatever his nationality, he's a co-conspirator," the chief replied, stepping over to the 180 and peering inside. "What might you be carryin', today?"

"I don't have a clue what you're talking about."

Finding no contraband inside the plane, the chief's expression darkened. "Where you been, anyway?"

"I don't see why that's any of your business. But as a responsible citizen, I don't mind telling you that DB and I were fishing, up in Georgia."

"I don't see no poles in here."

"Now, it's true that Georgia is a bit behind the times. But, it turns out that they do have fishing poles, with reels and everything."

The chief's mouth turned down at both corners. "I don't think you're very funny. Suppose you tell me why you got life jackets on this airplane?"

"I sometimes fly fish spotting missions for trawlers."

The chief hooked his thumbs in his belt, like a prosecutor who'd tied up a witness in court. "You don't need two of 'em to spot fish. And I happen to know you weren't spotting today—I already talked to Captain Buxton. You haven't been fish spotting for more than a week." He smiled at the trap he'd set and sprung on me.

"I never claimed we were fish spotting today, counselor. I already told you, we were in Georgia. We needed two life jackets because DB and I flew back over the ocean. We were looking for whales."

The smile flaked off the chief like dried formula from an ugly baby's face. "You expect me to believe you were lookin' for *whales?*"

"You prefer mermaids?"

Jelly wasn't amused by my flippant attitude. In fact, she looked plain terrified.

The chief didn't find me funny, either—both his hands balled into fists. "You sass me again and I'm gonna knock you into next week, boy."

Now, I know dogs can't understand more than a few rudimentary words of English, but I swear that Tailskid chose that moment to step between the chief and me.

"If you don't believe me, ask Captain Buxton. I spotted a whale out by his trawler the first time I flew for him." Spurred on to loquacity, I added, "They're Right whales, here in these waters to birth their young."

The chief said, "Don't think I ain't gonna talk to Buxton again."

"You're going to be talking to my lawyer, if you don't take those cuffs off Mrs. Rawlins right now."

"Don't tell me how to treat niggers in my jurisdiction, Jewboy! I'll put this bitch in jail for the rest of her natural born days, if I see fit!" At the chief's threatening tone Tailskid began to growl, deep in his throat.

"Maybe you never heard of the Civil Rights Act, Chief. If you bother this woman again, I'll have the ACLU down here so fast it'll make your pointy head spin. You got a problem with something I do, you come after *me*."

The mention of civil rights lawyers threw cold water on the chief—he calmed considerably. "What do you care what happens to a spook, anyway?"

"Jelly is my friend. I'd bet the house and farm that this good woman never broke a law in her life, and I'm willing to put my money where my mouth is. How about you, Chief?"

He expectorated a brown stream in reply then reached for his keys to turn Jelly loose. "I'm gonna keep a mighty close eye on you, from here on. Because I know damn well you're up to your ponytail in trouble. You even fart inside my city limits, I'll put you in jail so long mushrooms'll be growin' out your ase-hole."

The chief seemed well satisfied with his part of the exchange. At least he did until he noticed my dog, leg lifted in ironic salute, rinsing dust off his boot. Tailskid governed his life by a simple motto: *If you can't eat it or screw it, piss on it.*

———————

Jelly and I stood side by side and watched the patrol car throw twin rooster tails of sand into the air as it accelerated away. Still quaking, she shook her head. "You do *not* want that man as an enemy."

She was the second woman I'd recently heard express that sentiment. "I've had worse enemies."

"Not around here, you haven't. Chief Pistle is a nightmare."

"He's just a small town cop, Jelly."

"He is a Southern police chief, and that makes him a man with power. He's also a Klan leader."

"I know things aren't perfect here, but you're making this guy sound like Bull Connor or something."

"I'm grateful to you for getting me released, Slats, but don't you dismiss me—I know what I'm talking about. After hearing your 'pointy head' comment, I figured you knew the chief was in the local klavern."

Born and raised in Central Florida, I found it hard to swallow that we were home to a KKK chapter. "Are you sure about what you're saying?"

Jelly turned to face me, one tear tracing a slow path

down her cheek. "He was wearing a hood the night he killed my Henry."

———————

I required several things right about now: I required insight into the chief's background and habits; I needed a safe place to temporarily retreat; and most of all, I craved softness in a hard world. I knew I could get all three from Darla, so I hangared the 180, made sure DB got home, and headed for town.

All dogs love getting their face into the wind. Most are satisfied sticking their heads out of car windows. But I'd discovered that Tailskid liked his airflow undiluted. That crazy mutt had taken to motorcycle riding, tucked between my knees on the BSA, front legs wrapped around the fuel tank. When we got going fast enough to flatten his ears in the wind, he'd throw his head back and let out unearthly howls, a canine banshee set loose on the world.

When we arrived, I peeled him off the tank and set him down. Darla had heard me coming and was already waiting outside. I introduced her to Tailskid, and she took one look at him and asked, "Why does he have a hard-on?"

I shrugged. "He really likes riding on motorcycles." The dog wagged his tail in vigorous agreement. "Besides, the same thing happens to me every time I get within half a mile of you."

Darla slid her hand down the front of my jeans, arching her eyebrows. "Gee, you're right. What can I do to help?"

"Umm…"

She shot a quick glance at the porch swing, sighed wistfully, and then said, "I guess we better go inside, seeing as how it's broad daylight."

Huskily, I gave the response every guy makes to a sexual invitation: "Okay."

"What is it with men? Every time the blood rushes to their peckers, they lose the ability to say more than two syllables at a time."

"You're right."

Darla laughed, shaking her head. "Wait out here a minute."

Like a good soldier I obeyed my orders, with little comprehension of why they'd been issued, until I was given the go-ahead. "Come on in, Slats."

I stepped through her bedroom door. Darla was on her hands and knees, bare bottom facing me, looking over her shoulder. "Tell me your brain is working well enough so you don't need an instruction manual, complete with pictures, to know what comes next."

I nodded, "Uh huh."

I shucked my clothes and climbed onto the bed behind her. I knew Darla intimately enough by now to start foreplay at the obvious spot. I reached around to her perkies, which at this moment were cooperating with gravity. I tickled a nipple with my forefinger and nuzzled her neck, whispering, "Do I need that manual?"

"No-o-o-ohhh..."

"*Now* who's reduced to *monosyllabism*?"

"I love it when you talk dirty, Slats."

In response I slapped her pale bottom, and then tweaked her other nipple.

Darla laid her head on the bed, arching her back and

presenting herself. I moved closer, fitting myself to her, sliding along her silken loins.

"You're smoother than a cirrus cloud."

Her only response was to reach behind and open herself fully. I obliged her, slipping into place languidly—Darla's entire body shivered beneath me. We were both so aroused that it took only a few slow thrusts to surpass the peak.

I remained draped around Darla until our breathing slowed. Finally, we rolled onto our backs. Darla looked over with lidded eyes, one corner of her mouth barely upturned.

"In recognition of an outstanding and *up*standing job, I hereby award you the Purple Penis."

"And I, as a duly appointed officer of the United States Air Force, present you the Turgid Nipple with Fig Leaf Cluster."

Darla laughed merrily, then threw a shapely leg over me and climbed on as if I was a horse. "I hope it is okay for an officer to be on the bottom."

"You may ride me hard and put me away wet."

———————————

We'd gotten dressed and gone into the kitchen for a post-coital beverage. Darla glanced out the window, did a double take, and then started banging on the glass. "Hey! Stop that, you hairy little bastard!" She pushed past me and out the back door.

I followed her onto the porch, only to find Tailskid and Darla's poodle doing precisely what we'd just finished.

"Get him away from my Coquette!"

"What can *I* do? There's love in the air," I laughed.

Darla wasn't put off so easily. She ran to the love-struck couple and tried to separate them. The hair on the back of my dog's neck stood up as he started growling furiously, and Darla quickly backed away. Tailskid didn't like to be interrupted when he was laying pipe.

"You better teach that four-legged boner some manners!"

"If it makes you feel any better, he'd never bite you, Darla. And I hope you'll forgive me for also pointing out that Coquette ain't exactly being held down."

Darla stared furiously at me for a moment then threw her head back and let loose a guffaw. "I reckon you're right, Slats. How'd he get in here, anyway?"

I pointed at the hole that Tailskid had scooped out under her backyard fence. "He's an incredibly intelligent dog with digging skills and a perpetual hard-on, which makes him a force of nature that can't be stopped. We might as well leave them to their… romantic interlude."

"More like manic intercourse, if you ask me."

Darla brewed a pot of coffee and brought a couple of mugs to the table. I had a serious matter on my mind and, knowing how touchy the subject might be, framed my question with typical Kisov diplomacy.

"Was Piss Bubble in the Klan while you were married?"

"You barge in here, have your way with me, let your dog screw my pooch, and then ask me something like *that*?"

"Just tryin' to make small talk, Darla," I lamely joked.

"Jesus, Slats!"

"Look, I'm sorry. But I had another run-in with him, and he almost arrested my landlady. I had to threaten to bring in the ACLU before he uncuffed her. Jelly told me about the KKK. I find it hard to believe that in this day and age there's active Klan around here, but I had to ask."

"What'd she say?"

"She claims the chief killed her husband, and that he was wearing a Klan robe when it happened."

"Who was her husband?"

"His name was Henry Rawlins—it would have happened fifteen or so years ago."

Darla's face screwed up in thought. "I remember reading something about a black man hanging himself back then. There were rumors it wasn't a suicide, but there's always rumors floating around this town. That was before I was married, though."

"How about the chief—has he ever been in the Klan?"

"Now, I'm not saying Bobby Joe isn't prejudiced. That man hates anyone who isn't whiter than a preacher's shirt. But I can't believe he's in the Klan."

Darla didn't sound overly convinced of this, even as she said it.

Seventeen

As so often happens, I was thinking about Meat. He had this way of reducing any subject down to its most basic principle—we called these distillations *Meatisms*. One of my favorites was: "Don't piss around when you gotta take a shit." I decided to apply this particular Meatism when it came to obtaining guns for the Morales family.

I rode my Beezer down to Vero Beach, where I found several pawnshops on Old Dixie Highway. I chose one called Jimmy's Ring & Pistol. Inside I found a fat guy sitting behind a counter, gnawing on a meatball sub.

"What can I do ya for?"

"I'm looking for a couple of guns, Jimmy."

"Name's Mike. Jimmy croaked a few years back. I took over his shop. And his house. And his wife."

"Sounds like you got the package deal."

"If you'se lookin' for guns, you've come to the right place. But if you're a convicted felon, don't tell me, 'cause then I can't sell you guns."

"My record is cleaner than your shirt."

Mike looked down to find a considerable amount of

spaghetti sauce smeared over his bowling shirt. "What kind of guns are you lookin' for?"

"I'm a sportsman, Mike. I find myself in need of a good hunting rifle, and a handgun with which to dispatch wounded game, should I fail to make a clean kill with the rifle."

"Then allow me to show you our Huntsman Collection." Mike sidestepped once, extended his pinkie finger delicately, and gestured toward a gun rack.

He had a pretty decent selection of long arms—I looked over the entire rack, before pointing out a Winchester carbine. "Let me see that one," I said.

"You've got a good eye. That's a Model 94 in .30-30 caliber, pre-64." He handed it to me.

I worked the lever to make sure it was unloaded and, leaving the breech bolt open, peered down the barrel. The rifling was sharp, and the action seemed tight. It had a little exterior wear, but that only served to lower the price.

"I like it," I said. "Now, what do you have in a .38 Special?"

Mike opened the case, noting, "I've got both Colts and Smiths."

"I'll have a look at that Military and Police."

He handed over the Smith & Wesson, with a standard four-inch barrel. A quick examination showed it to be in similar condition to the Winchester I'd selected.

"Looks good to me, Mike. You got ammunition here, too?"

"I got enough ammo to retake Tarawa. How much you want?"

"Gimme four boxes each of .38 and .30-30."

Mike complied, did a little toting on a scratch pad, and then said, "That comes to a hunnerd seventy-three dollars and twenty-two cents. We like cash on the barrel-head, here at Jimmy's."

"That sounds just a wee bit steep. What do you say to a buck and a half? You throw in some stout twine to use as a sling, so I don't lose The Gun That Won the West off the back of my bike on the way home."

"You got a deal," Mike nodded, and I peeled off three fifty-dollar bills. "You want a receipt?"

"That won't be necessary, Mike. I'm not much for paperwork."

"Hey, we got a sayin' here at Jimmy's: 'You got iron, you don't need paper.'"

I took back roads on my return to Farth because I didn't want to explain to any law dogs why I had a high-powered rifle strapped to my back. At a red light on the edge of town, I caught the attention of a family on vacation from Ohio— the three boys in back pointed and stared, and their startled mother reached over to lock the doors. I made it safely back to the ranch and stowed the weaponry, idly wondering whether Slats Rodgers had ever done any gunrunning.

I didn't wait long to transfer the guns to Chico Cay. I invited Oso along, figuring that this was a job better suited to him than DB. He showed up at the appointed time with his luggage, which consisted of a pair of blue jeans rolled up around a toothbrush and an ounce of weed.

While performing my preflight, I noted, "You're the only guy I've ever run across who packs lighter than me."

"I take only the important stuff, ese," Oso displayed his gold teeth in a wide grin. "Besides, since I was a little kid I stole shirts from my older brother. This is like a visit and a shopping trip, rolled into one."

"Maybe you better take those shirts early, before I teach everybody to shoot."

"Carlos won't hold it against me. But my mother—*ay!* She'll beat my ass if she catches me."

"I've seen her in action. That woman is not to be messed with."

As soon as we took to the air, Oso pulled a joint from his pocket and lit it. "It will be very good to see my family. It's been long time, amigo." He handed over the joint and I took a single hit then tuned the ADF to WQAM.

With the dulcet tones of Carly Simon washing over us, I said, "Family is the most important thing in life. Your mother may be strict, but she's the glue that holds your family together. I like her." I added, "I just hope I never have to wrestle her again."

I had become accustomed to navigating over the sea. I could accurately judge the wind at cruising altitude by watching the whitecaps below and noting my drift. Estimating the wind at fifteen miles per hour out of the north, I crabbed three degrees into it to hold my desired course. As we continued, a cloud bank appeared on the horizon, probably centered over Grand Bahama Island, a signpost indicating my navigational accuracy. I leaned comfortably back in my seat—some pilots may disagree, but I always enjoyed flying in the Bermuda Triangle.

With fair weather, magnificent scenery, and the finest marijuana to speed us on our way, Chico Cay all but sprang at us from the horizon. I alerted the Morales clan by diving from altitude and screaming over their roof at full power, and they boiled out of the house like hornets. I crossed the controls and sideslipped the Cessna, stopping the rapid descent at the last moment with a quick stab of power, and then setting us down light as a feather. Before the prop even coasted to a halt, Mrs. Morales was at the passenger door.

"*Ha pasado tanto tiempo desde que estabas en casa, mijo! Te he extrañado tanto!*"

Oso threw his arms around her. "*Yo también te extrañé, Mamá.* It's good to be home."

I could relate to this homecoming, having experienced my own not long ago, and I busied myself with locking the controls and tying down the aircraft. I grabbed the tarpaulin in which I'd rolled the guns, and Julieta—always ready to moon over me—took our bags and followed close on my heels. I shot a quick look at Mrs. Morales, wondering whether it might be wise to hide the ammunition, at least for now.

As Oso was enfolded by his family, we enjoyed a round of coffee. But the guns seemed to exert a sort of malevolent gravity—the family's attention was dragged unwillingly to the tarp. So I unrolled it, revealing the lever action and pistol. A weighty silence gripped the room.

Mrs. Morales spoke first: "This is unprecedented in our family. Never before have we owned weapons. It seems… unworthy of artisans such as ourselves." They all nodded upon hearing her words.

Except Oso. He shook his head, saying, "Times change. We should have known this years ago, before Papa was killed—times *always* change. It takes an outsider to teach us this; it takes Slats."

Oso looked at each member of his family, his gaze finally settling on his mother. "Well, he's no outsider now. We won't get our product to market without him. And maybe we won't even *survive* without his help. If we have to defend what is ours, then we better learn fast." He picked up the revolver, offering it to me. "Show us how it works. Show us how to stay alive, amigo, if evil comes to visit again."

So before we'd even been in Chico Cay for thirty minutes, I led them through gun handling and dry firing exercises.

I declared the next day to be the Chico Cay Fourth of July, despite it being a few months out of synch with the calendar. It was time for some American-style fireworks, and I trotted out the ammunition as we adjourned to the sandy berm I'd made to use as a bullet backstop.

Figuring a carbine was easier to shoot accurately than a handgun, I started them out on the Winchester. For safety's sake, and to get them used to the loading process, I had them load only one round at a time.

"Who wants to be first?" I asked. They shuffled uncertainly, looking at one another, before Carlos stepped forward.

"I am the man of the family. I will be the first," he stated.

I thrust the Winchester into his hands, handing over a single cartridge. He slipped it into the loading port.

"Remember to always keep guns pointed in a safe direction. Now, kneel behind this table and point the gun toward one of those empty cans I've set up. Work the lever to move the cartridge into the chamber. Rest the gun on the table, and aim like I showed you last night. Take a deep breath and let half of it out. Don't yank the trigger—instead, squeeze with your entire hand."

The carbine bucked in his hands, the family flinching at the loud report. Carlos didn't hit the can, but a nearby spout of sand from the backstop showed he hadn't missed by much.

"Good, Carlos."

"But I missed…"

"It was a near miss. If that had been a man, you'd have wounded him, maybe even killed him. It was a good first shot, my friend."

Carlos nodded, and I handed him another cartridge. He loaded it, again steadying the Winchester against the table.

"This time, take aim and squeeze most of the pressure off the trigger. Pause and take your deep breath, let some out, make sure your sight picture is still good, *then* squeeze off the last little bit of trigger pressure."

Carlos took his time, followed my advice, and was rewarded with an airborne can. "I hit it!"

"You're a natural. If you were in the army, they'd make you a sniper." Carlos beamed at me, and I clapped him on the back. "Okay, take a few more shots, then let's see how you do, Tomas."

One at a time, I let each member of the family take a few shots. The results varied, but most of the Morales clan would never earn a sharpshooter badge. But they learned the basics of shooting, and they all had firearm safety drilled into their heads from the start.

Mrs. Morales provided the real surprise. She must have had a strong strand of martial DNA woven into her genes, because she took to shooting like a cat takes to mousing. After practicing only a few rounds, she could send cans flying in quick succession with the Winchester. Nor was her skill limited to only long arms. She had a similar way with the revolver—both single and double action—as if she'd been shooting for years.

I turned to her in astonishment and said, "Your name isn't Dolores Morales, it's Annie Oakley!" After this was translated and explained, Mrs. Morales giggled like a girl.

"No one is more surprised than me. I love shooting these guns! And I feel more secure, having them here. Thank you for bringing them, and for schooling us in their proper use. We are truly in your debt, Mr. Slats." It was the first time she'd unbent enough to call me anything but Mr. Kisov.

The only one who seemed less than pleased by this newfound matriarchal skill was Julieta. Just loud enough for me to hear, she muttered, "I have become an endangered species."

———————

That night we had another fine meal, cooked by the mother-turned-gun moll. After we'd stuffed ourselves and proceeded to the coffee course, Mrs. Morales took center stage.

Raising her cup, she said, "To Mr. Slats! You have proven yourself to be not only a fine transporter, but also a good friend. I hope you will accept this as a token of our esteem." She handed me an irregularly shaped package.

I unwrapped it to find a good-sized sack of marijuana and a bundle of hundred dollar bills. "I thank you, but this really isn't necessary, Mrs. Morales. You have been more than generous with me."

"You went to a lot of trouble, expense, and risk for our sake, bringing these guns to the island. We want to give you something you like and appreciate. Forgive the money, which is a crass gift, but you shouldn't have to pay for our protection out of your own pocket. The true gift is the sinsemilla—this may be the finest art ever produced by our family. Please, enjoy it with our sincere regards."

I opened the sack and an intoxicating scent wafted out to envelope me. The buds were a riot of green shoots intertwined with delicate pistils of red and orange, all dewed with sticky resin. Each was a jewel of ineffable organic beauty.

"This marijuana is almost too beautiful to set to the match. Thank you all very much." Each one smiled and nodded at me. "I may not even need my airplane to fly back to Florida," I said, and they all laughed.

Before Oso and I departed, Mrs. Morales took us aside.

"We have become more than friends, and it's time to stop being so formal with one another. I almost feel as if you've become another son to me. Perhaps you could call me Mama instead of Mrs. Morales."

She'd caught me off guard, and I looked down, shuffling my feet. But as always, my sense of humor took over. "My mother would box my ears if she ever caught wind of that. Could I call you Mamo, instead?" Her brow knitted in confusion, so I clarified my request. "It's a contraction of *Mama* and *Morales*."

Her consternation cleared, and she wrapped her arms around me. "*Mamo* it is, Slats."

Eighteen

I haven't yet spoken about the money I was making—I still find it hard to believe how quickly it accrued. I'd made five thousand dollars each for the first two flights, but afterward they insisted on upping my take to ten percent of the load's wholesale value. That amounted to ten thousand per flight, and the value of sinsemilla was rising fast. Money was piling up faster'n bat guano in Carlsbad Cavern. My biggest problem was what to do with it all.

Initially, I'd opened a savings account at Farth Trust and Repository, into which I'd deposit money from military disability payments and my legitimate flying. But there was no way to explain the kind of money that had begun to pour in from illicit sources. I was akin to a flying prostitute, with no visible means of support. After several runs to Chico Cay, I'd accumulated a considerable wad of cash, which I temporarily kept buried beneath the dirt floor of Jelly's barn.

I knew I had to keep my bundle as small and concealable as possible. When smaller bills built up, I'd ride the Beezer to Vero Beach and, going to a different bank each time, change them for hundred-dollar bills. I also asked Oso to pay me in hundreds. But keeping my nest egg in a dirt vault with a hay door was risky.

So I rented a safe deposit box. Looking toward the future, I insisted on a good-sized one. After every Bahamian flight, I'd tuck the trusty short-barrel .38 that I'd carried in Vietnam into the waistband of my jeans, throw a leg over the Beezer, and blat down to the Trust and Repository with pockets full of hundreds. I'd lug my safe deposit box into a private room, and squirrel away another big chunk of change.

I paid cash for everything. I withheld a few bucks from each check, so as to appear to be living from my established income. But I'd feed the small potatoes back into the safe deposit box, right along with the next big harvest. My savings account had thus started to accrue nicely, as well. Like a good citizen, I dutifully paid my taxes.

I did keep a few thousand dollars on hand in the hangar. My brushes with the chief weren't lost on me, and I figured that some rainy night, I might just need bail money.

———————

I'd put aside enough money to pay off the Cessna but just hadn't gotten around to placing it in Wilco's hand yet. So I pushed the 180 out of the barn late one morning and took off, pointing the nose toward the Airpark. Timing my arrival well, I sat down beside Wilco, who as usual was presiding over lunch.

"Well, I'll be dogged! Pull up a stool, son, and let's see what the Cow Patty can do to your stomach lining."

"I don't think anything can bust my gut today; I feel too good."

"Why is this day different than any other day?" At this unlikely location for a Seder meal, Wilco had asked the most significant of the Four Questions.

"Because it's payback time, pal," I answered, handing him a slim roll of bills.

"Feels a little light," he joked. Then he slipped the rubber band off and started counting hundreds. The smile melted off his face, and he said, "I might have been a bit premature. There's a thousand bucks here, Slats. That's more than you owe."

"I included interest." He started to protest, but I shook my head. "You got me back into the air faster than it'll take to digest today's lunch. You can't imagine how much I needed that. But if it will make you feel better, you can buy lunch," I grinned.

"Hell, I'll buy lunch for the house." The regulars appeared shell-shocked. "Beer for my men and horses!" he added, earning himself a standing ovation.

"You made the right choice, Wilco. If you hadn't accepted this money, I would have had to pay you off in flight time."

"Flyin' is the only thing that turns my stomach more than the food here. I'll definitely take the cash."

Patty snapped her gum, mumbling, "As usual, I don't get nothin' but more work and insults."

I looked up at her, nodding. "Y'know something? You're right, Patty. On behalf of every unappreciative male that has ever walked in here, I apologize." I handed her a twenty. "I hope you'll accept this modest gratuity in the spirit which it's intended."

Astonishment broke over her like a wave on a coral

reef, and she bestowed upon me the highest compliment a waitress can pay a customer. "You ain't no stiff, after all."

Wilco and I conversed companionably over our grilled hockey pucks. At one point, he told me, "Dickey Houghton flunked his second-class physical and lost his Commercial license and now he can't tow banners any more. I reckon somebody else will have to service his customers now."

"Is there much to banner towing?"

"Not really. Snagging 'em off the ground can be hazardous, but after that, it's pretty damn boring; just grinding up and down a section of beach. Of course it's seasonal, demand only lasts as long as tourists are around."

"You had my attention with the word 'hazardous,' Wilco. Who can teach me about the banner business?"

"Why screw around when you can go straight to the maestro? I'll put you in touch with Dickey. Just one thing, Slats: if you're serious, you're going to need a tow hook on the 180. I can install it for you, but it's going to be expensive."

"An airplane is just a hole in the sky that a pilot shovels money into," I sadly noted.

Wilco punched me on the arm. "I'm just kidding, Slats. That thousand you gave me entitles you to complimentary tow hook installation. I believe I even have one in my parts bin."

Three days later my aircraft sported a new tow hook, and I was waiting in the shade of my wing for the banner master's arrival. A sawed-off stump of a guy with a crew cut and leathery face marched across the tarmac, stared feistily at me, and snapped, "I don't know if I want to fly with any pilot who was trained by the Air Force."

"If it's confession time, Father, forgive me for I have

sinned. I was just reflecting that I don't appreciate having to fly a plane with a tailhook. Makes me feel like I've been demoted to swabbie."

He barked laughter and stuck out his hand. "I'm Dickey Houghton, and anyone who thinks that way about the Navy can't be all bad. So says this old Marine war-horse."

Dickey had shot down eleven Japanese aircraft from the cockpit of a Hellcat before being downed himself and held as a POW for the final months of World War II. He'd flown thousands of hours in lightplanes since then, and his specialty was banner towing. Right off the bat, we saw eye to eye about flying.

"Wilco tells me you did a tour in Vietnam as a FAC. Hell, son, if you can do that kind of flying, picking up banners ought to be a cinch."

"Leadeth me to the river, sir, and let me quaff the waters of knowledge."

"Here it is in a nutshell. Banner towing is like women— the only real skill is in the pickup. The rest just comes natural." Dickey fell silent.

I waited for him to continue but he just sat there, apparently contemplating his navel. "And…" I finally urged.

"That's pretty much it, son. But if you want a more visual lesson, I've already set up a practice banner for us." He led me to the edge of the Airpark, where two poles about eight feet high had been erected, with ten feet of nylon rope stretching between the tops. The banner lay unfurled, face down on the ground.

"Here's the straight skinny. You take off, throw the towline and grapple hook out your side window, then circle around and come at this rope with the hook trailing behind the plane. Do pickups into the wind, with your airspeed about thirty miles per hour above stall, from an altitude of twenty feet or so. Just as you fly over the rope, haul sharply back and hit full throttle. If you time it correctly, the grapple will dip down, snag the rope, and start peeling the banner off the ground.

"Now pay attention—this is the critical part. After your initial altitude gain, you have to nose over and dive before leveling off. If you have managed to snag the banner, you're going to need speed and power to counter the sudden drag as it comes off the ground. Otherwise you're going to stall and crash, and when you wake up, your legs are going to be folded underneath the instrument panel like origami. *If* you wake up…

"Let me emphasize this again: whether you've caught the banner or not, you must *nose over and dive*. It's the same principle as when we landed Hellcats on an aircraft carrier. We always went to full throttle as we touched down, just in case we missed the arresting wires and had to go around. You understand what I'm saying?"

"Yes, sir. Keep my energy up: with very little altitude and maximum drag, I better have full power and at least a small margin above stall speed."

"Excellent. Maybe I've been underestimating you Air Force boys."

"We might be ugly, but we ain't stupid," I assured Dickey.

"The rest is just common sense. Max airspeed is eighty-five, or you'll tear up the lettering. Your plane is going to wallow like a pig, so be patient with her. If you have engine trouble, first thing you do is pull the cable release and drop the banner. Try not to do that over a bunch of bikini-clad girls at Spring Break, though. Mashed up young-leg makes us all look bad."

"Can we try a pickup or two?"

"Never flew one of these, before—looks like a Chevy truck, compared to my MG Midget of a Super Cub. But don't worry, I never met the plane I couldn't fly. Airplanes are like women—you just lay your hands on 'em, and the rest comes natural."

Dickey stuck his head inside the cockpit. "You got this set up nice and simple—I like it. But where's the other set of controls? Hell, doesn't matter—take the right seat." I never thought I'd be relegated to observer in my own airplane, but I kept my mouth shut and climbed aboard.

Dickey got the fan turning, taxied to the end of the runway, and ran up the engine. He pulled on two notches of flap, took off and climbed to twenty feet then tossed the grapple out the window. He brought us around in a tight circle, straightened out, and came at the rope. In well-choreographed movements, he did precisely as he'd instructed, and we found ourselves climbing sharply with full power. Dickey waited briefly then pitched over and dove before leveling off. I could feel the plane slowing like a bicycle ridden into mud, and I knew we'd snagged the banner.

He made a slow circuit of the field, and I spotted a group of airport bums pointing up at us. Dickey brought the aircraft around and pulled the cable release, dropping the banner within feet of the pickup point, then shot a landing. We taxied over to the ramp, our audience awaiting us.

As we climbed out, they burst into spontaneous applause. I was puzzled as to why as they'd all seen hundreds of banner pickups over the years. Dickey just spread his arms wide, bowing low like an actor on a stage.

One of the group handed over a Polaroid picture he'd snapped, as a memento of the occasion. There, sprawled across the banner in six-foot letters, was the following message: DANGER: AIR FORCE PILOT FLYING. I smiled crookedly.

But I did redeem the good name of the Air Force by successfully snagging the banner on my first attempt. And for his part, the resident Marine made it up by promising to recommend me to his customers.

Nineteen

Darla was due at the ranch soon, and I'd spruced up the place. Since my place was a barn, this basically consisted of chasing a raccoon out and spreading a little fresh hay around on the floor. I thought it looked pretty nice.

I'd spent more time on the 180, scrubbing her down and hanging one of those pine tree-shaped air fresheners on the altimeter knob. I intended to introduce Darla to the miracle of flight, and I wanted the occasion to be memorable.

I'd also embellished my aircraft, painting an apotropaic eye on the left door just below the window. Mimicking the eyes painted on the prow of Roman sailing vessels two thousand years ago, it was intended to ward off evil. My eye had a fierce slant to its brow and an angry red iris, to strike fear into the hearts of my enemies. The letters SK were stenciled below the eye: once the Shit Kicker, always the Shit Kicker. I thought the emblem enhanced my Cessna's already sleek lines.

I heard Darla's pickup rattling down Roadapple Lane, and went out to meet her. We embraced, and when we came up for air there was Tailskid, squatting down and letting loose.

"Your dog is not well-acquainted with Emily Post," Darla dryly observed.

"What do you expect? He lives in a barn. You should do what I do: just consider it a one-gun salute from the troops."

Peering into the shady interior, she said, "So this is your hangar. Where do you hang your hat, in the house?"

"Not exactly. Step this way." I headed for the tack room and opened the door. "Voila!"

Darla leaned in and stared at my cot, table, and hot plate. "Well, this explains a lot," she said.

"It's got indoor plumbing," I replied, pointing towards the water pump.

"Where's the bathroom? Or has your dog already demonstrated the required technique?"

"The outhouse is … *out*, where outhouses belong."

"Grown men don't live like this, Slats!"

"I probably never should have read Thoreau when I was a kid. *Walden* made a big impression on me."

Replying in female sign language, Darla placed her hands on her hips.

So I quit kidding around and spoke from the heart. "It's quiet and peaceful here. No mortar rounds are exploding. I can swim in my own pond, and little guys with rifles aren't trying to kill me. My roommate is beautiful and undemanding: all she asks for is a little fuel, every now and again." I took Darla's hand. "Right now, trees make good neighbors for me."

She stroked my cheek tenderly. "I guess it makes sense."

I led her over to the Cessna. "This is the mechanical woman in my life. Don't get jealous."

"Why is your airplane scowling at me?"

"Maybe I should be telling her not to get jealous," I joked. I explained the principle of apotropaic eyes to Darla.

"These initials look a little out of place. You're not a monogram kind of guy," Darla noted.

"It doesn't stand for Slats Kisov. It stands for Shit Kicker, my FAC nickname."

Darla shook her head. "How did I get involved with a longhair named Shit Kicker who reads Thoreau and knows about apotropaic eyes?"

"'I will lead the blind by ways they have not known, along unfamiliar paths will I guide them.' So sayeth the Lord, in Isaiah 42:16."

Darla wrapped her arms around me and kissed me hard. Then she leaned her head back and asked, "You gonna take me flying, Rabbi?"

"Yes, I am. But first, like any longhair in good standing, I'm going to offer you another new experience." I took her hand and led her into the tack room, then brought my bong out from its hiding place.

"You're a dope fiend."

"Ummm…" I stammered.

Darla laughed at me. "I'm just yanking your chain, Slats. You can't work around Oso very long and not become familiar with marijuana. Never smoked it myself, though."

Like the military man I'd once been, I explained the proper use of the Bong, Mark One, to her. "Think you'd like to give it a try?"

"I've always said I'm open to new things. Yeah, I'll try."

I pinched off a tiny piece of bud and packed the bowl. Darla positioned the bong and, as I held a flame to it, began to draw. The water pipe burbled, filling with smoke, and

Darla eased open the carburetor hole and inhaled deeply. She held it briefly, and then exhaled. Squinting her eyes and looking inward, she said, "I don't feel anything."

"You're a first-timer; it'll take a while to have an effect."

I took a turn, and then packed a second small hit for Darla, explaining, "It takes two bookends to hold up an encyclopedia." This time she settled back after exhaling, a dreamy look coming over her. I tuned the radio to a country station, in deference to Darla's musical taste, and she began to nod her head in time to "Cowboy Boogie."

"I love this song." Darla stood up and began to sway languorously to the music.

"I never saw a one-woman line dance before," I said, amused.

I was less amused when she motioned for me to join her. "Come on, it's time you learned to boot scoot."

I shook my head. "I'm Russian. We only do that Cossack squat-and-kick thing."

Darla closed her eyes, continuing her dance. I bided my time, watching her sensual performance. When the song ended, she said, "Well, if you won't line dance with me, then waltz me into the atmosphere."

"*That* I can do." I grabbed her hand and guided her to the plane. In no time the 180 was pushed out and pre-flighted, and I started the engine.

Darla squirmed down into her seat. "You were right, Slats—planes give even better vibrations than motorcycles."

I pulled on a couple notches of flap and gave her the gun. With only two lightweights and half fuel on board the tail came up quickly, and I popped her off the road and accelerated in ground effect. Just as we hit seventy-five miles per hour, I pulled back on the yoke and hung us from the prop in a steep climb.

"Oh...ohhhhhh! This beats the roller coaster at Six Flags!" Darla's head swiveled as she looked around in fascination. As we reached fifteen hundred feet and leveled off, she said, "My God, you can see to the ends of the earth. No wonder you love flying so much."

There is nothing a pilot likes as much as giving a first hop to someone who thoroughly enjoys the experience. Darla wasn't scared at all; in fact, she thrived on flying. She beamed at me, as wide-eyed and excited as a little girl, and through her unfettered joy I experienced my own love affair with the sky anew.

We flew over town and circled her house. Darla purred, "I've had dreams for years about flying, but they were never as good as this. I feel disconnected from the ground, and yet more connected to the world than ever before. You once told me flying made you part of the godhead. Now I understand what you meant."

I added power and began to climb, heading out over the ocean. I took us up to six thousand feet, where the air was smooth as spun glass. A thin layer of flat-top clouds lay spread before us. I eased us down, letting the wheels stir the mist, as if we were landing on vapor. As we overflew the edge, I pushed the yoke forward and dove steeply toward the water, like a car going off a cliff.

Darla squealed in delight, as a view of the ocean far below filled the windscreen. "We're masters of air, earth, and water!" She opened her arms, as if to embrace it all.

"You understand me a lot better now," I said.

Darla leaned over to bestow a soulful kiss, one that

quickly turned passionate. She looked at me with suddenly-glazed eyes, and then pulled off her shirt.

"What do you think you're doing, young lady?" I asked.

"Getting naked," she replied. "Just seems like the thing to do, in an elemental situation."

"Is the Goddess of Nudity applying for membership in the Mile High Club?" I laughed.

"What's that?"

"It's an unofficial club started back in 1916. The only requirement is that members have … *conjoined*, while airborne."

Darla, having finished her aerial striptease, threw her clothes backward into the cargo compartment. "Sounds like an upstanding civic organization. Let's join."

"I know you're serious; these things never lie." I tickled a nipple, and Darla tittered. I slid my seat back a little, saying, "It's gonna be tricky to shed clothes and fly at the same time."

"I'll help." Darla reached over and yanked my shirt over my head, and then started to unbuckle my belt.

"Help, police! I'm being disrobed by a madwoman!" I cried unconvincingly.

"You're about to be deflowered in midair by a madwoman," she panted, while depantsing me.

"Weed has turned you into a nymphomaniac. *Reefer Madness* never warned about this."

When Darla had stripped me bare, she unfastened her seat belt and—carefully guiding her right leg past the controls—straddled me. Facing rearward in a position that would have cramped a yogi, she was contorted but undaunted.

"Are we still a mile high?" she asked.

"Feels a lot higher than that," I replied, kissing her again. "I think I need oxygen."

Darla sank lower, engulfing me, and we moaned a duet.

Keeping one hand on the yoke, my other hand roamed over Darla's soft flesh, always returning to a nipple. She began to undulate slowly in the confined space, and I occasionally peered around her to check for other aircraft that might happen along. As Darla's pace increased, the plane began to rock in time with her, and she giggled at the motion.

"Don't laugh at my plane in the middle of an aerial *ménage à trois*."

"Bet her eye ain't scowlin' now," Darla gasped.

Pinned delightfully to my seat, I could move only my hands and feet. Wishing to play a more proactive part in this ballet of aeronautical lovemaking, I began to gently pull back, and then push forward, on the yoke. With every pull the G-force would notch up a bit, and Darla responded with increasing yelps of pleasure. As her pace quickened, so did my rhythm on the controls, the G-force steadily climbing.

G-force meshed with g-spot, and Darla screamed out in release. Unfortunately, this coincided with a large amount of back-yoke and a subsequent loss of airspeed. The Cessna trembled—much like Darla—then stalled and pitched sharply over. Unprepared and unrestrained, Darla fell backwards onto the yoke and throttle, mashing both fully forward.

The good news was that this broke the stall. The bad news was that we now entered a full-power vertical dive. With Darla sprawled on the controls I couldn't level us off, and we quickly screamed past maximum allowable airspeed. Structural failure now became a real possibility.

I had no option but to crack Darla on the bottom, as hard as possible. Desperation lent me strength, and even from my unfavorable position I managed to knock her clean off the controls. I immediately chopped the throttle and, easing very gently back on the yoke to keep from overstressing the aircraft, brought us back to straight and level. Darla ended up draped over her seatback, a scarlet handprint glowing on her upturned tush.

"I've been bad, Slats; spank me again!" she quivered, still in the throes of climax. Darla didn't have the vaguest clue how close we'd come to disaster.

I'd survived some of the most dangerous flying in Vietnam during my tour of duty, but who could have predicted that my riskiest flight of all would involve this sort of…gunfire?

Twenty

I flew the 180 up to Gainesville, after being summoned for a routine medical check to determine my status regarding disability benefits. Arriving with plenty of time to spare before the exam, I walked the mile from the airport to the University of Florida, to pay my alma mater a visit.

As I neared the campus, I was caught up in nostalgia for a past that seemed much further away than only a couple of years. A ruckus on University Avenue tore me from my reverie. A barricade had been thrown up, with students on one side facing police on the other: an anti-war protest was in progress. A student harangued the growing college crowd, over which hung a thin pall of anger and marijuana smoke. I joined onlookers, local citizens who appeared to be puzzled by a breakdown of the tolerance that usually existed between local cops and students.

Then a guy in an Army uniform, but with hair almost as long as my own, began to talk about excesses the military had committed. He was a member of an organization I'd never heard of before, Vietnam Veterans Against the War.

"The rules changed during my tour of duty. Our leaders

created so-called 'free fire zones,' in which we were encouraged to use force against people who were not clearly identifiable as combatants.

"It was not unusual to rake entire villages with .50 caliber machine gun fire, if those villages just happened to lie in one of the free fire zones. Where once we'd sought to win the hearts and minds of the South Vietnamese people, we now tried to increase the body counts by which our leaders measured success. Resentment against US forces skyrocketed.

"It wasn't just Vietnamese civilians who resented these changes in the rules of engagement, either. Rank and file servicemen like myself were being forced, we felt, to commit atrocities. Our leaders were making war criminals out of us."

The students booed with every revelation made by the speaker. But he wasn't just another uninformed protester calling soldiers baby killers; this was a combat veteran, a man who'd earned the right to express his opinion. While I might not agree with every point he made, he'd certainly paid the price to speak his piece.

It was almost time for my appointment, and as I turned to leave, the police were bringing up water hoses. I could hear them spraying the protesters as I walked away, the screams of the students, and cheering from some of the townies. I wondered if the Army veteran was being sprayed, and I wondered if I'd ever called down an airstrike in defense of his unit.

I strolled the few blocks to the Veterans Affairs Medical Center, mulling over what I'd witnessed. The docs poked and prodded me at length, then determined what I already knew: though I'd recovered from my wound, my veteran's disability payments were fully justified and would continue.

As I left the examining room, I collided with a tall man walking down the hall. I looked up to apologize, then froze in my tracks.

"What's the matter, never kissed a black man's dashiki before?" he asked.

"Wha…?" I exclaimed.

"Erudite, as always."

I pounded R&R on the back. "Where the hell did you come from?"

"Feels like the far end of the earth," he said wearily. "But you're a sight for sore eyes, Slats."

"I couldn't have been more surprised if I'd run into Ho Chi Minh." Though R&R was happy to see me, he seemed subdued. My warning antennae came up, and I asked, "Are you okay?"

"As okay as anybody in a VA hospital can be," he shrugged. "But you're the guy with the wound—I hope it ain't givin' you trouble."

"I healed up real good. I'm just here for a routine exam. The VA is making sure I didn't spontaneously regrow a nut."

"Uncle Sam, doin' his usual dumbass thing," R&R shook his head. "Like the song says, 'This isn't what the governmeant.'"

"Ain't it the truth? Hey, c'mon outside. I got something for you that requires a little more privacy."

"If any other longhaired guy said that to me after bussin' the hem of my robe, I'd run the other way as fast as I could." He laughed halfheartedly.

I led R&R over to North Lawn Park. "We can get away

with more out here on the UF campus," I said, liberating a joint from my pocket.

"Lookee there!"

I lit up, and passed it to him. "Try this."

R&R inhaled deeply, held his breath, and then blew out a stream of smoke. "I've never tasted anything like this before." He took another hit, adding, "Nothin' ever slammed me this hard, either. This stuff is takin' the top of my head off, like a round from a ZPU."

"Not your average stink weed, that's for sure. I wish you had your guitar with you—we could show those college kids what 'higher learning' is all about."

R&R's face fell. "Don't play no more, Slats. I got the music knocked right out of me in Vietnam."

"Huh?"

"I smashed my guitar against a tree, like some kind of bush-crazed Pete Townshend."

"Why?"

He looked inward for a moment. "I don't think I could tell this to anyone else. Those shrinks at the VA will sure as shit never hear the whole story. But I can talk to you."

I'd never seen R&R look so miserable. He took another hit to fortify himself, and then passed the joint back to me. "I was almost on my way back to the World. Another few flights and I'd have been *gone*. Then Operation Jefferson Glenn came along.

"The 101st Airborne was helping ARVN troops destroy rocket installations along the foothills of the Truong Son Mountains. The good guys came under fire, so I did what I'd done hundreds of times, called in a gaggle of fighter-bombers. I was in communication with the ground grunts—those guys gave me the coordinates, and I marked the target. Only…" he swallowed.

I passed the joint back, giving R&R all the time he needed to gather his thoughts. He took a couple of big hits, and then continued. "Only this time, I didn't hit no fuckin' gooks. The ground grunts started screamin' to stop, and I started screamin' at the Phantoms to break off, but it was too late.

"I hit our own guys. I took out a whole patrol, Slats." Fat tears formed in my friend's eyes. "I incinerated God knows how many of our own boys." R&R broke down and cried like a baby, and there was nothing I could do but hold him while he let it out.

When he finally settled down, R&R wiped his face on his sleeve. "You ever think about Meat?"

"All the time," I nodded, holding up my hand to show him the ring I'd never taken off. "Every time I look at this."

"Well, there's worse things than dying in Vietnam." R&R told me he was being treated for post-Vietnam syndrome.

"I've never heard of it."

"The shrinks are starting to call it PTSD now, short for post-traumatic stress disorder. In World War II, they called it battle fatigue. Some guys get addicted to adrenaline, do dangerous stuff. A lot of them experience depression, or develop some kind of anxiety disorder. Some guys even have hallucinations."

"If that's PTSD, many vets I've met must have it. Hell, *I* exhibit some of that behavior."

"Whatever they call it, to me it ain't nothin' but plain old culpability knockin' at the door. They got me on Valium now, but all that shit does is make me feel numb and weak.

Maybe I need to get back to smokin' weed—that stuff of yours makes me feel better than anything those pill-pushers are throwing at me."

"In that case, allow Dr. Kisov to prescribe his special PTSD medicine." I handed him all the weed I had on me. "I'm also extending an invitation to take the cure at my place in Farth. I'll personally fly you down in my deluxe charter aircraft, extend the hospitality of my treatment facility, and then fly you back to wherever you need to go." I assured him, "Seriously, it's quiet and peaceful, and I can get my hands on as much good smoke as you want. I think you'd like it, R&R."

"Can I have a rain check? I'd take you up on it right now, but I have to report to my new boss on Monday."

"You've already found a job?

"Yep, I just finished training."

"So come down for a day or two. I'll make sure you're back in plenty of time to start your new job."

I was gratified to see R&R relax enough to flash a genuine smile. "That's real nice of you, Slats. I'd love to see your hometown, metropolis that is must be."

Twenty-one

It didn't take R&R long to pack a bag and meet me at the airport. As he walked onto the ramp, he started to chuckle upon sighting my 180. "Jesus, *this* is your 'deluxe charter aircraft?'"

Assuming my most dignified expression, I said, "I'll have you know that at the Airpark, this is the closest thing we have to a Learjet."

"Farth must not bear a whole lot of resemblance to Westchester County Airport." He peered in the window at the instrument panel. "But your 180 does remind me a lot of an O-1."

"Hell, the best thing about her right now is that there's no set of controls where you'll be sittin'," I joshed.

"No, the best thing is there ain't no launch rails on this plane."

"I can't punch any holes in that statement. If there's one lesson that Vietnam taught me, it's this: 'Don't draw fire; it irritates the people around you.' And nothin' draws fire quite like armament hanging from your wing."

"You're singin' to the choir. Amen, brother."

R&R threw his bag in back and we took off, heading southeast. He was quiet for a long spell, before turning to me. "I can't tell you how much better I feel, after getting some of that off my chest. It sure is good to be with you again, Slats."

"The feeling is mutual. But you still aren't going to fly my plane."

"Then I'll smoke this all by my lonesome," he replied, pulling one of my joints out of his pocket. But after drawing on it several times, he generously reconsidered and passed it to me.

"So, what's this new job you mentioned?

R&R looked a bit uncomfortable. "I just finished training with the BNDD."

"What's the BNDD?"

"It's better known as the Bureau of Narcotics and Dangerous Drugs."

What a character my friend was; I almost fell off my seat laughing at his joke.

But R&R didn't even crack a smile. "I ain't kiddin'—I'm their newest plainclothes officer." Pulling out his wallet, R&R flipped it open to reveal a shiny new blue-and-gold badge. "But that's only a temporary position. I was really hired because of my aviation background. I'll eventually become their go-to expert on aerial smuggling."

It was my turn to swallow. Under the circumstances, I did the only thing I could—I presented my hands for cuffing. "I'll go peacefully, Marshal. You got me fair and square."

"I'm going to let you slide this time," he magnanimously waved me off, leaving a ropy trail of smoke in the cabin. "We both know that marijuana isn't a narcotic, and it sure as hell isn't dangerous. But I might have to confiscate any more of this I run across," he said, holding up the remaining roach. "Besides, someone's gotta fly the plane."

"Life is full of irony," I smiled, shaking my head. "The guy who introduced me to marijuana is now a narc."

"Don't hold it against me, Slats. I *am* under a psychiatrist's care," he ruefully replied.

It didn't take long to reach the ranch. Jelly was hanging some wash to dry as we landed, and she came over as the prop coasted to a halt.

"Sorry, Slats, I didn't know you had a guest."

"Miss Jelly Rawlins, I'd like you to meet my best friend, R&R."

"'Scuse me, ma'am, but Men-*a*-chem here isn't at his best with introductions. I am BNDD Agent-at-Large Malcolm R. Rehnquist, and I'm pleased to make your acquaintance." R&R bent low to bestow a kiss on the back of her hand.

Jelly flushed, but recovered herself quickly. "Welcome to my modest ranch, Agent Rehnquist."

"You are the first rancher I've ever met," R&R said, and Jelly blushed again.

"I don't mean to interrupt the moment, but what does the R stand for, *Malcolm*?" I inquired.

"Reinhold."

"You really missed your calling, R&R. With a handle like that, you should have become a lawyer." My comment broke them up, and I added, "We flew together in Vietnam, Jelly. That was before he became an agent, of course."

Just then, Tailskid raced up. Launching himself into the air from five feet away, he caught me at knee height, all but bowling me over with his enthusiasm. I mussed his unkempt head, saying, "It's good to see you too, boy."

R&R squatted down and scratched Tailskid behind one ear—the dog's head immediately tilted over forty-five degrees. "Look at that bank angle! Add that to his short-field takeoff technique, and it's plain to see this dog is a natural born flyer."

"Meet Tailskid: he adopted me on my first day back."

"Slats gave you a good aeronautical name, didn't he, boy?" Tailskid answered with one of his hundred-decibel barks, right in R&R's face. "But you could sure use a tooth-brushing. And a bath!" Upon hearing his least favorite word, Tailskid backed cautiously rearward.

"*Bath* is a cuss word to Tailskid," I laughed.

"I was just kiddin', boy. You don't smell any worse than we did in Vietnam. Come back over here and get some more scratchin.'" Good-natured animal that he was, Tailskid forgave R&R and returned to his side.

R&R helped me push the 180 into the barn, and I showed him around the tack room and swimming hole. He was uncharacteristically quiet until the short tour ended.

"I can see why you like this place so much. You found yourself an idyllic corner of the world. It's got the few things a man needs, and no bullshit distractions." He added, "I like your landlord, too."

"Jelly's a special lady. Don't know how she manages to hold on to that—she's had sorrow in her life." I told him about Jelly's husband Henry, and his lynching by the Klan. "The guy who led the killing is now police chief of Farth."

"A lynching, in this day and age? Christ, the South hasn't changed much in the last hundred years."

"The chief and I don't exactly see eye to eye, either.

He welcomed me home by pistol-whipping me."

R&R rubbed his face. "How... *biblical*. Trouble in paradise is an old story."

I flew R&R to the Airpark, where we picked up some takeout and beer before strolling downtown to eat. We sat on a park bench, popped our tops, and unwrapped our burgers.

R&R took one sniff and said, "Jesus, Slats, this stuff stinks even by Vietnam standards."

"That's why the restaurant is known to one and all as the Cow Patty. Slosh their grub around in enough beer, though, and it gets more palatable."

"Think a six-pack is enough?"

I didn't get a chance to answer him before DB and Gene showed up. Gesturing toward them, I said, "R&R, I'd like to introduce you to some friends, Gene and DB." Turning to them, I added, "R&R and I served together. This guy could fly a whorehouse, if you bolted a big enough engine to it."

Gene shook hands. "Pleased to meet you. And I thank you for your service to our country, son."

DB leaned close, rasping, "It is a pleasure to make your acquaintance."

Stiffening as DB's breath roiled over him, R&R quickly caught himself and said, "The pleasure's all mine, gentlemen." But I noticed that he brought the previously reviled hamburger up close to his face for use as an air freshener.

DB set up the omnipresent chessboard, and he and Gene started a game. Pushing a white pawn forward, Gene asked, "What do you think of our fair township, R&R?"

"It's small, quiet, and friendly, and I can't tell you how pleasant that is after Vietnam."

"It's a mighty nice place, with the exception of a few people. But what city can say otherwise?" The words were barely out of Gene's mouth when the chief sidled up.

"Hey, speak of the devil," I observed.

"I see you're hangin' out with the usual losers." Then, staring pointedly at R&R, he said, "Don't believe I've seen this darky around here, though."

"Who are you calling darky, you slack-jawed ofay shit-bird?" I'd never seen anybody get R&R's back up so fast; he was usually as calm as a country preacher.

I was considerably less surprised at the chief's instantaneous rage. "I'm Chief of Police Pistle, and you're *this* guddamn close to spendin' time in my jail! Let's see some ID, boy, and I mean right now!"

R&R was half out of his chair, and if I was any judge of body language, he looked ready to launch himself like a Sidewinder missile. The chief's hand had already strayed to his revolver when I stepped smoothly between them. "Have a little respect for a fellow officer of the law."

The chief flashed one of his cow hit-by-a-stunner-at-the-slaughterhouse looks. "What in the hell are you goin' on about, hippie?"

"Why don't you 'tin' the chief, R&R?" I suggested.

Slowly straightening from his half-crouch, R&R towered over the chief. He reached into his back pocket, pulled out his wallet, and flipped it open to reveal his badge.

The chief's brow furrowed as he slowly spelled, "B...N...D...D."

Back in control of himself, R&R said, "Say, you really know your alphabet. Can you count, too?"

"Now, R&R," I interceded, "humor only confuses the constable."

"That wouldn't seem to be a difficult job," he replied.

"What's them initials mean, anyway?" the chief asked.

"I like to think they stand for Badass Nigger Doing his Duty. But most folks just say Bureau of Narcotics and Dangerous Drugs."

"A guy who's hangin' out with the biggest dopehead in Florida is tellin' me he's a narcotics agent?" Though I'd seen the chief splutter before, it still tickled me every time.

R&R held his shirttail up, showing the .38 tucked into his waistband. "If my badge doesn't convince you, perhaps this Detective Special will."

The chief's eyebrows shot up; I don't think anyone had ever threatened, however obliquely, to put on-duty holes in him. "Maybe I better call your superiors to see if your story checks out."

"You can call your mommy, if it makes you feel any better. But don't ever jack me up again. I've run into guys like you all my life; you're just another dumb fuck in a pickup truck."

The chief's only response was to let go an angry stream of tobacco juice. But I noticed it hit the grass well away from R&R.

As the chief stalked off, I mouthed, "Badass Nigger Doing his Duty?"

R&R shrugged. "Nothing else came to mind in the heat of moment."

"That's okay; punctuating your statement with a Colt

revolver made up for it. You really got ol' Piss Bubble's goat."

"Piss Bubble… That fits Bobby Ray Pistle to a T," Gene chuckled.

"He came real close to getting a lesson in PTSD. Anger management ain't exactly been my forté, lately," R&R admitted.

"Well, I know a little something that'll help you manage your anger. But let's get off the street first, Agent Rehnquist."

DB, an astonished expression pasted onto his face, still held a pawn mutely in his hand.

"Nice meeting y'all," R&R said, as we turned to go. "We'll have to do this again, real soon."

We adjourned to an empty lot, with a good field of vision for security purposes, before firing up a joint. "You really Florida's biggest dopehead?" R&R asked.

"I do try," I said modestly. "Y'know, we probably should have invited the chief. Now there's a guy in need of a good anger management technique, if ever I saw one."

"I wouldn't piss on him if he was afire. Besides, I doubt a cracker like that does anything but dip worm dirt and drink beer," R&R replied.

"He's got other hobbies. He also enjoys hitting women. He smacked my girlfriend around when they were married."

"You're dating the chief's ex-wife?"

"I am. Vietnam must have given me a taste for living dangerously."

"You two are destined to butt heads."

I pointed at the scar on my noggin. "He's had his shot at my head. Remember that pistol-whipping I mentioned? First time we met, he went upside my head with that gun he carries around on his hip. He loves that old pistol."

"And I thought this place was peaceful."

"Farth may well be the Garden of Eden. But I reckon that makes Piss Bubble the snake."

"Perhaps you should learn to be a little more circumspect, Slats."

I held my finger up in the air like a learned philosopher, reciting one of my favorite quotes. "'There are three kinds of men: some learn by reading, a few learn by observation, and the rest of us just have to piss on the electric fence.' I think King Saul said that, right after losing to the Philistines."

R&R laughed, and then smacked himself on the forehead. "We forgot to pick up the rest of the beer when we left."

"You also left your hamburger behind."

"That thing was too lethal to eat. Besides, I don't want to spoil my appetite—Jelly invited me to dinner tonight."

"Is that a fact? You work pretty fast, with that shiny badge and your … *gun*."

R&R snatched the joint from my hand and took another hit. "My gun is no snub nose," he sniffed. "It's a Buntline."

I didn't see R&R until mid-morning the following day. "You're looking fat, dumb, and happy. Stay up late?"

"My daddy taught me that it ain't polite to kiss and tell. Gotta say, though, that I haven't felt this relaxed in quite a spell. You weren't kiddin' when you said your 'treatment facility' would be good for me."

"That makes me a happy man, R&R."

"The only bad thing about this visit is that it has to end so quickly. It's time for me to go back to Gainesville to start my job."

"I figured that that announcement might come soon, so I got you a parting gift." I handed R&R a fat baggie of the best sinsemilla I had. "I hope this *medicine* will stand you in good stead."

"I don't ever want to know where this stuff came from. In my new profession, that's known as 'plausible deniability.'"

"Government speak."

"I can't thank you enough, Slats. The Lord was lookin' out for me, when He let me trip over you at the VA."

"Come back anytime." I said, rolling out the welcome mat for future visits.

Twenty-two

Just about the time a fellow named D.B. Cooper was leaping out of a 727 with a bundle of cash, I met Dr. Elliot Everett for the first time. He introduced himself by tripping over the grounding wire, while I was fueling my Cessna at the Airpark. I turned to find a gentleman wearing a sport coat and wire-rimmed glasses, peering down at the cable that had ensnared his ankle.

I climbed down from the ladder and handed him the fuel nozzle. "Hold this while I untangle you and reground the plane. I'd hate for all three of us to go up in a fiery explosion, when we've just met."

"Might you be Slats Kisov, by chance?"

I reached for the hose and resumed fueling. "How do you know my name?"

"Captain Buxton told me to look for a man with the most battered airplane at the airport."

"You got me there," I laughed.

"I've got to admit, I'm not much for flying, and I can't swim a stroke, so I want something that's not going to drop me in the water. I'm Dr. Everett, by the way."

"You want to charter my plane?"

"Yes. I'm a marine biologist teaching at a small college down the coast, on my annual pilgrimage to study Right whales. Every winter, they calve their young in coastal waters. I've been hanging around the inlet since yesterday, pestering everyone about whales. The captain got tired of it and sent me here."

"You're a marine biologist that can't swim?"

The doc looked abashed, admitting, "I guess you could say I'm on the theoretical side of the fence."

I laughed again, and then said, "I spotted a Right whale a few months back, while fish spotting for the captain. Beautiful creature, she was."

The doc's eyes shone. "I fell in love with them the day I saw my first, back when I was fifteen. This is pretty far south to encounter one, though; most don't come further down than the waters of northern Florida. We may have to fly up the coast to find them."

"This plane has a range of almost eight hundred miles, if we throttle back some. And going slow is better for reconnaissance purposes, anyway."

"Sounds like you've done this before."

"If finding whales is anything like locating Viet Cong, I'm your man."

"You flew for the military?"

"Hope that ain't a problem."

"I was in the Navy myself, back in the early sixties, Mr. Kisov."

"Well, this ex-Air Force bug smasher won't hold that against you. And call me Slats, Doc."

————————

Next day, the doc and I found ourselves airborne and

paralleling the coast. As we flew north, keeping an eye out for whales all the while, we got to know one another a little.

"If you don't mind me asking, what did you do in the Navy, Doc?"

"I was part of a team at Point Mugu, California, investigating the use of aquatic mammals as military aids."

"You mean as weapons?"

"More like assistants. We worked mostly with bottlenose dolphins, which we trained as harbor guards. Several of my wards ended up watching over our ships at Cam Rahn Bay."

"I never heard anything about that."

"The program was secret at the time, and talk still isn't bandied about much. Dolphins were also trained to assist divers, and to locate lost items like armament accidentally dropped from ships or aircraft."

"I always knew dolphins were smart creatures, but I guess I never realized just how intelligent they really are."

"For a while, we also worked with beluga whales, and that's where I came into my own. Belugas are even smarter than dolphins. They can also carry much bigger loads, and dive deeper and faster. But belugas are creatures of the arctic climes. That and their relative rarity put an end to whale use in the Navy, much to my regret. So when my enlistment was up, I took up whale research full time as a civilian."

The doc stiffened in his seat, staring off into the distance. Then he reached for the binoculars hanging from the strap around his neck, bracing his arms so as to get a steady look. Unfortunately, he chose to brace himself on the yoke, and the pressure he exerted on the controls caused us to bank sharply. As the wing dropped Doc dropped his binoculars, the strap wrapping itself around the yoke. Attempting to unsnarl it, he pulled on the strap, which put us into an uncoordinated steep right turn.

"Jesus Christ, let go of that strap before you spin us into the sea!" I brought us out of our downward spiral, and then continued, "There's nothing over there but waves. So let's set up some air rules right off the bat. Rule number one: don't move nothin' but your eyeballs and your pointing finger. I'll handle the controls, and you are in charge of observation. If you see something that needs to be investigated, just point at it and I'll take us right over. The way things are going, we're more likely to circumcise a whale with the propeller than we are to observe him."

The doc cleared his throat and said, "I'm truly sorry. I seem to have a way of getting tangled up in things. I shall endeavor to control the unfortunate tendency."

"That's okay, Doc. But you'll forgive me if I keep a weather eye on you."

We were off the coast near St. Augustine when I spotted a puff of vapor. I inclined my head, saying, "Over there—I think it's a spout."

"You found one! And there's a calf with her, too!"

We overflew them, and I banked right to give him an unobstructed view, throttling back and pulling on a couple of notches of flap. As we slowed to circle mother and calf at low altitude, Doc marked the location on his map, jabbering excitedly all the while. He seemed more cranked up than a kid with a new sled on Christmas. I smiled to myself, muttering, "Rosebud."

"Eh? Oh, excellent idea, Mr. Kisov. We'll christen the

mother Rose, and her calf Rosebud," he said, scribbling furiously in his notepad. The doc had constructively misunderstood my comment.

But unlike Charles Foster Kane, this man would never become jaded.

———————

Every day for a week, the doc and I flew back up to the waters off St. Augustine Beach. Rose and her bud had found the undersea freshwater vent located three miles offshore. Most of these so-called submarine springs were mere drizzles, but this tremendous outpouring rose to produce a large pool of lighter-colored sweet water on the ocean surface. For centuries, everything from sailing ships to U-boats had used this spring to replenish their drinking water. Our whales had found themselves an aquatic oasis.

It didn't take long to find them on successive days, as they never seemed to stray far from the spring. Even the doc couldn't explain why creatures of the sea enjoyed such close proximity to fresh water, but we certainly took advantage of their preference—the ability to locate them so easily maximized our observation time. By the end of the week, Doc had more experience with these two than all his previous Right whale sightings combined.

On our last day, we circled the pair for quite some time, the doc snapping roll after roll of 35mm film. Finally, I tapped on the fuel gauge to get his attention.

"We're gonna have to head back. I always like to maintain a little fuel in reserve: there's nothing less useful than air in a gas tank, Doc."

Though disappointed, he acquiesced. "Quite right, Mr. Kisov. But I'm sorry to have to break off this study. I've never had such a ringside seat to watch whales in their natural environment."

He started to wind the rest of the film around the spool, so he could place it in a canister, but somehow the doc got his sleeve twisted around the mixture control. Belatedly remembering his pledge to stay away from the instrument panel, he withdrew his hand. This yanked the mixture back to idle-cutoff, and the engine died.

The sudden silence galvanized me into action. Shoving Doc's arm forward, I yelled, "Mash this red knob all the way down and keep your hand on it, or we'll end up sleeping with Davy goddamn Jones!"

As the mixture control went forward, the engine caught again, backfiring so violently I thought the muffler would part company with the aircraft. I shot a furious look at the doc, preparing to royally ream him out. But his face had so ghastly a pallor that I swallowed my comment.

While working to free his sleeve from the mixture control, I mumbled under my breath, "These friggin' legit flights are gonna *kill* me."

I made the doc sit on his hands, like a misbehaving little boy, as we flew back to the Airpark. He was still apologizing when the chief stalked up to us on the ramp.

I introduced him: "This is Chief Pistle, Doc, titular head of our two-man police force."

"If it ain't the hippie and his latest accomplice…"

Still feeling guilty after his aerial faux pas, Doc pleaded, "I didn't mean to get tangled up in anything, officer."

"Well, you're about as tangled as you can get!" shouted

the chief, shoving the doc up against the fuselage and patting him down.

"He ain't chargin' you with mishandling the airplane, Doc," I explained. "He thinks you're a smuggler."

The doleful look he shot me would have been laughable under other circumstances. While Dr. Everett may have been one of the smartest people I'd ever met, he was naïve when it came to the real world.

"See, the chief labors under the delusion that I smuggle drugs, and that anyone who flies with me must be helping me. I've demonstrated many times that I'm a retired military pilot who now engages in legitimate civil flying, but this flatfoot just doesn't seem to get it. Of course, he doesn't have anywhere near the intelligence of Rosie the Whale."

The chief whirled unexpectedly on me, and I didn't see his fist coming until too late. Down I went. "Don't you start that whale shit on me again, boy!"

"The only thing lower than whale shit is your IQ." I grinned at him, adding, "You ever hit me again, Piss Bubble, and I swear to God I'll knock you right on your fat ass."

He took a threatening step toward me, but to his credit the doc moved between us. "There has been a serious misunderstanding, Chief Pistle. My name is Dr. Everett. I'm a college professor who hired Mr. Kisov to assist me in conducting whale research. We've just returned from a flight up to St. Augustine, where we've been observing a Right whale named Rose and her newborn calf, Rosebud. I have notes and film to back me up, if my word isn't sufficient."

The chief turned toward Doc, only now noticing the academic gear with which he was festooned. "Let me see some ID, buster." Doc complied immediately, the chief perusing the credentials with his customary squint and lip movements.

The doc helped me to my feet, inquiring, "Are you all right?"

"I've been hit harder by Vietnamese bar girls," I said, dusting off the seat of my jeans. The chief threw the identification card down and stomped furiously back to his patrol car. I slapped Doc on the back, adding, "I should have realized a professor would know how to bleed air out of an over-inflated adolescent."

He grinned shyly. "I've had worse trouble from recalcitrant students, Mr. Kisov."

"I keep tellin' you, Doc, call me Slats."

Twenty-three

If there was anything my time in Vietnam had taught me, it's that one never knows what turn life might take. A good case in point was my shopping trip, in search of something I'd never needed before. Christmas was around the corner, and I wanted to buy Darla something nice.

I suppose I could have shopped locally, but that would have given me few choices other than the Woolworth or Jimmy's Ring & Pistol. Instead, I flew the 180 down to Miami and had the taxi driver drop me off on Collins Avenue. Perplexed by the job at hand, I wandered around until I spotted the Parfumerie Parisian. I stepped inside and froze—I was the only one in the place not formally dressed. I could not have felt more out of place if I'd suddenly found myself standing in Hanoi.

A pretty little saleswoman took pity on this country boy and glided over on high heels. Her nametag, which identified her as Regina Louise Castlenuevo, was almost as big as she was.

"Welcome to Miami's finest perfumery. You seem somewhat ... *overwhelmed*. Please allow me to assist you, sir. And be assured that I can make this experience a painless one."

"You don't realize what a godsend you are," I smiled gratefully. "I've never been perfume shopping before."

Miss Castlenuevo's eyes flickered over my blue-jeaned and flannel-shirted form, before she smoothly replied, "I'd never have known it, had you not confessed." The sparkle in her eye and tiny smile on her lips put the polite lie to her fantastic statement.

"I did take the precaution of scraping off my boots before I left the ranch." Her laughter encouraged me to add, "It wouldn't do to introduce indecorous odors into the par-*fu*-marry."

She led me over to a counter. "Do you have a price range in mind?"

"I might look rougher than forty-grit sandpaper, ma'am, but price is no object. I just want something nice for a special lady."

"We'll try out several scents, and you tell me when we find one you think might suit your lady."

She pulled glass stoppers out of a number of small bottles and held them under my nose, but they all struck me as overwhelming—I couldn't imagine Darla wearing any of them. Intuitively, Miss Castlenuevo recognized that her selections weren't connecting.

"Don't despair; let's try something a bit more subtle," she suggested, "Perhaps an *eau de toilette* would be more suitable." I must have left my poker face in the tack room, because she whispered, "Toilet water is merely perfume with a bit less panache." Laying a delicate forefinger over her lips, she considered the display case for a moment, and then withdrew a bottle. "What do you think of this?"

I took a short sniff, and was engulfed by the most mesmerizing scent I'd ever encountered. Inhaling deeply now, I was transported—if heaven exists, it must smell just like this.

"Never in my life have I smelled anything so intoxicating. That's the one for Darla. What's it called?"

"It's known as Ciara, and it's one of my favorite scents. You have excellent taste, and I'm sure that your lady friend will like it, too."

"I'd like a big bottle, please."

"A little goes a long way."

"I'd buy a fifty-five gallon drum, if you had it. If I could smell this for the rest of my life, I'd be a happy man."

"The largest bottle we have is five ounces. Will you be placing this on a charge card?"

"I prefer to use cash."

While she was ringing me up, I leaned close and quietly asked, "Would you happen to know a place where I might find a more intimate kind of gift?" One of Miss Castlenuevo's eyebrows lifted. "You know, something kind of, uh … *naughty*."

Handing me back my change, she suggested, "Washington Avenue is two streets over, and a few blocks north of here, you'll find a Frederick's of Hollywood. That would be a good place to start."

"Thank you for all your kind help. You've not only made this an educational experience, you've also managed to make it fun."

She beamed at me. "Your friend is a very lucky woman."

I followed Miss Castlenuevo's simple directions to Frederick's of Hollywood, made another quick purchase, and then caught a cab back to the airport and winged my happy way home.

Ma was wedged between us, on the bench seat of Pop's pickup. We were taking that most Jewish of annual migrations, heading to a Chinese restaurant for dinner on Christmas Eve. Although Vero Beach was just a hop and a skip for my motorcycle, Pop's speed was curtailed by the most relentless mechanical governor known to man, a Hebraic wife.

"Where do you think you are, the Indianapolis 500? Slow down before you kill us all!"

"What? I'm doing thirty-seven miles an hour. If we slow down any more, by the time we get there the restaurant will be closed for New Years." Pop threw an arm around my mother's shoulder and gave her an affectionate squeeze, causing him to swerve slightly in his lane.

"Keep your eyes on da road! I didn't get away from Germans and Russians only to get killed in the *goldeneh medina*, while you are pitching woo."

"What am I gonna do wit' you, Minka?" He leaned over to plant a kiss on top of Ma's head.

"You want me to get in the back while you pitch more woo?" I asked.

"Sarcasm from you I don't need, boychik. Just because you've been to Vietnam doesn't mean I should listen to that wisenheimer talk," Ma remonstrated, pinching my cheek fondly.

Pop backed his foot incrementally off the accelerator. His smile proclaimed: *It doesn't cost a thing to make my wife happy, and besides, what could be more pleasurable than a few extra minutes spent joshing around with my favorite people in the world?*

In due time we arrived at the Happy Good Eat, where we were greeted by the proprietor himself.

"Now I know it Christmas. My favorite Jews here: Orange Jews, Apple Jews, and Grapefruit Jews." Jimmy Yee emitted the squeaky yips that passed for his laughter.

My father, immersing himself in the tradition which dictated his reply, said, "So, now I guess you gonna get that mythology book out and make me a drink?" He was referring to a mistake Jimmy had made years ago, in which he'd confused the word *mixology* with *mythology*.

"How hard is it to mix black and tan?" Jimmy yipped again, and the two shook hands. "Welcome to my place. Come, I save best table in house."

Jimmy showed us to the table, disappearing then reappearing again with almost magical speed, bearing bottles of Guinness Extra Stout and Bass Pale Ale. He demonstrated his mixology skills by pouring a glass half full of Bass, which he topped off with Guinness, producing an impressive froth on top just as Pop liked.

"This not Hollywood: you no blow foam off beer like cowboy," Jimmy cautioned, slapping Pop on the back.

"Do I look like a guy who would waste a good head like this?" Pop asked, tipping back the glass and taking a grateful swig. "You pour a good black and tan, Jimmy, and that's no myth."

Turning to Ma, Jimmy said, "I bring best General Tso you ever eat—chicken very crunchy, just way you like." To Pop he said, "Mandarin Beef, sweet meat to counter sour beer." Then he turned to me.

"You back from Vietnam—I'm very glad. How you doing, Slats?"

"I had a pretty rough time, sir, but I'm doing well now. It's great to be home."

"I hope you not develop taste for Vietnamese cooking."

"Not a chance, Mr. Yee. You know what I want."

"You betcha. Together we break kosher law—Szechuan Pork, so spicy your breath take paint off father truck on way home." Jimmy paused, peering back in time. "I flee China when Communists take over in 1949. See many bad things on way. I put behind me, here in USA. You put behind, too."

"As a wise man I know would say, 'You betcha.'"

Jimmy nodded and squeezed my shoulder. "Food here before first glass of beer gone," he said, before vanishing again.

Ma turned to me, wearing her most insouciant expression, and I instinctively braced myself. "So, when are we going to meet the *shiksa?*"

"This is the way you kick off a dinner conversation?" Pop inquired.

"What? A mother is interested in the woman her son is seeing. Besides," she shrugged, "it seems like a fair question on a *goyishe* holiday."

Pop took a breath, ready to dive right into the deep end, but I interrupted. "Let us not pitch woo straight out the window."

My folks swiveled their heads toward me, and then burst out laughing. "Forgive a nosy mother, Menachem," she shrugged, and I smiled at her. Then, in typical Minka Kisov fashion, she bowled right on. "Now, about this shiksa…"

Chuckling, and knowing she'd never let up, I said, "Her name is Darla Pistle. I met her the first day I was back from Vietnam, when Gene bought me breakfast at The Hair of the Dog. She's a waitress, very intelligent, with a great sense of humor and an equally great sense of adventure. She's also pretty easy on the eye," I summed up.

"She sounds like a very nice woman, and I'm glad you found each other," Ma graciously admitted. If I was surprised that Darla's Christianity didn't put her off, I also realized Ma knew that to restrict oneself to Jewesses would bring the number of eligible women in Farth down to zero. Ma was nothing if not practical.

But so was my father. "Pistle? She's not related to that putz of a police chief, is she?"

"Not any more, Pop."

"What?" It wasn't easy to confound my father, but I'd managed.

"She's his ex-wife."

"Oy, *gavalt*! Is this why you've been in trouble with the law lately?"

"Might have a little to do with it," I admitted.

"Trouble like this you don't need; that guy is a Cossack!"

I didn't like the turn this discussion was taking, so I employed a bit of misdirection. "Pop, he used to smack Darla around. Better he should hit me than her."

That silenced my parents. In my family, striking a woman was an offense exceeded only by hurting a child.

"My son is involved with the ex-wife of a *momzer politseyskiy*—what next?" Pop was mixing his languages more thoroughly than the cooks in Jimmy's kitchen stirred their ingredients.

"Relax, this sounds worse than it really is. Our family has survived much more serious times. You both endured the worst that Hitler and Stalin could throw at you, and I've just returned from a place where everybody was trying to machine-gun me. By comparison, Chief Pistle is no more than a pesky horsefly. I like Darla a lot, and a putz's petty jealousy won't stop me from seeing her."

Seen in this perspective, my parents could do nothing but nod, and I congratulated myself for putting them at ease. And, for successfully ducking my legal issues.

Then a waitress, bearing a tray heaped with Chinese food, diverted our attention in a more culinary direction.

The next day found human, dog, and motorcycle joined as one, blasting down the back roads toward Farth. Tailskid, head thrown back as he laughed into the wind, knew damn well where we were headed. I hoped my own anticipation was better veiled.

We pulled into Darla's driveway and, before I could switch off the engine, Tailskid leaped off the gas tank. He ran to the fence and dug right in, commencing to reopen the Tunnel of Poodle Love.

I started up the porch steps, and then froze. Darla was standing in the screen door, wearing only an elegantly upswept hairstyle with a tiny sprig of mistletoe woven into the strands. I loved her love of nudity.

"Hey, what if I'd been the pizza guy?"

"Then I'd hope you brought a generous serving of… *pepperoni*."

"Is that any way to talk on a religious holiday?"

In a breathless Marilyn Monroe voice, Darla replied, "Holidays always make me crave pepperoni."

"Too bad; all I brought was a salami." I untucked my shirt and shook a couple of small packages out, adding, "Well, a salami and these."

"For me?"

"I think they'll go really well with that outfit."

"And all I got you was a spark plug and some ignition points. Get in here, before I catch my death."

"We can't have that, can we?"

I stepped inside and, in deference to the mistletoe, planted a soulful kiss on Darla. Then I stared pointedly at her nipples, standing at attention from the cool breeze. "Maybe you should open this one first."

Darla unwrapped the box and read the label. "You bought me something from Frederick's of Hollywood?"

"It's my favorite place to shop."

She slipped the top off and peered inside. "What a pretty necklace. I love this cute little bell."

"There's an inscription on it."

"'My Heart-Chime.' Oh, Slats."

"This isn't just a necklace, though. Look here, when you unclasp this part."

A charming pink color suffused Darla's face. Looking shyly up, she breathed, "Oh my gosh! Are those…?"

"I hope you don't think it's too weird a gift."

"Silver nipple clamps—I love them!"

"As soon as I saw this, I thought to myself that whoever designed it must have had you in mind. And it'll go great with this." I handed her the second box.

Darla eagerly tore it open, squealing, "Perfume!"

"I don't know much about perfume, but I sure like this one. I hope you do, too."

Darla drew the stopper and inhaled delicately. "That is the most heavenly scent I've ever smelled." She gave me the smokiest of looks. "I guess it's time I finished dressing.

Will you help me?" she asked, holding up the clamps.

I gently eased them on. Then Darla dabbed a bit of Ciara on her finger and touched the hollows of her neck ... the underside of her breasts ... her bare cleft. Taking my hand she led me toward her bedroom, silver bell tinkling softly. She paused to glance back over her shoulder, eyes agleam. "You are the dearest man."

What guy wouldn't like hearing that?

Twenty-four

DB and I rang in 1972 the right way, with a flight to Chico Cay for a load of ripe product. As I followed what had become a well-worn path in the sky, I noted the first distant buildups to the southwest.

"See that cloud bank? That's tropical storm Dari, brewing in the Caribbean."

DB clutched his life jacket a little tighter than usual. "There is a hurricane coming?"

"It's just a depression now—she may not get much stronger. I won't let her catch us unaware."

"My mother always warned that the anger of a woman was truly dangerous," he said, his voice even more gravelly than usual.

"She should know something about that subject." My friend rolled his eyes.

DB peered furtively off our right wing for the rest of the flight, but we enjoyed smooth air all the way to touchdown. Mrs. Morales met us at the runway, nearly dancing with anticipation.

"Did you bring me anything?"

"You're like a little girl on her birthday," I teased. "I brought lots of it, Mamo."

Eyes sparkling with pleasure, she hugged me. "Thank you, Slats. I have had great difficulty saving the last box of pistol ammunition for defensive purposes. Now I can practice, practice, practice!"

"Sounds like you're trying to get to Carnegie Hall. Did you save your brass?"

"Yes." She held up one finger and quoted me: "Reload— shooting is expensive enough, already." She laughed, and then gestured toward the house. "Come! I have prepared *cafecito* and food for my boys."

After we'd satisfied our hunger and thirst, Mrs. Morales buttonholed DB and me. "Let us go shooting. I wish to show you something I've been working on." We grabbed the revolver and a couple of boxes of ammunition and followed her to the range.

Mamo slipped six rounds into the cylinder, tucked the S&W into her waistband, and pulled her shirttail down to conceal it. "Set up two cans, widely spaced," she directed. After I'd returned to her side, she added, "Those are two intruders; tell me when to react."

I took a step back, waited a few seconds, and then said, "Blast 'em!"

Hands blurring, Mamo yanked her shirt up with the left and slapped iron with the right. The pistol steadied for a moment, then a double action shot rang out and a can leapt into the air. The muzzle shifted quickly, and then a second shot rang out. For an instant, both cans were simultaneously airborne. When I looked back at Mrs. Morales, she'd already tucked the gun back under her shirt.

She laughed at the expression on my face. "Am I getting better?"

"You can outdraw Dillinger and shoot straighter than an FBI agent!"

She smiled, and then her natural modesty resumed control. "I owe it to your teaching, Slats."

"You have far exceeded anything I could teach you. You're the greatest natural pistol shot I've ever seen."

She downplayed my comment by observing, "I hope I never have to switch from cans to people."

That night after dinner, I stepped outside with the Morales brothers for a smoke. Tomas rolled a joint big enough to be hanging from a launch rail, got it fired up, and passed it around.

"I swear, every time I come back here you guys have even better weed than the last trip. I don't know how you do it."

"We do the experiments. We pinch off top branches to make the plants bushy, we change the fertilizer, the amount of sunlight, the amount of water," Carlos said. "We get more flower tops, more resin."

"Very good—*muy potente*," Tomas added.

"You are truly agricultural artists, and I'm glad that it is going so well for you."

"Not everything is so good. We see the same boat, a few times now—always three men. They have fishing poles, but they do not look at the sea. They watch our island."

"Is there anything unusual about their boat? Is it painted a strange color, or does it have markings, anything that makes it stand out?"

Carlos' brow creased in concentration. "No, I don't think so. But one man, he always wears a blue hat." He struggled for the right English words. "I think they call it a Panama hat."

I thought about this for a moment, then suggested, "I think you should keep a sharp watch for this boat."

"We already do that."

"It might also be wise for Mamo not to practice shooting if the boat happens to be nearby. These men are probably nothing to worry about, but it's always best to hold your cards close to the chest."

The blue hat wasn't much to go on, but it was all I had and I filed it away.

I had also brought Julieta a present. We'd been working on her English each time I visited, with the help of simple books I'd bring. She, in turn, was teaching her mother. Julieta was a bright girl who absorbed everything she read, so I'd found a set of World Book Encyclopedia for her. These would not only greatly improve Julieta's English, they'd give her a broad education about the world.

The brothers helped me transfer this hundred pound load from Cessna to house. As I said, Julieta is quick: she took one look at the literary cornucopia and threw her arms around me. "Thank you, Slats! Thank you!" I knew that she would bury herself in these books frequently, just as I had as a kid.

"How do you know these aren't for Tomas and Carlos?"

"They have their own reading material," she countered, referring to the salacious magazines her brothers had occasionally requested in the past. I shot a look at them, one now busy examining the craftsmanship of his shoes, while the other contemplated the infinity of the cosmos with head laid back.

I tactfully replied, "Well, there's learnin' and then there's education."

They laughed just as Mamo emerged from the kitchen, drying her hands. "What's so funny?"

"I was just explaining some simple facts of life to your children, ma'am."

―――――――

The first item on my checklist for our return flight, as always, was sunglasses. I took off and throttled back for cruise-climb, the six-cylinder engine burbling reliably. I squirmed onto the cushion, enjoying the solid feel of this aircraft through my own seat. This Cessna might essentially be a flying pickup truck, but she ran smooth as a Swiss chronometer as she bore us steadily upward. I let my mind roam where it would, something that's always been easiest to do while at the controls of a good airplane.

Importation day usually lifted my spirits as high as I could climb the 180. But today I could think only of the men in the boat. And of Mamo, whose life should not have to take so martial a turn at this late stage. DB must have felt this too, for he was uncharacteristically silent as we bounced our way through the remains of tropical storm Dari.

But Mamo was only doing what she thought necessary. If this peaceful horticulturist felt that she needed to steel herself for battle, then perhaps it was time for me to gird my own loins. On future flights, I'd tuck the .38 into my waistband.

Twenty-five

I started the month as usual, by dropping in on Jelly to pay rent. Jelly was not a demanding landlady. In fact, I usually had to talk her into accepting the money. While I did so, she'd make a pot of coffee and bring out some freshly baked pastry. I always enjoyed paying my debt to this particular society.

But today Jelly was clearly upset, and she initially evaded my questions. So I sipped my coffee and gave her time to gentle down, before suggesting, "Tell me about it, Jelly. Maybe I can help."

"Nobody can help me out of this." Never had my friend sounded so mournful.

"Sometimes it feels better to just get things off your chest."

She took a deep breath. "The tax collector was out here yesterday. I need to come up with a lot of money by next month."

"I don't understand."

"I'm behind in my taxes. I wasn't able to pay them last year." Tears welled in her eyes.

"I can always scrape up a few dollars. You can come to me anytime." What's the point of having money if you don't use it to help your friends?

"You don't understand. I missed a payment of two hundred seventeen dollars, but now they're telling me I owe the balance of my mortgage, plus a penalty." At my confused expression, she explained, "Some addendum to the deed where the county can call the rest of the debt, due immediately. Slats, they say I have to come up with almost seven thousand dollars in thirty days! That's more money than I've seen in my entire life. I'm going to lose the ranch. I'm going to lose my house. I'm going to lose Henry's grave." She laid her head on her arms and wept.

Men come better prepared for war and pestilence than we do for a woman's tears. But I did know enough to put my arm around her. "We'll figure something out, Jelly. If there's one thing I learned in the military, it's how to deal with bureaucrats." She looked up, a glimmer of hope swimming in a sea of tears.

"Do I have your permission to make inquiries on your behalf?"

"You do," she sniffed.

"Okay." I shoved the rent money over to her. "But don't give the county a penny of this. You hang on to it for now."

"What should I tell them if they contact me again?"

I puzzled over a response that would camouflage my lack of knowledge with a mask of legalese. "You tell 'em this: 'My advocate advises me to hold all further payments in escrow, pending adjudication.'"

Jelly ventured a weak smile. "You've only been my 'advocate' for two minutes and you already sound like a lawyer."

"I got into enough trouble when I was in the Air Force and just naturally picked it up," I replied, managing to get a grunt of laughter out of her.

———————

I needed to get this right for Jelly, so I headed over to the library for research. I'd always loved spending time in libraries. One could learn practically anything, especially with the assistance of a good librarian. It took me much of the day to arm myself with knowledge, but feeling considerably buoyed, I jumped onto the BSA and headed home, stopping only to pick up a blank power of attorney form.

Bright and early the next morning, I headed for the courthouse. I followed the paper trail I'd blazed at the library, going from the Clerk of Courts office to the Recording Division, getting copies of pertinent records at each stop. Along with Jelly's signed power of attorney, I felt well armed, ready to pay a visit to the man himself.

My first impression of Bob Jameson could be summed up in one word: milquetoast. He'd been county tax collector for nearly twenty years, and unless appearances were deceiving, he must have done so by being the archetypal faceless bureaucrat. During that time he must have executed plenty of legitimate evictions, so he could not possibly fail to understand how atypical this one was.

We shook hands, and before exchanging a word I slipped a hand into my manila folder and passed him Jelly's tax notice. Head tilting over as he read it, Jameson resembled a curious squirrel.

"My name is M. J. Kisov, and I'm here on behalf of Mrs. Rawlins."

"I cannot deal with you. This is a matter for Mrs. Rawlins and the county."

My hand dipped into the folder again, and I produced the signed power of attorney form. "Mrs. Rawlins has authorized me to act on her behalf."

After examining the Power of Attorney, he said, "I will tell you the same thing I told Mrs. Rawlins. There is no recourse but for her to pay or vacate the premises, by the first of next month."

"That's not how I see things. In my view, Mrs. Rawlins has two much better choices. Choice A involves filing a petition before the county Value Adjustment Board. This option would allow Mrs. Rawlins and the county to keep things simple. The case will be heard by licensed appraisers, men who know about property value and law. Not only would this save a great deal of time, it would also save a lot of money on legal representation—for both sides."

Jameson seemed surprised to hear that I'd done my homework, but this was his turf and he tried to mark it now. "The county does not see things your way, Mr. Kisov."

Once more, I plucked out some records. I think Jameson was beginning to dislike my manila folder. "Here are copies of the Rawlins Ranch tax receipts that I obtained from the Recording Division. You'll note that taxes have been paid on time for the entire period of ownership. Calling the note due because of one late payment is unjust."

"That is how the county has always done business."

"You mean that's how the county has done business with *black* property owners, don't you, Mr. Jameson?"

Much like a schoolboy with a memorized poem, he

recited, "I can assure you that this county treats all land-owners with the same—"

I cut him off at the knees. "Save that shit for the court-room, Bob."

He glanced aside, and I knew by that simple gesture that my suspicions were correct. Someone—undoubtedly that redneck peckerwood of a police chief—had pressured Jameson into using Jim Crow tactics that were despicable, not to mention illegal in today's civil rights-sensitive era. I felt the taxman tottering, so I gave him a little extra push to see which direction he'd tip.

"Let's cut straight to the chase, Choice B. This would involve filing an action in circuit court. If you choose option B, I'll be bringing in an ACLU lawyer to prosecute this race-based outrage. Then I'll get an NAACP attorney, just to keep an eye on the ACLU guy. I wouldn't be surprised if Jesse Jackson himself showed up."

Jameson swallowed.

I continued, "By the time I'm done dragging this matter through the court system, and catering to the intense media scrutiny which will inevitably follow on its heels, you, sir, will be the most reviled man in Indian River County. You will also be unemployed." The taxman began to look ill.

I added the kicker. "Hell, Bob, you *might* even find yourself in jail." Bob Jameson started to hyperventilate. I fetched him a drink from the water cooler, patting his back as he sipped. Having no partner to assist me, I played the roles of both good cop and bad cop, and I was having the time of my life.

I adopted a most reasonable tone. "Look, Mr. Jameson, surely you can see that no one wins with Choice B. And I think I have a way out for both parties, one that involves no reporters, no lawyers, and no third parties of any kind. It's also fair and equitable, not to mention quick. Does this interest you?"

"I'm listening."

I have rarely enjoyed a ride so much as the one I took back to the ranch. Assuming a serious expression, I knocked on Jelly's door. It opened, and I said, "I know you weren't expecting your lawyer, but I have news."

She looked at me with trepidation. "Come in, Slats. I'll make coffee"

I led her to the couch, instead. "Jelly, I managed to get the county to lower their demands."

Jelly's reaction was more subdued than I expected. "Slats, I can't thank you enough for getting the amount cut down. But I couldn't even come up with two hundred dollars when I needed it."

I handed her the manila envelope; she opened it gently, as though it might be booby-trapped. But it held only papers, the top one bearing an Indian River County crest. It didn't take long for her to read, as it was short.

"I don't understand," she said.

"I simply made the taxman an offer he couldn't refuse." At Jelly's puzzled expression, I explained, "By the time I finished telling him about the ACLU and NAACP lawyers who were on their way here, and reminding him of the legal penalty for abusing his oath of office, I think Mr. Jameson may have had to change his boxer shorts.

"This is your tax receipt for $2,804.75, marked Paid in

Full. Your deed is underneath it. Copies are on file at the courthouse, and I've taken the liberty of making others, as well. You can use them for Christmas tree ornaments, if you want."

She looked up at me and started to speak.

I silenced her with a shake of my head. "I know what you're going to say, so don't even bother. You can pay me back a little at a time, or after you inherit a bunch of money from a rich uncle. Hell, you can never repay me for all I care. The important thing is you get to keep your rightful place in this world."

Tears formed in her eyes, but I held up my hand. "One more thing, and I'm not going to listen to any argument on this point, either. I will continue to pay rent, including the occasional cost-of-living increase. I'll even try to get it to you on time from now on."

Jelly hugged me. "Thank you, Slats. Thank you for letting me stay with Henry."

My face grew hot.

But I just said: "Who else would let me and my airplane live in their barn?"

It felt fine to be in a position to help Jelly. I'd be lying, though, if I didn't admit it was also very satisfying to stick it to Piss Bubble.

Twenty-six

Although I still appreciated the solitude of the ranch, I was now spending many of my nights in town with Darla. She understood me, and tolerated my strange ways. She never talked about getting married, because life with the chief had not turned out well. As for me, I was quite satisfied with the status quo. As a pilot, I know that when you're following the right heading, you keep her well trimmed and on course.

I showed up at Darla's place tired from my successful effort with officialdom, only to be met by an unexpected verbal broadside.

"Tailskid knocked up my Coquette!" Darla put her hands on her hips. "What are you going to do about it?"

I figured that humor was the best response. "I'll get my shotgun and see that they're married right away."

"It's not funny, Slats!"

"Look, nature tells dogs to procreate, and they just naturally follow orders. As a responsible dog owner, I promise to find a good home for Coquette's pups."

"What about the *next* time he breaks into my yard and rapes my dog?"

"I hardly think the word 'rape' applies."

"You've got to have that little bastard neutered, Slats!"

"I'm not gonna do to my dog what some bastard half-did to me!"

"Then I'll find some drunken, disbarred veterinarian with a rusty scalpel and blood in his eye, and those hairy dog-oysters will be nothin' but an ugly memory!"

I'd never heard Darla sound so shrill, and I snapped to attention, executed a neat about-face, and marched out of her house. I gave the bike a furious kick, and then proceeded to redline the tach in all fours gears on my way out of town.

I didn't even make it home before regretting my words. But she'd chosen the one subject that really gave me the willies—testicular liquidation. Just thinking about it made me squirm.

So, Tailskid was going to be a father. There were probably shotgun-armed dog owners all over Farth seeking the violator of their beloved bitches. As I rode up to the ranch I could see him dragging his ass down the side of the road while managing to simultaneously wag his tail in greeting.

"Nobody's takin' *your* stones. Just try to use 'em like you got some smarts, okay?"

———

I was unable to sleep, despite repeated attempts to knock myself out with weed. Finally, I rode back to Darla's house—it must have been after two in the morning.

Darla was a sound sleeper, and I had to knock loud and long before she peered sleepily out the front door. She was too tired to be pissed. "I have to be up at five. Why are you banging down my door?"

"My mother says you should never let the sun go down on your anger."

"The sun went down seven hours ago."

"Then, you should never let the sun rise on your anger."

"You woke me up at oh-dark thirty to impart such pearls of wisdom?"

"I woke you up because there's no way I'm going to be able to sleep until I tell you how sorry I am for my behavior. I further apologize for disturbing you on a workday. I'll go home now and leave you to what little is left of your rest." I turned toward my motorcycle, only to hear the sound of the door opening.

"Get in here, you imbecile."

I followed Darla to her room without a word, afraid to damage the fragile truce that had just been declared. She climbed into bed and turned her back to me. I stood there awkwardly for a moment then quietly removed my clothes and slipped in beside her.

"You better keep your hands to yourself, if you know what's good for you."

I took this pronouncement for the gentle goodnight buss on the cheek it was.

———————

I clawed my way out of nightmare, gasping, heart hammering. I was lost in nothingness. But Darla was right beside me, smoothing my brow, murmuring, "Shhhh, shhhh... everything's all right."

I tried to speak, only managing a croak from my dry throat. "Where...?"

"We're right here in my bed, Slats—the safest place in

the world." I lay gratefully in her arms.

"You kept yelling something about bird dogs and meat."

"The Bird Dog is the airplane I flew in Vietnam, and Meat is a guy I flew with." I fell into silence, which stretched out.

"And?" she prompted.

"Meat has been on my mind lately. I helped save his life once, after he was shot down. I felt…" Darla nodded encouragement, waiting for me to find the right words. "I felt as if I'd adopted him. I can't explain it any better than that. In some strange way, Meat had become my responsibility."

"That's not a bad thing, is it?"

This was nearly impossible to force out, but I pressed on. "A couple of weeks later, Meat was well enough to return to duty. The very next day, he crashed. I was watching when his wing came off. Tonight, I watched him burn again."

Darla put her arms around me and held me close.

I felt better, having shared the worst of Vietnam with Darla. I was lucky to have found a woman like her, and I tried in my clumsy way to let her know it.

"We should take a little road trip," I suggested.

"What do you have in mind?"

"Have you ever been close up for a rocket launch?"

"I've seen a couple go from here, if I looked up at the right time. I've never been to the Cape, though."

"NASA is launching Skylab this evening. It's going to be the last flight of a Saturn V rocket, the biggest one we have, the one they used for moon shots. Let's blast up there on the bike!"

"I've heard that traffic can be bad for one of those launches."

"People are getting pretty jaded about space these days, Darla—it probably won't be too crowded. If it is, I'll do a wheelie down the side of the road, while you hang on with one hand and flip the cage-drivers off with the other."

"All right, Mr. Kisov, you're on!"

We made the forty-mile trip in half an hour, locating a nice little park straight across the Indian River from the launch pad. It was empty enough for us to find a quiet stand of trees, right on the water. I spread my blanket under a live oak with a privacy curtain of low-hanging Spanish moss, and we spent the time until launch catching a buzz and necking. The columnar tribute to the gods of science hulked above the palmettos across the river.

Via Darla's transistor radio, the local station alerted us to the countdown, and by the time the launch commentator reached *All engines running* a glow illuminated the launch pad, flames licking at the first stage. Then the orange glow intensified to a pure, radiant white, and seven and one half million pounds of thrust erupted from the engine nozzles. There was a pause before the rocket lifted, and then it inched upward, taking time to clear the gantry before accelerating rapidly. It was streaking like a comet now, a comet with a tail of fire rather than ice, and arcing to follow the curvature of the earth. Reaching for a place where no winged craft

195

could follow, it was suddenly just ... *gone.*

I escorted Darla to dinner at the Thirsty Turtle, a nice little joint in Cocoa Beach that catered to locals. In the continental manner, I ordered for the lady and for myself: "We'll have fish and chips, with a vinegar garnish on the side. And please bring us a carafe of your finest draft beer, to sample while we wait."

Doing a little quick figuring in my head, I observed, "It would take about half a million Cessnas to match the power we just witnessed."

"How like a man to love a big number."

"What do women love?"

She dropped her voice. "Big members."

"Should I place an order for oysters?"

"You don't require the assistance, sir!" She batted her eyes.

"You're not going to strip off right here in the Thirsty Turtle, are you?"

"Not unless our waitress is replaced by a particularly good looking waiter."

"I think that big rocket thrusting skyward gave you a case of the hornies."

"Slats, are you happy?" Sometimes women have this abrupt way of dropping a monkey wrench into the conversational machinery.

Sensing the serious nature of this question, I quickly ran over a selection of possible responses. I opted for honesty. "Yes, I am," I replied, thinking brevity might also be wise.

"Are you sure?"

Okay, brevity was out. Instead, I reached for her hand. "You are a very special woman, Darla. I'm lucky you tolerate a rough old cob like me." She scoured my face for any trace of teasing, but there was none to be found. I added, "You please me."

An enigmatic smile softened Darla's expression, and I leaned over to kiss her. "But I'm still not going to castrate my dog."

"You please me too, Slats," she kissed back. "Most of the time."

Twenty-seven

I could hear him coming a mile away. He tore up Roadapple Lane, locked the back wheels and skidded wildly sideways. The car didn't quite come to a halt before he popped the clutch, performed a three-quarter donut, and then eased up to the barn door.

I stuck my head inside the window and asked, "Is this vehicle standard government issue?"

"Hell no! I got some credit, and then I found a dealer." I raised an eyebrow, so R&R clarified, "A *Chevy* dealer, Slats. Anyway, next thing I know I'm beholden for a Camaro to the tune of seven grand."

"You owe your soul to the company store?"

"You got that right. But she'll fly faster than any O-1 ever flew. You hear that engine? That's a 350 with four-bolt main, wearing a Holley four-barrel—head's been flowed, too. Might not be the biggest mill on the road, but she's hacked, jacked and stacked." Like all pilots, R&R loved a good spec list.

"You sound like every redneck motorhead I've ever known. Maybe we should try her out, though. There's a closed airport nearby, with four thousand feet of decent runway to race on." The spark that ignited in his eye was good to see, as few things seemed to really engage R&R these days.

"First things first, though. Welcome back to my modest aerodrome." I led him into the cool barn and got him a glass of my favorite drink, warm well water. "You've got a hungry look in your eye, R&R. Are you thinking about women, or Marlboros, or what?"

In a terrible Spanish accent, R&R snarled, "Marlboros? We don't need no stinkin' Marlboros!"

"Well, this is no carton of coffin nails." I said, handing him a wrinkled paper sack. "And I wrapped it myself!"

He grinned, pulling out a fat baggie filled with colorful buds.

"You shouldn't have."

"What else does one get the BNDD agent who has everything?"

"DEA."

"Huh?"

"Whoever is in charge of government-speak has renamed us the Drug Enforcement Administration."

"Well, this is still known as the finest sinsemilla in the western hemisphere." Then, looking evasively in both directions, "Just don't forget to forget where you got it."

Holding his right arm heavenward, R&R pledged, "Plausible deniability, all the way. If tortured, I promise to point my finger at the MFAF."

I broke up at his reference to the Mexican Free Air Force, as we smokers used to call ourselves back in Vietnam. "Then enjoy this in good health."

R&R grew serious. "You'll never know how much this stuff helps me."

"I have a pretty good idea, buddy. I use it the same way."

Later that afternoon, we set off for Valkaria Airport. I would never admit this to R&R, but I was uncomfortable with his driving. No pilot is truly relaxed as a passenger in any machine, and R&R wasn't cutting me any slack. He lit those tires up at every opportunity, taking all bends in the road sideways, always on the ragged edge of traction. I thought that big V8 might strip the tortured tires right off the rims. On the long straight R&R had it over a hundred, but thankfully he had to slow down at a dogleg in the road, midway to Valkaria.

I studied R&R's face as he drove. His concentration was fierce, but there was little enjoyment to be found. He was deadly serious—I didn't see even a flicker of a smile the entire time. This was not the same carefree man I'd known in Vietnam, and I was becoming truly concerned for my friend.

We pulled into the airport lot; a few cars were already there. A mucous-colored Road Runner was showing its ass to a Mustang Mach 1, both blasting down the runway as if they meant to take flight. We watched several more drag races, a T-bucket then a Merc going down just as decisively to the Road Runner.

At a break in the action, we sidled up to the kid driving the Plymouth. R&R asked, "You packin' a 383?"

"No, this is a Superbird with a 440," he proudly claimed. "Why? You runnin' yours?"

"I'm always ready to test my mettle...and my metal."

The kid just scratched his head.

He pointed toward the far end of the runway and said, "See those stakes with white flags on either side? We only race that far because you need time to slow down or you'll run right off the end."

They fired up their respective cars, doing a few mandatory burnouts to heat the tires and beat their chests. Clouds of tire smoke filled the air. *Any more and they'll have to go on instruments*, I thought. As he edged up to the starting line, R&R waved me over.

"C'mon, Slats; take the ride!"

I considered declining, on the grounds extra weight would lessen his chances of winning. But instead, like the Sierra Hotel military pilot I'd been, I put on my game face and climbed aboard. "Shit fire and save the matches!"

A cute little tenderoni, who just had to be a majorette, twirled a bandana over her head and brought it sharply downward. A cubic inch cacophony broke out—it sounded like a B-29 taking off.

As R&R and I launched off the line, the Camaro briefly broke loose and fishtailed, allowing the Road Runner an early lead. But despite the horsepower deficit, R&R stuck to him like snot on a fingertip, doing precise gear changes as he hit redline on the first three. We were winding it up in fourth, the flags coming up fast, when the Road Runner started to back off. Not R&R, though.

R&R was a superbly coordinated man with a keen competitive spirit, one who had apparently decided that he was not going to lose. He kept stompin' it all the way, and at the last instant we rocketed past our decelerating opponent. R&R finally lifted his foot off the gas, and we started to slow. He hit the brakes hard, and I could feel the tires tremble at the skidding point. But even as R&R downshifted into third, the end of the runway hurtled at us and we shot off into the grassy overrun.

The car spun vertiginously, at least six times. Luckily for us, we missed the gopher tortoise holes that could have hooked a wheel and overturned us. As we slid to a halt in a cloud of dust, I congratulated myself for keeping my intestinal contents inside, where they belonged. I'd glanced at the firmly-pegged speedo as we crossed the line—we were doing more than a hundred-twenty miles per hour.

R&R wore the expression of a wild man. But even as I watched, he mastered himself, physically tamping down his thoughts. He revved his engine and did several donuts in the opposite direction we'd just spun, explaining, "Screwin' my head back on, after that spinout." We kicked it back down the runway.

The kid shook R&R's hand, saying, "I ain't been beat in a while. That was pretty nuts. You got some big balls." That wasn't how I would have put it.

As scared as I'd been for my own hide, I was even more alarmed about R&R. I'd served with him, I knew him well, and this was not the same man. He'd held the throttle open far too long for a kiddie-car race. R&R was every bit as serious about this race as he'd been about combat flying. It was almost as though he was back in Vietnam. For a second or two, the word *suicidal* had flashed through my mind.

I made sure to medicate R&R thoroughly before we headed back to town. He couldn't leave well enough alone, though, driving sedately through Farth until reaching the police station. Happy at finding the town's sole patrol car in

its designated parking slot, R&R demonstrated his enthusiasm by performing a donut, which went so well that he
did another. Then he kept the tires lit up for two blocks,
fishtailing wildly up Sumpter Street while cutting loose a
very credible rebel yell.

But this person was a stranger, an actor playing the role
of R&R.

We arrived at the ranch, and R&R idled up to the barn. I
opened the door so he could stow the Camaro under the
Cessna's wing—concealment seemed like a good idea, considering the police station buzz job. R&R shut her off and
we listened to the cooling engine sing its mechanical lullaby.

"Well, you beat the local champ, tore up the pavement
in front of Piss Bubble's office, and wore about half the tread
off your back tires. Are you tight for the night?"

"I guess."

"You know we can have a serious talk any time you
want, right?"

"Shit, that's how VA shrinks start conversations."

"I'm no shrink. I'm your friend. And I've got few enough
of those left."

"What's the matter? Did I scare you tonight?"

"Yes, you scared me! You almost spun a Camaro in and
bought me the farm."

"You've been in spins before."

"It's not the spin that amazed me, it was the recovery."
Then, more seriously, "I knew I was nuts to go down that
runway with you, but I did it anyway."

"Why?"

"Because I wanted to see you in action. And that's what it was like, as if you were back in action. Back in Vietnam."

"Like I was having a flashback? Is that what you mean?"

"I don't know about that stuff. But I know you. You were way too serious for some dumbass dragstrip in Buttfuck Bend, Florida. You acted like lives depended on the result."

"What are you talking about? Whose life?"

"*Yours*, I guess."

R&R started to say something then closed his mouth. He looked at me a long time, and as well as I knew him, I couldn't say if he was curbing a sharp reply or simply digesting my remark. Finally, he said, "I'm just workin' through things my own way. I don't know how else to do it. Okay, Slats?"

I nodded at him. "Okay."

Throwing a few things into a backpack, I told R&R, "I'm going to Darla's, so you and Jelly can enjoy some privacy." I added, "I changed the sheets in the tack room, in case you get into trouble and need to bail out." His withering look made me laugh as I roared off on my nice safe Beezer.

Next night, R&R wanted to drive and smoke. I couldn't refuse, although I did ask him to keep it under a hundred. He just smiled and nodded absently, so I made sure to empty my bladder before climbing aboard.

R&R joined me, saying, "This is always a good idea, before strapping on either a plane or a Camaro." Never one to be left out, Tailskid helped water the turf—we all bonded in ancient male ritual.

R&R snapped his fingers. "Dogs love to stick their heads out of car windows—let's take ol' Tailskid along."

"The way you drive, if he gets anywhere near an open window, he'll be sucked out by hurricane-force winds."

"Okay, okay," R&R grudgingly conceded, "I'll keep it under a hundred. A little bit under..."

Tail wagging, Tailskid jumped into the back seat. Unprejudiced, he was as happy riding in a car as he was clinging to a motorcycle gas tank—he was up for anything, anytime, anyplace. I rolled down the windows for him, hoping his low center of gravity would keep him grounded. I also hoped Tailskid wouldn't see the leather seat as a blank canvas for his own particular brand of splatter art.

We swung onto the road and R&R immediately nailed it, the 350 bellowing like a bull rhino. Tailskid threw his head back and howled accompaniment. A true redneck, he enjoyed powerful machines; the faster we went, the happier he seemed. We were doing a hundred and ten down US 1 when R&R looked in the mirror and said, "Shit, we've got company."

Sure enough, Farth's finest was behind us, lit up like a cat-house on New Year's Eve, the siren's wail lost in our engine song. If R&R was nervous, it sure didn't show. He slammed on the brakes and started downshifting, forcing the cop to stomp his own brake pedal to avoid a rear-end collision. The cruiser door opened, but instead of the chief, Officer Carling stepped out. He looked mighty pleased with himself.

Bernard Carling was Farth's only other serving police officer, which made Piss Bubble's title of Police Chief rather grandiose. The chief could be pretty threatening; Carling was anything but. His mild ways and given name led to the use of an obvious nickname, one I now invoked. "You're about to meet Barney Fife."

I should mention that Carling also had the misfortune to own the world's worst toupee. It matched neither the color nor the texture of his small remaining patch of natural hair. In fact, it appeared to have been stamped from some kind of space-age polymer similar to AstroTurf. You found yourself talking to the rug rather than to the man. Like a nineteenth century English painting, the hair-hat seemed to stare at you no matter where you stood.

Carling marched up to the car, crowing, "I *knew* I'd catch up to this car sooner or later. Let's see some paperwork!"

R&R took one glance at the hairpiece and went right into action. He flung the car door open and leaped out, causing Carling to jump back and drop his ticket book. Quick as a cat, R&R snatched the toupee off Carling's head, yelling, "I'll save you from that weasel, officer!" He threw it to the ground, stomped on it a few times, and then stood on it.

Carling was momentarily paralyzed, thrown completely off guard by the bizarre behavior. Looking back and forth from R&R to the ground, he seemed unable to decide if he should be angry or cautious about the madman standing on his headgear. "People have been shot over less than that!" he observed petulantly.

"Save it," R&R said, flashing his DEA badge. "I'm on undercover assignment, and you're drawing unwanted attention toward me. I assure you that if I'm going somewhere at this speed, there is an excellent reason for it."

Carling pointed at Tailskid. "And I suppose that's one of those drug-sniffing dogs?"

"He does have a remarkably sophisticated nose."

"My nose isn't too bad, either. I smell something suspicious coming from this car."

"If you're talking about the marijuana, don't be an idiot. Marijuana is the focus of the DEA's investigation."

"I'm going to have to check into these claims, Agent Rehnquist."

"You will mention this to no one. If you fuck with this investigation any more than you already have, I will see you brought up on charges." R&R stared nails at him, adding, "And I will also see that the story of your 'scalping' is spread all over your jurisdiction. Your reputation will be sealed for all time to come... *Barney*." Carling's face fell, and R&R began to pace. Passing by me, he winked and said, "Allow me to consult with my confidential informant."

R&R led me aside, asking if I wanted to mess with the guy's head a little. I looked over at Carling, frantically combing the dust out of his trampled toupee. I told him I had a better idea, and quickly laid it out.

R&R took up where he'd left off. "You might be in a unique position to help this investigation, though. At the same time, you'd be helping yourself."

"I don't know anything."

I wanted to sing out a heartfelt amen, but I chose a different tack. "You know a lot about Chief Pistle, the target of our investigation."

Carling's jaw dropped open. "The chief, involved with drugs? No, that couldn't happen," he stammered.

"We know it's been happening for a while. You two are thick as thieves... have been for years. A sitting police officer cannot possibly be so blind and so stupid to miss what's going on. This fact is not lost on the DEA." I almost broke up at the notion of me using the DEA to threaten a police officer.

"I still say I don't know anything about that." He hastened to add, "But I'll cooperate with any official investigation, of course."

R&R took over. "We know the chief had Klan affiliations in the past. Is he still associated with the KKK?"

"I don't know."

"Now, Barney, do you think I'm stupid? The chief would never hire the only other cop on the force unless he was a like-minded soul."

His blank stare let me know I was talking over his head.

"Are you telling me that you're not in the Klan?"

Carling squirmed a little. "Will you keep my name out of this?"

Both R&R and I relaxed, realizing we were about to hear the music. "I can guarantee it," R&R assured him. To spread some jam on the biscuit, he added, "Think about this: if Chief Pistle is as dirty as he looks, then who do you suppose will get first consideration as his replacement?"

Barney's facial expression clearly reflected the progression of his thoughts. "Okay, so I used to run with those boys, a little," he admitted. "But since civil rights came on strong, a lot of the old members have dropped out."

"But not all of 'em, eh?"

Barney was only too happy to spill more beans. "Not the chief."

"Is the KKK funding itself with drug money?"

"Those guys are into some serious hate. But I can't see any of 'em messing with drugs—they hate hippies."

"Then maybe the chief is motivated by simple greed."

"That doesn't seem to fit the guy."

"You just throw out the facts and we'll connect the dots."

"Whatever you say…" Once Carling started to cooperate, all his reservations crumbled.

Kickbacks, intimidation, beatings, most of it directed toward black citizens: he was very forthcoming about the chief's activities. He was more shrouded concerning his own. I found out that Jelly had in fact been targeted because of me, and that the chief was deeply angered by my interference. I'd made a serious enemy in Pistle, Carling assured me, and he thought the chief would be even angrier if he knew I was cooperating with other law enforcement agencies against him.

"Of course, the only way he can find that out is through you, and you won't be talking, will you?"

"No. And you know I'm telling the truth; I have more to gain from you guys than I do from him."

"You remember that. I'll contact you if—make that *when*—I need more information."

A couple days later R&R returned to Gainesville, and I moved back into the barn. Everything looked exactly as I'd left it. Either R&R had managed to stay out of trouble with Jelly, or he'd learned something about housekeeping since Vietnam.

Twenty-eight

I'd been telling Gene about my dog's dalliance with Darla's poodle, and the resulting batch of scruffy but cute puppies. Gene, a man with his ear to the rail when it came to talk around town, smiled enigmatically.

"That dog of yours does get around. He's a randy little Englishman."

"Darla calls him things that don't sound nearly that classy."

"Makes me wonder what the chief is gonna call him?"

"The chief?"

"I understand his best huntin' dog just had a litter of pups. They don't look much like their mama, though."

"No?" I wheezed.

"Penelope—that's the proud mama's name—is a registered German Shorthaired Pointer. But the puppies will never be registered with the AKC."

"You gonna tell me why, or just sit there grinnin' like a cat with a carp?"

"Because they look like him," Gene pointed at the offending animal, currently engaged in wolfing down the last of my chili dog. "A whole lot like him."

Tailskid burped, and then lazily reached a foot up to scratch his ear. I defended his honor: "Does he look guilty to you? Because he sure doesn't look guilty to me."

"Slats, he has committed *peccadilloes* with many of Farth's leading canine elite. He's a walking advertisement for Spanish fly. He spends more time engaging in acts of love than he does sleeping."

"Other than that, he's a pretty good boy."

Tailskid strolled over to the nearest tree, hiked a leg, and proceeded to simultaneously urinate and defecate.

"You ever see a dog do that before? He's a natural-born showman, one who lives only to entertain."

"He mostly likes to entertain female dogs."

Tailskid yawned cavernously then lay down for a nap, his conscience unstained by notions of sin.

Gene changed the subject by asking, "What are you and Darla doing this Saturday?"

"Besides cleaning up egalitarian skid marks? We have no plans."

"My buddies are getting together for a session. I've been practicing the harp." Gene and his friends had a pretty good band that did occasional gigs. He knew how much I loved the blues.

"Where's this going down?" I asked.

"A little bar called Farzo's Joint, about twenty miles north of here, up in Stone."

"Sounds like I need to take a motorcycle ride."

———————

"I'm Farzo, and this is my joint. Tonight we bring you a

band so cool that they have no earthly use for the air conditioner. Ladies and gentlemen, The Undertakers!"

The drummer set the beat, the bassist slipped in, the guitarist took it up, and finally Gene began to sing.

> The hard ways of this world
> are more'n I could bear,
> if not for my sweet woman
> though no longer is she there.
>
> I see her in my mind's eye
> as clear a sight to find,
> though I buried her many years ago
> yet she lives, within my mind.
>
> For five short years, we dwelt in paradise
> we spent eternity together, the time of our lives.
>
> We never tied the marital knot
> only jumping the broom,
> but she was my blushin' bride
> and I her devoted groom.
>
> I druther dwell in memory with
> my spirit, my common law wife,
> than spend ninety and nine more years
> draggin' through a common life.

When it came time for the second chorus, Gene instead chose to blow the harp. His plaintive wail touched a place deep inside me, and I leaned over to take Darla's hand.

"They're very good," she whispered. "Gene can really play that harmonica."

"He writes his own stuff, too. If I could play like that, I'd do gigs all the time. The only embalming Gene should ever see are audiences embalming themselves with alcohol."

"The world also needs embalmers," Darla said.

"The world has enough people in the death business."

"I *would* rather see him play than come at me with a needle."

"You got that right."

During the break I slipped out the door behind the bass player. I'd watched him onstage, head thrown back and shoulders hunched in that characteristic way that bassists have, loose right hand fingerpicking … slapping … muting the strings. Just now, I'd caught him touching an Ohio Blue Tip match to the joint grasped in his left. He looked calmly up at me, and said, "A white boy in Stone? Tell me you ain't a cop."

I pulled a pin joint out of my shirt pocket. "Would a cop be carrying this?"

"No, sir, I don't believe he would. It does look a mite undernourished, though."

"We won't even need all of this."

I touched match to spliff, got it going well, and handed it over.

The bassist took an experimental hit, rolling the pungent smoke over his tongue like a weedy oenophile. Tilting his head back, the bass player exhaled a stream of smoke. His head swiveled down, a big smile on his face. "Oh, yeah, this is good ganja!" He had a bassist's spatulate fingertips, but his lungs must've been modeled on Louie Armstrong's.

"That is without a doubt the best grass I ever smoked."

"I guess I should have introduced myself. My name is Slats. I'm a friend of Gene's." I stuck out my hand.

"They call me Shiny, 'cause I sweat when I play." Shiny gave me some skin, slow and silent, bluesman style.

"How come nobody else is out here for attitude adjustment?"

"Those guys are great musicians, but when it comes to this stuff, they're squares. Except Chitlin, the drummer—he'll get high after the show is over."

Right about then we heard Chitlin do a little rattle on his snare. Shiny said, "Time to start up again. Thanks for letting me try some of this stuff."

As we headed back I slipped him a couple more pinners, so he could stay fueled for the night. "That's mighty nice of you; I'm fixin' to slap that E string clean off my Fender!"

———————

Since I was piloting the Beezer, I'd allowed myself only one drink. Darla, however, enjoyed several beverages. We danced wildly when the musical stops got pulled, and we slowed down when the band mellowed. The Undertakers had taken over the Joint: they controlled the audience musically with the same ease as I guided my Cessna. We were only too happy to surrender control—the blues had snared us all.

Gene carefully guided the pacing of the night, reminding me of the conductor of the only classical orchestra I ever saw. When he wasn't wailing on his Hohner, he used it enthusiastically as a baton. For a man with one lung, he showed real energy and stamina. Gene was truly in his element—tremendously energetic, yet completely at peace.

After the second set, Gene plopped down gratefully at our table. "Darla, you are a vision of loveliness. Slats, I'm so glad you could make it."

"Gene, you're workin' the room better than Sinatra. You make the rest of us look like a bunch of pikers."

"I can't help it—music always grabs me by the lapels and gives me a good shake."

"You play one mean blues harp."

So Gene gave me a quick education. "Technically, this isn't a blues harp. This is a ten-hole Hohner Marine Band, about the simplest harmonica there is. But it sounds downright greasy," he chuckled.

"We should have used blues to conquer North Vietnam, instead of guns."

"My mama was a religious woman—she thought blues was the devil's music. But my daddy always said, 'Blues in him, and it got to come out.'"

"Your father sounds like a pragmatic man."

"That he was! And it's time for his musically sin-drenched son to get up and do the last set." He leaned over to kiss Darla's hand, winked, and then whipped out an A-harp like it was a straight razor. "Time to put the evening down so painlessly that nobody will realize what's happened till we're gone."

Darla and I were just tearing past the St. Sebastion River Preserve on my BSA when the lights and siren came on behind us. This was getting to be too common an experience for my taste. I leaned the bike on the stand as the chief marched up.

"Well, well… Looks like we got us a drunk driver who's speedin'," he crowed, flicking his eyes toward Darla.

"I'm not drunk, but I can't be sure about my speed because the wind blurred my vision and I couldn't read the speedometer."

"You were tippin' ninety-six!" He flipped open his ticket book and made a mark, carefully reading the printed caption: "Excessive speed in a duly posted zone."

"Is that all?"

"I got a more important bone to pick with you, boy. Your dog has ruined my Penelope."

"My dog boned someone named Penelope? Hey, I make it a policy never to interfere with his love life." As I said this, I looked over to see Darla hide a grin.

Dim as the chief's bulb was, none of this was lost on him. He banged a forefinger on my chest, snarling, "Penelope is a registered huntin' dog. When covered by a registered male, pups are worth a couple hundred dollars each! But I won't see none of that, because she was worn out instead by a litter of mongrels!"

"How much is a mongrel worth?" I asked.

The chief had a ready answer. "They ain't worth shit, which is why I put 'em in a sack and drowned 'em." Darla inhaled sharply, and the chief smiled at drawing blood.

I knew immediately he was stating a fact. I started to reply, but Darla beat me to it. "You really drowned a litter of puppies just because they're mixed?"

"Far as I'm concerned, that dirty little sumbitch is guilty of miscegenation. I'll deal with him in due time."

"You touch…"

"I've heard it before," the chief interrupted. "If I touch your dog, you'll knock my dick in the dirt."

"What I said before was, you touch me and I'll knock your dick in the dirt. Now I'm adding this: if you touch my dog, I'll beat you to a bloody pulp with a piece of rebar." I looked him straight in the eye. "And if you ever touch Darla again, I'll kill you before sayin' hello."

The chief looked startled at being so boldly addressed. "You got a big mouth for such a skinny little bastard." To demonstrate his testosterone level, he thumped me once more in the chest, this time with the ticket he'd written.

I took it, saying only, "Don't forget what I said."

───────────

It galled me to have to pay yet another ticket. But I usually stayed on the right side of the law, so the occasional stride over the line could be taken with impunity. I swallowed my pride and paid my fine, using the visit as a chance to reconnoiter the jail. I'd seen that it would be pretty difficult to break out of this place. But, of course, keeping people inside is what jails are designed to do.

In high school, I'd been fascinated by escape artist Harry Houdini. His book had explained many useful things: the art of misdirection; utilizing the cover of night, where possible; the fundamentals of locksmithery. It turned out that I need only slip a bathroom window clasp with my knife blade to get inside. Silently, I crept through the darkened halls, making sure I had the place to myself. Entering the chief's office, I made a quick circuit without finding the object of my desire.

I did locate a locked desk drawer, however. Prepared for this possibility, I slipped several items out of my backpack. I inserted the piece of stiff wire into the keyhole and felt for the tumblers, while gently applying turning pressure with a little screwdriver. I manipulated the tumblers for a few moments, until resistance on the screwdriver handle suddenly vanished. The lock clicked open, and there lay the chief's legendary .45 caliber horse pistol.

I yanked the heavy Colt from its holster and unloaded it, then took it back to the cellblock. Pulling a portable torch from my pack, I lit it and set to work about two inches from the end of the seven-inch barrel. Though it took a long time to heat the steel, I was in no hurry. When I had a section glowing cherry red, I stuck the muzzle between a couple of bars in the nearest cell then hauled on the grip with all my strength. It felt it shift, and I bent it upward at a thirty-degree angle. I then applied heat several inches further down the barrel, stuck it between the bars again, and bent the barrel back downward thirty degrees.

I admired my artwork as the metal cooled. The barrel had a neat S-bend with nicely-radiused curves—my metal shop teacher would have approved. But somehow, it didn't seem quite finished. So I pulled out a hacksaw and cut the hammer off, complete with firing pin. Now I'd achieved a beautiful flow, from cursive barrel to streamlined frame. Though I've never been keen on mementos, I slipped the hammer into my pocket.

I carried the modified revolver back to the chief's desk, reloaded and holstered it, and then locked it safely away. I wiped down every surface I'd touched, shouldered my pack, and slipped back out the bathroom window. Hell, I even politely relocked it!

I took the hammer home, filing out the saw marks and neatly beveling the edges. I drilled a small hole through the base, chamfered it, and then laced it to my aircraft key with a piece of leather thong. I also blunted the firing pin; it wouldn't do for my new key fob to stick me in the soft parts when pocketed. And I hoped my message to Piss Bubble was clear: you touch my dog, I'll circumcise more than your hogleg.

Twenty-nine

People often made the mistake of thinking that Oso, a poor immigrant dishwasher, must be dumb. Nothing could be further from the truth—he had a well-developed business sense. Said business might be illegal, and conducted only three times a year, but it nonetheless dealt in large sums of cash. And it was growing steadily.

Oso had found what he called "good customers," people who were only too happy to pay top money for the best stock. Though they would have happily bought ten times as much as the Morales family produced, these customers had to be satisfied with the family's small production. Quality, not quantity, was our byword—we were a boutique operation.

I thought I had problems concealing my illicit income, but Oso's difficulties put mine to shame. I was here to collect the fourteen thousand dollars I'd earned for my last flight; Oso'd had to figure out how to make a hundred and twenty-six thousand dollars look legit. He'd apparently been mulling the problem over for a while.

Oso passed the joint to me. "Slats, what do you do

with your money?" he asked out of the blue.

"I keep most of it in a safe deposit box. I don't know where else to put it."

"The business is changing. There is so much money coming in, it take a lotta time and effort to launder it."

"*Launder* it? You sound like a tax lawyer," I laughed.

"You can laugh, but that's how people get tripped up in this business. I must try to figure out a way to make so much money look right. Look … *legitimate*. That's the word."

In his way, my friend was every bit as smart as his brother DB. But Oso had street smarts, which added another level to his intelligence—cunning.

"So, what are you going to do, invest in the paving business, like a mobster?"

"I don't know about other businesses. But I'm learning about bonds and stocks, things like that."

"Are you pulling my leg?"

"No. Last time we sell our crop, I buy something called bearer bonds. A big sheet of paper, very fancy drawing on it, almost like paper money. You buy one for five thousand dollars, put it away somewhere safe. Every six months, you cut coupon off the bottom and cash it in. They make five percent a year, good for twenty-five or thirty years, tax free. When the coupons are gone, you turn in fancy picture and get your five thousand dollars back."

"You sound like an investment counselor."

"Here's the thing: we've got so much coming in, before long it will be a full time job just to cut the coupons. I'll need bigger investments, paper stuff … I don't know, bond fund or blue chip stocks, something like that."

"Where did you learn about this?" I asked.

"Reading *Forbes*," he shrugged, and I laughed. "So, I'll give you a choice. I'll pay you cash, just like always, or I'll give you three bearer bonds."

"Your math is off, Oso; that's more than you owe me."

"The family will write it off as a cost of doing business. Besides, you're worth every penny. It a grat…gratu…"

"*Gratuity*? The Morales family is giving me a tip?"

"*Si*, a tip." He showed me a bearer bond, issued by the city of Miami to finance improvements in the electrical grid. He said they were fully guaranteed by the municipality, held a triple-A rating, and were about as safe an investment as one could make. The most recent coupons were still attached, uncashed.

"Sooner or later, Slats, you're going to have a problem with your money too. But it's up to you; I give you cash or bonds, whichever you want."

"Won't I have the same trouble explaining how I got the bonds?"

"For your amounts, we'll make a cover story. Rich old uncle?"

"Hell, no."

"Of course you don't! He just died from a heart attack, up in, uh…Minnesota. You inherit everything."

"What about the money from future flights?"

"You're a very smart investor. You put the interest into more investments."

I grinned at him. "You've made your case, Oso. I'll take the bonds, thank you very much. In fact, if you have others that are just as safe, I'd like to…*launder* some more of my money. "

"I got a shitload, Slats. I'll cover whatever you want.

We put our money to work." Oso laughed, showing his gold teeth.

"God bless America!" I agreed.

Oso picked me up later, and we paid a visit to the bank. To the three bonds he'd given me earlier, I now added twelve more. I gave him sixty thousand dollars in cash, and he gave me a quick tutorial in how to cash in the coupons. I did keep a ready supply of cash in the box, though. One never knew when he might find himself in need of a fiscal parachute.

"I've been worried that a safe deposit box might not protect me against inquiries by the law, if the chief ever got smart. I feel safer, now."

"It is safer. You always know how to make the flying safe. I will take care of this new danger, cops on the lookout for money. Between you and me, we'll stay ahead in this game."

"Do you have more of these bonds, Oso?"

"I have close to a hundred thousand worth."

"If you don't mind hanging on to them, I'll take 'em all as payment for future flights."

So I traded my big safe deposit box in on a smaller one, and started to fill it with colorful, coupon-bearing artwork.

———————

My economic task complete, I took a swim in the pond to celebrate. As usual, Tailskid followed me around the perimeter. He barked enthusiastically to warn me when the resident alligator surfaced. But this eight-footer had been around long enough for me to know he was more curious than aggressive. I'd be considerably less trusting if he was still around for the start of mating season, however.

I climbed out to dry myself, and found Jelly on the bank eyeing the alligator uneasily. "You crazy, getting into a swimming hole with a gator that size?"

"Tailskid lets me know when he gets inquisitive. Besides, we have an understanding. I don't hunt him, and he extends the same courtesy to me."

"Keep an eye on that dog; he's an alligator tidbit if I ever saw one," Jelly advised. "And you best be careful around Ol' Gabriel too, Slats."

"You named the gator?"

"I did. I call him Ol' Gabriel because, if you ever hear him blow his horn, it'll be time for the Promised Land."

"I heard him bellowing in the middle of the night, once. At least I think it was him."

"My old auntie would have said it was a haint, calling out for somebody's soul," Jelly joked.

"More likely Ol' Gabriel is callin' for a girlfriend, unless I miss my guess."

Jelly's laughter pealed like a bell, and I joined in. But then her hand shot to her belly, and she chirped in pain.

"What's the matter?"

"I've been having stomach pains lately, but they're especially sharp today."

"You should see a doctor."

"I already have an appointment with Dr. Logan."

Thirty

The following week, right about the time Jane Fonda was sliding her pert ass onto a North Vietnamese anti-aircraft gun, I stepped onto Jelly's porch with rent money in pocket. I didn't even get my knuckle on the door before she called out, "Come on in, Slats."

I entered, shaking my head. "Am I that predictable?"

"You are one of the most unpredictable people I've ever known. Except on the first of the month..."

I found that she already had company. "I didn't know you were here, Mabel. I'll just leave this, and let you ladies carry on with your visit." The two had known each other since the first grade.

"No, don't go just yet. I have news that concerns you, too." Jelly got up and poured me a mug of coffee.

Mabel slid her chair over to make room, saying, "Good seein' you again, Mr. Kisov."

"I sure wish you'd call me Slats, ma'am. Every time somebody calls me 'Mr. Kisov,' trouble is always close behind."

"You ain't in no trouble with me. You a godsend to Jelly."

"I'd say it was the other way around. Who else but Jelly

would have opened her door—well, her barn door—to someone who dropped out of the sky one day?"

"She's a good woman; both of us got that part right."

I sipped my coffee, watching Jelly over the rim as she struggled to find the right words. Then she did what she always did—she squared her shoulders and spoke plainly. "I have cancer in my colon." Her eyes misted, and Mabel reached over to take her hand.

My blood chilled. I'd been around injury and sudden death; I knew intimately the damage wrought by bullet, shrapnel, and flame. But I was wholly unacquainted with malady. I sat staring at my friend, and I saw she was afraid.

My instinct was to fight. "Can it be treated?"

"It has a pretty good hold already. The doctor is checking into something called chemotherapy, which I guess is some kind of drug. But it has bad side effects. He says radiation is out, because the colon is so sensitive."

"You have to use whatever weapons you have, in any kind of war," I said. "But this sounds expensive. I know you don't want to hear this, but if you need some money…"

"I am already so far in your debt I could never repay you. The last thing I need is to die beholden."

"Don't say that! I have more than I need for my simple ways. I don't care about money. What I'm short on in this world are friends. Please let me help, Jelly."

Jelly reached out to cup my cheek. "The one thing I am *not* short on is friends." She took us both by a hand and smiled. "You two are more than friends, you and Mabel are my family. If I need something, I'll let you know. But Dr. Logan tells me the new Medicaid program should cover this. Now, don't either of you worry about me."

She may as well have told us to fly to Neptune.

I didn't know much about Dr. Logan, and it didn't help that I held a pilot's instinctive distrust of pill pushers. But this doctor's exemplary ways quickly won me over. He turned out to be a most dedicated physician, and his patients enjoyed an unparalleled standard of treatment. I think he saw in Jelly a reflection of his wife, who'd succumbed to leukemia many years ago, and that he took personal affront in cancer's decision to again lodge in so helpless a host.

First things first: Dr. Logan recommended a surgeon of his acquaintance in Vero Beach, a man with both skills and the wisdom to charge patients on a sliding scale commensurate with their income. Dr. Remshaw examined Jelly, evaluated the X-rays and other diagnostic tests, and then confirmed Logan's suspicion that it was too late for surgery. Colorectal adenocarcinoma produces incredibly fast-growing tumors, and is also resistant to chemotherapy. Both doctors reluctantly concluded that the only treatment indicated was palliative care.

So Dr. Logan took up the fight again, with the limited weapons at his disposal. If he could not treat the disease, he could at least treat the symptoms. When Jelly lost weight, Logan had Mabel entice her with her favorite dishes. When she got diarrhea from the rich food, Logan gave her Loperamide. And when Jelly began to pass blood, the doctor transfused her.

Jelly's main symptom was pain. Logan, a physician of the old school, first prescribed low-dose codeine tablets to alleviate the discomfort. But as the cancer gained a firmer hold, he gradually ramped up the strength of the analgesics. He progressed to Hydrocodone before long, and then to Dilaudid.

I believe Dr. Logan's most effective technique was his bedside manner. He inspired trust with his compassionate care, while using humor to ease the patient's mind. More than once I saw Jelly forget the nagging pain which now filled her days. Most of all Dr. Logan impressed me with his dedication. And his willingness to respond instantly to Jelly's needs—night or weekend—really won me over. He provided his home phone number, he made house calls, he did literally everything in his power to ease Jelly's way.

But cancer was as remorseless an adversary as I'd ever run across.

———————

"See how I'm making a tent shape with her skin?" Dr. Logan pinched a little flap up with thumb and forefinger. "You just smoothly and firmly push the needle in where the door would be." He made a tiny, practiced jab into Jelly's arm. I winced at her expression, but pills were no longer strong enough to do the job. Mabel and I needed to add subcutaneous injections to the list of medical procedures we'd already learned.

"I'm sorry, Jelly. It seems like I'm always sticking you with something."

"Don't worry, Doctor; morphine kills the pain of the shot, too," she smiled. "I guess I'm a fallen woman now; I went from teetotaler to drug addict in one fell swoop."

"That's the bad news. The good news is that you get

two lollypops for being such a tolerant patient." He smiled at her, earning himself a peal of laughter from Jelly. I did not understand how this woman managed to retain her sense of humor.

Either Mabel or I were always at Jelly's bedside. Darla also lent a frequent hand. Sometimes she'd bring a dish meant to tempt Jelly's almost nonexistent appetite, but more often Darla just kept her company. Medicaid was paying for necessary medical procedures, but I'd quit trying to get them to spring for ancillary services like home care. I quietly paid out of my pocket, meanwhile assuring Jelly that Medicaid must be the most generous government program since the Oklahoma Land Rush.

I'd developed a real admiration for Mabel. She was a friend in the truest sense of the word, willing to bend over backward to help in any way she could. She put her own life on hold, to be there in Jelly's time of need. And Jelly *was* in need—the prognosis was dire.

"The cancer has spread to her lymph glands," Dr. Logan told me. "This is a bad sign. You need to know that her time is growing very short, Mr. Kisov."

"Doc, isn't there anything else you can try?"

"I've pulled every trick I know out of my hat. All we can do is try to keep her comfortable." He reached over to give my shoulder a squeeze. "If you're a praying man, it can't hurt."

"I'm not much on religion, Doc. Seems like prayer mainly helps the people who are doing the praying."

"There's a great deal of truth in that, sir. But what's wrong with a little help for the supplicant? Caregivers shoulder one of the most difficult jobs imaginable."

"I'm sure not cut out for it."

He turned to look me squarely in the eye. "I've been a doctor for forty-three years, son. You and Miss Mabel are doing as fine a job of it as I've ever seen."

Darla had brought some freshly picked wildflowers, which she placed in a vase by Jelly's bed. She arranged them quickly but artfully, sponged Jelly's brow with a damp washcloth, then put the fan in the window to direct cool evening air into the room. She sat beside me, and Jelly beamed at us.

"You two were meant for each other. You both know that, don't you?"

My hand sought out Darla's, and our fingers intertwined. "Yeah, we know it, Jelly. I quit lookin' around after our first date."

"You damn well better have quit looking," Darla observed dryly.

I put on a frown. "I keep a sharp lookout for your left jab," I said, earning a punch on the arm.

Jelly took a sip of water. "Listen up now, Slats. Do the right thing by this good woman. Don't keep her waiting too long."

"Yes, ma'am," I said, scuffing the floor with my shoe.

"Don't give me that scolded schoolboy act, either," she smiled. Then, abruptly changing the subject, she noted, "The power of attorney I signed for you a while back is still good." I paused a moment, trying to absorb this non sequitur. "Don't look at me like my clutch is slipping, there's a point to what I'm saying. I want you to be the executor of my will."

I started to make the standard denial one makes in such a situation, mumbling something about this not being the time for such a discussion.

But Jelly gently hushed me. "Now is precisely the time, while my mind is still clear. I need to make my wishes known."

"Of course I'll be your executor. I didn't nearly get my fill of acting like your lawyer, last time around," I assured her.

"You were good at it, too," she smiled. "But I'm not concerned with physical possessions; taking care of those few things is simple. I'm talking about more important matters. When my time arrives, I want to lie with Henry."

Jelly was referring to the tiny fenced graveyard near a stand of trees, not far from the pond where I swam. There, Henry Rawlins had lain at rest under an inexpensive concrete marker for almost two decades, shaded by a massive live oak and watched over by the plots of several well-loved family dogs. I had foreseen this talk, and prepared for it.

"Do you feel up to a little trip, Jelly?"

"I don't have to ride on that motorcycle of yours, do I?"

I laughed. "Actually, I had a more basic form of transportation in mind."

Which is how Jelly found herself lying in a scrubbed and blanket-padded wheelbarrow, wobbling through her yard toward the pond, pushed by a skinny guy who was better at piloting airplanes than he was one-wheelers.

"I feel a little like an old Eskimo woman being put out on the ice," Jelly joked.

"Don't be silly; this is Florida, where would we find ice?"

She let loose a peal of morphine-lubricated laughter.

"Maybe you're gonna feed me to Ol' Gabriel instead, just like the dear departed go to the vultures in Tibet."

I pushed her not to the pond, but instead to the picket fence. Darla opened the gate and we went straight to Henry's resting spot. Jelly had fallen silent.

She was staring at the new granite headstone, on one side of which the concise description of her man's lifetime was engraved. The other side was blank as morning sky. A short inscription bridged the two: *Love is immortality.*

After a pause to let her reflect, I said, "We all kicked in on this marker, Jelly. We should have done this for Henry a long time ago."

Jelly spoke very softly. "Where have I heard that quote?"

Darla said, "It's from a poem you once read me by Emily Dickinson."

Jelly was weeping now. "This is such a beautiful gesture, I just don't know what to say."

"You don't have to say anything." I kissed her cheek. "Except that you'll promise to leave this side of the marker smooth, for as long as possible."

But Jelly wasn't able to keep that promise. She slipped away the very next day.

When it came to the next step, there was only one man to call. Gene immediately took everything in hand: he prepared the body, he located a simple pine casket, and he hired two diggers. Then, in his capacity as lay preacher, Gene led the service.

"Folks, we're gathered here today to see Jelly Rawlins off on her final journey." He had a faraway look in his eye as he peered backward in time. "I knew Jelly back when her last name was still Watson. The fact is, I rented the place right next door to her folks' house, and I listened to nonstop jazz coming from her daddy's Victrola, if you need proof of my claim. I watched Jelly grow from a toddler to an upright young woman, and I was there when she tied the knot with Henry.

"Jelly was as fine a woman as you'll ever know. She came from good people, she married a good man, and she had the fortune to live her life surrounded by other good people. She believed in helping others, and she did so often.

"She didn't hold with fancy ways. Jelly was a down-to-earth woman who enjoyed living simply, and I'm not going to stand up here and try to wax eloquent over her. You want eloquent, you just study on the way she conducted herself throughout her life, and the way she approached death—that is the very essence of eloquence.

"The thing in life Jelly most valued was her marriage to Henry Rawlins. The only true injustice in her life was that she and Henry were able to share far too little time together." Gene looked down at the double-plot, and said, "Well, now you get to spend eternity beside one another. May both of you rest easy, in the peace you so richly deserve."

The diggers lowered the casket into the grave and Gene threw a handful of earth on top, to begin the covering with love. Then he pulled a harmonica from his coat pocket and blew a mournful rendition of an old Civil War tune, "The Vacant Chair," part blues and part hymn.

He carved the heart right out of my chest with that music.

Thirty-one

The only task left to me was to carry out Jelly's final wishes. So I read her last will and testament to the only person Jelly had told me to summon for the occasion, Mabel.

I, Jelly Rawlins, being of sound mind if deteriorating body, do leave to my lifelong friend Mabel Frasier five acres of her choice from my ranch. It is my request that the executor help her build a small cabin there, where she may dwell rent free for the remainder of her days. And may it be a long, happy life! I also leave to Mabel my pickup truck of questionable parentage (perhaps the executor could turn the occasional wrench for her).

To Slats Kisov, who dropped out of thin air one day to light on my land and in my heart, I leave the remaining thirty acres, including house and barn. I hope you'll continue to fly from this place, where you've become as familiar to locals as the hawks with whom you share the sky. And I hope someday that Darla will come to live here with you.

I can't begin to thank you both for allowing me

to remain at home, where I belonged, for as long as humanly possible. I consider this the most valuable gift of my life—no one ever departed God's green earth feeling more loved.

Mabel and I looked at each other shyly. To be praised in this manner was almost too sweet to bear.

"Jelly and I talked about her plans to leave you some property. She wanted to leave you more, but she thought you'd never give yourself permission to accept it."

"She was right. To tell you the truth, I don't feel all that good about five acres, let alone more."

"It was Jelly's wish that you become financially independent. She said that your income as a midwife, along with the food you'd be able to grow on your own place, would allow that. She called it 'true freedom.'"

"I can hear exactly the way she would have said it." A tear rolled down Mabel's cheek. "Well, my oldest boy is a fine carpenter. Jimmy will know about costs and such. We'll just have to see if I can scrape up enough money for a snug little shack."

"Jelly was way ahead of us, here. She already contacted Jimmy, and we took up a little collection for materials. My dad donated some of the electrical fixtures and plumbing stuff. Jimmy told me what to order, and it's stacked out behind the hangar right now. All you need to do is pick out your land."

"I have to think on this awhile."

"Let's take a walk." I led her down Roadapple Lane, to the corner of the property closest to town. "I thought this might be a nice spot. You have easy road access, and utility access, too. The acreage is pretty; some is woods, but the rest is clear enough for a nice big vegetable garden. You're close enough to visit any time you want, and far enough for privacy. But if you prefer another spot, just say so. And as far as I'm concerned, you're welcome to more than five acres; take as much as you need. I only want what Jelly wanted, for you to be content."

Mabel looked at me. "You sure about this, Mr. Slats?"

I smiled back. "As sure as I can be, Miss Mabel."

"Then this plot looks fine to me." Then, shaking her head sadly, "But there goes your neighborhood."

———————————

So we held a good old-fashioned house-raising. The first order of business was for Jimmy to walk the terrain and get the lay of the land. Mabel wanted her place built in the shade of stout trees, but close to a clear patch so she could step conveniently out to pick fresh vegetables from her garden. Jimmy found just the spot, angling the cabin in his mind to match the surrounding growth, and then laying out a string perimeter with practiced ease.

I was put to work as a pack mule with Mabel's other son Jesse, a Vietnam vet turned Orlando cop. Mabel had requested a simple one-bedroom design, about four hundred square feet in size. Jimmy and his helper were skilled carpenters, and they knocked the floor and frame together in a few hours then started on the roof trusses. Jesse and I transported corrugated metal roofing sheets to the site, where they would crown the trusses.

"I love the sound of rain dripping on a metal roof. Such a comfortin' way to fall asleep," Mabel said.

Jimmy assured her, "It makes for a sturdy house, too. A small well-built cabin, stiffened with a metal roof, can withstand a hurricane hit better than most buildings. It's strong, but it has flexibility built in." While Jimmy hammered the roof trusses into place, the backhoe arrived and began digging a hole for the septic tank. By sundown, the water line had been laid from my well, and the potbellied stove was installed in the little parlor. Mabel's belongings had arrived, and she was scurrying around trying to find a place for everything.

We'd get electric and telephone hooked up as soon as possible, but for now Mabel could do without these niceties. She intended to begin her residency immediately. Or, as she put it, "I ain't spendin' another night under somebody else's roof, not when I got a fine roof of my own, a kerosene lantern, and a thunderpot. No sir, I'm stayin' right here!"

"What's the first thing you're going to do in your own place?"

"I'll go visit Jelly. She was my best friend in the world, and I need to thank her right."

I nodded my head in agreement. But Mabel reached up to enwrap me in a powerful hug. "Your name is right under hers, on that list, Mr. Slats. You're helpin' me now almost as much as you helped Jelly. I know this cost you some money, right along with the sweat of your labor. Thank you, Slats. For everything."

With Mabel around Jelly will be just a little less gone, I thought, as I watched her tiny yellow light bounce resolutely away in the darkness.

Thirty-two

I'd been distracted before takeoff by images of our POWs stepping off transports at Clark Air Base, on their way back to the United States. The look on their faces as they finally stepped onto free soil stirred my soul. I'd probably seen several of these guys go down with my own eyes. I didn't give a hoot in hell about fancy treaties being signed at official ceremonies. Getting our captured personnel back was the real end of the war. My thoughts were thus occupied as I flew over the Atlantic, DB and I exchanging little conversation.

Which is how I was taken so thoroughly by surprise as I overflew Chico Cay. A boat had been dragged on shore near the house and several armed men milled among the Morales family.

"What are we going to do, Slats?"

"We can't take 'em all on with a short-barrel .38. I don't see any alternative; we have to land peaceably." Regretfully, I bid my trusted S&W goodbye and tossed it out the window.

As I taxied up, I could see Carlos and Tomas sitting with their backs to the wall, tied up. Carlos looked battered—he must have put up a fight. Two of the men had pistols in hand, the one wearing a ridiculous sport coat and a blue Panama hat shouting at Carlos. A third man relaxed in a chair. He looked almost as though he were sipping coffee in a Paris café, except instead of a cup of fine Arabica, the Morales' Winchester carbine was placed on the table in front of him. I saw no sign of Mamo's revolver.

"Search them," said the sitting man, whom I mentally nicknamed Boss. Hat, who seemed inclined to barely controlled violence, pushed me roughly over the table and patted me down, then shook his head. The quiet one, Harpo, merely looked on.

"You are *my* chauffeur now, gringo." Boss reached casually out and swiveled the Winchester until the muzzle pointed squarely at Julieta. "Or am I going to have trouble from you?"

I instinctively realized that this was not a man to push. Instead, I opted for shuck and jive. "I just like to fly and get high, man. I'm what you call a peaceable dude." I held up my ponytail.

"That's all I want you to do, fly another load to America. Except this time, my brother will go with you," he nodded at Hat. "He'll tell you where to land."

"You can't land a load like this just anywhere…"

"That is not for you to worry about! You will go where you are told," he airily waved his hand, "like a good chauffeur."

"Sure, I'll fly whatever you want, wherever you say."

Boss muttered an aside in Spanish. I caught the word *mariposa*, which technically means butterfly but actually was a slur on my manhood. Hat and Harpo laughed disparagingly, while I just nodded and grinned like the village idiot. If they wanted a hippie version of Stepin Fetchit, well, here I is!

Boss indicated the Morales family. "Do you like these people? You should remember we'll hurt the women first, if you don't do what I say." He grinned widely, adding, "It wouldn't be the first time we taught a lesson to them, eh brother?" Hat laughed hoarsely. DB inclined his head to get a better look at Hat, his eyes curious, appraising.

Hat stepped over to Julieta and caressed her hair. "This your sister?" he asked DB. "I not hurt her… *too* much."

"She is just a child," DB pointed out.

"If she bleed, she can breed," Hat replied with a lascivious grin. Carlos began to struggle again, and Hat answered him with a swift kick in the solar plexus. I felt like slitting this bastard from crotch to sternum, but with considerable difficulty I squelched my anger. Harpo looked on, intent but silent—I half-expected him to pull out a horn and start honking, at some point.

Hat was in a talkative mood, though. "We've been watching. We know it's time to come here when the harvest is in. We going to make much money from these people," he grinned. "*Again.*" DB looked up again, recognition and fear now evident in his eyes.

"Enough talk," Boss cut him off abruptly. "Get that marijuana loaded; it isn't going to fly itself to the States." I set off with Harpo to pile the weed in and tie it securely down, thinking furiously the whole time.

They had the advantages of weapons and hostages, and they didn't care how big a mess they left behind. But I also realized these men would be weakened when they split up.

Best of all, the most violent and unpredictable of the lot was coming with me. Julieta and the others were temporarily safer while we were gone.

And I did have a single edge—the ability to think in three dimensions. I mulled over the limited options available to a prepared if unarmed man. In the end, I decided to do what I always did—improvise!

In short order, Hat and I were sitting side by side in the 180, he holding a pistol on me as I ran her up and checked the magnetos. The airplane was in apple pie order, but Hat was showing unease for the first time. I recognized the apprehension of a first-time passenger.

We taxied to the end of the landing strip, and I purposefully hit every pothole and clump of weeds on the way, bouncing the small plane around like a tractor traveling over broken road. Hat kept the gun pointed at me, but his other hand was gripping the edge of the seat tightly. I wondered: *If he hates taxiing this much, how is he going to feel when he gets in the air?*

Over the engine, I hollered, "Buckle up for safety!" Hat looked uncomprehendingly at me, so I grabbed my own belt and fastened it ostentatiously. "You don't wanna get hurt while committing multiple felonies, right shitbird?"

When he complied, I immediately shoved the throttle to full power, and the big Continental let out its characteristic bellow. Hat's eyes widened as the aircraft surged forward, and then goggled as we took the air. I stood her on her tail, nothing but sky visible through the windscreen, grinding upward at just under stall speed. The impact of unfamiliar motion and sonic assault seemed overwhelming to him.

I advised, "Put that goddamn gun away, before you shoot yourself in the dick." Hat turned to look, and I mimed putting the pistol back in his shoulder holster, which he did. I climbed to only a thousand feet before abruptly leveling off in the rough, hot air.

I began to subtly work the controls, magnifying the effects of the turbulence. I rolled the wings a little, first right and then to the left. When I threw in some pitch changes, Hat clung to his seat with a two-handed death grip. Finally, I introduced a sickening little yaw with the rudder pedals, to churn the contents of his stomach to a froth. For good measure I closed the cooling vents, and the temperature in the cabin started to rise.

As we Dutch-rolled our way westward, I kept up my cheerful, obscene patter. "This is great, isn't it asswipe? Just me and my dipshit buddy, out on a pleasure junket." Hat looked over, beads of sweat oozing from his pale face. He wasn't nearly as aggressive as he'd been, and we were only ten minutes into the flight. I sent another brisk little shudder running through my Cessna, suppressing a smile when Hat responded with something between a hiccup and a wet burp.

I had Hat's stomach percolating enough by now that I started a gradual climb to altitude. I kept the plane jiggling the entire way up to eighty-five hundred feet. "Take that jacket off, you hemorrhoid, before you drip pus all over my plane," I urged as we leveled out, fanning my face to indicate cooling effect. He shrugged out of the coat, and when I put my hand out he placed it there trustingly. I casually tossed it back over my shoulder on top of our fragrant cargo, and then grinned at him. "You know you're the only guy I ever met who egressed through a bunghole instead of a birth canal?"

I shoved the yoke forward and the bottom dropped out. The map lying on the instrument panel magically levitated in the negative G-force, and blue water filled the entire windscreen. "Hold on, this ol' hoss is gettin' away from me!" Then I yanked merrily back on the yoke, sinking deep into my seat cushion, positive G making me feel like I weighed five hundred pounds.

That was it: Hat tossed his cookies all over his lap. "Geez, are you all right? Maybe you picked up a dose of the clap while committing your last rape." I wiggled the wings a bit and he let loose again. I slid the aircraft through quick changes in all three flight axes, and it was as though I were wringing water out of a washcloth. I'd never seen anybody vomit so much, and my best friend was bulimic.

After that performance Hat just slumped in his seat, as miserable as any human I'd ever seen. He was as disgusting as any human I'd ever seen too, coated in his own sour slickness like a mothballed carbine in cosmoline. My glance slid to his holstered pistol, but I knew there was a limit to what I could get away with. So I sent another sine wave running sickeningly through the plane, and then reached over to snatch the hat off his head.

"You think you're going to steal a bundle, tap that little girl, and then shoot her whole family, don't you? All in a day's work, right? To a thief…a murderer…a despoiler of innocent souls."

Hat's only response was to drool bottom-of-the-gut dregs down his shirtfront.

"You strike me as a philosophical man. Well, contemplate

this." I tipped the aircraft vertically onto its right wing, Hat's face flashing into astonishment. Then I reached over to pop the door open and, curling my fingers as I pulled my hand back, snagged the release on his seat belt. He went out the door like a champagne cork leaving the bottle, assisted by a nudge I gave the rudder pedal.

I'll say one thing: the guy sure had a great set of lungs. I could hear his protracted scream for almost ten seconds as he swan dove toward the Atlantic, one and a half miles below. I rolled her back onto an even keel, reached over to slam the passenger door, then dusted off my hands. The only vexing thing was that his pistol went with him.

I flew straight to the ranch, got the plane tucked safely in the barn and, for the first time, warehoused a load of weed large enough to send me to prison for a very long time. But that was nothing compared to the Morales' trouble.

I had tossed my only firearm into the sea. I knew of no one from whom I could quickly borrow another, so I grabbed the next best option—my Air Force survival knife. I pulled the now-empty plane back out of the hangar and headed for the Airpark, where I quickly topped off the fuel tanks.

There was only one man I could rely on for help, and I thanked God he was pulling dishwasher duty when I ran over to the Hair of the Dog. I filled Oso in quickly on the situation.

"Please tell me you can get your hands on a gun," I said.

"I stay away from them, Slats. Only guy I know who has a gun is you."

"That means we'll be bringing knives to a gunfight."

Oso's expression grew foxy, and he stepped over to the cook's station. He pulled a heavy butcher knife out of the rack, running a fingertip along the nine-inch blade. "You shove a big knife into somebody, you can mess 'em up pretty bad."

I took Oso and his knife—plus a towel—back to the Airpark.

"*Jesús Cristo* … this plane stinks!" Oso exclaimed when I opened the door.

"Yeah, well, the last guy to sit in that seat didn't like flyin' very much."

"Where is he?"

"He … left. The good news is he took some of the puke with him."

I wiped up as much of the remainder as I could with the towel then indicated the neatly folded clothing in back. "These are your new threads, my man." I held the jacket up to his chest; "This coat is definitely you."

"What was this guy, a pimp?"

"Just be happy I got him to remove it *before* he got sick."

We took off and headed for Chico Cay as I outlined my plan to Oso. Except it wasn't really a plan—it was a very short opportunity to improvise, before gunfire broke out. Basically, I told him to get near one of the strangers, surprise him, and then kill him. I offered Oso the use of my survival knife, but he politely declined on the grounds that it was "too small." So I tucked it into my waistband, knowing my chances of getting to wield it were slim-to-none. But it comforted me, nonetheless.

As we approached the island, Oso donned his new

clothes. They were a bit baggy, but that shouldn't be a problem for the short time he might expect to fool the remaining hijackers. I circled once to assess the situation, prayed irreligiously not to fuck up, and then shot a landing on the packed sand.

Boss was near the house; I couldn't get close to him. But Harpo was off all by his lonesome. I taxied up to him, pulled the mixture control back to idle-cutoff, and then watched the prop coast to a standstill.

Oso proved himself a fine character actor. He slouched in his seat, blue hat pulled low. Wiping his face with a sleeve, he then opened the door and stepped stiffly down. He hunched there a moment, hands on his knees, indistinct in the shade under the wing, muttering a prayer.

Harpo laughed, and then spoke the first words I'd heard from his mouth. "You don' like de flying, Manolo?" he inquired, walking toward the plane.

Oso waited until Harpo stopped in front of him. Then, uncoiling like an adder in a single lithe motion, Oso thrust his knife up under the unsuspecting man's ribcage. The blade went in up to the guard and Harpo toppled backwards, Oso landing astraddle him.

"You think you fuck my sister? I fuck your heart with this blade!" Oso gave the knife a furious twist and blood fountained from the wound. Harpo's mouth worked for a moment, like a hooked fish thrown onto a riverbank, before he gave a single ghastly exhalation and lay still. His raping days were done.

Boss stood there for a moment, frozen. Here is where Hat's gun would've come in handy—I could have pumped a quick round or two in his direction to slow him down.

Instead, recovering quickly, Boss looped his arm around Julieta's neck, pulled his pistol, and put the muzzle squarely to the startled girl's temple.

"I'm going to blow her head off right in front of you!" he screamed, and Julieta's knees sagged in terror.

I yelled, "Hold on, we can still do this deal!"

"Where's my brother?" Boss screamed.

"He's okay. He's with the weed, back at my little landing strip," I desperately asserted. "It looked like the place he wanted to land was being watched. I'll take you to him, right now."

I could almost see the wheels turning in Boss's mind, as he weighed my words. "You lie. My brother would never give up his hat." His gaze swiveled to Oso. "And this prick who stole it just cut my best friend in half." He swung the muzzle suddenly towards Oso and snapped off two shots. Oso went down and lay very still, a fact I noted even as the pistol swung my way.

But another voice interrupted Boss. "You deal with me first, *pendejo*." It was Mamo, squarely facing Boss, standing with feet slightly splayed and the sun at her back.

Boss said derisively, "What are you going to do, woman, poison my porridge?"

But Mamo was not to be so casually dismissed. "I've known you were coming for a long time now, and I have prepared for your visit." Mamo slowly raised her left hand, showing it to be empty, before easing it down to lift her shirttail. I don't know how or when she'd managed to get hold of her revolver, but there it was, nestled comfortably in her waistband.

Boss did an actual double take—in different circumstances, it would've been amusing. But then he started to laugh. "Who do you think you are, Joan Wayne?"

"You laugh, and yet you hide behind a small girl. You are a *cabarde* who is about to join *him*," she thrust her chin towards Harpo's body, knife handle still protruding obscenely from his abdomen.

One does not call a *pistolero* a coward, not without consequences. "I will kill your daughter, then you and the rest of your bloodline," he hissed, gesturing with his pistol.

"Vas a usar esa arna o le vas a chupar el pito, puto?"

Upon hearing this, Boss's face twisted in fury. Julieta, now convinced she was at death's door, let out a tremendous sob as Boss started to swing the muzzle toward her head.

I never saw Mamo's hand actually move. In one instant, it was beside her hip; in the next it was extended outward, holding a smoking revolver, a sharp report echoing off the wall of the house. Boss' head snapped rearward, highlighted by a burst of red mist, before he went over backward, taking Julieta with him.

I thought Julieta had been hit, too. But I dismissed her from my mind, pulling my knife as I rushed toward Boss to slice his throat, if he still drew breath. One look sufficed to tell that Boss's breathing days were over; a sizable piece was missing from the back of his skull, along with much of his brain. Switching mental tracks, I called out, "You still with us, Oso?"

"I ain't gonna die—take care'a Julieta!"

I sheathed my knife and knelt beside her. I could find no trace of blood, and though Julieta's respiration and heartbeat were fast and shallow, that was understandable. I took her head gently in my hands, only to have some of her long brown hair come loose in one palm. I looked more closely, dreading what I'd find.

The bullet had shorn off a hank of her hair, but left Julieta otherwise untouched. I sat back on my heels, marveling at how narrowly it had missed tissue and bone. By a quarter of an inch? An eighth, perhaps? Mamo must have had no more than a crescent slice of the hijacker's head to aim at, but she'd certainly made the most of the shot.

Julieta stirred softly now, and Mamo cried, "Thank you, Jesus!" The brothers, still tied and gagged near the house, visibly relaxed as well.

And the family took their first collective breath of freedom.

Thirty-three

The immediate threat had been dealt with, and against all odds the Morales' were all still breathing. Oso had suffered a through-and-through wound to the fleshy part of his thigh. I was glad Boss had been using full-jacket ammo, because it drilled a nice neat hole. I let it bleed a bit to make sure the inner wound was washed out, before disinfecting and bandaging it. Oso squawked pretty loud when I poured peroxide into both ends of the bullet hole, but Mamo's first aid kit didn't contain painkillers.

But now we were left with a major cleanup operation. Carlos and Oso were both out of action, so Tomas and I undertook the task. We dragged the two bodies to the shore, near their boat. Few things are more difficult to move than a fresh corpse; no matter where you lift or push, the body "gives" in every possible way. And they're heavier than would seem possible—the term *dead weight* was coined for good reason.

We collected their guns, clothing and other discarded gear, right down to the empty cartridge cases. We hoisted everything aboard, and tied the bodies together using stout nylon anchor line from the boat, making sure to leave the anchor attached. Then we shoved the boat into the surf. As Tomas started to climb aboard, I held up my hand.

"I'll take it from here."

"But I want to help!"

"You have helped, my friend. But I'm going to handle this part. I'll go a couple miles out and deep-six everything, and then swim back." Tomas, a poor swimmer, could not argue with my logic. I stripped to my shorts, threw my clothes onto the sand, and fired up the Evinrude. Waving to Tomas, I headed east in the little Chris-Craft.

A mile out, I started tossing guns, knives, and clothing merrily out in every direction. At the two-mile point, I killed the engine and faced the worst part of the job. I knew from my Vietnam experience about "floaters," which is what we used to call submerged bodies that had bloated enough from decomposition to rise to the surface. To eliminate that likelihood, I used Oso's knife to thoroughly perforate the thoracic cavities of both men, getting quite bloody in the process. Then, with less emotion than running over a squirrel would have stirred, I wrestled the bodies onto the gunwale and committed them to the deep. I watched as they sank into the murk, knowing that these waters had enough sharks and scavengers to process them very quickly.

I started the engine and motored partway back, before stopping again. I opened the fuel tank, and then used the hatchet I'd brought to chop large holes in the bottom of the hull. The boat sank beneath me, leaving me floating in the warm Caribbean water, and I struck out for the island. Taking great pleasure in the physicality of swimming, I sluiced the unpleasant experience off as easily as I did the blood, and by the time I reached shore, I felt just fine.

There was nothing left to do but celebrate our survival. Mamo, of course, handled the cooking. Oso and Carlos—who was bruised and contused but not seriously injured—reclined in places of honor. Tomas and DB set about erasing any remaining evidence of the hijackers from Chico Cay, right down to clearing their footprints with brush, like Indians in a western.

I hopped over to Nassau to find some painkillers for the Morales brothers. Knowing that under-the-table business is best done across the tracks, I went to the poor side of town. The first pharmacist I encountered rolled his eyes when I said I had no prescription. But when I flashed a fifty, he forgot all about other kinds of paper and handed over a small bottle of codeine tablets.

By the time I returned to the island, all was in readiness. I handed codeine out to Oso and Carlos, shrugged and swallowed one myself, and then was led to the head of the table. While the ladies were busy with the food, I took the opportunity to fess up.

"I dumped the bodies, after putting holes in 'em so they won't surface."

"Where'd you learn to do that?" Carlos inquired.

"Watchin' *The Godfather.*"

"They sleep with the fishes now," Oso said, and everyone laughed.

The codeine must have been kicking in, because everyone seemed relaxed for the first time today. Hell, I was feeling pretty calm myself, as a joint made the rounds.

Mamo and Julieta entered, bearing platters of wonderful *arroz congri oriental, con pollo* that she'd whipped up. "What's so funny?" Mamo inquired.

"Oso was just saying that if he'd known that you could shoot like that, he would have behaved better as a child."

"It's true: he was sometimes a bad boy, very headstrong. But today you see how strong his head really is. He came to this place of guns and death, disguised as an enemy, armed only with a kitchen knife. And he kill that *violador* who come to hurt my baby. Who try to hurt all my babies!" She spat on the floor, something I never thought I'd see this controlled, polite woman do.

This sparked a memory, and I asked, "Mamo, you said something in Spanish to the last man standing, which made him very angry. What did you say?"

She hesitated for a moment, and then surrendered to the twinkle in her eye. "I'm not sure what made him so mad. All I asked was: 'Are you going to shoot that gun or suck its dick, faggot?'"

The sibling's eyes goggled simultaneously, and then they all but fell off their chairs laughing. I howled until tears came to my eyes. All the while Mrs. Morales sat as prim and proper as a DAR member.

When I could finally take a breath, I noted, "And then you drove the point home." She looked at me soberly for a moment, and I thought I'd gone too far. Then, a crack in her veneer, which widened into a grin and shined warmly upon us.

Unnoticed by everyone, DB had remained silent thus far. He sure got everyone's attention, though, when he said,

"That was the man who killed Papa."

Mamo turned to him. "What are you talking about?"

"You weren't there that day. You never saw the bandits. I saw only one of them clearly, but today I saw him again."

"You were a little boy, how can you remember this?"

"I don't know, Mama. I still see it in my mind, the day that Papa was shot. I had to hear this man's voice, and allow for the passage of time, before I could be sure. But I tell you now, from the depth of my soul, you have avenged Papa's murder and vanquished his killer!"

Mamo stared at him for a long time, but it took DB's next surprise to fully convince her of what he'd said.

"I'm hungry. When can we eat?"

"What?"

"I'm starving, Mama."

She began to cry: I don't think Mamo had ever expected to hear those words from her youngest son again. She cried while she fixed him a plateful of food.

Hell, I nearly cried when DB dug in with a vengeance. It did my heart good to see my friend enjoy food. Mamo whispered in my ear, "This is your doing, Slats."

I watched DB from the corner of my eye. I wasn't completely sure that he was right about Boss, but DB was one of the smartest people I'd ever met, so I didn't entirely discount his judgment either. He was absolutely convinced though, and with this knowledge, his PTSD had evaporated, taking the bulimia with it. DB had overcome his phthisis.

As the food was passed around, Oso—serving as straight man to my stand-up comedian—said, "What happened to the guy that left with you, Slats?"

I hesitated, before admitting, "I, uh…defenestrated him."

A rapid exchange of Spanish followed, before DB said, "Even I cannot translate that word."

"'Defenestrate' is Latin; it means, *to throw from a window*."

There was a long pause as this information was processed, before another burst of laughter swept through the room.

Carlos asked, "Are you tellin' us that you threw him out of the airplane?"

"First I calmed him down."

"How did you do that?" It was Tomas's turn to question.

"We flew for a while down low, where it's hot and the air is rough. I rocked him in the plane like a mother rocks her child…except a little harder. *Much* harder, in fact. He grew very sick. I never saw anybody throw up so much. Even you would have been envious of the way he puked, DB."

"Not any more," DB answered around a mouthful of food. His mama immediately heaped more rice and beans onto his plate.

"Then I took him up high, to get him cooler and more comfortable, and I…" Here I used my left hand as an airplane and tipped it over, then employed my right to mimic a long downward arc. "They *all* slumber on the seabed tonight." Again, everyone swirled in gusts of laughter.

"I guess we bury the hatchet with that bunch, eh?" Carlos noted.

"Mamo buried the hatchet…right in Boss's head," I retorted.

Julieta had been nearly silent after her ordeal, and I

recognized someone who was processing her first brush with mortality. I felt much better when she chirped, "You all joke, but look what happened to my hair!"

There was more merriment tonight than ever before, during my time with the Morales family. To the uninitiated, it might seem an inappropriate time for such high spirits. But I'd seen this behavior before many times, in Vietnam. We'd done what had to be done—we'd helped one another, and against all odds everyone had survived. So we proceeded to have a raucous party. There wasn't a drop of liquor to be found, but there was a plethora of good weed, as if our spirits weren't high enough already. We partied half the night under the benevolent gaze of Mamo.

It wasn't until late that Mamo drew me aside. "My bible says somewhere: *I was in prison, and you came to me.* I have you to thank for my children, Slats. I will never forget." I bussed the cheek of this peaceful mother who'd been driven, for reasons beyond her ken, to master pistolry of all things.

Seems like I'd set free my own POWs.

Thirty-four

I got Oso back to Florida and made sure he was examined by a good physician. To me that meant one man, Dr. Logan, and he wasn't pleased when he uncovered a gunshot wound on his patient's leg. My explanation that it happened outside the country didn't exactly calm him, either. But his cursory look quickly turned into professional assessment.

"Who dressed this?"

"That'd be me, Doc."

"Well, you did a pretty good job of it," he grudgingly admitted.

"You can't spend time in Vietnam without learning first aid."

He wiped the wound down with disinfectant and put a clean bandage on it. "This must be painful; here's a prescription for something to dull it. Stay off the leg for a while. I don't know where this happened, but my best advice is to stay away from there in the future."

"Thank you for helping me, señor."

But Oso couldn't stay off the leg, at least not yet, because there was still the little matter of five hundred pounds of sinsemilla in my hangar. He popped more codeine to help him through the next couple of hours, and we beat feet back to the ranch, with me at the wheel since Oso had a bum clutch leg. My sphincter unclenched only when I saw the place was cop free.

I got the Bronco into the hangar, and we quickly transferred the weed. Oso might be in pain, but he was highly motivated to get this load moved to a safe location. I'd driven the Bronco back out, when I spotted a dust cloud that could only mean an approaching vehicle.

"I take it from here, Slats."

"It's too late to leave by road without being seen."

"Is there another way out of here?"

"Not without driving over barbed wire. Y'know, maybe it's best to just leave casually, headed away from town. If you're chased, then go off-road."

Oso gave me a thumb's up, climbed in, and mashed down on the clutch. "God damn!" he yelled. "I should have bought an automatic!" The Bronco bucked uncertainly away, Oso cursing his poorly-functioning leg lustily, as I hurriedly made sure no incriminating evidence had been left in sight.

The vehicle came into view, and my sphincter immediately clenched again. It was the chief's car, and I prayed he wouldn't chase after Oso. To my relief, the chief pulled up in front of the hangar and got out. I noticed he now carried a .45 automatic, but if he suspected I'd performed the *bris* on his pistol, he never mentioned it.

"Wasn't that your beaner buddy's car I saw leavin'?"

"My door is always open. To my friends, that is."

"Now, that ain't very nice. Whatever happened to good ol' Southern hospitality?"

"I'm a little short on that, right now…unless you've come to pay respects to Jelly and her husband?"

"Naw, that ain't it. But now that you mention it, how'd you end up with the jig's ranch, anyway?" He showed his tobacco-stained teeth in a lascivious grin. "You weren't tappin' that dark meat, was you boy?"

"Either curb that tongue here on my land, or climb back into that prowl-car and drive off it."

"That ain't very neighborly considering that I come all the way out here just to give you some news about that other spook friend of yours."

"Who might that be?"

"That fella in the BVD, or whatever. The drug agent."

He was talking about R&R, and I instantly went on alert. R&R had never responded to my attempts at contact when Jelly took ill, nor had he attended her funeral. I just figured he'd been working hard.

"What about Agent Rehnquist?"

"He's dead."

I managed to keep my face a mask, though behind it I reeled. Something told me I could believe him—bitter experience had demonstrated that sons of bitches like the chief were always eager to deliver terrible news.

"You got anything else you want to say?" I inquired, surprised at the steadiness of my voice.

"You can't even work up some grief over your buddy? I thought that you Jewboys was sensitive to nigger doings."

"Time to go," I said quietly.

"I'd like permission to look around, first."

"Go right ahead. *After* I see your search warrant. No warrant, no search."

"I reckon you know what's best."

"What I like best is the sound you make when you shut the fuck up."

He didn't look pleased at hearing my words, and he didn't get any happier when I added, "You ever come onto my land again without a warrant, I'll pin you to the shithouse wall with a pitchfork." I paused a moment, then added, "Bet you'd make a nice sound then, too."

The chief, red-faced and fuming, got into his car and drove off. I knew that what really vexed him, though, was his failure to get a rise out of me about R&R.

What vexed me, however, was how perilously close to discovering our operation this *mo*-ron had stumbled. I filed a seed of an idea away for later consideration, as I had much more pressing matters to look into.

The Vero Beach Library had records on microfiche from the major newspapers. I was there within the hour, with the last four months of the Gainesville Sun stacked beside the reader. It didn't take long to find what I was searching for.

Federal Agent Killed in Raid

The Drug Enforcement Agency today released the identity of the agent killed in yesterday's deadly raid. Agent Malcolm Rehnquist, working undercover while helping to bust a local gang involved in drug sales, died on the scene from multiple gunshot wounds. Witnesses say that a drug deal turned sour, and Rehnquist found himself surrounded by angry gang members. Despite his poor position, Rehnquist pulled his service weapon and attempted to arrest the subject of the investigation. He died in a hail of gunfire. According to his unit commander, "Rehnquist's actions reflect well upon his dedication to duty and his bravery, and are in the best traditions of the DEA."

I dug for more information, and then ran what I learned past my inner translator to decipher the government-speak. The terseness, the same phraseology and non-facts repeated by different spokesmen, led me to believe a cover-up was in progress. Putting this together with R&R's desperate unhappiness, I came to the conclusion that he knew exactly what he was doing.

He found himself a situation which allowed him to end things quickly, decisively, and ... I don't know, *acceptably*. He'd pulled a pistol in the full knowledge that it would be his last action in a life that had come unraveled.

I mourned my friend. And I wondered how much of what tortured him might also be found in me. If I was right that R&R had committed suicide, might I also be at risk? He was a strong man, and he'd succumbed to the pressure.

But there were also differences between us. He'd been in-country longer than me, and he'd had much worse experiences. How does a man deal with accidentally killing his own people? I believe R&R had used suicide by criminal to come to terms with his guilt.

I'd taken another tack, immersing myself in the things I loved. Perhaps if R&R had continued to fly, he might have exorcised some of his demons. Maybe simply continuing to play the guitar would have eventually brought him back to himself.

I would never know.

Several days after our near-fiasco, I asked Oso to accompany me to Stick Marsh. The seed had taken root in my mind, and I wanted to demonstrate my latest idea to bend the smuggling odds in our favor. So we went out to a typical spot for an airdrop.

"Let's say this is the next delivery flight, and you've just gathered the last sack. As I'm leaving the area, I spot a vehicle heading straight for your location and report it over the radio. What do you do?"

Oso thought for a moment, and then said, "I drive off in another direction, run away."

"What if several cars are headed your way?"

"That is worse. But I know this place like the hollow of my girlfriend's thigh, so I head for the swampy area and try to get them stuck while following me."

"I have a better idea. You stay right here, and turn your back for a minute."

I started the Bronco and drove off the trail, parking up against a palmetto bush that was taller than the car's roof. I tugged the canvas bag I'd brought out of the car, dumped the contents on the ground, and unfolded the camouflage net to its full length. Then I unrolled it right over the car and adjacent bush. It would have been much easier to do this with assistance, but I'd precisely rolled and folded the net so as to permit one man to do it alone. While the camouflage net itself did a pretty good job of concealment,

I used the machete from the bag to chop off a few palmetto branches and enhance the effect. Then I dropped to the ground and rolled under the net.

"Okay, look around."

Oso turned around, but the grin didn't stay on his face for long. He looked this way and that, knowing that I must be very close but failing to locate me. Finally, his gaze settled on the right spot and he discerned the underlying shape. The grin returning, he said, "That a good trick, ese!"

"Back in Vietnam, these camouflage nets helped us keep a low profile. Tell me: even if you were alert and on the prowl, could you have cruised right past me?"

"Sí, easy."

"This trick could come in handy someday. Suppose we practice it a few times?"

"*This* is why you are so good at the job, hombre. You're full of tricks, like a boxer, you keep movin', and then, counterpunch out of nowhere. You are the Roberto Durán of smuggling."

I showed him how to roll the net carefully and stow it in the bag. Then we drove around for an hour, letting Oso set the clumsy net up alone and put the palmetto branches in place. As always, he was a quick study.

He promised to make the camo net a part of his checklist, from now on.

Thirty-five

By the time Gerald Ford tripped into the Oval Office, I'd made the ranch-cum-airport my ideal home. Mabel made it clear from the get-go that my aerial operations didn't bother her in the least. In fact, she'd accompanied me on flights a number of times. Mabel—a stolid woman if ever one existed—wasn't cowed at all by flying. She seemed to regard the Cessna as a particularly fast pickup truck, unusual but useful.

My life had fallen into a routine: a bit of fish spotting, some banner towing during tourist season, occasional cargo runs to bring music to the Bahamians, and my favorite legit airtime of all—whale patrol. The common denominator was flying—I spent a lot of time in the air. The sky had come to feel more like home than home itself.

And let's not forget my main aeronautical task; weed runs out of Chico Cay. The loads had grown ever larger, and much more lucrative. In fact, I'd had to start overloading my aircraft in order to accommodate them. No problem, as a 180 will carry an overload, but you had better pay close attention to balance if you do.

This meant airdrops took longer, and that the trail of sacks could string out for half a mile after DB ejected them. I'd started circling back to make two runs, to shorten the distance Oso had to chase after bales. Both our exposure times were thus increased.

The bellow of my engine rang out frequently, like a lion's roar, proclaiming this land as my own. And to declare my regard for the friend who'd so thoughtfully provided this sanctuary, which I now called Jelly Roll Field.

I'd never really enjoyed night flying. As an old-time contact pilot, I only trusted flight in visual conditions. So I undertook the next modification in my smuggling technique with a degree of trepidation. But, as with many things one studiously avoids, night flying ended up providing an entirely new perspective on my favorite activity.

DB was even less happy than me about our new flight schedule. "This is very inconvenient, Slats. It will cut into the ten hours of sleep I need every night," he complained.

"I thought Oso was the hibernator in your family."

"Ten hours is just a nap, for him," DB sulked.

"Look, you can sleep the whole way across the Atlantic—I'll wake you up to kick the smoke. Even if you stay up until we arrive at Jelly Roll International Airport, you'll only be awake for ten minutes."

"I'm not sure I like the idea of flying at night. What happens if the engine quits? How will you land the airplane then?"

"Oh, don't worry about that. The Air Force taught us all about night flying, DB. If the engine quits, you immediately go to best glide speed and descend from altitude. When you get close to the ground, you turn on the landing light. If you don't like what you see, you turn it off."

DB rolled his eyes. "If flying doesn't work out for you, then maybe you can write jokes for Rodney Dangerfield."

I laughed at DB's wry sense of humor. "'Hey, I don't get no respect.' Okay, here's the straight skinny. We only fly on clear nights with at least a half-moon; visibility should be good. We raid the chicken coop while everybody's asleep. Our exposure—and Oso's—will be minimized."

"You sure this will work?"

"If it doesn't, we won't repeat the experiment."

It was put up or shut up time. DB and I sat in the idling Cessna at the end of the Morales strip, with a well-warmed engine and a load of fine smoke. The moon was full, with a scattered layer of cumulus clouds at an estimated ten thousand feet. I looked over at DB, who nodded.

I shoved everything up into the kitchen, and the big Continental engine let out its characteristic howl. We bounced down the strip and into the air, throttled back, and set up a cruise climb to altitude.

We flew completely blacked out, no lights outside or in, so my night vision was in full swing. Not that I needed it much. Visibility was fantastic—there was plenty of light by which to fly. I could steer by familiar stars, and I could clearly see the ocean surface, which looked more like a calm lake tonight. There wasn't a breath of wind or a hint of rising thermal: it felt more like underwater swimming than flying. I'd never experienced a more ethereal beauty. Time seemed to stand still.

When we leveled off at altitude, I trimmed the airplane carefully so as to require no pressure on the controls whatsoever. I let go of the yoke and demonstrated this to DB—the plane continued on straight and level, as though on autopilot. When I leaned a little to the left, the aircraft banked harmoniously in that direction. I corrected our course by leaning back to the right.

It felt as though we were suspended, floating, with the world shifting around us. When the moon passed behind a cloud, moving rays shot out in all directions; moonlight beaming through the wispy edges diffracted into delicate pastel rainbows. It looked like an immense, animated Rising Sun flag.

"This is unlike anything I have ever seen, Slats."

"Makes me wonder why I never liked night flying."

"My mother has always been disappointed by my lack of faith in God. But seeing this, I find the concept much easier to accept."

I could only nod, then fall silent. And wish that R&R was here, plowing a moonlit wake through the Atlantic skies with me, carrying a load of Bahamian weed that would have made him grin from ear to ear.

I'd always admired Charles Lindbergh's audacity, winging his way across the Atlantic in a single-engine plane. Our aircraft, though separated by almost fifty years, were really very similar: high wing, strut-braced monoplanes of about two hundred-thirty horsepower. Lindbergh had written in *The Spirit of St. Louis* about his feelings of disconnection from all things earthbound—I understood him now. If DB hadn't been there to ground me, I might never have found my way back to the earthly plane of existence.

On a more practical level, I used the ADF to check my position. I was right where I expected, so I turned everything back off to enjoy the solitude. Always, when I needed light, I used the red-tinted cabin fixture—it preserved my night vision, and was also less visible from outside.

The crossing seemed to take no time at all. I roused myself from my reverie and reported our imminent arrival over the radio. Homing in on Stick Marsh, I saw the wink of Oso's flashlight, and I paused before giving DB the go-ahead.

"Barf 'em, buddy!"

DB started tossing bales out as fast as he could. Midway through, he paused and yelled, "Go around!"

Using Oso's light as a navigational fix, I circled back to our starting point and DB finished kicking the five hundred-fifty pound load.

"Towel two two," I reported to Oso.

While DB buttoned up the cargo door, I turned us toward the ranch. We ended the flight with a smooth, unruffled touchdown. We'd never even broken a sweat in the cool night.

"You did a good job of 'puking.'"

"Not bad, for only practicing three times a year," DB replied.

"Night flying works out well, doesn't it?"

"I have to admit, it was a beautiful and easy trip. You are the Mozart of aviators."

———————

But Mozart turned into Salieri just before dawn, when Oso

awakened me to report the loss of a sack.

"I looked for a while in the dark, then figured I should get the big load out, before worrying about the last sack."

"You want me to help you find it?"

"If you do the driving, I'll be okay. My leg hurts pretty bad." Oso tossed down another codeine tablet, as if to emphasize the point.

"Let me get a few things together, and I'm with you."

We found ourselves rolling into Stick Marsh just as the sun broke the horizon. We were in stealth mode, sneaking in the back way down a little used trail.

For perhaps the thousandth time, I mused on Oso's suitability for this job. He was a natural born tactician, thinking like a soldier in the field, and he could quickly adapt to changing situations. He had real wisdom, too. His choice of a Bronco for our ground vehicle was a good case in point. It was big enough to carry any load the Morales farm could produce, but it was old and faded enough to be anonymous on the roads. It was the off-road capability that came in so handy, though. And it had never been more necessary than now.

"You know where we're going, right?"

"I'm taking you right to the place where the other sacks dropped. But I don't know where you guys pitched the last one."

"I'm hoping that you just miscounted, and that you already have all twenty-two of 'em in storage."

"You remind me of something my grandfather said long time ago, to a crooked tax collector in Cuba. He told that guy that he couldn't count to twenty-one unless he was naked." Oso grinned gold, and I laughed.

We might have been joking around, but we were also on full alert as we approached the drop zone. "That's the tree I stood under last night. Both your runs looked good, straight down the road. I don't know how the weed was lost."

"Hell, it probably just bounced under a palmetto. We'll find it fast and get the hell out of here. And maybe rethink the wisdom of flying these loads in at night."

I parked us in the faint indentations that Oso's tires had left in the grass, only hours before. We started walking at the southernmost point, working our way up the length of the drop zone. We weren't far past the Bronco when Oso spotted it.

"There, hombre!" Sure enough, the sack had come to rest in the weeds. I picked it up and we started toward the Bronco, when Oso grabbed my arm and said, "You hear that?" We halted, and now I heard the sound of an approaching engine.

"Time to go," I hissed, and Oso responded with a burst of speed equal to mine, though accompanied by considerably worse language. I threw the weed in back of the Bronco, and then paused briefly to listen.

None-too-gently, Oso urged me along. "Hurry up, Slats! We gotta get the fuck outta here!"

I held up my finger to silence him a moment. "Sumbitch is comin' down the same path we used," I said, before scrambling behind the wheel.

Oso thought a moment. "There ain't many trails out in this section. We could go into the swamp, but it's been raining enough that even the Bronco might get stuck."

"Tell me you have the camouflage net, buddy."

Oso's face lit up. "Right behind your seat, hombre!"

I started the car, and said, "Then let's go to ground." I headed off the path at a ninety-degree angle for sixty feet or so, and then backed into a big clump of palmetto. I dragged the net out and unfolded it, and with Oso's help unrolled it over the Bronco and some of the undergrowth.

"Roll down the windows; they might reflect right through the net. And retract the antenna; that chrome will gleam in the sunlight. I'll get some palmetto branches and cover the windshield." He didn't need encouragement—he could hear the engine as clearly as me. I distributed a few branches quickly then lay down and rolled under the net just as the car came into view.

I heard it roll right past the place we'd cut off the path and continue down the trail. When I judged that it was out of sight, I rolled out and wove more palmetto branches into the net. We were pretty well covered, so I rolled back under.

Oso whispered, "It's that goddam cop! How did a pendejo like him figure this out?"

"I don't know. Maybe somebody was crawdad fishin' last night and spotted the plane."

"What are we gonna do?"

"Hunker down right here and wait him out. And while he's out of sight, I'm going to give you a graduate level education in the art of camouflage."

"Okay, hombre. And while you show me, take *la Inglés* there to school, too."

I told Oso that the human eye is naturally drawn to straight lines, which are rare in nature, and that we use palmetto branches to break them up. When the cruising police car wasn't nearby, I'd roll out and touch up a problem area with another branch or two. It wasn't long before we were superbly concealed—I'd have felt okay even if the Viet Cong were looking for us, instead of the doltish chief.

I stopped myself there. The chief might be a dolt, but he obviously had a modicum of instinct, and it was slowly but surely leading him ever closer to our trail. I may have underrated him, not a wise thing to do with an enemy.

"Should we put more branches on?" Oso asked, interrupting my reverie.

"No, we're in good shape. There's an old saying in the military: *Perfect is the enemy of good enough*. Let's just stay submerged like a submarine, until he gets tired and goes home."

"Okay, ese. I got codeine to stop the pain. We sure got enough weed to keep us happy. And there's this," he leaned into an open window and produced a bottle of sangria. Pulling the cork, he took a sip and passed it over. "I've even got some crackers in here, somewhere."

"I'll be happy if the cracker stays out there." But getting into the spirit of things, I added, "There's a couple of orange trees nearby, probably the remains of an old orchard. I'll get us some fruit, pretty soon. Hell, all that's missin' is music."

Oso sighed. "That would be nice. But we can't have everything in life."

So, we sipped sweet wine and took our leisure, smoking occasional hits when the chief was searching elsewhere. His appearances became more sporadic as he widened the search pattern, but his tenacity impressed me—I'd definitely underestimated the man.

It was late morning when he stopped the cruiser within sight. Oso had nodded off. I watched from concealment as the chief examined faint tire tracks then inspected both sides of the trail. Finally, he jumped up and down in sheer comic frustration.

"Guddamn cocksucker sumbitch!" he screamed. Yanking his .45 auto, he fired all seven rounds off in rage, one bullet spanging off a tree trunk and keyholing through nearby vegetation. Then he climbed back into the cruiser and, furiously spinning his wheels, tore off down the path. Oso continued to snore softly.

I nudged him gently, and then not so gently. Finally, Oso's eyes blinked open, and he stretched like a well-fed cat. "Guess I took a little nap."

"You slept right through the chief emptying his pistol in every friggin' direction!"

He shrugged. "You know me, ese; I need my beauty sleep."

"Sorry I disturbed you. You want to return to the land of Nod?"

Oso's brow furrowed in concentration, before he answered, "No, let's put this weed to bed first, my friend."

And so we did.

Thirty-six

Darla now stayed with me much of the time at Jelly Roll Field, and I was happy to have her around. She had undertaken a stealth renovation of the house, keeping it simple and tasteful. The tasteful part bloomed from within—the simple part was in deference to me.

I switched on the radio to hear the latest from Paul Harvey about something I'd thought might never happen, the end of the war. Apparently, the handwriting was on the wall: Vietnamization had failed, and the US was frantically beginning its final pullout before communist forces took Saigon. Very soon South Vietnam would cease to exist.

To his credit, Gerald Ford had decided to clean up of one of the war's injustices, namely the orphans and abandoned children of mixed race who were the innocent result of our involvement. Ford initiated Operation Babylift, gathering several hundred of these kids together to inaugurate it with a flight to the US on a huge C-5A Galaxy.

Stunned, I listened as Paul Harvey described the crash which ended that first flight, only minutes after takeoff. A serious malfunction had resulted in the failure of the hydraulically-assisted control system. The pilots had done a marvelous job of wrestling this aluminum overcast of an airplane about and heading it back toward Tan Son Nhut. But as they slowed for landing they'd been unable to keep the plane under control, and it plowed into a rice paddy. Seventy-eight children perished in the crash, and many more were badly injured. The Air Force had no plane to spare for at least ten days to get the survivors to the States.

Which was where American businessman Robert Macauley stepped in. He'd been so moved by this news that he immediately chartered a 747, scraped together a team of volunteer doctors and nurses, and headed for Vietnam.

"How did Mr. Macauley pay for this?" asked Paul Harvey. "He mortgaged his home, the roof over his own family's head. And now you've heard the rest of the story!" Harvey concluded with his traditional signoff: "This is Paul Harvey; good-day."

Darla dabbed her nose with a tissue. "Those poor babies!"

"I hate to say it, but that's pretty much what happened every time we tried to do anything good in Vietnam."

"Maybe... But that businessman, Macauley...he sure did some good."

"You've got to respect the man's humanity."

Most of a year had passed, though, before I read the real story, at least for one little girl. She'd been badly burned in the crash, and had received extensive medical care from the Air Force. One leg had been too shattered to save—the doctors had had to amputate it. Finally, she had healed sufficiently to be released from the hospital at Homestead Air Force Base, south of Miami. Her first action upon taking temporary residence at a nearby orphanage was to run away. She'd been missing for two days, and authorities were worried, because even that far south, it was uncommonly cold.

When I sought her out, Darla was putting flowers on Jelly's grave. She'd paused briefly to clean up after Tailskid, who regarded the entire world as his toilet.

"Kings in old England used to appoint a trusted person to an unusual but influential position, sort of a keeper of the royal privy. But for the life of me, I can't imagine how I ended up as *his* Groom of the Stool." She indicated the offending creature with her chin.

I laughed, "Well, you'll never get laid off that job. It's what you might call a full time position."

"What's bothering you, Slats?" Even as I wondered how Darla knew that I was uneasy, she added, "Your face is an open book."

"I can't get that lost kid out of my mind," I admitted.

"It's heartbreaking. But what can *you* do about it?"

"I can do what I was trained to do, search from the air. Maybe I can help to find her before she dies alone in the cold and wet."

"Sounds like your mind is already made up."

I found myself winging south through intermittent drizzle. My thermometer indicated forty-two degrees, and I was using the cabin heater to fight off the cold. The thought of a little girl spending a third night out in this weather made me nudge the throttle up. *I need visibility*, I thought. *It's like I'm on a mission.* I shook my head, as if to clear cobwebs.

Darla had refused to stay behind. I shot a look out of the corner of my eye, and caught her staring at me, smiling.

"What did I do now?"

"I love you, Slats Kisov."

It was so startling a non sequitur that I just swallowed, and then turned my gaze back to the horizon, squinting like Sky King. That got a good laugh out of Darla.

It took just over an hour to reach Homestead Airport, a nice little place with gliders, skydiving, and a grass runway that beckoned to me. It also held several news vans in the parking lot, and a Dade County Sheriff Department helicopter squatting by the fuel pumps. I secured my aircraft and, avoiding the media like they were contagion-bearers, strolled over to talk with the pilot of the copper chopper.

He told me he'd completed several search flights. Late yesterday, he'd covered a swath of the Everglades nearest the orphanage. The current thinking was that the child must be hiding somewhere in Homestead, and he was concentrating his efforts today over the city. He filled me in on what little he knew, including the location of the orphanage from which the girl had fled. Darla wandered over to the search coordinator to see if she could lend a hand, while I hoofed it to the nearby orphanage.

When I explained who I was and why I was there, the Mother Superior was more than willing to help. She called Sister Margaret in to show me the room that the girl had occupied, if only for an hour.

"You must have a good heart, to come so far on such a task. But why do you want to see her room?" she asked.

"I need to learn something... *anything* about her, Sister."

"We don't know much about Bian. We're not even sure of her exact age, though she looks to be four or so. The Air Force nurse who dropped her off says she hardly talks, but she seems to understand English well enough."

"What's her physical condition?"

"She was burned over thirty percent of her body, and has been fighting recurring infections. It's from the crash landing in the rice paddy—the Vietnamese use excrement as fertilizer, I'm told."

"Yes ma'am, I know. I spent most of a year in Vietnam with the Air Force."

"Bian's right leg was mangled in the crash, and had to be amputated below the knee. She's just received her first prosthesis; I've been around enough of these cases to know her stump must be very painful."

"So I know what to look for from the air, what was she wearing?"

"She came to us with very little in this world. She was wearing a gray dress, medium length to cover her scars. She does have a decent coat, though. It's red, bright red, almost like a fire truck."

"That's a plus, Sister. Red is highly visible from the air, especially at this time of the year."

"She'll be cold, poor child, so I suspect that she'll be wearing it buttoned up to the chin."

"Sister, could you to give me a moment alone? I want to see if I can … get into her head a little." Sister Margaret stepped out of the room.

I sat on Bian's bed, staring out the only window in the tiny room. She'd been looking west, toward the Everglades. The fleeting patches of sun a couple days ago probably would have seemed familiar to her, perhaps like her memories of Vietnam. Here, she'd known nothing but strangers, uniforms, and pain. But perhaps a familiar sight, and a memory of home, drew her toward the unknown.

I left her room and descended the stairwell, just as she must have done. I turned left on the landing toward the exit and found myself looking at the eastern edge of the Everglades.

I dropped to my knees to get a child's perspective, and could clearly see a gap in the vegetation, the start of a trail. I stood and followed it, then closed my eyes. Burrowing as deeply into the mind of a young girl as I could, I took a fresh look down the trail. To a hurting and exiled orphan, this might have looked like a path to freedom. I took my bearings, like the pilot I was, then marched back to the orphanage.

I reported my conclusions to the distraught nun. She nodded and said, "It's my fault that she's been lost; I should have stayed with her."

"Don't blame yourself. I think she's been waiting for the opportunity to run for a long time."

"Are you a religious man, Mr. Kisov?"

"I guess I'd consider myself a spiritual man."

"I will pray for Jesus to lead you straight to Bian."

"Thank you, ma'am; I'll need all the help I can get. Besides, I reckon we Jews should stick together." I winked at her.

Sister Margaret laid her hand on my arm. "Bian means *Hidden* in Vietnamese, Mr. Kisov. Please, lead her out of hiding."

I got myself back to the airport and into the air as fast as possible. I then headed toward the orphanage at low altitude and circled the building several times. I took a deep breath, throttled back, and pulled on two notches of flap—I wanted to go slowly enough to get a real good look at the terrain.

I followed the same path I'd walked only a short time before. Even from four hundred feet, I could see the Everglades stretching all the way to the horizon in front of me. I flew through patches of drizzle, under a fifteen hundred-foot ceiling, and the first living thing I spotted was a twelve-foot alligator. How could a four-year-old possibly survive three days in this inhospitable place?

The path was fairly distinct at first, and I trusted my instincts to track it well into the swamp until it forked. I followed the northernmost leg first, as it was better defined. Taking a circuitous route, it doubled back on itself to avoid the worst of the wetland. The areas to either side were overgrown, so I felt certain the girl had pressed on down the path, if she'd come this way. More than a mile in, the path grew indistinct and then faded away altogether, though the ground did seem more firm here. I began a standard expanding-square search pattern.

Using the end of the trail as a starting point, I flew west for thirty seconds, then turned ninety degrees and flew north for thirty more. Turning east, I flew a leg for one minute, then south for another minute. I kept this square spiral pattern up for half an hour, ever expanding it, until I felt I'd gone further in every direction than Bian could possibly have walked. There wasn't a single sign of her.

So I headed back to the fork and followed the lesser of the trails, until it, too, disappeared. I set up another expanding square pattern, with a similar result—no kid, no spoor. Stumped, I climbed for altitude to get a more global view, which showed me nothing whatsoever. Almost two hours into the search and I was back to square one.

I flew back to the orphanage, and switched tactics. I chose a slower but more thorough pattern, the creeping line search. Starting at the Everglades' edge, I flew a north-to-south leg six minutes long, turned west for thirty seconds, then south-to-north for another six minutes. Thus I worked my way slowly westward, using the same basic pattern one employs to mow his yard, thinking Bian may have followed the sun.

I was burning daylight and getting nowhere, wondering if I'd gotten the child's mindset completely wrong. But I decided to stick to my guns in the belief that she'd instinctively gone to familiar ground. I could think of nothing to do but tack a couple small expanding-square searches onto the northern and southern terminuses of my "grass-mower" search pattern. Nada, and much of the day was behind me now.

I didn't understand how she could simply disappear like this. She could not possibly have traveled further than my search had taken me. I tried again to place myself in her mind, and then it came to me: Bian didn't *want* to be found. She hadn't gone far, because she was weak and in pain. She was hunkering down under cover, behind the best windbreak she could locate. And she had no intention of surrendering.

I flew back to my starting point, the orphanage, and then started anew down the main trail. At the fork I took the northern leg again, flying slowly up one side of the path then back down the other. When I saw nothing, I slowed a bit more and stubbornly repeated the search along both sides of the path. Again I saw zip, but I nonetheless began a wide circle of the area where the path gave way to vegetation. On the third circuit, I thought I saw a flash of red.

I altered my orbit, now circling over the new area of interest. There it was again, a brief glimpse of scarlet. I circled several more times until I was sure that something lay concealed under a bush, and I marked the location indelibly in my mind.

This was no naturally-occurring red, not during this drab time of year—it had to be Bian. I must have passed right over her earlier in my search, but she'd insistently remained concealed. So now, as I started searching for the nearest patch of ground suitable for landing, I radioed the airport.

"Homestead Unicom, Cessna Three Six Lima. I may have spotted the girl. I'm going to land and try to pick her up. Suspected location is approximately four miles north-northwest of the airport. She is near the end of the trail leading from the orphanage into the Everglades. Start search parties toward that area."

The best place I could find anywhere close to the girl looked none too good. I was glad I'd used much of my fuel, as less weight meant a shorter ground run. I made several passes, judging the best place to touch down, hoping the ground wasn't so marshy I'd nose over onto my back. I thought there was enough room to land; hell, maybe even enough to take off again!

I dragged the 180 in low and slow, using full flaps and some power. When the touchdown point I'd chosen came into view, I crossed the controls and sideslipped like a madman. Just above the ground I used a burst of throttle to help straighten out, and then plopped her right in. Keeping the yoke full back, I dumped the flaps and put more weight on the wheels, to decelerate faster. She squished and skidded to an almost-stop, and I pivoted her neatly around with another burst of throttle then killed the engine. I'd have to take off in the opposite direction. There was a tall tree on this end that clearly said *no way.*

Donning my backpack, I set off toward the place I'd marked in my mind. It was chilly, and I drew my denim jacket more tightly around me. It didn't take long for my boots to become soaked, adding to my discomfort. *She's been out here for more than two days,* I thought. And then, unbidden; *Maybe she didn't show herself because she couldn't.* I pushed that notion far back in my mind, and moved faster to keep warm.

It took about half an hour to find the end of the trail I sought. Orienting myself, I walked south-southwest approximately sixty yards and there she was, curled up under a dwarf cypress. I thrashed through the vegetation toward her, making a lot of noise, but she didn't move a muscle. I knelt down, reaching out to touch her arm.

Her eyes blinked open, and a shudder passed through her little body. I smiled, hoping I wasn't merely the latest in a long line of strangers to barge unwelcome into her life. She just looked at me.

"My name is Slats. I've been looking everywhere for you, Bian." I helped her sit up, took off my jacket, and tucked it around her. "I'm so glad I found you. Many people are worried about you." She just kept up her wordless stare.

"Did you see that airplane fly over? That was me. I knew I'd never find you if I looked from the ground. Vietnamese people are very good at hiding—especially children." I poked her gently in the stomach. "But no one can hide from me when I'm in the air." While she made no response, she didn't seem frightened.

"You must be hungry and thirsty. Here," I said, pulling some supplies out of my pack, "drink some of this first." I unscrewed the top and handed over the canteen, and she took a long pull. By that time I had the wrapper off a banana-flavored Moon Pie, and I offered it to her.

She tore ravenously into it, wolfing down several quick bites. Then she did something that moved me to my roots. She offered me a bite. Not a word accompanied the offer, but it was the truest communication as far as I was concerned. I accepted her polite gesture, biting off a piece and saying, "Mmmmmmm, I *love* Moon Pie. Thank you, Bian." Her only response was to continue eating.

I removed my watch cap and pulled it over her head. "You must be freezing. I know I am. But my airplane has a heater—it's nice and warm. Would you like to see it?"

For the first time I saw fear in her eyes, and I cursed myself for being an idiot. Of course she was afraid! The only time she'd ever been in a plane, it had burst into flames and burned off her leg.

"You don't have to worry about this plane; it's not like the other one you were on. My plane is small and friendly, kind of a pet. It would never hurt anybody, especially a nice little girl like you." While she didn't look fully convinced, her fear abated somewhat.

"Why don't we just take a look at it? We can start the engine and get warm, at least. Okay?"

She nodded, and I was so pleased with her response that I reached down to give her a hug.

"I know your new leg must be hurting. How about I give you a piggyback ride to the plane?" That phrase seemed to stump her, so I mimed someone climbing onto my back and hanging on. She nodded again, and I slipped my backpack onto her. "You can be in charge of our food and water."

I helped her to stand, then turned around and squatted down. She trustingly moved close and put her arms around my neck, and I stood up. When I hooked her legs with my arms, she groaned in pain, and I quickly let go of her right leg.

"I didn't mean to hurt you. Does it feel better if we just let this leg hang down?" In my peripheral vision, I saw her nod.

We set out for the plane, and I gave her as steady and soft a ride as I could. Though I shivered in my thin flannel shirt, my heart was certainly warmed. With a glow in the thin clouds to the west serving as my compass, I quickly located the plane. I slowed, giving Bian a moment to look it over.

"I know she looks old and tired, but that's just on the outside. I think she looks just like a kitten, ready to jump up and play with a string. And that's what she is, too, a kitten that comes to life in the sky!"

Bian looked awestruck at the notion that a machine might also be an animal. Perhaps she'd known a cat somewhere in her short journey through life. If so, I'd struck upon a lucky reference that put her at ease. I put her carefully down next to the passenger door and, rummaging in the pack, found a piece of beef jerky to distract her.

While Bian gnawed on it, I did a quick preflight. She watched everything I did, as though she understood it all. When I'd finished and was standing beside her again, I reached up and petted the plane fondly.

"This airplane is my friend, Bian. She wants to help us get to a warm, safe place. And she can do it too, if we both trust her. Will you help me do that?"

Bian looked from me to the Cessna, and then reached up to stroke the fuselage. Again, she nodded her acquiescence.

I boosted her into the right seat and strapped her down. "This is the airplane's way of giving you a hug." I ran around and climbed inside, fastening my own belt. "Don't be scared, I'm going to start the engine so the heater will work."

I fired up the big Continental, letting it chug at low RPM in what I hoped was a friendly purr. It didn't take long to warm up enough to start blowing hot air. "Feels good, doesn't it? But the heater works even better in the air. You ready to try?"

I could talk about kittens and friendly airplanes till the cows came home, but Bian was still terrified. Her face reflected it, and so did her body language. But I'm damned if she didn't nod her head anyway. My impression was reinforced—this was a most unusual little girl, and I reached over to squeeze her hand.

Then I dismissed her from my mind. I had a difficult takeoff in front of me, and I needed to concentrate. The last thing I wanted to do was put Bian through another crash. I pulled on two notches of flap, set the trim, and ran my eye over the gauges a final time.

"Here we go!" I stood on the brakes and pushed the throttle smoothly up to full power. The aircraft trembled for a moment, and then I let off the brakes. We squished forward all too hesitantly, slowly gaining momentum. One wheel bounced through a watery hole, throwing up a huge splash and causing the plane to swerve. I stabbed the rudder sharply, realigning the nose with the narrow runway, and then glanced at the air speed indicator. We were passing fifty-four miles per hour, and the end of the strip was hurtling toward us. Though we were barely above stall speed, I yanked back hard on the yoke to haul us off the ground, and then leveled us out at an altitude of several feet.

We were able to stay in the air because of ground effect, a natural assist to low-flying airplanes. We accelerated in ground effect faster than we could on terra firma. I aimed her straight at the trees that filled the windscreen. They looked like a giant flyswatter, poised to strike us. I was glad that Bian could see only the instrument panel—she didn't need this particular view.

At the last possible moment, I hauled back on the yoke. Though we were below climb speed, we nonetheless ballooned upward, and the trees disappeared under the nose. I leveled off abruptly, just before she stalled, and found my ass all-but-dragging through the treetops. I let her accelerate again for a few seconds, and then eased her up just below the cloud deck.

Releasing the breath that I'd subconsciously held, I smiled at Bian. She didn't look convinced. But she did enjoy the strong blast of hot air I directed toward her from the vent. "The kitten likes you, Bian. Feel her warm, friendly breath?"

She relaxed enough to peer out the side window. "We're higher than the tallest tree. I can even see the place we're going to land. It's big and has no trees, so it'll be easy to land there. The kitten could do it by herself, but I'm going to help her anyway. We're a team, and now you're part of the team."

I radioed Unicom again, to tell them the child was safe and to start calling in the searchers.

Bian looked up at the clouds scudding by, not far above us. She looked down at the swamp through which she'd so laboriously trodden, the place that very soon would have killed her. Then she looked at me, a stranger in an incomprehensible land. Yet she didn't look at me like a stranger. Hope—and I think some trust—was written on her face.

Thirty-seven

Everyone was on hand: reporters, searchers, curiosity seekers and hangers-on. This was the last thing that Bian needed right now, and I briefly considered going elsewhere. I needed fuel though, so I had no choice but to land in their midst. I chose the grass strip again, thinking perhaps that I could dodge behind the hangar and offload Bian before she was inundated. But this airport was simply too small to offer any chance of cover, and I reluctantly taxied to the ramp. I hurriedly shut down the engine before one of the idiots rushing toward me got into a losing argument with my propeller.

I had only a moment to ready Bian for the confusion outside. "Don't be scared. Lots of people have been looking for you, and some of them are here. They're like me, though, very happy because you are safe." Her only reply was to look more frightened than before the takeoff.

Then I spotted Darla and Sister Margaret, pushing their way through the crowd. "I see the cavalry coming, Bian. You can trust these people—they're going to help you."

I cracked my window as the women came up to the

plane. "She's scared spitless. Go around to the other door and keep people back until I can get there."

Then I turned to Bian. "I'm going to walk around to your door, and then we'll get you out of here."

I slipped out, shoving one slow-mover out of my way, and clawed around to the other door. Darla gave me a quick kiss on the cheek. "You did fine, Lieutenant."

Sister Margaret was glued to the side window, smiling apologetically at Bian. I said, "Try to gain me a little space here, and I'll get her out."

Opening the door, I leaned in to whisper, "We're going to go in there." I pointed at a little shack, adorned with a faded sign that proclaimed *Learn to Fly*. "I'll be with you the entire time."

She nodded, and when I turned around she immediately grabbed me around the neck. I lifted her out, being careful to leave her leg hanging. I started to move forward, Bian all but choking me in a death grip, when a particularly insistent reporter and cameraman blocked the way.

"Can I have a moment of your time, sir? How did you find the girl? Is she all right?"

I wasn't sure which question to answer, so I equivocated. "I just flew around until I spotted her."

"Why isn't the little girl walking? Is she hurt?"

"She's missing a leg, and she's been lost in the woods for almost three days."

The reporter opened his mouth to yammer more nonsense, and I put a scowl on my face that would have warned off a wiser person. Then, suddenly, a priest I'd never seen before stepped between the reporter and me.

"I'm Father Bob. The Sisters of Mercy Orphanage is

part of my ministry. I'll answer several questions, but then I must insist that we get this child inside to be treated."

"How did she get away from the orphanage?"

Father Bob was more than equal to his assumed PR task. "The child was frightened, and she ran away. It's as simple as that," he responded.

Disgusted and impatient, I put down my head, butting both reporter and cameraman aside as I headed for the sanctuary of the shack.

The good father smoothed over my abrupt departure. "We'll get back to you as more details come to light. Until then, we thank you, gentlemen of the press."

As he came through the door, Father Bob was considerably less guarded. "*Gentlemen* of the press, my padded seat!"

I set Bian down on a chair. Sister Margaret came over to hug her. She turned to me with tears in her eyes. "I don't know what I would have done if you hadn't … Thank you for bringing her back."

Father Bob slapped me on the back. "That's as fine a job of shepherding as I've ever seen, son. You also pulled the church's bacon out of the fire. Tell me you're a good Catholic."

"I'm a bit lapsed, Father. By two thousand years." At his vacant expression, I explained, "I'm Jewish."

He laughed. "I know of another Jewish man who also has quite a reputation as a shepherd."

Sister Margaret reached under Bian's dress and began to unfasten the prosthetic harness. "Her residual limb is obviously very sore. It takes a long time for an amputation to toughen up, but it will. We'll just have to take it slowly." When she pulled the leg free, the stump sock was bloody, and she wrapped it in a wet towel to soften it before removal. Sister Margaret retrieved half a codeine tablet from her medical bag and ground it into a glass of water. "This will taste bad," she scrunched up her face, "but it will make the pain go away."

When the sister had finally removed the sock, Bian's stump looked more like hamburger meat than flesh. Darla recoiled, then got hold of herself and knelt down to talk with Bian as the sister continued administering first aid.

"My name is Darla. Slats and I are good friends. And now I'm your friend, too." She offered her hand, and Bian understood what that meant. She and Darla shook hands, gravely.

While the ladies big and small were thus occupied, I asked Father Bob, "What will become of her now?"

He shrugged. "We nurse her back to health, and then try to find her a good home with loving people to parent her."

I looked over at Bian, who was studying Darla with huge, expressive eyes. She had a wild mop of unruly curls, and a complexion that reminded me of my morning coffee, milky and sweet. Her face was somehow untouched by all she'd suffered.

"How difficult will it be for an injured child of mixed race to find a home?"

"Sadly, it won't be easy to find a family for her."

Unbidden, another question slipped from my mouth. "What about a single person?"

"That is *never* done."

"Why?"

"Our children may only be adopted by married couples. Personally, I don't see the reason for this, but that is the policy of the Church, and I'm afraid that there are no exceptions."

Sister Margaret had Bian's stump cleaned and dressed by this time. I asked, "What now, Father?"

"I suppose it's time to take her back to the orphanage."

Bian obviously understood. A single tear slid down her cheek, the first I'd seen in our short acquaintance. Darla continued to hold her, and Bian wrapped her arms tightly around Darla's body. Sister Margaret tried to take her, and Bian resisted, but she was too weak from her ordeal to prevail.

"We can't leave her like this, Slats. Can't we go back with her, at least long enough to get her cleaned up and put to bed?"

"Of course we can!" I said, and four smiles beamed my way.

A hot meal, a dry place out of the weather, and the milk of human kindness can make all the difference in the world. Sister Margaret had shooed me out of the bathroom, scolding, "We have women's business to attend to, sir!" But I stayed just outside the door, listening to Bian splash in the tub like any normal kid. The only difference was a lack of reply to the women's comments.

"Has the ban on males been lifted, or am I to be permanently barred?"

"You can come in now." Bian sat on the edge of the tub wrapped in a towel, while Darla rubbed furiously at her hair with another one.

As the bandage was being reapplied, I inquired, "Does everything look all right, Sister?"

"The residual limb has been set back in the healing

process. But I've given her an antibiotic injection. She's a strong child—she'll be fine."

"Then I'm happy."

"It's getting quite late, and the weather is pretty bad. We have room at the inn, so to speak, if you'd like to avail yourselves," the sister said.

Darla's face immediately rearranged itself into a plea. Bian's face simultaneously did the same thing.

"I don't know, Darla might have to work tomorrow…" I teased.

"Keep jokin' and I'll slap the funny right out of you!" Darla threatened.

I held up my hands in surrender. "I hope you're happy now, Sister. Jews have moved in—there goes your neighborhood."

I carried Bian upstairs, following Sister Margaret as she showed Darla and me to adjoining rooms connected by a bathroom. "It isn't fancy, but it's clean. And it's right next to Bian."

"Is it all right if Bee stays with us until she falls asleep?" Darla asked.

"She already has a nickname? It took me weeks to get a nickname when I joined my squadron."

"Bee's a fast mover, a necessary skill when you're forced to run with the bulls," Sister Margaret observed. "Of course she can stay with you. Though I can't imagine how she's managed to keep her eyes open this long."

Sister Margaret turned to stare out the window, at the rain-lashed palm trees and frigid puddles forlornly reflecting the street lamps. "I can provide medical care and food and clean sheets. But you've delivered her from… *that*.

You've given her a fresh chance at life. It's a kind of rebirth, and that's no small thing." Smiling almost like the Mona Lisa, she added, "You're a saint, Mr. Kisov."

"I know Catholics recognize lots of saints, but I bet I'm the first St. Menachem." The sister laughed, and then eased the door shut.

"I've always suspected you were a saint. A tainted saint perhaps, but a saint nonetheless."

"And I thought Shit Kicker was a good nickname."

Darla looked at me with mock disdain. "I'm changing my suggestion to Tain't a Saint."

"Let's compromise; call me Saint Shitkicker."

"Hush your mouth, Bee is listening to every word."

I looked down at this scarred, scabbed, and scrubbed little girl. "You won't tell on me, will you?"

She shook her head. We all lay down together on the bed, Darla and I watching as Bee's eyes blinked, grew heavy, and finally closed in sleep. Darla wasn't far behind, and I spread a blanket over the two of them, and then slipped contentedly beneath it.

———————

When I awakened the next morning, Bee hadn't moved a muscle. It would have required an Old Master to properly paint her. She was truly beautiful, her face a marvelous genetic blend, alive with intelligence—I could not take my eyes off her. Would others be able to discern her beauty, or would she languish in this place as Father Bob feared?

Then I regarded Darla. Even in her sleep-tussled state, she looked especially attractive this morning. There was a peaceful repose, a ... *satisfaction* about her.

She reached out in her sleep to touch Bian, and I thought it the most maternal gesture I'd ever seen. As Darla's eyes blinked open, I reached out to take her other hand.

She smiled at me, and then at Bee. "What a wonderful way to wake up."

"You mean in bed with an unmarried man, beside an innocent babe, in a building owned by the Catholic Church?"

Her smile widened. "Yes."

"What would Sister Margaret say?"

"That it's good for Bee to be around people who love each other so deeply."

I looked at Bee. "What will happen to her?"

"I don't know, Slats. I'm frightened for her."

"Maybe that's why I can't stop thinking about Jelly." I squeezed Darla's hand. "She was a prescient woman, you know. She once told me that I shouldn't keep you waiting too long."

"Have you been smoking weed this early in the morning?"

"I never drew a more sober breath. Will you marry me, Darla Pistle?"

She was flabbergasted. "I…we…you…"

"That's quite an impressive list of pronouns you're compiling."

"Are you sure about this?"

"I've never been so sure of anything in my life. I woke up this morning beside the family I was meant to have. Be my wife; let's adopt this child."

"The answer is a most emphatic *yes*."

"Then I've got things to do!" I enthused. "But I'm not ready to start, just yet." And I wriggled back into the bed, allowing Bian's warm breath to fan the coals of my happiness.

———————

I needed to talk to Father Bob before things progressed any further.

"I have an important question: how long does the adoption process take?"

"Normally, it can take months. But for a child *in extremis* like Bian, that could be considerably shortened if the church—which is basically me, in this case—is convinced that the parents are good people. But I must say again that there are no exceptions to the rule about children going only to married couples."

"That's one reason I asked Darla to marry me."

"Is that so? Congratulations to you and your soon-to-be wife! I have never seen folks take to one another in the extraordinary way you three have."

"Which is why my next question is so important: exactly how long after jumping the broom will we have to wait?"

"Virtually no time at all, provided you have a suitable home."

"We have two choices. I own a little house on a thirty acre parcel outside of Farth, and Darla has a place in town."

"So housing will be no problem. Exactly when do you plan to get married?"

"This afternoon, I hope."

He chuckled, but I kept my face straight. "Are you serious?"

"I suffer from gamophobia: one thing I never joke about is weddings."

"That's marvelous! The Lord is shining his benevolent smile on us all today! I even know of a rabbi who may be able to perform the service on short notice."

"That's a nice offer, but we have a man in mind already. *If* you're willing, that is."

It took a moment for this to sink in. Then the father took a boxer's stance, throwing a few jabs and punches. "I'd like to see someone try to stop me!"

———————

Sister Margaret was pinning up Darla's hair in simple, classic style. She'd also managed to locate a nice dress that suited Darla, and a white shirt for me, to offset my jeans and boots.

"It's about time you made an honest woman out of me," Darla said.

"Honest? You railroaded me into this."

"Then how come you're smiling?"

"You ever heard the old saying, 'If you were born to be shot, you'll never be hung?' Well, the hangman's rope will never caress my neck."

She shot me a patented Darla look from the corner of her eye, observing, "Maybe it's a good thing you tossed your pistol into the sea, too."

The sister paused in her hairstyling. "You shouldn't even be in here, Slats. Don't you know that it's bad luck for the groom to see the bride before the service?"

"What kind of luck does it bring when the couple's child sees the bride before the ceremony?"

Sister Margaret cleared her throat primly. "That is outside my particular area of expertise, Mr. Kisov."

"And I thought that all nuns did was hit boys' knuckles with rulers."

"I'm thinking of doing that right now."

"In that case, I'll just practice turning the other cheek. Which should be a very useful skill in marriage."

Darla interrupted our banter. "Oh, no! What about rings?" Apparently, I hadn't thought of everything.

But the sister came to the rescue. "Use this," she said, pulling off the ring she wore as a Bride of Christ.

"Oh, no, I couldn't possibly do that," Darla protested.

"You don't realize how much this day means to me, Darla. I'd consider it an honor if you'd accept my gift."

"Are you sure?" Trying it on, Darla said, "It fits like it was sized for me. This is a generous gift, one that I'll always treasure. Thank you, Sister."

The nun turned to me. "Are you one of those men who prefer not to wear a ring?"

"No, ma'am. Get the Mother Superior down here, so I can pry that ring off her finger!"

Sister Margaret turned to Darla. "You sure you want to marry this guy?"

I felt Meat's presence then, an unusual occurrence on the ground. I looked down at the stainless steel ring on my right pinkie. "Y'know, I could probably force this over the correct finger, but I might need a dab of fifty-weight oil."

"We better try it first, before the ceremony," the sister replied. Then, in a stage whisper to Darla, she said, "I don't want to give him an opening to back out."

It ended up fitting, but only after a struggle. Darla observed, "Wearing a ring that small is almost like being branded. Some stuff just shouldn't wash off."

———————

When I'd thought of weddings, which admittedly wasn't often, I'd never pictured one quite like this. For one thing, I hadn't known it would happen only eight hours earlier. Also, with the notable exception of the bride and groom, everyone was Catholic: a priest was conducting the service and the witnesses were all nuns. Not to mention that beside us, wide-eyed and taking in everything, stood my daughter.

And the strangest thing of all was that I wasn't the least bit nervous. This felt superb. I looked at the ring girl—now temporarily on crutches rather than her prosthetic leg— concentrating on her job as though her life depended on it.

Darla caught me mooning over Bee, read my mind, and then squeezed my hand. "What in the world would have happened to her if not for you, Slats?"

"If you ask me, I think she needs a mother more than a father. Together, we'll make a fine family."

Darla was close to tears. Luckily, I had prepared a distraction.

"You know the old rhyme, 'Something old, something new, something borrowed, something blue?' I figured Bee was new, and my jokes were old..." Darla nodded her head emphatically in agreement, and I chose to ignore her. "The sister's ring is borrowed—all I needed was something blue. So I went shopping." I spun around and hollered, "Hit it, Sister!"

The amplified scratch of a needle on vinyl echoed through the room. Then—for what I'd have wagered was the first time ever—blues music pealed forth from the speakers at the Sisters of Mercy Orphanage in Homestead, Florida.

"This is Earl Hooker's plugged-in version of 'Sweet Black Angel.'" I stooped to pick up Bee, then continued, "I chose the song because it reminds me of this beautiful little girl. We've got our own sweet black angel now, Darla."

If I'd really meant to stop Darla from crying, I missed the mark by a country mile. She burst into tears, and Sister Margaret joined right in.

Even the good Father gave a short snuffle. "You'd make a fine man of the cloth, Mr. Kisov."

"You must be well-regarded by the Lord to get away with that claim, sir. Anyone else, and He'd hurl lightning bolts!"

The Father held out his hands. "No bolts from the blue? Then I think we're ready to begin. Gather round, folks, it's time for this couple to 'jump the broom,' as Slats put it.

"I've never been asked to perform a service quite like this one. I hardly knew what religion to call on for inspiration: Slats' Judaism, Darla's Baptist upbringing, or Bian's heritage, which is probably at least half Buddhist. Then I realized it didn't matter. It's not important because, in His wisdom, God has ordained this marriage.

"It is a coming together of people from completely different walks of life, a joining born of love, and pleasing to His eye. Out of war's terrible crucible, nourished from fire and ash, three branches on humanity's tree entwine, and in so doing, gain strength."

Father Bob placed Darla's hand in mine, and then smiled at Bee. "To seal this union, I spoke with the Monsignor this morning, and he gave me special dispensation. The moment you exchange rings and embrace, the adoption of Bian will be complete. You will be a family, not only in God's eyes, but in the secular vision of the law, as well.

"We come now to the most pivotal questions of your lives. Do you, Slats, take this woman, Darla, to be your lawfully wedded wife, to have and to hold, in sickness and in health, in good times and woe, for richer or poorer, keeping yourself solely unto her for as long as you both shall live?"

"I do!"

"And do you, Darla, take this man, Slats, to be your lawfully wedded husband, to have and to hold, in sickness and in health, in good times and woe, for richer or poorer, keeping yourself solely unto him for as long as you both shall live?"

"I do!"

Father Bob squatted before Bian. "Do you take these good people to be your mother and father?"

Bee nodded solemnly in agreement. The father whispered, "Do you have the rings?" Bee reached into her blouse and fished out the pouch that Sister Margaret had tied around her neck. Father Bob retrieved the rings, and then handed them to us. "Place these symbols of your love upon one another. As they encircle your fingers, may they remind you always that you are surrounded by love."

We exchanged rings, mine going on without too much difficulty thanks to Sister Margaret's judicious pre-greasing.

"I now pronounce you husband, wife, and daughter. Whom God hath joined together, let not man put asunder."

———————

The press waited outside in force; only Father Bob's strict insistence on privacy had kept them at bay. Now it was time to fish or cut bait.

"Can't we just slip out the back and disappear?" I asked.

"You can do as you please, but the Fourth Estate is relentless, and if you duck them, they will seek you out. If you say nothing, they're just going to make things up. If I were you, I'd make a short statement, then tell them your honeymoon awaits and fly off. They're like children—they'll love the drama, but before you are even out of sight something else will snare their attention."

He was right, so I reluctantly stepped outside.

Reporters rushed forward, and cameras began to flash. One especially intrusive newsman forced his way forward, yelling, "Mr. Kutsoff! Mr. Kutsoff! You're being hailed as a hero for your incredible rescue yesterday."

I figured to go with what I knew—humor. "I'm no hero. I just got lucky and stumbled over the only patch of red in the Everglades for a hundred miles in any direction."

Another reporter shouted, "One unverified report says that you landed out there to pick her up? Is that true?"

"My mother taught me never to ignore a lady in distress," I said.

"Some say she wouldn't have lasted one more night outside. Is that true?"

"I'm no doctor, so I can't answer that question. I can tell you she was cold, wet, hungry, and in pain."

A woman reporter with a sappy expression observed, "And less than twenty-four hours later, you've adopted her. That certainly sounds heroic to me."

In my best John Wayne imitation, I drawled, "It just seemed like the polite thing to do, ma'am." She laughed.

"Did you get married today just so you could adopt the little girl?"

Only a few questions in and already I began to grow testy. But I kept my face carefully neutral, and related, "Darla Jean Pistle and I have been in love for years. All I did today was to rectify my tardiness in changing her last name."

A television reporter elbowed him aside. "Was adopting the crippled girl your way of paying for the atrocities we committed in Vietnam?"

I would just as soon have slapped this idiot as answer him, but I pressed onward: "Bian is an intelligent, endearing little girl, and both my wife and I fell instantly under her spell. This incredible child is a survivor and a fighter, and the only crippling injury she faced—having no family—has now been remedied."

He began to ask another question, but I stepped on it like a cockroach. "I want it understood that—"

Father Bob seemed to come from nowhere to take me by the arm. Calming me like a spooked horse, he explained, "Gentlemen, I believe that Mr. *Kisov*—that's K-I-S-O-V—is not comfortable hearing the word *hero* applied to himself. And I know that you will all understand how anxious he and his family are to celebrate the momentous events of the day. He'll be available to answer more questions later, but for now, let's all wish them well." Still holding my arm, he guided me to sanctuary inside the orphanage.

"Thanks for saving me from myself," I said.

"I probably shouldn't have lied and told him that you'd be answering more questions later, but at the time I thought it was the best way to put an end to his inexcusable rudeness."

I patted his shoulder. "Say ten Hail Marys, Father. And five Oy Veys!"

Thirty-eight

Father Bob insisted on driving us to the airport to see us off. He'd had another brainstorm about fooling the press.

"Reporters might be rude, but they're pretty savvy. They'll know you're going to eventually leave by plane, and they'll have the airport staked out. That's why I recruited a little help." Riding behind us in the orphanage bus were Sister Margaret and two other nuns, plus a few of the orphans.

"I've heard the phrase *soldiers of God*, but I've never seen a battalion in action before."

His grip on the wheel tightened. "If it takes nuns and orphans to run interference on the press, we'll fight perfidy with innocence!" The entire orphanage had been caught up in Bian's saga.

"Did you ever serve in the military, Father?"

"You might say that—I was schooled by Jesuits," he laughed.

The bus rolled to a halt near the back road to the airport. Darla and Sister Margaret got our baggage out, while Father Bob outlined the rest of his plan.

"I'll go ahead with the other nuns and the children. Sister Margaret will accompany you to your plane, which I asked the owner of the flight school to move behind the hangar. I'll do my best to distract their attention for a few minutes, while you get ready to go."

"Father, I just came down here to help find a lost kid. Two days later, I'm married and absconding with her." Donning a confused expression, I looked upward and asked, "What happened?"

He chuckled. "Apparently, He had other plans."

"I suppose I can deal with the demotion to copilot."

"You take good care, son." He climbed into the driver's seat and headed for the entrance.

With Bee clinging to my back, I led us cautiously up the back road, and then dodged through brush to approach the hangar from the rear. There sat my 180. I peeped around the corner of the building and spotted the now-parked bus. I threw the bags in back then preflighted the aircraft. The three girls said their goodbyes, exchanging hugs.

It was only as Darla opened the passenger door that she slapped her forehead. "There's only two seats. Where is Bee going to sit?"

"You will sit in your accustomed place. Bee will sit on your lap."

"And we'll both buckle up together?"

"No, we can't do that. If we have to decelerate fast, you would squash her." I poked Bee. "That's why I also visited the Army-Navy store during my shopping expedition." I showed them a couple of long canvas straps with buckles that I'd purchased. "You'll be belted in, and Bee will be strapped to you, papoose-style."

"Will that work?"

"Many Vietnamese women carry their children like this, and I see no reason it won't work well in the air, too. Bee's only problem is that her seat has more bone than cushion to it."

Darla seemed convinced. "I'll accept that as a round-about compliment about my weight." I got them both settled and belted, then turned to the sister.

"Sister, thank you. In the blink of an eye, my life has changed almost as much as Bian's. I'm happy, deep-down happy."

"This is a winner for everyone, Slats. Go with God."

I did as much of the pre-takeoff check as I could with the engine off—I'd finish the rest while taxiing. Sister Margaret kept watch, peering around the corner of the building.

"The orphanage car is pulling in," she reported. "It's going around to the far end of the cement runway. The father is pointing at it. And they're off—it's a reporter stampede!"

I started the engine and, keeping it throttled back, let it warm. Sister Margaret flashed a thumb's up, a sign that the out-of-shape reporters had all staggered over to the decoy car. I taxied unobtrusively over to the near end of the grass runway, and then gave it the gun.

Like a flock of startled geese, the reporters' heads swiveled as one. But it was too late—the Cessna's tail was already coming up as we accelerated. As we broke ground and angled upward, they must have realized they'd all been had—by a *priest*!

It was quiet in the plane for a moment, and then our collective breath whooshed out as one. "I've got to hand it to Father Bob. That plan was better executed than most military operations."

Bee looked out the window as we flew toward home. Then she softly said, "I am safe now."

Darla and I glanced at one another in astonishment. Yet somehow we intuitively knew not to make a big deal out of these first words.

Darla said, "Yes, you're safe. We have a house on a little ranch—it's almost like having our own country." Darla hugged her. "No one will ever hurt you again, Bian Kisov."

———————

I landed on the road and taxied up to the barn. I was out the door before the propeller clattered to a halt, unbelting the ladies and assisting them from the plane. As I set Bee down, Tailskid raced up. He spotted Bee and, uncharacteristically, curbed his excitement. He sat down nearby, enthusiastically wagging his tail.

"This is your new brother." Bee giggled, and the dog's ears perked up. "See? He loves to make people laugh. His name is Tailskid, and he's waiting for you to call him to you."

Gingerly, Bee extended her hand. "Tail…skeet."

Tailskid bounded over to lick her hand, then her face. Bee's laughter only encouraged him to redouble his efforts.

"He likes you, Bee! But his name is Tail*skid*," I enunciated.

"Given his interest in the ladies, I think Tailskeet is much more accurate," Darla observed.

About then I spotted Mabel chugging our way, wearing a grin like a cowcatcher. Tailskid ran to escort her.

"Lord Almighty, just look at this pretty child!" She squatted down to eye level. "Can I give you a hug, honey?" Bee nodded, and Mabel enwrapped her like a warm quilt.

"Mabel, this is Bee," Darla said.

"Honey Bee—I like that. You can call me Aunt Mabel, if you want." Then, holding her arm close to Bee's, she added, "If we ain't related, we sure must have been dipped in the same inkwell."

"We've got our own rainbow here, and *you* are the pot of gold at the end of it, Bee."

We all went into the house. Bee took her time examining each room, with Tailskid dogging her steps. She looked serious as a drill sergeant inspecting the barracks. When we finished with the house, she insisted on seeing the barn and then Mabel's cabin, too. We wound up the inspection back in the living room.

"I live here … long?"

"*Mi casa es su casa*," I said, and she cocked her head at me.

"Men can be confusing," Darla instructed her. "He means that you can live here forever."

And with that, Bee smiled serenely.

Thirty-nine

Darla undertook further renovation of our house, and in no time at all, she'd redone the second bedroom for Bee.

I took to marriage and fatherhood like a tick to a bloodhound, and though I'd never suspected that such feelings were inside me, they were beyond denial. I took great delight in introducing Bee to her new extended family, my kith and kin. My folks were ecstatic over instant grandparenthood. Bee learned new phrases in Yiddish and Russian: she was the only Vietnamese person I'd ever met who understood words like *bubbeleh* and *krasavitsa*.

Bee and Gene took to one another, too. Bee called him *Bác* Gene, a term of respect for an older male relative. Gene puffed visibly upon receiving this honorific, and with Bee's help he composed a blues tune with Vietnamese lyrics.

But it was Aunt Mabel with whom she forged a special bond. Bee visited her cabin every day to help milk the goat, as well as to care for Frederick Douglass, Mabel's old tomcat.

In a land not unlike her native Vietnam, Bee settled happily into a new life. Nourished with love and wholesome food, her wounds healed rapidly. Armed with prosthetic leg and ever-toughening stump, Bee was soon hiking tirelessly around the ranch. I also taught her to swim—she was frisky and quick as a tadpole. As her physical condition improved, so did her state of mind. Bee got the hang of English, at least as it's spoken in the South, and in almost every way she continued to bloom.

Yet there was a melancholy about her at times. She had been through hell and come out the back door, and that has lingering effects. I knew PTSD when I saw it, and I knew it didn't resolve itself in a year, if ever.

———————

I'd ridden the Beezer to town, Bee tucked safely between my arms astride the tank, just as Tailskid liked to ride. We were headed for the Hair of the Dog to have breakfast with my folks. Darla was going to meet us after stopping at the realtor's office.

Darla had quit her job after tying the knot, but we still liked to patronize her old employer. They would make me breakfast at anytime of day, and the coffee refills were always free. It also gave me a chance to parley with Oso about the upcoming junket to Chico Cay.

Darla bounced in with her feet barely touching the ground. "I sold the house! And I got my price—this meal is on me," she enthused. Eyeing the helmets underneath the table, she said, "I thought we were going to wait a while before Bee started going on longer rides."

"The weather's so nice, and the road was calling. Besides, I took it easy, didn't I, Bee?"

"We never go over ninety," Bee said with a straight face.

Darla frowned, but was unable to hold her expression

long before breaking into a grin. "I guess I should be grateful he kept it under a hundred."

"So, congratulations on selling; I guess that means we're rich!"

"This is *my* mad money. Who knows what I'll decide to do with it?" she said with a twinkle in her eye.

"What is mad money?" Bee asked.

"That's money meant for something wild or crazy. It's a very American concept."

"What are you going to do with the mad money?"

"I think I'll buy lunch, and then ... put the rest in my bank account."

"Doesn't sound very mad to me," I interjected.

"You should put your money to work," said Oso as he emerged from the kitchen. "Let me invest your nest egg; I'll hatch it into big, pretty flamingo."

"Oso!"

"*Hola*, Bee Bee! What do you want to eat today?"

"Guess."

"Hmmm, let me think." Oso held his hands together like a meditating Buddhist and chanted, "Stack of pancakes ... lots of butter, syrup ... side of bacon." This required zero prescience, as Bee ordered the same thing every time. "We only have twelve plates in this restaurant, so I'd better wash dishes for a group this big."

As Oso returned to the kitchen, my folks entered. The ever-expanding table got another round of greetings, none more enthusiastic than Bee's. As always, Pop's hello involved a bear hug and double-cheeked kiss.

"Zadee gives kiss that shakes the world," Bee quipped.

"What does Bubbee give?" my mother asked.

"Cookies that shake the world!" Everyone laughed.

Darla's replacement strolled over, flipping open her order pad. As Bee prepared to speak, Minnie smiled. "I already know what you want, honey. How about y'all?"

"I'll have what Bee's having," I said.

Darla agreed, "Tack on another."

My folks made it unanimous. "Pancakes for the house!"

"Don't forget the coffee," Darla added.

"Yes, coffee," Bee nodded seriously.

"*Milk*," Darla and I simultaneously countered.

"Well, well! Looks like a meetin' of the *U*-nited Nations or somethin'." The chief strolled up to spread his own special brand of cheer, trailed by Deputy Carling.

"What do you want?" I inquired tonelessly.

"Just keepin' in touch with the electorate."

"You weren't elected to anything," I pointed out, assuming his position in the Klan didn't count. "And, you're interrupting our Sabbath brunch."

"What the hell is a 'brunch?'"

"It's not quite breakfast, and not quite lunch."

"Sounds like some kinda Jew thing."

"Congratulations: you have correctly surmised that the word 'Sabbath' relates to religion. Now, why don't you leave before we ... *infect* you."

Darla put her hand over mine, tapping our rings together softly. It was a gesture we sometimes used toward one another; Darla called it Menachem Morse code. I guess the message this time was an affectionate warning.

I was all for affection, but in my growing anger I ignored the warning part. "We're celebrating Darla's house sale." The chief's frown was immediate, as I'd known it would be, because the chief lost that house to Darla in the divorce. "Yes, sir, the UN—as you so amusingly put it—is on firmer financial footing today than it was yesterday."

The chief scowled at me, and I realized it wasn't the house that angered him. He seemed too angry for that alone. I think he was furious about me marrying Darla, and bringing home a ready-made family. In some weird way, the chief figured I'd robbed him. This man thought like a pissing dog: once he'd marked a piece of ground, it belonged to him.

"You ain't funny, boy."

"And you're about as welcome as a turd in church. Take a hike."

The chief's expression grew murderous, his gaze shifting to Bee. "Hey, tell me somethin': which one runs stronger in her, the nigger blood or the slope blood?"

In a reaction so fast it took even me by surprise, Pop screamed, "You get out of here or I break you in half!" He stood up and made a grab for the chief's lapel, a move the chief instinctively and wisely ducked. Though no longer young, my father was built squat and solid as a fireplug. He rarely got mad, but when Pop began to thunder like Almighty God, you had better watch out. "Everybody knows you're a crooked *zhopoliz!*"

Carling tugged at the chief's arm, muttering warnings in his ear, and the chief allowed himself to be led away before the situation spiraled out of control. I performed a similar function for my father, and we again sat down. It took a while for Pop's spluttering to wind down.

Bee looked scared, so I patted my lap and she came meekly over to me. "I'm sorry we got mad. But we just don't like it when someone talks bad about you."

Pop also was apologetic, but unbowed. "I don't care if he is a cop—nobody talks like that to my granddaughter."

"Is he Communist, Zadee?"

My father, always quick to get over his anger, laughed loud and long. "I wish you say dis while he was still here."

"Why do you ask that, Bee?" I inquired.

"Because he act like men who come to village: he has gun and he yell a lot. It looks like he want to shoot somebody, just like men who call themself Communists." Bee's accent always got stronger when she was upset.

"This is not Vietnam, Bee. This is America, and we don't have Communists in power. The chief is mean and he's dumb, but he does not have the power to hurt you." Placing my hand over my heart, I leaned in close and whispered, "I promise, with all the power vested in me by Skykitten." I used our secret name for my Cessna, stemming back to our first meeting in the Everglades.

"He call me bad names."

Bee's grandmother reached out to take her by the hand. "Don't let him label you, Bee. Never let anyone tell you who or what you are. You know here," Ma touched Bee's head. "And here," she laid her hand over Bee's heart.

"You're going to hear stuff like that in school sometimes. When you do, just remember what Bubbee said. And whenever some bucketmouth starts in on you, you tell them something like this: 'I'm a gook, a spook, a Jew with one shoe. So what?' You'll use up every insult people like that can think of and they'll be clean out of ammunition."

Darla put her hand over mine, tapping her approval. "Then show them your backside. And put some wiggle in it!"

I tapped her right back.

Forty

In Florida, hurricanes are a fact of life. More summers than not the state is swiped by at least one major storm, bringing not only high winds, but thunderstorms with incredible levels of rain. During a close strike, the electricity might be out for days, and roads can become impassable too. When I was a kid we'd ride out the storms at home, using kerosene lanterns and a camp stove as our appliances. First, Ma would prepare a feast with all the perishable food in the refrigerator, and then we'd make do with stored provisions like rice, nuts and dried fruit, all washed down with warm water. If your house took a hard hit, you might need to be self-sufficient for a couple of weeks as roof-patching and other repairs took place. And it certainly didn't hurt that Pop owned a hardware store!

A hurricane is a fickle creature: it might fizzle, or it might grow to a monstrous size. Hell, it might just hover right overhead, like Joe Btfsplk's thunderhead. Now, with the hindsight provided by two years of marriage, I understood why hurricanes were named after women.

Coming on the heels of 1977's piddling hurricane

season, this year's storm season was intense. It began early, and the storms kept marching through until late in the year. We had a great new meteorological tool in GOES, the weather satellite launched several years back, which took detailed photographs of hurricanes as they formed. But even these high-tech pictures weren't in real time—there was a delay involved.

Tropical Depression Kendra formed quickly in the Caribbean, just south of Cuba. Forecasters were keeping a close eye on it—hurricanes were rare so late in October, but not unknown.

The possibility of a personal disaster had long haunted me: an island the size of Chico Cay could literally be scoured clean by even a moderate storm. Now I faced a difficult decision, and I couldn't ask the Morales's opinion on how to proceed.

Should I fly down there and evacuate them? They were still several weeks away from harvesting the latest crop, and I couldn't see Mamo running away. On the other hand, I *could* see, in my mind's eye, the devastation that Kendra might soon inflict upon my second family. And, if I didn't have enough worries already, there were five of us and my plane was a four-seater.

I tuned my shortwave to NOAA Weather Radio, to monitor the latest forecast. The news wasn't good:

For the Caribbean Sea and the Gulf of Mexico:

The National Hurricane Center has issued an advisory on the tropical depression located 70 miles south of Havana, Cuba and moving very slowly to the northeast. Locally heavy rainfall and high winds are spread across a wide area. The depression is expected to develop rapidly into Tropical Storm Kendra. Environmental conditions are conducive for continued development, and a hurricane warning has been issued for Cuba, the southeastern United States, and the Bahamas. Formation chance through 48 hours high, 95 percent.

The storm had generated itself while almost at a standstill, allowing it to build rapidly over the still-warm Caribbean waters. The latest GOES photos showed a tightly-wound knot, accelerating as it spiraled off toward the northeast. I slipped into military mode, weighing my decision analytically. It was a no-brainer: leave now and try to save lives.

Including my own… I mean, how many people evacuate *into* a hurricane, via airplane?

I quickly threw together emergency supplies: extra fuel, as many lifejackets as I could locate, some food and water. And rope, lots of rope. I notified Oso about my plan, and promised him that he'd hear from me as soon as possible after my return.

Darla latched onto me like a barnacle, and asked, "Are you out of your goddamn mind?" I pretended not to see Bee nod in my peripheral vision.

I squatted down next to her. "Sometimes you just know that you must try to help someone. The day I heard you were lost in the Everglades was like that. So is today. Four people I love are in trouble, and I think I can help them. I know you're just a little girl, but can you understand that?"

Bee frowned in consideration, and then said, "I understand, Daddy."

I kissed my girls and, before running out to the plane, said, "An Apache medicine man once told Geronimo that he'd never be killed by an enemy's bullet. Despite fighting many battles, that fierce warrior died in bed at the age of eighty. In the air, nothing can touch me—I am Geronimo!"

———————————

I knew I should be anticipating conditions and making contingency plans for my arrival. But instead I was sitting, yoke in hand, with an idiot's grin plastered across my face, winging my way toward adventure. I was unlikely to ever face a more challenging bit of aviating.

At the halfway point, the winds were picking up considerably. They'd swung more westerly, so I scooted right along with a groundspeed of one eighty-five. I looked down to judge my drift angle by the waves, as I had many times in the past, but never had I seen the Atlantic so rough. I adjusted my crab angle to seventeen degrees, to hold the desired course into the crosswind. As I got closer, I encountered rain bands and had to let down to fifteen hundred feet.

I wasn't even sure where to take the Morales family. Did I fly a couple at a time to Nassau, or Andros? Could even a big island like Andros shrug off a direct hit by a hurricane? The more I thought about it, the more convinced I became that there wasn't time for two trips, nor did anywhere in the Bahamas seem truly safe. No, I figured that I'd better just cram everyone into the Cessna and head for the barn. If I could even land in weather like this!

Too many questions, I told myself. *Just concentrate on flying the plane, and take things one at a time.*

In a rare instance, I had all the avionics and radios going at the same time. I needed to be able to cross-check my navigation, or transition to instruments, at the instant when necessary. I used every bit of assistance at my disposal and every fragment of contact flying knowledge I possessed. Unfortunately, the ADF was largely useless—low frequency AM transmissions were scrambled by all the lightning.

So I borrowed a technique from aerial navigators of yesteryear. Knowing that winds this high made accurate dead reckoning navigation all but impossible, I purposefully aimed for a point north of the island. When I judged that I'd flown the prescribed distance from my last known fix, I'd turn ninety degrees to the right and follow that course upwind. In other words, I purposefully planned to miss my mark, knowing I had to turn right to find it. The island should be somewhere along that line…theoretically.

So there I was, scudding along under low-lying clouds and staring hopefully at the choppy waters. And like magic, the island emerged out of the mist, just about where I'd expected. I roared overhead and began to circle, as Mamo and Julieta ran from the house and began to wave madly. I wasn't paying them much attention, though.

I was looking at the short, rough runway carved into the sand. It was already pretty wet, and I risked nosing over on touchdown and stranding myself, along with them. But at least I wouldn't end up in the Atlantic. Just in case, though, I shut down the avionics and turned off the master switch.

As Meat would have said, "Learn not to burn."

I didn't like doing landings toward the sea, but the wind gave me no choice. I set up an approach with two notches of flap, carefully trimming the aircraft. As there was a bit of crosswind from the left, I did a forward slip into it to compensate. The plane almost seemed motionless in the air, so intense was the wind. I touched down precisely on the threshold, offsetting the contact with gluey sand by applying backpressure on the yoke. The Cessna rolled quickly to a stop, and I taxied back to the approach end of the runway, and then swung the nose around into the wind before shutting down.

The first words from Mamo's mouth were, "It is very good to see you, Slats!"

"You too, Mamo. But where are Carlos and Tomas?"

"They are harvesting the most mature plants."

"You're kiddin' me, right?"

"We don't know what will happen. Except that the crop might be ruined. Thinking it better to have a premature product than none at all, I sent them to the reaping." She shrugged. "Besides, it gave them something to do. Men require tasks."

"My task is to take you out of harm's way. We'll be overloaded, so there's no room for weed."

Mamo just flashed me a less than tolerant look.

"I'm not joking. We have to save our lives. Get everyone together quickly, forget about weed or luggage or anything else, and let's get out of here while we still can."

"As God wills!"

In due course, the brothers finished their task and returned to the house.

"How's the crop, boys?"

"The best of it is in the bags."

"We can't take any of it. We're already going to be over-weight just with people, so nothing extra."

There was a rush of Spanish between them. It grew more heated, and Mamo began to shout and gesticulate. Julieta, threatened by yet another breaking storm, moved her chair to the shelter of my lee side.

But my fuse was also growing short. "What is there to argue about at a time like this?"

"Which one of us will stay here, so that the product can go. Carlos says he's the man of the family and must stay. I say I am the head of the family, so *I* stay. "

"Are you out of your minds? I'm not leaving any of you here so that a sack of marijuana can ride in your seat! The wind's picking up and we must go—now!"

But Mamo crossed her arms—there was no talking sense to her. I eventually concluded that it was easier to just leave with the extra poundage. If we waited much longer, we weren't going anywhere.

"Fine! But no more than seventy-five pounds—that's it!"

A bit more Spanish, and the matriarchal nod was given. I refueled from the jerrycans then tossed them aside, while the brothers loaded the weed into the back of the plane. When I looked at the load, it looked like more than a hundred pounds to me.

I'd told them to pile most of the sacks behind the two seats, then tie them down. You can get away with over-loading an airplane by a fair amount, but it is vital to keep the balance correct. So I needed to concentrate the weight close to the center of gravity. The sacks would come in handy one way, though—several folks would be using them as seat cushions.

I'd given the seat assignments careful consideration. I put Mamo in the right seat, with skinny Julieta on her lap (I'd brought along the restraint straps I'd used with Darla and Bee a couple of years ago). The brothers were seated on the weed facing rearward, Carlos on the left to offset the weight of the two passengers on the right seat. I had to use rope to tie them down, and I told Carlos to keep his knife handy to employ as a quick-release, in case of a crash.

As Carlos climbed inside and settled onto his uncomfortable seat, I noticed him trying his best to conceal a bag. "What's that? I said no baggage."

Mamo answered for him. "We always keep some money on hand, for emergencies. We can't leave it here."

I hefted the bag—it must've weighed close to forty pounds. I peeked inside to see bills of every denomination, tied up in neat bundles. "How much is in here?"

"A few thousand, I guess," Mamo replied, her face set combatively.

"Is money worth your life?" I asked. Then, gesturing toward her children: "How about their lives?" She looked less certain, and I slipped the bag from Carlos's grasp and tossed it onto the ground. I laughed and said, "At least nobody will be killed by a flying moneybag. Now, strap yourselves down tight!" I went round to climb into the left seat, as Tomas scrambled into the back.

I started the engine and let it warm. "Listen to me carefully. This is going to be the hairiest takeoff I've ever done. If I can't get her into the air, we're going off the end of the runway, and we'll most likely flip over. If that happens, don't panic—a plane will float for quite a while. Take a deep breath, unfasten yourselves, and get out as quickly as you can."

I turned on and tuned in every device in the cockpit, tested the controls, set the trim, and tightened my belt as much as possible. Then, saying a silent prayer to Charles Lindbergh's recently-departed spirit, I stood on the brakes and pushed the throttle up to full.

The Cessna answered with a belligerent howl.

Forty-one

I've always had a tendency to imbue airplanes with human characteristics. But this time my 180 reminded me more of Tailskid: intelligent and friendly, but at the same time cocksure. The Cessna shook in her own propwash, gathering her skirts.

I looked out over the ocean, noting that the wind had shifted slightly and was now blowing straight down the runway. It looked to be gusting well over fifty miles per hour. But as an aircraft carrier moving at full speed gives an assist to launching aircraft, so would the wind help shorten our takeoff roll. Our chances still looked slim to me, though.

Then I noticed the squalls, shredding the tops off the storm-tossed waves as they moved over the surface. The gusts were coming in increments that I could time. A big one appeared a thousand feet out, and I waited…waited… then released the brakes. The runway, now a soggy quagmire, sucked greedily at the wheels—it took a moment before we began inching forward. But though we barely seemed to move across the ground, thanks to the wind we had decent airflow over the wing and control surfaces. I got the tail up and we started to accelerate faster, but already the water seemed to be reaching out for us. Worse, it looked as though the waves might get us before the wind gust arrived. We'd passed the point of no return—it was too late to abort the takeoff—so I concentrated on using literally every inch of available runway. We'd barely made it to jogging speed when the end of the runway disappeared beneath the nose so I yanked hard on the yoke.

I swear I felt the wheels spank off the face of an incoming wave. It deflected us upward a few inches, and I let off most of the backpressure on the yoke. We were trembling on the edge of a stall, but maintaining critical clearance over the wavetops. At that time the gust swept over us, and like a blood transfusion to a sick man, the wing responded with a surge of lift. The trembling ceased, and I gingerly allowed her to accelerate in ground effect until we hit best angle of climb airspeed, then started upward.

I looked over at Mamo and Julieta. Both women goggled at me; never had they resembled one another more closely. I burst out laughing.

"What is funny about any of this?" Julieta asked.

"Nothing in this world feels better than cheating death."

Mamo's expression soured. "I give the glory to God."

"And I would have left the extra cargo on the island, not made Him work so hard uplifting us." Mamo tried to hide her sardonic smile.

I took up a heading that included a thirty-degree crab angle into the wind. With no way to check my accuracy until we got much closer to a radio station, I concentrated on threading my way around cloud buildups and lightning flashes, always compensating for these detours to maintain the desired track. My navigation didn't have to be exact, because it would be pretty difficult to miss the entire state of Florida.

I kept the airspeed down to a hundred twenty-five miles per hour. It wouldn't do to overstress an already overloaded aircraft—structural failure has a way of spoiling your entire day. Carrying all this weight and cruising slower than usual, the aircraft felt mushy and unresponsive. I kept the plane just under the cloud deck, at about nine hundred feet. We were being tossed around, and the first of the clan succumbed to the turbulent air. I heard gagging sounds from my right.

Julieta exclaimed, "Oh my God, you puked down my neck!" Which was immediately followed by an over-burbling from Julieta's own stomach. And then a similar, sympathetic response from behind. I thought I'd planned for every contingency, but sick sacks had completely escaped my mind. Lord, just when I figured things could not possibly get worse, I now faced a full-immersion baptism!

"Somebody is going to clean every bit of this up when we get to Florida!" I yelled.

All I got in response was another chorus from the Upchuck Choir.

I shook my head, thinking to myself: *Now I've seen everything. The entire Morales family is throwing up, except for DB.* I cracked the side windows open, willing to take whatever rain came in with the fresh air.

Turning my concentration back to flying, I looked down at the waves, and then added another five degrees to my crab angle. If the wind continued to increase, then I'd be looking out the side window to see the direction we were actually moving.

It seemed to take forever to make our bouncing, wheezing, puking, and farting way across the Atlantic. My beautiful aircraft had been converted into a flying privy. But she was a trooper, soldiering along without a missed beat through conditions that would have imperiled her even if she'd been chained to the ground.

I'd been fiddling with the ADF, trying to latch onto a signal, and finally got a college station from Melbourne called WFIT. The backdrop of rock and roll lent further surrealism to this flight. Every time lightning discharged the needle swung wildly, so the fix was far from accurate. But the needle behaved itself enough to indicate that I was somewhere near Melbourne.

I kept a sharp eye out for any sign of the coast. Now I was down to seven hundred feet, and I slowed to a hundred, giving me a better shot at avoiding any obstacle that might loom suddenly out of the mist. The one thing I didn't worry about was being spotted as I came ashore. I knew that law enforcement personnel were hunkered down, like every other sane person on the Florida coastline. Only crazy people were out and about today.

The first thing I spotted was a high-tension tower, its hazard light winking red. *What a strange place for a high-voltage line*, I thought, and then realized it was a launch tower. I'd made landfall over Cape Canaveral, of all places. It was a good thing nobody was chasing me today—NASA had radar powerful enough to track a hummingbird over Maryland.

I turned south into the teeth of the gale, edging back out over the ocean to avoid entanglements. I kept the beach in sight off my right wing, using it as a sandy compass to point my way home.

I thought about the upcoming landing. Everything up till now had been practice for what promised to be the most daunting several minutes of my flying career. I had one big advantage: the wind was aligned with the strip, just as it had been at Chico Cay. There were more perils than I cared to think about, though they could all be summed up quite simply: *I'm flying in the middle of a friggin' hurricane*!

Reaching Sebastian Inlet, I turned west-southwest toward the ranch. For only the second time, I was bringing more than mere ounces of weed onto Jelly Roll Field. But there was no question of dropping the weed anywhere, and I sure wasn't going to attempt two landings in these conditions. Hell, if I could land once without killing somebody, then I'd consider myself royal-flush lucky.

I shut down the avionics and turned off the master switch, while I gave quick instructions to Carlos and Tomas about how to proceed after landing. Sick as they were, they promised faithful assistance. I handed Mamo my knife and told her to cut Julieta's straps then run for the house as soon as we stopped.

When I hit the mainland I followed SR 512 the last eight miles, and then executed a circling approach to Road-apple Lane. I lined up and began my descent, using two notches of flap and plenty of power to keep us moving in the incredible headwind.

"You got that knife ready, Carlos?" I yelled.

"Si!"

I spotted the barn, and said, "Here we go. Hang on!"

I cut the power back, and we almost stood still in the air. It was an illusion, though, as the airspeed indicator showed us doing eighty miles per hour. I trimmed all the pressure out of the controls, pushed the yoke forward and, like a helicopter, we started to settle vertically.

Strangely, this was the simple part. The wind was straight down the strip and all I had to do was keep the wings level in the rough air. A touch of rudder here and there to keep aligned, and the mains settled onto the ground. I stood on the brakes, dumping the flaps to help stick us to the ground, and then eased the power back and allowed the tailwheel to settle. We ended in a three-point attitude, with the engine running at partial throttle. I continued to apply brakes, using the controls to "fly" the plane on the ground while debarkation commenced.

As she sawed at the straps, Mamo said, "That was easier than I thought it would be."

"The hard part comes when we turn and try to get her into the hangar," I said. Then, to Carlos and Tomas: "Remember my instructions!"

"I remember. Go, Mama!" Carlos shouted, and the women took off like spooked deer.

The brothers sprang out, Carlos running under the right wing and hooking his fingers over the tip. Tomas ran for the hangar, using the key I'd given him to open the double doors as wide as they would open. Then he ran back to the plane and, adding his weight to Carlos', nodded at me to indicate they had a good grip.

Edging the throttle forward, I started turning left. As the aircraft swung out of alignment with the wind, I counteracted with the controls. We were so far beyond the maximum allowable crosswind that it would require every trick I knew to beat it. As the plane presented more and more broadside, the wind slapped at the vertical stabilizer trying to weathervane us around. I could feel the gale reaching under the wing to flip us. Both brothers had to put all their weight on the wingtip to keep it down.

Then a big gust hit. I felt the right wing come up, and I looked over to see air under all four feet—the brothers were hanging by their fingertips. The thought flickered through my mind: *Let go, before you end up in the prop!*

But Carlos' legs seemed to sprout arms. The arms wrapped themselves around his thighs and took a firm grip. They were stout arms, black arms, and they held on tighter than anacondas.

The wing remained poised in the air, but it climbed no higher. Finally, the gust subsided and the right wheel bounced back onto the ground. I instantly returned to taxiing for the hangar. My wing handlers kept hold, sidestepping toward the open door while I drove the plane straight toward the waiting shelter. Just as she came even with the door the handlers let go—there was a slight jar and then I was through, yanking the power instantly back to idle, lest I run her through the back wall.

I sat in the familiar barn, the engine gently burbling. It felt strange to be out of the wind's grasp. I tried to let go of the yoke, but my left hand was cramped into such a death grip that I practically had to pry it off. I cut the switch and listened to the most satisfying wind-down of an engine I'd ever heard.

I climbed stiffly from the cabin, as weary after flight as

I'd ever been. Carlos and Tomas stood on either side of our rescuer. Soaked to the skin and grinning like the Cheshire Cat, Mabel put her hands on her hips and said, "You must be crazy if you think today is good for flyin'. You ought to be up in Chattahoochee, takin' that mental cure!"

For once, words failed me. I just went over and planted a big kiss on her forehead. "You saved my airplane. You're in my will."

"Keep flyin' like this and you be needin' a will."

"You talk sense, Mabel. I hereby give up flying in hurricanes."

"Now *you* talkin' sense."

"Would you tell everyone we're okay? We'll be inside shortly."

I did a walk-around, finding only one bit of damage. The stamped-aluminum wingtip had been shorn off in squeezing past the hangar door—Wilko could easily repair it. My Cessna seemed to regard me with an apotropaic eye. It had done a pretty good job warding off evil, after all.

We stored the weed behind some bales of hay and swept out the cabin. Then we passed a fat joint around, silently pondering our trip. Carlos put the roach between his lips and gave a last inhale as I clapped my thighs and said, "Let's go inside and drip all over Darla's nice clean floor."

We wrestled with Kendra one final time, and then I kicked the door open and yelled, "Honey, I'm home!" Bee and Darla latched onto me, and I feebly protested, "You're gonna get wet."

"Right now, I don't care. But in a minute, I'm going to kill you," Darla replied.

"You can kill me later. First, I'd like to make some introductions that are long overdue."

Now sheltered from the deluge, my disparate families swirled into one.

As the storm raged outside, we were safe in our lantern-lit cocoon. My eye fell on the bag resting beside Mamo's feet. "How did that get here?" I asked.

"Tomas might have picked it up, when you were climbing into the plane," Mamo admitted.

Tomas avoided my stare.

"I made him do it," Mamo confessed. "It represents the sweat of our brow. If we couldn't bring our possessions with us, then we can at least use this money to replace them."

She upended the bag onto the table. The soft thump of money bundles hitting wood was punctuated by a solid clunk. There, nestled amongst the bricks of cash, gleamed a blue steel revolver.

"You brought your *pistol*?"

"It is a family memento that means a great deal to me."

"You weren't happy merely overloading the plane. That four out of the five people on board were illegally entering the country wasn't enough. Adding a hundred-twenty pounds of marijuana at the last minute didn't quite satisfy you, either. So you threw, what, a hundred thousand dollars into the mix? And *then,* on top of it all, you arrive with a gun? I count at least seven felonies!"

Mamo looked nonplussed, and then offered, "Well, sure, when you say it like that, it sounds bad."

I burst into laughter. "You're even crazier than I am, Mamo."

"It seemed like the right thing to do, at the time."

My laughter redoubled, and I could barely breathe let alone speak.

Julieta added, "Cubans know how to make a grand entrance. The seething storm, the dramatic coming ashore with mysterious cargo, the bag of treasure: it's like a Wagner opera."

"And Slats gets half," Mamo sang in a falsetto.

I nearly choked on my laughter, while the Morales family regarded me with amused tolerance, like a demented-but-harmless uncle. When I managed to throttle down my amusement, I looked at my ring and said, "This isn't quite how I imagined the meeting of my two families."

———————

I didn't need to figure out how to contact Oso. He was at my door early the next morning, having detoured around or driven over every obstacle separating him from his goal. On his first visit, he was mainly concerned with dangerous cargo: the weed, the gun, and the money. These he tucked into his Bronco and took safely away, while the tail end of Kendra still lashed the area. He did leave a thoughtfully large fistful behind for me.

It was only while watching him drive off that reality hit me smack between the eyes: I was now out of a job. There went my main source of income, not to mention the exuberant risk that I'd craved since leaving Vietnam. I was only twenty-nine and, for the second time, forced to retire. Faced with so serious a downturn in my fortunes, there was only one thing to do; I went to the tack room to sample the latest crop.

Oso came back a while later for the most important cargo, his family. We all adjourned to the hangar for a business discussion. Oso began: "Sometimes in this world, things change. Probably there is nothing left on the island. Even if the house is still there, the soil is now salted. So, I think maybe we need to relocate."

"We are refugees again," Mamo said.

"But this time we have money. And I have learned how things work in America. I will get false papers for everyone, and we will find a place to make our art."

"I'll help any way I can," I offered.

Oso looked at me, smiling. "You still think only to help us. You, who get our crop to America and help us make all this money, who save my family and put yourself out of business at the same time, you want to help us more."

"It's not like I'm penniless. You've been very generous, and I'm quite happy," I said. "Unless you're trying to tell me my investments have dried up."

"It has been a while since we talked about the investments. They are doing pretty good; you got no worries. We want to talk about your retirement package."

"Retirement package?" I echoed stupidly.

Mamo took over. "To begin, we give you permanent access to our… artwork. A lifetime supply!"

"Really?"

"Unless you want to start buying that brown, seedy stuff," Oso said.

I shuddered. "No, that won't be necessary. I accept your wonderful offer."

Mamo said, "When we begin operating again, we will be needing a… how did you say it, Oso?"

"A 'quality control person,' Mama."

"Si, a quality control person, to ensure we stick to the highest standards."

"I was born for that job."

"Second, there is the matter of your severance pay," Mamo smiled. "That bag of money you wanted to leave on the island? Half is yours, almost fifty-six thousand dollars."

"I thought you were kidding last night. I can't take that."

"You already did—I added it to your investment portfolio. Soon as the electric and phone come back on, anyway," Oso grinned.

"About those investments, are they at least holding their value?"

Oso looked downright smug. "Holding their value? Right now you are worth more than four hundred thousand, and more comes in every day."

"Guess me and Darla'll move to Califor-nigh-ay, and buy the mansion next to the Beverly Hillbillies."

"I'm not jokin', Slats. This investing thing is great. We double, even triple, some of the money. Best part is, it comes out clean as Mama's sheets from the wash."

I was stunned. Money worries were definitely a thing of the past. A safety barrier had been erected around my family. The Morales's generosity truly touched me, enough that I had to turn to wisecracks.

"At most, I only expected a gold watch..."

"That's how Fidel would do it, back home. And it would be fool's gold!" Oso piped.

They all laughed, and then Mamo said, "God knows one of His good children when He sees him. Blessed are the selfless."

"First the nuns call me a saint, now you," I shook my head.

"Yeah, St. Pullas," Oso said.

"Huh?"

"You pull our ass out of the fire." Mamo smacked him on the back of the head for his blasphemy, and Oso ruefully added, "It's good to have you back in hitting range, Mama."

"Do you have any ideas about where to settle?" I asked.

"I know some people near Pahokee. It's right on the lake. Lots of Latinos, and that Okeechobee soil is very fertile," he grinned.

"And that's barely fifty miles away by plane. Keep me informed, Oso."

"I will. But for now, I'll get these illegal immigrants off your hands." With tears from the women and hugs from the men—and a big kiss from Julieta—they climbed into the Bronco and drove away.

I waved them off, feeling like a conductor on the Underground Railroad must have felt a hundred years ago, passing endangered folks along to a new start in a free land.

Forty-two

About the same time that Iranian students were taking over our embassy in Tehran, we found out that Darla was pregnant. Bee caught the baby bug immediately, of course, telling all her friends at school that she was going to be a big sister. Mabel had been involved from the start too, both personally and professionally, and Darla had already asked her to handle the delivery. As will happen in small towns, word spread quickly—we'd been back-slapped and well-wished by nearly everyone, except for the less desirable element which, unfortunately for this town, dressed in a police uniform.

The chief had never liked me. As far as he was concerned, I was a hippie Jewboy who didn't take himself, let alone anyone else, seriously. The chief believed in his heart that I smuggled weed, but he'd been too inept to prove it, and now he'd blown his last chance. If that wasn't enough, I'd not only befriended people of color in a small Southern town, I'd had the audacity to adopt one. And worst of all, I'd married the woman who had rejected him.

The chief was not the sort of man who dealt well with

loss. He was the sort of man who, once he'd stamped his name on any belonging, felt like it was his for life. When word of Darla's pregnancy reached him, the chief was not happy.

I'd gone to Captain Hook's to celebrate. Virginia, the one-armed owner for whom the bar was named, staked me to my first vodka. My money was no good—my glass was refilled several times by voluble patrons and I needed only one quarter to run the pool table all night long. The prospect of being a father again made me feel like a million bucks.

And then the chief walked in. He moved carefully, like a drunken man who was used to the feeling. He sat on a stool and slapped the bar loudly, demanding, "Gimme a longneck!"

"Comin' right up," Virginia replied.

He took a long draft, and then peered around the bar and spotted me at the pool table. He snatched up his beer and wobbled over. Then, right in the middle of my game with Wilco, he put a quarter in the table and started racking 'em up.

"What the f…" I started to remonstrate.

But Wilco grinned and said, "It's okay, Slats; go ahead and play him."

"We're playin' for five bucks," the chief stated.

"I never play pool for money."

"I said we're playin' for five bucks!"

"Challenger's don't get to make that call."

"Men gotta compete for somethin'."

"I compete for fun."

"That's why little girls jump rope."

Wilco interrupted us to quietly say, "I'll cover your bet, Chief."

The chief looked annoyed at failing to stir me up, but drank his beer while I broke. I sank the four ball, then said, "Looks like I got small ones." Then I added two more to my total, calling each shot, before missing.

The chief sank an easy twelve ball, and then missed his next, instead sinking the nine in an unintended pocket.

He started to line up his next shot, and I said, "You didn't call that last one."

"I sank that one on purpose," he lied.

Whereupon Wilco piped, "What do you say we double the bet, Chief?"

He couldn't very easily say no, so he just nodded. He missed the next shot, and I sank three more, the last unintentional. "Your shot," I gave the table to the chief, who looked at me like I was nuts for sticking to the rules.

He missed again and I cleaned up the table, ostentatiously sinking the eight off a bank. "Looks like you owe Wilco ten bucks."

"You think you're so damn smart, don't you? The hero, back from the battlefield but still rescuin' damsels in distress. You ain't nothin' but a dope-smokin' piece'a shit."

"But I play a mean game of billiards, don't I? Speaking of which, don't 'men' generally pay their debts when the competition is done?"

The chief was already red-faced; now the spittle started to fly. Slapping down a sawbuck, he yelled, "I know you're flyin' that shit in, too. You been lucky up till now, but I'll catch you one'a these days."

"The only thing you could catch is your dick in a zipper."

"Plus, you live with niggers. Jews got no respect for common decency," he slurred.

"Color doesn't matter. The only thing that matters is how someone thinks and feels and acts. My little girl is one of the purest souls I've ever been around. The sewer runs inside you."

The chief's face twisted in hate. "Worst of all is that you ruined Darla. She was an upstanding white woman once, but now she's going to bring a mongrel into this world, to go with that first one you picked up. And that's a goddamn shame."

"You showed your appreciation to that 'upstanding white woman' by beating her. You are a perineum." Knowing that four-syllable words stymied him, I explained, "You know, that funky patch of skin between a dick and an asshole."

I spoke out of pride, in the belief that this pitiful man could no longer threaten me. I spoke not only as the winner of the pool game, but also of the smuggling game. And I'd won the biggest prize of all—Darla. In snagging her, I'd dug my spurs into him. In starting a family with her, I'd bested him. By making Darla happy, I'd insulted him in the worst possible way. I think the chief felt cuckolded.

Drunk, angry, and confused, he spun on his heel and stomped out the door.

"Hey, where you going? You still owe us twenty-five cents!"

"What for, interest?" Wilco asked.

"It's for the pool game he interrupted."

Wilco laughed. "Don't worry. I would have paid fifty bucks to see the expression you pasted onto his face." Wilco frowned, then added, "Don't take him lightly, though. The chief is mean and stupid, and that's a dangerous combination."

I only wish I would have listened to that advice.

———————

Next morning, Darla and Bee were off to see the obstetrician for a routine exam. I'd gone fish spotting in the Cessna—I figured that today's flight ought to pay for a couple of week's worth of diapers, anyway. I stopped by the Airpark to refuel before flying back to Jelly Roll Field. I was just finishing when Wilco came running over.

"Some woman named Mabel has been trying to get in touch with you. She says she needs to see you, pronto."

"What's up?"

"I don't know any details. She sounded pretty upset, though."

I hopped into the 180 and beat feet over to the ranch. I landed and taxied right up to Mabel's cabin, just as she was coming out the door. My heart jumped into my throat when I saw that Bee was with her. She was scared out of her mind.

"Daddy!" she hiccuped.

"What's wrong, Honey Bee?" She was crying too hard to answer. I held her close while Mabel explained.

"Darla's in the hospital, over to Vero. She's mighty beat up, Slats, but the doctor says she's gonna be all right."

"What happened?"

"That sumbitch done it!" I'd never heard Mabel curse; she was generally a soft-spoken woman.

"Who?"

"That chief. I could just kill him!"

It was as though ice water had been poured over my head; I literally went cold all over. "Get hold of yourself. Exactly what did he do?"

She took a deep breath, and said, "Near as I can determine, he stopped Darla and Bee on their way to the doctor. He was yellin' and screamin' like a crazy man, sayin' he was gonna beat some sense into Darla, then he'd start in on Bee."

Bee let go of my neck. "He started hitting Mama, Daddy. I just ran away. I couldn't think of anything but getting somebody to help, to stop him from hurting Mama." She threw her arms around me again, sobbing her heart out.

Mabel took up the story again. "Bee run off into the woods and cut back this way. After a while, she came back to the road and somebody gave her a ride. I called the ambulance; they took Darla to the Indian River Medical Center, over to Vero."

I hugged Bee even tighter.

Mabel said, "I had to call the law, too. I figured better the sheriff than the police."

"That was smart." I looked at Mabel, standing there helplessly. "I have to go to Vero, Mabel. Can you watch Bee?"

"I keep her till you're back, and Tailskid too. That chief come pokin' 'round here, I'll take a hatchet to his ass! The dog can eat what's left, for all I care."

I picked up Bee and carried her into the cabin. "I have to go to see Mama, Bee. But I'll be back soon, with news about her. Until then, Aunt Mabel will take care of you." I stared into Bee's pained eyes, and said, "Everything will be all right. You hear me?" She nodded, and I kissed her.

Mabel followed me to the door. "I didn't want to say the rest in front of Honey Bee. Slats, Darla lost the baby." Only then did she break down and cry.

The trip to Vero was a blur. I found myself standing next to a hospital bed, an ER physician at my elbow. Darla was unconscious, her face swollen and stitched, and a patch over one eye. Finger marks stood out clearly on her neck, and an IV was inserted into her arm.

"Your wife received a severe beating, including a fractured nose and cheekbone, some abrasions to her eye, and a concussion. The assailant also dislocated her left shoulder, and she has internal bleeding from repeated blows to the midsection." He laid a hand on my shoulder. "I'm very sorry to tell you that the beating resulted in a miscarriage. I'm no detective, Mr. Kisov, but it looks to me as though the assailant concentrated on her abdomen. Her pregnancy was quite obvious, making this a particularly vicious crime."

"Is she going to be all right?"

"Your wife is an otherwise healthy woman in the prime of life—she will recover quickly from most of these injuries. I'm afraid she won't be able to have any more children, however."

"Was the baby a boy or a girl?" I whispered.

"It was a boy."

"Could I be alone with my wife for a while, Doctor?"

"Yes, sir, you surely can." He cleared his throat, and then added, "I'm very sorry for your loss. My wife is expecting right now, and…" he trailed off, shaking his head.

I nodded my acknowledgment.

I spent quite a while sitting beside Darla, holding her uninjured hand. I didn't say a word, but I tapped out a near-continuous Morse message on her ring. The sun had moved through a considerable arc before my thoughts turned to comforting Bee. I made sure the nurses had Mabel's and my phone numbers, and then headed for the airport.

As I neared the ranch, I could see a car driving fast enough down Roadapple Lane to raise a big dust cloud. I automatically throttled back to get a better look without drawing attention to myself. Drawing a bit closer, I could scarcely credit my eyes: it was a Chevy Caprice with a red gumball light and bearing the familiar insignia of Farth's finest. The car slowed considerably, and then cruised sedately past the ranch before picking up speed again and continuing north.

I'd been numb for hours, but now my jaw clenched like a vice. I had the irrational urge to introduce my aircraft to this police cruiser, Kamikaze-style, but I had Bee and Darla to consider, so instead I slowed even more. I kept the chief surreptitiously in view from behind and to the right, his blind spot.

It didn't take Einstein to figure out he was looking for me. This guy either had balls the size of watermelons, or he'd gone completely insane—he wasn't even trying to hide his actions. The memory of a story my father once told me came to mind. When he and my mother were fleeing the Nazi invasion, Pop saw a Russian pilot use his propeller to chew the tail assembly right off a German dive-bomber. If I came in from behind, perhaps I could settle over his car and take his head clean off with my aluminum scimitar. It wouldn't do the plane much good, but if I did crash, I stood a decent chance of surviving. With careful piloting and a dash of luck I might be able to pull up a few feet and let him crash, then land deadstick.

I knew this much, though—I'd waited too long to deal with the bastard. It had cost the life of my unborn son, a stain on my soul I could never wash away. I was responsible for Darla's sterility, as well. I, a warrior tested in combat, had failed to protect the people I held most dear in this world. I'd played with a snake, throwing around insults and defacing guns, but instead of attacking me, the serpent had bitten the woman I loved.

I started downward, shutting off the master switch at the same time. I didn't know where the chief was going, but he was headed there at about seventy-five miles per hour. As I neared the road, I started banking to intercept him. I also began to sideslip, to help keep the car in sight for as long as possible. I knew at some point he would disappear beneath the nose, but for now he was keeping a steady speed and I should be able to accurately close if I wasted no time. I wasn't thinking at this point so much as I was calculating—I'd converted myself into a sort of glide bomb.

I lined up with the road, at the same time I reached the maximum slip angle manageable without snapping into a spin. The car vanished from sight under the nose and, concentrating as hard as I ever had, I willed my plane to intersect his car at so precise a point that I'd open the roof like a can of tuna … right along with his skull. I turned off the fuel valve, knowing that the engine would run for half a minute on the gas already in the lines.

I came out of the slip perfectly aligned with the road and continued descending the last few feet. I was completely out of his sight, with the engine throttled back so far he had little chance of hearing me. If I was correctly placed, the chief's final sight would be a shadow closing over his car, the Angel of Death come to call.

I came pretty close—the landing gear neatly straddled his car, but I missed the roof with my propeller. Instead it chewed through the hood, while the fuselage banged down hard on his roof, partly crushing it. I tried pulling up, but the impact had broken my plane's back and I had no control. I was now a hood ornament.

The chief instinctively veered off. My Cessna and I skewed sideways with him, and as the car rolled over it tore my left landing gear away. The wing smashed into the ground and snapped off, and I was tossed around inside like Las Vegas dice. I must have hit my head, because my memory of the crash after that is pretty fuzzy.

I'm glad I had the foresight to turn off the electrical system, because when I came to my senses I was staring at fuel-soaked dirt, up close and personal. I shook my head to clear it, seeing that the wing tank had split wide open and deposited almost thirty gallons of highly flammable avgas onto the road.

I seemed to be having trouble with my left hand, so I reached over with the right to release the seatbelt. I fell out onto the road, screaming in pain as I hit. I don't know how I'd missed seeing the bone that was sticking out of my forearm—you'd think something like that would attract one's attention. The dirt and gasoline jammed into the wound weren't helping, either, so I struggled to my feet.

The chief's car had rolled a few times, ending up on its wheels. I limped to the midway point between plane and car, figuring I was far enough away to avoid bursting into flames myself if either one caught fire. I could see the chief through the glassless windshield, slowly stirring back to consciousness.

"Bastard's harder to swat than a cockroach," I grumbled.

"What'd you say?" the chief croaked.

"You aren't dead."

"You tried to kill me. I'm a sittin' police chief!" he said in astonishment.

"You should have left my family alone."

The chief was fussing with his seat belt, which seemed to be stuck. Since he wasn't shooting at me, I knew he must have lost his .45 in the rollover. Instead, he tried to soothe me with words. "You gotta un'erstand, I was raised agin mixin' of the races." This was about as close as he could come to reasonable logic.

"You are one hard-hearted prick. That's going to rebound on you, someday." I turned abruptly on my heel, heading back to what was left of my plane. I retrieved my flannel shirt and the survival knife I always carried—plus the fob from the ignition key— and then stepped into the woods. I cut a section of sapling about four feet long, tied the shirt around one end on the way back to the plane, then soaked it in the gas puddle under the wing stub.

I backed well away, dropped the sapling on the road, and then fished a matchbox from my pocket. Aligning myself upwind, careful to keep my fuel-soaked left side as far away as possible, I struck the match one-handed and lit the makeshift torch. Then I touched it to the gasoline-trail leading from the point of crash, watching the gas catch fire and wick over to my wreckage, like a fuse. The plane whumped into flames.

Giving the conflagration a wide berth, I limped back to the car, stopping ten feet short. With precious little calm remaining, the chief quavered, "What in hell do you think you're doin'?"

"Showing you what it feels like to be a victim." I waited a moment for this to sink in, and then tossed the torch onto the hood.

With no fuel puddled there, the torch lay inert, the flame already burning down. The chief just stared at it, willing it to go out. But fumes rose from the smashed carburetor, through the propeller slashes, and soon the tiniest trace of white smoke wafted upward. As it grew heavier, a tongue of flame licked out, and having tasted oxygen, it ignited rapidly. While the chief commenced his dreadful aria, I stepped back from the twin infernos. Each still contained an unexploded fuel tank, and I had no intention of joining the chief in a duet.

Killing is never pleasant. But Vietnam had taught me that it is sometimes necessary. I pulled the fob out of my pocket, fingering the amputated hammer from the chief's revolver almost like a rosary. And I lay down to await my fate, while the fires—and the chief—slowly expired.

Forty-three

Mabel later related that she'd spotted me tailing the chief from the air. And that she'd called the ambulance for the second time that day, after the smoke column rose.

The attendants found me lying in the road, and initially thought that I was dead. They revised their medical assessment from deceased to injured when I stirred feebly as they approached. They figured I must have been thrown from one of the incinerated vehicles, though they didn't know which one.

The truth was that I'd fallen asleep. I was worn out following combat, and my injuries felt better if I lay still in the sun. As he opened his medical bag, the EMT asked, "Do you remember what happened?"

I knew that I might be in serious trouble. Should I be frank about everything, or would it be best to play my cards close to the vest? Opting for the latter, I replied, "I'm not sure."

The driver said, "Well, it's a first for me, an accident between an automobile and an airplane." He pointed toward the wrecks. "Do you know which one you were in?"

"All I know right now is that I'm hurt."

The EMT administered a shot of morphine. "Relax, while we splint your arm and bandage your wounds. I'm sure it will come back to you."

They took me to the same hospital where Darla was being treated. The same ER doctor was still on duty, and he cleaned, sutured, and set my injuries before deciding to err on the side of caution and keep me overnight for observation.

I was banged up and drugged, but I still couldn't sleep. I lay waiting for Darla to awaken, and dreading it at the same time. How does one tell the woman he loves that her womb is as dead as her unborn child?

I was pondering these matters when a fit older man in uniform stepped into the room. "Mr. Kisov, I'm Sheriff Barnett. I'd like to speak with you, if you feel up to it."

"I'm trying to figure out what I'm going to tell my wife when she wakes." I nodded at Darla.

He looked surprised to hear that my roommate was also my wife. "I was sorry to hear about her loss, sir. I assure you that the Sheriff's Department has already begun an investigation into that crime." He paused, and then asked, "Do you feel well enough to answer a few questions?"

"Sure."

"Here's what we know right now: this morning your wife was severely beaten, and the police chief of Farth is the main suspect. Hours later, your airplane crashed into the chief's car on Roadapple Lane, and he was killed in the ensuing fire. Can you add any details to the little we know?"

"I can't tell you much, Sheriff. I have a small ranch. I

use my barn as a hangar, and a short stretch of Roadapple Lane as my runway. I was flying back home after my first trip here to see Darla. I remember something about trying to shoot an emergency landing, and almost being down safely, and then everything went to hell in a hiccup. Things are pretty blurry after that, until the EMTs showed up."

"The doctor tells me you hit your head pretty hard. He also says your memory might become clearer, given time."

"I sure hope so. I can tell you one thing: this has been one of the worst days in my life, and I was shot down over Vietnam."

"I came ashore on D-Day, and I've been in law enforcement for twenty-eight years. I've seen my share of bad days, and yours is right up there." He stood up and said, "I won't intrude any more today. But this is an ongoing investigation, so I'll have to ask you not to go anywhere without informing the Sheriff's Department."

————————

But the day's vicissitudes were far from finished. When Darla stirred back to consciousness, I was her first sight, clad in a hospital robe, reclining in a hospital bed, be-tubed, and bedecked with a cast.

"What are you up to now?" she slurred, higher than me for once, thanks to legal narcotics.

"I had a minor crash."

"Motorcycle?"

"Airplane."

She was really stoned, only now becoming aware of her own tubes and bandages. "Was I with you?"

Since she was feeling no pain, I thought this might be

a good time to break bad news. "No, you weren't with me. Don't you remember what happened?"

Her eyebrows knit in concentration. "I...I was going somewhere. With Bee, I think." Then her head jerked up in maternal alarm. "Where is she? Oh, my God!"

"Shhhhh... Bee is fine, Darla. She's with Mabel." She sighed and laid her head back down.

It hurt like hell, but I struggled out of bed, dragged a chair beside her, and took Darla by the hand. "You were on your way to the obstetrician's office, and you were pulled over."

She took over, saying, "I remember...it was Bobby Ray...he hit me."

"He beat the hell out of you. And he'd have done the same thing to Bee, but she ran off to find help."

"Bee did that?"

"I've never been more proud of her."

I watched the thoughts flit across Darla's face, first pride in Bee, then puzzlement, and finally consternation. Only now did she think to examine her own abdomen, finding it flat and featureless. Tears sprang to her eyes as she looked up.

The only response I could manage was a mute shake of my head.

Darla unleashed a moan of pure anguish. I sat there, impotently holding her hand, as unable to help her as I was to stay my own suffering.

Ultimately, this was my fault. I'd made an enemy of the chief. I'd actually enjoyed messing with him, and I'd failed to perceive his true depravity. Now, my unborn son and my wife had paid the price. I'd had *years* to open my eyes to the truth; I'd waited four hours too long.

The nurse responded to Darla's cries with Valium, while I sat there holding her hand. It took forever for the drug to take effect, and for Darla's sorrow to recede. I leaned down to whisper in her ear exactly why she need never fear her ex-husband again, just as she fell asleep.

And still I sat there, my hand holding hers, envying her unconsciousness.

The following morning, I was awakened by Officer Carling, Farth's only remaining police officer. He strode in accompanied by a plump man with a good haircut, who stepped authoritatively forward and stated, "I'm Ron Lambert, State Attorney for the Nineteenth Judicial Circuit Court of Florida. I'm here to see you arrested for the murder of Police Chief Robert Pistle." Lambert turned to Barney Fife and melodramatically said, "Officer, do your duty."

Barney stepped forward with cuffs in hand, and I nodded. "Let's go." Then he glanced down at my cast-encased left wrist.

"I think we can trust Mr. Kisov not to make a break for it. He's barely able to walk, let alone run," Lambert noted. Then, turning to me, "You don't seem very surprised by this."

I nodded at Barney. "His predecessor committed infanticide yesterday. Nothing the law in this town does will ever surprise me again. Now let's go, before my wife wakes up. She's seen enough of her family snatched away to last a lifetime."

So they took me to jail, where Barney scraped together

enough guts to administer a 1970s jail haircut. Dangling my pelt by the ponytail, he escorted me to a cell, saying, "What goes around, comes around. That's for the chief, buddy boy." I stepped into my new home away from home, and the iron door clanged shut.

Forty-four

I hadn't been behind bars long, but it was more than enough time to realize that I didn't like jail very much. The food was bad, the company was worse, and the hours stretched longer than Crystal Gayle's hair. For days I'd had no visitors, no exercise, no weed, not even a book to help me pass the time. About the best that could be said was that my body had begun to heal.

But I'd certainly had time to think about my story. I didn't know how much, if any, incriminating evidence had survived the fires I'd set. So I worked on polishing my slant on the crash. I'd indicated to the sheriff that I'd experienced engine failure. I now decided to make that a partial engine failure, the prop still turning but with very limited power, to account for the slashes cut into the hood. A partial engine failure could easily be explained by carburetor ice.

I doubted much of the instrument panel would have survived intact, but the switch positions were all correct for an emergency landing. The chief hadn't fired his gun, and the torch had undoubtedly burned. I couldn't think of a single thing about the scene that defied logical explanation.

All the while, unseen folks were hard at work on my behalf. Late one morning, an impeccably dressed gentleman was ushered in to see me. "Good day, Mr. Kisov. My name is F. Leonard Frank, and I'm an attorney for the Southern Poverty Law Center."

"Pull up a stool, counselor. I don't get many visitors at The Rock."

"Yesterday evening, I went before Judge Hunter in Okeechobee. This morning, I served a writ of habeas corpus on Officer Carling. As of now, you are officially released on bail."

"Then let's get out of here, Mr. Frank."

He smiled at me. "You can call me Leo." We breezed through the stationhouse and climbed into his brown Ford. "Where would you like to go?"

"I'd like to see my wife and my little girl, if that's all right with you. We can talk on the way."

I found out a lot on the way to the hospital. Such as, my father had put things in motion by contacting the SPLC. Good ol' Pop, an intelligent and pugnacious man, if ever there was one.

And I discovered that Leo had come to his position honestly. The Klan had lynched his grandfather and namesake, a Jewish factory director from Atlanta, in 1915, after he was falsely convicted of raping and murdering a thirteen-year-old Christian girl. His jailers put up no resistance, allowing hooded assailants to unlock Frank's cell and drag him away.

I observed, "The Klan could learn something about the law of unintended consequence."

Leo shot me a look of reappraisal. "I see parallels between your case and my grandfather's. This sort of thing really yanks my chain."

Leo wasted no time in considering how to defend me. "I'm thinking the best defense will be a strong offense. Specifically, trying to stop this case cold during the grand jury hearing, rather than wait for trial."

"I'm a little ashamed to admit that I know more about the military system of justice than the civil system."

"Grand juries are different than trial juries," he lectured. "They are the first to hear accusations against an arrestee, to see evidence, to hear witnesses when they deem it necessary. Unlike trial jurors, grand jurors can ask questions and interact with the prosecutor and the witnesses. When they're satisfied they've heard all pertinent facts, they vote. If they return a 'true bill,' you go to trial. No true bill, no trial, and you walk out of that room free as a bird."

"What makes you think they might not indict me?"

"For one thing, the fact that Chief Pistle has been a dirty cop for his entire career, if I'm to believe the stories I've heard."

"Sounds like Mabel told you about Jelly and her husband Henry."

"Among others. She says it's common knowledge that Pistle was a Klansman, and introducing common community knowledge is permissible. If, of course, we can influence the jury to call the right witnesses."

"How can we do that?"

"Understand that one of the things grand juries do is oversee public services, such as police departments. So we make sure the jurors are exposed to allegations of misdeeds committed by Farth's police force, particularly by Chief Pistle. I'll use newspaper stories to raise a stink. There are influential editors in Florida that will eat a story like this for breakfast. It shouldn't be difficult to convince at least several of the eighteen jurors that departmental misconduct is at the core of this case. Especially if any blacks make it onto the jury—this place seems barely desegregated, and most black citizens are probably all too aware of Pistle's unfortunate proclivities."

"Are you going to call Carling to the stand?"

"Defense counsel is never seen or heard by a grand jury. I can't call witnesses—I can only advise you from the sidelines. But what I really want is *you* in the witness chair. Most times a state attorney calls the accused to testify, and the accused declines on the advice of his lawyer. This time, you're going to run for that chair so fast that Ron Lambert's head will spin. I think with a little coaching from me, we can have the jury eating out of your hand."

"Sounds positive…"

"The flip side is that one never knows what a jury will do. Especially if manipulated by a clever state attorney. Lambert may be insufferable, but he's a savvy prosecutor."

We pulled into the hospital parking lot. As I entered Darla's room, I was horrified. Her bruises were terrible, a purple-to-greenish yellow mask that covered much of her face. But this was merely a framework for her eyes: the hurt and loss radiating from them stabbed me like a bayonet.

Dr. Logan happened to be there, making arrangements for Darla's discharge. "It's good to see you out, son."

I was too stricken to respond politely. "Is she all right, Doc?"

"Physically, she's well enough to go home. Spiritually, she has a long row to hoe. But home is certainly the place for that."

Leo provided transportation, and then politely bowed out. Our homecoming could not have been entirely happy for Bee, either. Darla was stunned by events and strong painkillers, and by trying to deal with the loss of a baby. And I was withdrawn and sullen, blaming myself for everything that had happened. I tried to help out in the house, but all I seemed to do was get in everyone's way. Including Mabel, who visited frequently to help with cooking and with caring for Bee.

So I ended up spending a lot of time in the barn, smoking weed and staring at the place where my airplane was once housed. Without the solace of flight, I felt lost. Like a junkie craving heroin, I needed to fly, now more than ever, so I bought an issue of *Trade-A-Plane* and started perusing ads, allowing my unruly mind to sprout wings.

After ruminating for a few days, I put a few items into my backpack, stuffed five thousand dollars into the front pocket of my jeans, and slipped my survival knife into the waistband. Then I went inside to see Darla.

"What are you doing?" she asked.

"I'm going to see a man about a horse." Darla frowned, so I elucidated, "I need an airplane, Darla. There's one in North Carolina that sounds okay, so I'm taking some cash and hitching up there for a look."

"You're leaving?"

"You're able to get up now, and Mabel said she'd be happy to continue to help out while I'm gone. I'll probably be flying back, so this shouldn't take long."

"You can't go, Slats; you're out on bail. If they find out that you've left the state, they'll throw the book at you. How are you going to fly if you're back in jail?"

I sat next to her on the bed. "I feel like I'm going nuts. I need to fly to bring in some money for the family."

"You don't have to work. We have enough money to last us for the rest of our lives."

"It's not about the money!" I shouted. Then, more quietly, "I need to contribute ... *something*. I'm crawling up the wall. I feel like I'm still in jail. I need to fly." Such a basic truth bore repeating; "I need to fly!"

"So you're going to violate the terms of your bail and leave the state? Carrying enough money to buy an airplane? What happens if somebody tries to rob you?"

"That would be unwise," I gritted, lifting my shirt to expose the knife.

"Listen to yourself, Slats! Please don't go, not now, not like this."

"I'm goin'," I told her.

Her face closed like a vault. "What do I care? What *possible* difference can this make now? Do whatever you want!" She rolled over on her side and faced the wall. I reached out to her but stopped short of making contact.

So I found myself on US 1, thumb out and already feeling better. It didn't take long for a car to pull over. The middle-aged driver said, "You a serviceman on leave? Get in." He took me to Jacksonville, where I hiked over to US 17 and caught another ride northward.

We'd just passed Ridgeland in South Carolina, and

the sun was low in the sky, when I said to my current benefactor, "I'll get off anywhere along here."

"There's nothing but woods here."

"And that sounds perfect. Thank you for the ride, sir."

I walked into the pines until I came to a pond. I performed my ablutions Vietnam-style, and then applied my evening cologne...which smelled very much like DEET insect repellant. Properly groomed for dinner, I sat down to my repast, consisting of beef jerky and fruit leather washed down with the finest of tap water from my canteen.

I leaned back to enjoy an after-dinner pipe and watch the sunset, a better show than television will ever provide. I know I should have felt guilty, but mainly I felt relief. I'd hit the road, and I was as free as a man can get. If I so desired, I could travel where I wished for quite a while. I could stay on the road and sleep out in the weeds with a wad of cash in my pocket for a long time.

But I wasn't going to do that. I might be enjoying my little vacation, but I'd be right back in Farth in a few days, with or without an airplane. I loved Darla and Bee, and I knew that I would not leave them. Nor was I going to run away from my legal troubles. If the law dogs didn't take my explanation, they could send me back to jail. I'd done what I needed to do.

I filled another bowl and fired it up. Then, as the last of the light faded in the west, I wrapped myself in my blanket and crawled underneath a gnarly old evergreen. Sheltered by overhanging boughs, and cupped in a pine needle embrace, I fell into untroubled sleep.

Forty-five

My eyes blinked open in the pre-sunrise light, and I inhaled the clean pine-scented air. This was a red-letter day—if all went according to plan, then I might meet my next airplane today. I shouldered my pack, made sure my pocket was full and my knife unsnapped, and then headed toward the highway. Again, I thought about a drifter's life—the road beckoned to me.

But not as much as a plane did. I started walking, sticking a thumb out when I heard the occasional car approach. It didn't take long to get a ride in a stake bed truck. We passed through Ashepoo, Parkers Ferry, Ravenel and Rantowles. Driving on US 17 was like going back in time: there were still general stores open for business here, and I would not have been surprised to see a Waco biplane crest the treeline.

Navigation was simple: I stayed on 17 until it intersected 501, and then followed that road north for a few hours. Just outside Chapel Hill I stepped out to briefly stretch my legs, turning in at Horace Williams Airport.

I went into the only fixed base operation on the field, where the flight instructor let me make a local call. "Are you Dougie, who's selling the airplane?" I asked the guy who answered.

"Yep."

"I'm Slats; I called from Florida a couple of days ago. Can I take a look at it?"

"When do you want to see it?"

"I'm at the airport now."

"I'll be right over."

I love a motivated seller. Thanking the instructor, I strolled onto the ramp. I'd spotted a scruffy Super Cub on my way in, and as I got closer I saw that it had no flaps, a rarity among the type. This must be the one.

Piper had taken their venerable Cub and added a larger engine, bigger fuel tanks, and an electrical system, producing a masterpiece of an airplane. The Super Cub was built using 1930s technology, the fuselage made of welded steel tubing, the wings from wood and aluminum, and all of it covered with fabric. It was a knockabout workhorse, nicknamed the Poor Man's Helicopter because of its ability to operate from a field no bigger than a postage stamp.

This one was dog-tired. The fabric covering was so old that it was fraying in places. Was that a piece of duct tape patching the stabilizer? I already knew from the ad that the engine was far past overhaul time, and now I could also see that the instrument panel was sparse, the tires dry-rotted, and the plexiglass crazed.

And so must I have been, because I'd already fallen in love. Musty and dusty as the plane was, it smelled even more intoxicating than sinsemilla. I tried to get hold of myself—drooling with lust is not the proper way to negotiate.

A kid quick-marched toward me, trying but failing to conceal his eagerness. Until he got a little closer and looked me up and down with increasing disapproval.

"I know I must look a sight. I've been hitchhiking for two days, and I slept in the woods last night. I probably look like a bum—I came here before I even got a motel room.

"So let me establish my bona fides, right off the bat." I pulled my wallet out and started yanking cards. "This first one's my commercial pilot license, and the second is my Air Force ID." While he perused them, I added, "I brought this along, too." I pulled the flash roll from my pocket, riffling the end like a deck of cards to show it was composed of hundred-dollar bills. Dougie literally licked his lips when he saw my stash.

I grinned. "Now that we have that settled, how about we go for a ride? I prefer the captain's chair."

"Sure, yeah, let's go." Dougie bent to untie the tail, but I said, "Allow me to do the honors. If I miss anything, you speak up."

I did a complete walk-around, sticking my head into the engine compartment and crawling underneath the fuselage to look in those hard-to-see places. I paused dramatically next to the duct tape repair, but said not a word. Then we climbed into the cockpit, cranked up and taxied over to the runway, where I gave her a long careful run-up. She may have been past due for overhaul, but the engine ran smoothly enough, so I waggled the controls, set the trim, and gave her the gun.

The tail came right up and, after a short roll, she felt ready to fly. I eased the stick back, and we came off the ground easily. Immediately, I felt that she was wing heavy. I held left stick to compensate then switched the fuel selector to right tank to help balance her out.

Dougie noticed my actions and said, "You can feel that the right wing is a little heavy. The mechanic says she's slightly out of rig, that's all. I was waiting till I got her recovered to fix that."

Which made sense; I'd visually check it once we were back on the ground, to be sure. Otherwise, she felt pretty good, buoyant and light as a feather. I'd gotten used to the truck-heavy controls of my 180—this Super Cub felt more like a box kite with an engine bolted onto it. And it certainly felt natural to hold a stick again, rather than a yoke. As tired as this plane was, it intrigued me.

I did a couple of stalls and, no surprise, when she broke she fell off to the right. Given the condition of her fabric, I performed no spins or other radical maneuvers. I flew about half an hour, long enough to feel the right wing getting less heavy as the fuel from its tank was consumed. I turned back toward the airport and shot a couple of landings. Then it was time to shoot the shit.

First thing I did was sight along both wings. I thought I could detect a bit more washout on the right wing, indicating Dougie's rigging explanation was accurate. Which didn't stop me, of course, from harping on that and every other flaw: "To be honest, Dougie, the wing heaviness worries me."

"It's nothing, really. You're going to get her recovered anyway, and they always set the rigging after that's done."

"See, that's the thing. I know I've got to get an engine overhaul, and have the fabric replaced; now other problems are creeping up. Airplanes can end up being holes in the sky into which vast sums of money are shoveled."

"I bought her so I could accumulate hours cheaply, toward my commercial license and instrument ticket. She's done that beautifully, and I never had to put any money into her upkeep."

"Well, I do like the little plane. What's your asking price?"

"I'd let it go for... fifty-three hundred dollars."

"Not a chance, Dougie. That's what it'd be worth if the engine and fabric had half their life remaining."

"What do you want to pay?"

My turn to practice the grimacing and chin-scratching necessary for proper dickering: "I couldn't do much better than... thirty-nine hunnerd dollars."

"You're going to have to do better than that. I'll go down to... forty-eight hundred."

"It's gonna cost more than two grand to fix the problems I know about, and there's bound to be more that I'll find out about later. I couldn't see paying over four grand."

"I've got more than that into it."

So I educated Dougie about the true nature of aircraft ownership. "A pilot never really owns an airplane. What we do is pay for the right to keep it for a time, to enjoy the sky that it provides. In exchange for this privilege, your responsibility is to keep it in good shape, happy until the next payer comes along. Now, you got a bunch of cheap hours by forkin' over your money, and I'd bet the house and ranch that you got a new license tucked in your wallet, with the ink barely dry." Dougie tried hard to keep the smile off his face. "How much would it have cost you to rent a plane for the hours that you flew?"

"It would have cost a lot more," he conceded.

"Let's quit dancin'. I will peel forty-three of these hundred-dollar bills off my roll, and not one dime more."

"But that's way less than I'm asking."

"Only because you're asking too much. But if you can't abide my offer, just say so. No hard feelings. I will sleep in a cheap motel then hitch back to Florida."

Dougie's face did a Saint Vitus Dance as he considered the pros and cons of my offer. His vacillation encouraged me to pull the wad out of my pocket again. That was it—he caved in! "Okay, forty-three hundred," he grinned, sticking out his hand.

"The willingness to compromise will take you far," I told him, shaking his hand. "It's too late to do paperwork today. Can I have the airworthiness certificate, plus the engine and airframe logbooks, so I can look them over tonight? If there are any questions, I can check with my mechanic by phone. I doubt there will be any surprises, though, so if you'll draw up a simple bill of sale tonight, we'll head over to the FBO in the morning and consummate the deal. See you here at nine?"

———

Most small airports had someone equipped to assist with sales. The secretary of the flight school had blank registration applications on hand, one of which I filled out. She witnessed my cash payment to Dougie, made a copy of the bill of sale for us, stuffed these into an envelope along with a fiver, and fired it off to the FAA. The Super Cub was now officially mine.

I briefly considered insurance, but enough with the

ancillary crappola: I'd worry about insurance back in Florida. I longed for the isolation of a solo flight, and the chance to feel out this aircraft on a cross-country flight.

I'd already memorized the performance figures for this plane. It was capable of making the four and a half hour-flight to Farth without refueling with a tiny reserve left in the tank. But any decent pilot will tell you that you don't push an aircraft, not unless there's an excellent reason to do so…such as a hurricane threatening to drown your friends. No, I could afford the time for a fuel stop.

I strapped my backpack in the rear seat, folded my only navigational tool—the Rand McNally road map I'd used for hitchhiking—then herded the little plane into the air. I flew with the window slid back on my left, and the clamshell doors open wide on the right. Forget open cockpit—this was like flying a seat slung under a wing. I picked up 501, the same road I'd come in on, following it south-southwest at an altitude of nine hundred feet, low enough for the pine scent to waft in.

The Super Cub cruised at barely over a hundred, but that just gave me more time to savor pure flying. I passed Pittsboro and Aberdeen and Laurinburg, and then I was over South Carolina. I'd burned enough fuel from the right tank to make the wing feel lighter, but it got heavy again when I had to use fuel from the left. The soggy wing was the only detail to mar what was otherwise a beautiful flight.

I'd never flown a plane that felt so light and responsive—it almost seemed to be filled with helium. Any buyer's remorse I may have had now dissolved. I could be a happy man, sitting in this seat.

I left 501, angling south past Aynor and Hemingway

before turning to follow the coast at McClellanville. Navigation got even easier—all I had to do now was keep the water on my left and the land to the right. I flew over Fort Sumter, and the old mansions lining Charleston's Battery slid past my right wingtip.

This is where the first shot of America's most costly war had been fired. If my own generation had found angst in Vietnam, I could only speculate as to what it must have been like to fight against one's own countrymen. Plenty of those veterans had suffered from PTSD, except it had been known as "soldier's heart" back in their day.

Past the summer cottages lining Folly Beach, Kiawah, and Edisto. Over the congestion of Savannah to Darien, where the stench of the paper mills made my eyes water. If I had trusted the engine more, I would have angled out over the ocean to seek fresher air. I put in at Fernandina Beach airport to top off my tanks before continuing on into the more familiar stomping grounds of Florida.

If the air wasn't scrubbing me clean, it was at least removing some of the grime I thought might never wash off. I was looking forward to seeing Bee. And Darla, too... if she didn't greet me with meat cleaver in hand. Hell, maybe that's what I deserved for this stunt, though. If I went to jail, then they'd be stuck with this deteriorating antique. And a fitting tribute to me it would be—aging, careworn, crudely patched and cranky.

I stayed along the coast, getting vectored through traffic by Jacksonville approach control, then on past St. Augustine, Daytona, Cape Canaveral, and Melbourne. I had the radio off by now—I could find my way from here with eyes closed. I set down at the Airpark, leaving the aircraft in Wilco's capable hands.

Then, the new title-holder for 'Crappiest Plane on the Field' shouldered his pack and headed for home.

I came trudging up Roadapple Lane but nobody seemed to be around. Even Tailskid was absent, and he kept an eye on everyone's comings and goings. I whistled for him and heard a reply bark, but still no tail-wagging greeting. I headed in the direction of the bark, peering this way and that, and finally spotted him in the graveyard.

"Whatta ya waitin' for, boy, an engraved invitation?" I asked, stepping through the open gate. Tailskid came over, accepted a brief scratch, and then returned to the same spot and sat down again. "What did I do, interrupt the meal after the hunt?"

Tailskid wasn't eating, though: he was staring at a raw patch of soil, with a stone set into the earth beside it. He was watching over a tiny grave. I stepped closer to read the inscription on the marker.

Beloved Son

What kind of man was I, never to have even considered that a burial was necessary? Or that my wife and daughter needed comforting? All I'd thought about after release from jail was getting an airplane—what a selfish bastard! I stood rooted to the spot, tears streaming down my cheeks.

Until a small hand thrust itself into mine... It was Bee. She held on for a long time then looked up and said, "You told me once that I'd know when the time came to help somebody."

I wiped my face on a sleeve. "And you did, honey. You did a great job of helping your mother."

"I'm talking about you, Daddy." She pulled me down, until we were both seated on the grass. Then she crawled onto my lap and wrapped her arms around me, and we cried out some of our grief together. How a seven-year-old could possess such empathy, I don't understand.

I could barely bring myself to go inside the house and face Darla. I considered taking up residence in the tack room again. But her reaction was much the same as Bee's. We were all overwhelmed by the same sorrow; I guess we just reacted differently.

But we drew together now.

Forty-six

Showtime was here—the grand jury was convening this morning in Okeechobee. I hadn't been paying much attention to the outside world, so I was surprised when Leo handed me the editorial section of the *St. Petersburg Times*.

Hearing Set for Today

Menachem Kisov of Farth goes before the grand jury today for a hearing thought by many to be stacked against him. Kisov is charged with the murder of Robert Pistle, longtime police chief of Farth. This case is unusual, to say the least. Chief Pistle is the main suspect in a savage attack on Kisov's wife, who suffered a miscarriage. Hours later Kisov's aircraft struck the Chief's car, under circumstances that remain unclear. Pistle was killed in the ensuing fire, while Kisov was seriously injured.

    Chief Pistle has long been an anachronism in Florida law enforcement, apparently drawing inspiration from Bull Connor of Birmingham and his ilk. Civil rights came later to Farth than to almost anyplace else in Florida. Pistle was long suspected of being an active member of the Ku Klux Klan, and was notorious for his prejudicial treatment of minority citizens.

My intention is not to call for a specific verdict in this case. I wish only to see that Mr. Kisov receives what all citizens of Florida deserve, a fair and impartial chance for his story to be heard by a jury of his peers.

I passed the paper back to Leo, who rubbed his hands together gleefully. "This is exactly the sort of story I've been hoping for! The *Vero Beach Press-Journal* will jump all over this, and by tomorrow there won't be a grand juror that hasn't read up on the chief. We could not be in a better position to walk in there, today." He held up an admonishing finger. "But don't let your guard down. Emphasize what we've talked about, and keep your cool. If you need advice about any question, I'll be right in the hallway, and you can consult with me at any time. Make your request formal but polite, something like, 'I respectfully request permission to leave the room to consult with my lawyer before I answer that question.'"

We pulled into the parking lot of the courthouse and Leo slapped my knee confidently before we stepped out of the car.

I sat in a tiny, remote office with Leo for much of the morning, while the state attorney worked his mojo on the grand jury. This was nearly as gut-churning as waiting to fly a mission back in Vietnam. God knows what Lambert was telling those eighteen folks, slandering me in every way he could. The longer I sat there, the poorer I thought my chances were. By the time I was summoned, I figured the odds of going straight from this building to jail were about even.

I was introduced to the jury, sworn in, and then bluntly confronted by Lambert. "Did you willfully and maliciously murder Police Chief Robert Pistle, using your Cessna aircraft as a deadly weapon?"

The directness of his question took me by surprise. Nonetheless, I gathered myself and resolutely replied, "I ain't did nothin'." The grand jury seemed taken aback by my answer, a brief titter of laughter shivering through the back row.

"Mr. Kisov, I assure you this is no laughing matter."

"And I can assure you, I'm not laughing. The first and only thing I learned in jail was that no one's guilty. For me at least, that is true. I reiterate my innocence."

Our initial sparring satisfied, Lambert led me through the facts of the crash as the sheriff's investigation had determined them to be. I acknowledged most of what he said, making two things crystal clear: the fact that I'd never seen a police car until after the crash; and, that I was experiencing partial engine failure and thus locked into a given course of action, which in this case meant lining up on Roadapple Lane and putting the Cessna down in one piece.

"My memory is clear up to the moment I was about to touch down. Then everything went to hell in a hurry."

"Do you remember anything at all?"

"I remember falling out of the plane onto my broken

arm, right into a puddle of gasoline. I crawled away from the wreckage on the three appendages that still worked, as fast as I could go. I've seen pilots burn before, during the war, and I didn't want to be next to a wreck waiting to ignite."

"Did you see the police car?"

I squinted as if trying to see the distant past. "I saw a car, but I don't remember thinking that it was a cop car. It appeared to have rolled a few times—maybe the light had been ripped off."

"Was there anybody inside the car?"

"I don't know. I didn't hear anybody. But I couldn't see in very well, since I was down on the road. To tell you the truth, I was mostly seein' stars."

"All right, Mr. Kisov. I think this is a good place for us to break for lunch. We'll meet back here at one o'clock."

———

Lambert's stomach may have been full, but he went straight on the offensive. "Do you remember the fires?"

"I remember hearing the sound of fuel catching fire. It's very distinctive, a sort of *whump*. I was in and out of consciousness, but I heard that. I don't know which vehicle it was, though."

"Did you hear Chief Pistle screaming, as he roasted alive in his patrol car?" One older woman on the jury panel put her hand over her mouth and gasped.

Lambert pressed on. "Did you start the fire, Mr. Kisov? Did you willfully and with malice set on fire a human being, causing his painful and protracted death?"

I looked him straight in the eye and said, "No, sir, I did not." I swept my gaze over the jury, repeating, "I did not."

"So, you expect us to believe that you're an innocent victim of circumstance?"

"I don't claim to be a victim of anything. In my view, the only victims in this case are my wife and my unborn son."

"I wondered how long you'd wait to bring up this unrelated matter."

For the first time, he'd managed to drive a sliver of bamboo under my fingernail. "Unrelated? The chief's crimes that day drove every action that followed. His hand was on the throttle, and he guided the train down this track entirely on his own."

Lambert turned to the jury and said, "Chief Pistle's alleged crime is an entirely separate matter. The jury is looking specifically at the crash which resulted in the chief's death. The jury is directed to consider only the facts related to his death."

Lambert was turning back toward me when a middle-aged black man put his hand up. "Excuse me, sir."

Trying to hide his impatience, Lambert said, "Yes?"

"What you said is not completely accurate. Grand juries *can* look at circumstance, and we can follow up on testimony and evidence introduced by witnesses." The other jurors twisted toward him, fascinated to hear one of their own speak so authoritatively.

"Sir, part of my job as state attorney is to guide you through the maze of our laws."

"And you're doing a good job of that. But when I was selected as foreman, I thought I should familiarize myself with a grand jury's responsibilities, as well as its powers. I think Mr. Kisov's reasoning process drives straight to the heart of this case. I'd like to hear what he has to say." Several other jurors were quick to throw in with him, nodding their heads.

Lambert's jaw set briefly, before he shrugged and said, "All right."

The foreman turned to me. "What exactly were these actions on Chief Pistle's part?" Leo would be ecstatic: that was precisely the question he wanted me to prompt from the jury.

But I wasn't fully in the hearing room anymore. I'd flashed back to the aftermath of the crash: soaked in gasoline, arm broken, head full of hate for a man that had beaten my beloved wife half to death.

I took a deep breath. "You may not know that I happen to be married to Chief Pistle's ex-wife. For reasons known only to him, Chief Pistle stopped her and our adopted daughter that day. He pulled my wife out of the car and started to beat her mercilessly, right in front of my daughter. Then he told the child that she was next.

"Maybe the chief figured he could ignore Bee for the moment; she's only seven, and missing a leg. But Bee is the most precocious child I've ever met, and she slipped out the door and ran into the woods, looking for help. She made it all the way back to our ranch, and got Aunt Mabel—that's what she calls my friend, Mabel Frasier—to call the sheriff and ambulance."

"And how did you learn of this?"

"Mabel told me some of what had happened after I returned from that morning's flight. But I had to go to the hospital to learn that the chief had killed our unborn son."

Several of the jurors blinked back tears.

Ron Lambert opened his mouth again: "If you're

finished emotionally wringing out my jury, we'll…"

I came out of my chair like somebody had hit an ejection button, catching Lambert on the jaw with a right hook. Only his speed saved him from real injury, as he managed to duck like a prizefighter at the last instant. Nevertheless, he ended up on the floor with blood running down his chin.

"Take that man into custody! Take that man into custody!" Lambert shouted.

The bailiff, an older man who seemed half-asleep much of the time, only now moved into action. It was too late, though, as I'd tempered myself almost as quickly as I'd lost control and was now sitting peaceably.

The foreman stood, calling for calm from everyone. "Are you under control, Mr. Kisov?" he asked.

"I am, sir."

"Then can we move forward, Mr. Prosecutor?"

"If this *person* can manage to remain seated."

"I'm calm as a cactus. But don't disrespect my wife again."

"This is outrageous! I've never been threatened and manhandled in my own courtroom before!"

The foreman, now sounding more like a judge, said, "Perhaps this would be a good place to stop for the day."

We all knew wisdom when we heard it.

I reported to Leo in his temporary office. He was pleased when I related the foreman's mindset and his questions. "Now *that's* good news, Slats; he's become your best ally."

"And right after that was when I punched the state attorney."

"Has anyone ever mentioned what a delightfully bizarre sense of humor you possess?" Leo asked.

"I'm not kidding, Leo. I decked Lambert." I bent over, holding onto my head with both hands. "I blew it. I know I blew it. They're never going to believe anything I say now. From here on in, I'm just another nut job vet who can't control himself. I'm surprised that I'm not already back in a cell."

"Calm down, calm down. Why'd you hit him?"

"He spoke disparagingly about Darla, after I'd bared my soul to the jury. I lost it. I just lost it."

"This is not necessarily a game-ender, Slats. Big as grand juries are, sometimes they act more like a single entity. If so, they usually follow the most dominant member, which is the foreman. Did he seem outraged by your actions?"

"He called for calm, and then suggested a recess until tomorrow."

"That's not a bad sign. Don't despair; this process can be full of surprises."

"Lambert was trying to bait me, and I let him."

"Look at it this way: you taught him a valuable lesson. Next time he sets out to annoy somebody, he'll step back first."

I laughed. "You've been hanging around me too long, Leo."

———————

Next morning, Lambert began proceedings with an apology. "Mr. Kisov, I regret the phrasing of yesterday's last question. I meant no disrespect toward your wife, and I'm sorry."

I nodded, but otherwise remained aloof.

"Is there anything you wish to say, before we proceed?" he prompted.

"No."

Lambert shrugged then asked his first question. "Are you sorry about Chief Pistle?"

"What you are asking implies guilt, something I do not bear. Or maybe you are asking whether or not his death saddens me." I scratched the back of my head. "I have to be honest; the answer is no. I'm thinking of my family's safety when I say that I think he's better off... out of office."

"That's a very judgmental thing to say."

"In Vietnam, the chief would have been 'fragged.'" I looked at the jury and explained, "Fragged means killed with a fragmentation grenade, by one's own men."

"It looks like he may have been fragged, as you put it, right here."

"If so, he fragged himself."

"What do you mean by that statement?"

"It's a lengthy explanation."

"By all means, I'd like to hear it." Lambert bowed like a courtly gentleman.

"My explanation begins with a question. Why was Chief Pistle surveilling my ranch in the first place?"

Lambert asked, "Why shouldn't he? Your ranch *is* within his jurisdiction."

"Yes, it is," I readily agreed. "But in all the years I've lived there, I've never seen a police car pass by my place. So I ask again: why—only hours after brutally attacking my wife—was Chief Pistle surveilling my ranch?"

"The only man who can answer that question is dead."

"He must have been looking for me," I suggested.

"There is absolutely no evidence to support that contention."

"Maybe he was out looking for a bouquet of buttercups." The jurors all laughed. Then I said, "I know he was looking for me. In fact, he was *hunting* me."

"This isn't testimony, it's material for a pulp novel!"

"With respect, sir," the foreman interrupted Lambert, "we wish to hear the perceptions of the witness at the time these events took place." When Lambert clenched his jaw he immediately winced, then rubbed at it.

"I've been hunted before, in Vietnam. I'll say it again: the chief was hunting me. I know it now, and I would have known it then, if I'd spotted him before he saw me."

"You still insist you never saw the police car? I find that difficult to believe, Mr. Kisov. That would mean that you had an engine failure at precisely the same time Chief Pistle happened to be 'hunting' you. The odds of that happening are astronomical."

Lambert's smugness pissed me off. I didn't let loose with a fist today, but my mouth unleashed itself. "The odds of some cross-eyed buffalo-fucker shootin' me in the nutsack while I'm flying are also pretty long, but I won that lottery, too!" I shot back. I instantly regretted what I'd said, as that same older woman's hand once again fluttered to her mouth.

Before Lambert could reply to my observation, the foreman said, "I've heard you refer several times to having flown in Vietnam. I don't mean to pry, but may I ask about your service?"

"I was a Forward Air Controller, calling airstrikes down on North Vietnamese units."

"I am familiar with that job and its many hazards," he said. Then, peering back into the long ago and the far away, he softly added, "I was a Red Tail, once."

I sat back in surprise. The foreman was telling me that he'd been a Tuskeegee Airman, a member of the first all-black fighter unit in our military.

"I'm certainly familiar with your group's record against the Nazis, sir. It was matched by damn few, and exceeded by none."

"Son, some of my squadronmates developed what was then referred to as battle fatigue. It was no reflection on any of them, mind you, but it happened to a significant number of my comrades. I believe your generation refers to this phenomenon as post traumatic stress disorder." He paused to weigh his words. "I'm hesitant to ask this, but I think it may pertain to the case. Are you affected by PTSD?"

"I'm not sure how to answer that question. The war changed me. Who hasn't been changed in the heat of war?" The foreman subconsciously bobbed his head in agreement. "I've known a few guys who had PTSD, and I'd be lying if I said I didn't show some of the same behavior that they showed. I don't think it's affected me in life-changing ways, though. But how can a man accurately judge himself?"

"Thank you for your honesty. Now, to get back to your testimony, you were saying you never saw a car until after the crash. How do you think you came to collide with it?"

"I believe *he* hit *me*."

Lambert had lost control not only of the jury, but also of his tongue. "Preposterous! He's turning this hearing on its head—the victim now becomes the accused!"

"I was established for at least a minute on final approach, and moving slowly enough for a car to easily catch up. He purposefully positioned himself in my blind spot, below and to the rear—there is no conceivable way that I could have seen him. He, on the other hand, would have had an unobstructed view of me the entire time. All he had to do to avoid me was tap the brakes. He did not. Instead he stalked me and then rammed me."

"What would make him think that he could tangle successfully with an airplane?" the state attorney asked.

"You never met the chief, did you? Let's just say he wasn't exactly known for his intellect."

"Let us not talk ill of the dead," Lambert preached.

"My freedom is at stake, so let us talk honestly of the dead. Chief Pistle might be the only guy I ever met whose IQ increased after he expired."

"There's no way to know what truly transpired out there, is there Mr. Kisov? Your explanation is a stretch, to say the least. Do you have anything else to impart?"

"Only one thing: these events happened outside Chief Pistle's jurisdiction."

Lambert sighed. "We've already been through that. In fact, I distinctly remember you agreeing that the ranch was within the chief's jurisdiction."

"Yes, the ranch is within the police department's jurisdiction; however, the location of the crash—a mile and a half north—lies just outside that jurisdiction." I'd only tripped over this fact last night, myself. I'd measured it carefully on my sectional chart, not trusting my eyes: the crash had occurred a hundred yards or so past the city line.

Lambert's face fell, and though he recovered quickly and scrambled for the county map amongst his papers, I believe he'd already heard the chubby lady singing scales. I looked levelly at him. "I think the chief waited until he knew we were outside his jurisdiction. I believe he meant to kill me, and then go after my daughter. He must have been batshit crazy."

Peripheral motion caught my attention; it was the older woman's hand once again journeying toward her mouth.

"Ma'am, I'm truly sorry that my tongue has gotten away from me so often during this hearing, but you have to understand how riled up I am over this attack on my family. I apologize for any distress I've caused you."

"I have sons," she assured me. "I'll pray for your family, Mr. Kisov."

"Thank you, ma'am," I said with deference.

Then, turning to the foreman, I added, "I know these claims sound wild, which is why I'm urging you to call Officer Carling as a witness. He's in a position to corroborate much of what I have said."

Now, I'm certainly no judge of juries, but I have to say that this one didn't exactly look like they were searching for a rope to stretch my neck.

I told Leo about my testimony. The farther I progressed, the happier he looked. Until I came to the part about jurisdiction; then Leo sat back on his heels in utter astonishment.

"I am a defense attorney of long practice, one who pored over every facet of this case. How did that nugget escape me?"

I shrugged.

"Don't you think you could have mentioned it to me earlier, maybe on the way here?"

"I didn't want to spoil the surprise, Leo."

"This isn't an episode of Perry Mason. You must be very careful in presenting evidence to a grand jury."

"So maybe I was grandstanding. What should I have done differently?"

His face creased briefly in thought then relaxed into a smile. "Not a thing. You played it like Barrymore, Slats. Now we wait."

"They better not keep me waiting too long. I have important business to attend to."

"Pray tell, what could possibly be more important than the result of this hearing?"

"My new airplane is almost ready, over at the Airpark."

"Where did you get another plane?"

I shot a conspiratorial look both ways, then said, "I hitched up to North Carolina a while ago with five thousand bucks in my pocket, then returned in a flying wreck. Wilco and his fabric guy are working their magic right now—in a few days, she'll be ready for a test hop, and I'll have the sweetest little two-seater you ever laid eyes on."

"Are you certifiable? If you'd been caught, they would have been sure that you were on the lam, and you would have gone straight to jail."

"I can no more resist the urge to fly than a spawning salmon can stay out of the rapids."

Leo shook his head sadly, and I threw an arm around his shoulders. "Cheer up! I think you've pulled my ass out of the fire. And your grandfather would be mighty proud of you, Leo."

The grand jury listened for several days to the testimony of witnesses, from Sheriff Barnett on down. But it was Barney Carling who apparently sang longer and louder than a mockingbird at sunset. I'm sure he already considered himself The Chief.

Now, as the eighteen jury members and I were reunited, their faces didn't seem angry or accusatory. But all I could see in my mind's eye was the welcome Carling would give me when I returned to reinhabit the same cell I'd so recently vacated. The foreman stood to deliver the official judgment.

"Pertaining to the charge of murder in the first degree against Mr. M. J. Kisov of Farth, we of the grand jury return no true bill. The preponderance of evidence suggests that his explanation delineates the most likely train of events. An examination of Chief Pistle's actions and precise locations supports Mr. Kisov's claims. Your legal problems stop here, sir. Please accept our apologies for any interruption to your life, particularly in this period of mourning."

I released a breath so deep that I thought I might deflate. "I thank you all for so fairly evaluating the evidence and exonerating me. The system may be unwieldy, but it worked very well in your hands."

"Before you go, do you have anything you'd like to add?"

I briefly pondered the question. "As a citizen of Farth, I feel compelled to point out that Officer Carling is now poised to take over as chief. He is cut from the same cloth as Pistle. Not as violent, perhaps, but his name might just as well be Jim Crow as Carling. I think you should consider replacing him." In one swift thrust, I dispatched ol' Barney quicker'n Brutus done to Caesar.

In listening to this almost-but-not-quite-felon dispense civic advice so glibly, State Attorney Lambert's eyebrows nearly launched themselves off his forehead like hairy little

Willy Petes. That was fun to watch.

But the foreman asked seriously, "Do you have any alternates to suggest?"

"I do know of an Orlando police officer, Jesse Frasier, who hails originally from Farth. Jesse strikes me as an honorable man, one who could serve impartially. But I don't know whether he'd consider switching jobs."

"Well, Mr. Kisov, it seems you leave us with another important matter to investigate."

Forty-seven

Wilco stood grinning beside my reconstituted Super Cub. "That's the best news I've heard in along time, Slats. Congratulations on beating the rap."

"Getting off is good news. But seeing this machine— that's *great* news!"

And she was a beauty. The new fabric fit her like a cocktail dress. An overall beige, her rudder sported a glossy checkerboard of beige and red, with a flat-red antiglare panel extending forward of the windscreen.

The aircraft had been thoroughly reconditioned, in and out: a bit of corrosion touched up here, a trim cable replaced there. Best of all, Wilco had shoehorned a more powerful engine under the cowl. With a tow hook in back for banners, and a set of larger tires for operating from rough fields, she was ready to start earning her keep as a working airplane.

"Climb in, Wilco," I said.

"Not on your tintype. I'm trying to stay away from those." He pointed at my cast.

"Then I'm on my way to touch the face of God, to

paraphrase the wise man. If, that is, I can pay you Tuesday for an airplane today."

"What else is new, Wimpy? Go, fly. Celebrate your freedom." He slapped my back.

I kicked the tires and lit the fires, did a careful run-up, then pushed the throttle to the stop. The tail came up within thirty feet, and we levitated at about one hundred—I'd seen ducks make longer takeoff runs on my pond. Climbing at a thousand feet per minute, it didn't take long to reach two thousand feet.

I leveled off and tried some steep turns to the left and to the right. The wing-heaviness had disappeared quicker than a fart in a foehn. The controls were light and harmonious—this aircraft didn't just fly, it surfed on the wind. I could not imagine a more perfect marriage of engine and airframe.

I tried out a couple of stalls, and then some spins. She spun quite willingly either way; the instant I popped the stick forward and stabbed opposite rudder, she stopped spinning fast enough to make my eyeballs click. In a pinch, I could let myself down through a cloud deck this way. I whifferdilled and Cuban-eighted all the way to the ranch, grinning like an idiot in a pea patch.

Approaching my place, I felt nervous. The last time I'd seen this vista, a police car had dominated the view. Then, shaking off the memory like Tailskid does a stubborn piece of bio-refuse, I came in high and set up for a landing.

Lining up on Roadapple Lane, I crossed the controls and she fell out of the sky in a hell-for-leather sideslip— with a slab-sided fuselage like this to hang out in the wind, who needed flaps? Near the ground I gave her a brief burst of throttle to straighten out, eased the stick back to stall her, and then three-pointed gently onto the dirt.

I was in love. My aeroplane took off damn near vertically, climbed like a raped ape, maneuvered like a dragonfly, and then landed on a dime and gave back change. If Slats Rodgers were alive and kicking today, he'd be sitting at the controls of a Super Cub instead of a Canuck.

Hey, good enough for Slats Rodgers, good enough for me!

———————

Tailskid heard the plane. The sound of the engine might be unfamiliar, but any airplane was welcome as far as he was concerned. Bee was close on his heels, and Darla stepped onto the porch when I taxied up and cut the engine.

"Ain't she a beauty?" I yelled out the open doors.

Bee came near, poking suspiciously at the fuselage. "It's soft. What's this airplane made of?"

"Ceconite." At her puzzled expression, I explained, "That's a type of cloth."

Her eyes widened. "It looks like a kite."

"Flies like one, too. We'll try her out in a minute, but now I have some good news."

"I could see that on your face, Daddy. No true bilk."

"That's no true *bill*, Bee." I winked. "Although I think your way says it better."

Darla gave me a weary hug. "That's one thing off my mind, at least."

"I'll just take Bee for a short flight; she needs to be acquainted with the new rolling stock. We won't be long."

While we aviated, Darla threw together a meal. But

this was no last meal. It was quite the opposite, so she opted for steaks and a salad, with a bottle of wine for medicinal purposes.

"Can I try some wine?" Bee asked.

"I don't think so. I can just hear you in school tomorrow: 'I forgot to do my homework last night—I got drunk, celebrating my father's release from jail.'"

"Don't be silly, Daddy. When I need an excuse, I just feed my homework to Tailskid."

"You have to actually do the homework before you can feed it to the dog. Go."

We watched her walk away. "She's really something, isn't she Slats?"

"She already exceeds me in so many ways."

Darla must have detected something in my voice. "What do you mean?"

"Well, she showed more moxie than me when you were attacked."

"What are you talking about? You acted within hours. You vowed to let no man put us asunder, and you damn sure didn't."

"I'm supposed to be a warrior; I should have recognized the threat long ago."

"I *lived* with that bastard and I didn't see this coming. Bee did a fantastic job. That's what families are supposed to do. We're supposed to help each other… always."

I couldn't even look her in the eye, as I broached the one subject I hadn't yet been able to discuss with her. "It's my fault you'll never have another baby. I might as well have sterilized you myself."

Darla put her hand over mine, sending a light *tap-tap-tap*

with her ring, Morse code for the letter S. "I have just one question: Do you still love me, Shit Kicker?"

That was one subject I had no qualms discussing. I sent back the letter D: *tap tap-tap*. "With all my heart, Mrs. Shit Kicker."

"Then it's time you knew. I'm pregnant."

Epilogue

I was sitting in my favorite chair, the front seat of my Super Cub, patrolling high-tension power lines northwest of Miami. The electric companies had begun to do this recently, as it was quicker and cheaper than earthbound inspection. I'd gotten in on the ground floor, landing a contract for four routes, each three to four hundred miles in length, and each needing monthly attention.

How strange that I should end up flying over another endless green sea of trees, just as I'd done back in my first job. This time, though, nobody was taking a bead on me with a Kalashnikov. As the Grateful Dead once crooned, "What a long, strange trip it's been."

I loved these flights. I'd discovered my PTSD no longer pined for the rush that aerial smuggling had provided. Flying itself was enough to keep the demon at bay. These low-and-slow excursions, smoothing gently over the palms and piney woods of southern Florida, did the trick nicely.

Along with the smokier part of my therapy. While the marijuana on Jelly Roll Field these days was found only in small amounts, safely concealed deep within the barn, it did yeoman's duty soothing my fevered brow.

I'd come to accept that PTSD and I were going to be walking the same path for a long spell. I didn't fight it; I nodded to it. I bought a Smith & Wesson Model 64, a stainless steel .38 with a three-inch barrel and round butt. It was accurate as hell and small enough to carry anytime I wished. I'd piled up a sand berm behind the graveyard to use as a bullet stop, so I could practice. While I'd never be as good as Mamo, I'd gotten fast enough to give her decent competition when she came for a visit.

Sometimes, I'd find myself awake at all hours of the night. When I couldn't sleep, I'd lace my boots, tuck the S&W into my waistband, and walk my property line on night patrol. I didn't really expect more trouble, but you never know. The way I've heard it, the only folks who have seen the end of war are dead. I wouldn't just sit on my hands if another skirmish popped up somewhere out in the weeds. Neither would Darla or Bee—we'd do anything to protect little Kibby.

Looking down at my ring, rattling lightly against the throttle knob, I thought of Meat. This stainless fitting from his crashed Bird Dog neatly summarized the poles around which my world spun: family and flying. And I grasped a concept that may not make sense to another living soul. Family was the most important thing in my life. But flying was the most necessary. Flight was my meditation, my reward.

Flight was my sentence.